W9-DDI-393

To Jim Evans —
With gratitude for his
professional leadership and,
more important, many pleasant
memories from twenty years
of friendship.
— Robert G. Hays

EARLY STORIES
FROM THE LAND

EARLY STORIES FROM THE LAND

SHORT-STORY FICTION FROM AMERICAN RURAL MAGAZINES 1900 - 1925

EDITED
AND WITH AN INTRODUCTION
BY

ROBERT G. HAYS

IOWA STATE UNIVERSITY PRESS / AMES
in Association with
Harmony House Publishers

Grateful acknowledgment is made to the following publishers for permission to reprint stories appearing in this volume. "The Horse That Broke Him" is reprinted with permission of *Capper's*. "We Break the Mules" and "White" are reprinted with permission of *Farm Journal*. "Love and Roast Goose" and "The First Rig In" are reprinted with permission of *Wallaces Farmer*.

Authorization to photocopy items for internal or personal use, or the internal or personal use of specific clients, is granted by Iowa State University Press, provided that the base fee of $.10 per copy is paid directly to the Copyright Clearance Center, 27 Congress Street, Salem, MA 01970. For those organizations that have been granted a photocopy license by CCC, a separate system of payments has been arranged. The fee code for users of the Transactional Reporting Service is 008138-2894-5/95 $.10.

© 1995 Iowa State University Press
All rights reserved.
Printed on acid-free paper in the United States of America
First edition, 1995

Library of Congress Cataloging-in-Publication Data

Early stories from the land: short-story fiction from
American rural magazines, 1900-1925 / edited and with an
introduction by Robert G. Hays.
        p.   cm.
ISBN 0-8138-2894-5
1. Farm life — United States — Fiction. 2. United States —
Rural conditions — Fiction. 3. Country life — United
States — Fiction. 4. American fiction —20th century. 5.
Short stories, American.
I. Hays, Robert G.
PS648.F34E27 1995   94-29144
813'.0108321734 — dc20

CONTENTS

PREFACE

The genesis of this book goes back many years. It began, I think, when I was a boy growing up in rural southern Illinois. I remember looking forward to the magazines that showed up in our mailbox ever so often—not because I was interested in their technical articles about farming or cared about their advertisements, but because I found them eminently entertaining. In those days, I suppose, reading was more fashionable among young people than it is today; we had no television as yet, and movies were once-a-week luxuries at best. Radio had its limitations.

I remember *Capper's Farmer* and the *Kentucky Farmer*; but best of all, I remember *The Country Gentleman*. Its short-story fiction was so good that I recall some of it to this day!

We lived on what had been my grandfather's farm. But my father was a mechanic and blacksmith, not a farmer. We had no particular use for farm magazines unless they were entertaining. Like most country people, though, we typically got several. They all strove for maximum circulation—unlike today, with controlled distribution—and subscription rates were so low we may as well have got them for free.

Later, when I was in the Army and stationed at Fort Jackson, South Carolina, I had my first opportunity to take college classes. I took sociology and psychology courses at Columbia College, a Methodist women's school that welcomed taxpayer-funded male soldiers. My sociology professor gave us some kind of test one night that was supposed to indicate our socio-economic background. One measure it used was the number of magazines received in our respective households. I scored very high. That single measure, in fact, put me into the upper bracket of the test's total-score scale—ridiculous in light of reality. The experience taught me to question such surveys, but it also made me feel fortunate. Those many rural magazines, probably unknown to the academic person who created that test, really did count for something!

A few years later, as a student at Southern Illinois University, I liked to go to Morris Library during my rare free hours and browse through the magazine sections for occasional stints of fiction-reading. There, I discovered the old farm and rural magazines, in collections going back many years. Some of these provided truly excellent short stories; they helped me forget the demands of my classes and the stale reading in required texts. Here was a way of life entirely different from what I had known, preserved just as it had been described in stories for contemporary readers. This seemed to me to be something of value.

Fortunately for all of us, libraries give us wonderful repositories for these kinds of things. After joining the faculty of the University of Illinois, I soon learned that the campus library had a rich collection of farm and rural interest magazines dating well back into the 1800s. Collected in bound volumes and tucked away on shelves in a remote basement corner where relatively few patrons ever venture, they are a rare resource. This volume would not have been possible without that collection.

This book is my attempt to share with others some of the enjoyment I've gained from this particular kind of literature. The stories included were chosen from among hundreds that might have been selected. My first requirement was that a story was good reading; after that, it needed to be in some way descriptive of rural life in America in the period from 1900 through 1925. That single fact sets this work apart from other collections of short-story fiction. I believe that we can understand the future better if we know the past. These stories are a window on rural values during a time when the agrarian philosophy was a much more dominant one than it is today. They might help us understand those values better, and that understanding ought to be useful as we grapple with current issues of conflict between rural and urban interests.

Readers will be familiar with few, if any, of the authors represented. Most of them never became well known, although some were prolific writers whose contributions appeared often in the rural magazines of their time.

The collection is divided into six parts, a somewhat arbitrary division designed merely to call attention to the more common themes in the rural magazines of the period. Readers will find that many of the stories included could appear in other parts, as well. There is no magic to be found in reading the stories by clumps, as no pattern of continuity is implied. My only measure of success, so far as the reader is concerned, is that this collection may provide generous reading pleasure.

ACKNOWLEDGMENTS

I should express appreciation to a number of people whose names will not be mentioned. Among them are colleagues on the University of Illinois faculty who helped cover my responsibilities during a sabbatical leave that allowed me to finish this volume. Others include the scores of individuals who, through all these years, have built and maintained the university's library collection from which this work was drawn.

Shellie Robson and Bill Silag at the Iowa State University Press and Claude Brock and Bill Strode at Harmony House went far beyond the usual publisher's responsibilities to help get this book into print. Nancy Knieja keyboarded the stories into my computer, saving me many hours of work. And my wife, Mary, served as critical reviewer and major moral supporter, as always, throughout. I am greatly indebted to them all.

Urbana, Illinois
June 1, 1994

ROBERT G. HAYS

EARLY STORIES FROM THE LAND

INTRODUCTION

Rural America and Its Magazines, 1900-1925

RURAL Americans began the twentieth century with great hope. After decades of economic depression, they felt they could look ahead at last to a brighter future. They had been through the worst of times in the 1890s, facing new threats from worldwide marketing and old, familiar threats from drought and flood. They had learned they were vulnerable to exorbitant freight rates set by rich city men who controlled the railroad monopolies and to the acts of growing numbers of urban bankers who held mortgages on their land. Many, especially in the South, had learned first-hand the perils of tenant farming. But they also had learned the benefits of organizing granges and cooperatives in populist rebellion against what they saw as an unfair economic system, had learned that many voices expressing their grievances in unison were more likely to be heard than single voices crying out alone.

In that final decade of the previous century, the hard times rural America had endured for so long had spread to urban America, as well. Accurate figures are hard to come by, but perhaps as many as one in five American workers were unemployed in the mid-1890s. And although rural Americans could take little consolation in the fact that their misery was shared by so many of their neighbors in the city, they at least might hope that the rest of the nation would understand their plight better and be more sympathetic.

But now the new century. On the economic front, the upturn for rural America was swift and dramatic. The prices farmers received for their products and the value of their land nearly doubled in the first decade of the 1900s. Rural voters enjoyed new political clout. They believed they could influence public policy that affected their lives. They wanted obvious things like better roads and schools, and they also had come to appreciate more complex needs such as changes in the tax structure and cheaper credit and lower tariffs to improve their sales abroad. Still, the isolation of the typical farm family in the early 1900s would be difficult to overstate.

Unfortunately, the greater farm prosperity often had not been accompanied by the improved circumstances of daily life enjoyed by people in the city. Gas and electricity, telephones, plumbing in the home—these would remain foreign to most country households for years to come.

The same would prove true of good roads and highways. Even though rural families had more money to spend, getting somewhere to spend it—especially during times of bad weather—could present them with a nearly insurmountable challenge. The inescapable drudgery of farm life surely must have been equalled at times by its loneliness. The glitter of great cities remained far away and difficult to reach.

Only limited industrialization had reached the country, but in urban America the industrial revolution was in full swing. Factories produced consumer goods in staggering quantities. A few Americans became very rich; the working class, its numbers swelled by European immigrants, remained desperately poor. Working men and women in the cities struggled, just as their country counterparts had, for a fair income and better working conditions and found their best hope in labor unions. Again, like their rural neighbors, they gained strength through organizing.

Ironically, however, farmers by this time had lost much of their fervor for organization. They had learned from experience not to trust monopolies, and in some large measure felt a natural kinship with the working men and women in the cities. But farmers, controlling as well as they could their own levels of production, also had a natural bent toward unrestricted individualism. Thus the appreciation of unified voices that might have continued to serve them well was diminished. On the whole, rural America soon found itself in a position not unlike that of the proverbial hunter who shoots himself in the foot; it threw away its best chance for moving ahead in the new century on the strengths of its common interests and chose instead the route of "Let's go it alone." Urban labor, meanwhile, continued to organize and became a force that farmers came to view with suspicion.

But going it alone did not mean that rural Americans chose lives of isolation. They may have hated the railroads for rigging freight rates, but they loved them for the possibilities railroads offered for enriching country life. Life in many rural communities centered around the railroad station. The railroad was the lifeline of commercial shipping and receiving. It made travel into and out of the community faster and more comfortable, and it offered access to the telegraph. At a time when no other means of rapid communication was available, the telegraph was a crucial link to the rest of the world. And even more important, the railroad brought the mail.

Of all the changes occurring in early twentieth century America, the arrival of organized mail routes—Rural Free Delivery—probably had the most immediate day-to-day impact on rural communities. Farm families might not be able to enjoy all the comforts and conveniences of the city, but now they could share in its culture, delivered directly to their mailboxes in the form of newspapers, magazines, and mail-order catalogs. National magazines such as *Ladies' Home Journal*, the *Saturday Evening Post*, and *Collier's* helped open the minds of readers to social and cultural trends that otherwise may have remained obscure. *Munsey's*, *McClure's*, and *Cosmopolitan* entertained rural families with their popular fiction and exciting illustration. Readers also found in the pages of their magazines ample advertising for goods not readily seen in the typical village general store or small-town merchant's establishment.

Of at least equal importance to readers in the country were the more specialized farm and rural interest magazines, some of which had become quite good by the turn of the century. In the East, the well-illustrated *American Agriculturist* already was in its sixty-fifth year, published in Springfield, Massachusetts, and "designed for and adopted to the special needs of New York and Ontario, New Jersey, Pennsylvania, Ohio, West Virginia, Maryland, Delaware, and the South, wherein it largely circulates." It brought its readers a gratifying assortment of short stories, poems, serialized books, children's stories and puzzles, and general news and information important to farmers. *The Country Gentleman*, published in Philadelphia, also was well established. It combined the *Genesee Farmer* and *The Cultivator*, both of which dated back to the 1830s. The *Rural New Yorker*, begun in 1850, offered itself as "A Journal for the Suburban and Country Home," and enjoyed national readership. Its first issue of the new century included horticulture articles from New Jersey, Illinois, and Ohio as well as from New York, and reader inquiries and comment from Massachusetts, Louisiana, Colorado, Vermont, Oregon, and Connecticut.

In the South, Richmond's *Southern Planter*, a thick, old-fashioned journal of semi-technical information about crops and livestock, was commencing its sixty-first year. The *Southern Ruralist* in Atlanta and the *Progressive Farmer* in Birmingham were relatively young, but already showed the promise that would make them a powerful voice upon their later consolidation.

The *Ohio Farmer*, more than a half-century old, stated as its aim the improvement and betterment of "the farmer, his family and farm." It competed successfully in the Midwest not only with the Eastern publications, but also with the *Farmer's Review* and *The Orange Judd Farmer*, both of which had been around for some thirty years and were published in Chicago. The latter magazine was the "Western edition" of *American Agriculturist* and claimed to serve the territory "embraced in the states of Michigan, Wisconsin, Indiana, Illinois and the west and southwest, from the Mississippi river to the Pacific ocean, and the adjacent parts of Canada." Also published in Chicago was the highly-respected *Prairie Farmer*. It took pride in its readership in the "Western states." In a letter to readers on the front page of its first issue of 1900, *Prairie Farmer* credited its popularity to the fact that it depended heavily on correspondents drawn from "the most progressive farmers and stockmen in the Mississippi and Missouri valley states, and their articles teem with practical ideas gained from actual contact with the problems of the farm."

The number of rural magazines in the West and Southwest was relatively small in 1900, but would grow impressively in the next few years. Among the best of those in print at the time was the *Pacific Rural Press*, nearly three decades old. Published in San Francisco, it served primarily California farmers and especially the fruit and nut growers in that state.

On the whole, turn-of-the-century country magazines were remarkably similar in appearance and content. Most were regional publications with but limited national readership. But all made an honest effort to bring their subscribers practical and useful information, including national news that might have some impact on farm and small-town families in their respective areas of the nation.

The potential impact of any new technological development was not always readily apparent, of course. In May, 1908, the *Ohio Farmer* carried a single paragraph, buried on a back page in a column of news headed "minor items":

> The Wright Brothers of Dayton, O., have been conducting some interesting experiments with a real flying machine along the sea-coast near Manteo, N.C. Their ma-

chine made flights of from three to six miles at the rate of 45 to 60 miles per hour. It was wrecked during one of the tests, however, and the tests had to be discontinued.

By the end of the first decade of the new century, the typical American rural magazine demonstrated a keener awareness of the need to entertain its readers. It also sought to give them more thoughtful editorial content. *Successful Farming*, published in Des Moines, Iowa, challenged widespread rural conservatism in a December, 1911, editorial on "Woman and the Ballot." Women had shown their ability to compete with men in all areas of society, it said, and had earned the responsibility of full citizenship. But without the right to vote, women were "only counted in the census," required to obey the law but not allowed to help make it. "Give her the vote," it concluded, "and she becomes a citizen in fact as well as in theory." *The Threshermen's Review* that year ran a series of columns on ethics, ranging from the ethics of "car driving" to the ethics of food production and distribution.

A great many of the rural magazines by this time had turned to serialized novels as one way to entertain readers (and encourage subscription renewals), while a growing number also had added short-story fiction, poetry, and children's stories. The serials were especially important to magazines that used little other fiction, including the prominent *American Agriculturist*.

The country magazine editors also had begun to lend stronger voice to homespun rural philosophy. Rural readers no doubt felt comfortable with columns such as "From a Farmer's Window," a hallmark of *Farm Life*. That spirited and well-edited magazine merged with *The Agricultural Epitomist* in 1913. *Farm Life* also took forceful editorial stands, and was particularly outspoken in its opposition to organized labor.

The Country Gentleman, coming out weekly before switching to a monthly schedule in 1925, was among the earliest magazines to use short-story fiction to enhance its advice columns. It often ran instructional stories built around fictitious characters who learned important lessons through their experiences with real-life situations. Well-drawn and interesting characters learned the advantages of cooperative marketing, for example, or suffered the consequences of inadequate estate planning. These stories usually proved less entertaining, but they probably were educational for readers. The learn-through-experience formula became a staple of rural magazine short-story fiction for a time.

The automobile's popularity was growing as fast in the country as in the cities, or maybe faster. Rural magazine editors filled their pages with automobile advertisements, while the "Ford on the Farm" theme emerged often in stories, articles, and columns. *Farm Life* in 1913 promoted the five-passenger Willys-Overland touring car "with self-starter" for $985—somewhat expensive compared with other makes and models of its day. (A full decade later, the *Southern Ruralist* would be advertising Nash Motor Cars for $915, though a "mounted spare wheel" cost an extra $25; and *Capper's Farmer* advertised Chevrolet roadsters or touring cars for $525 and the Durant sedan for $750 as late as 1925—the same year the *Ohio Farmer* helped introduce the new Dodge coach with balloon tires as standard equipment for $1,095.) The array of automobiles coming on the market was astounding; new brand names appeared and disappeared almost over night, and vehicles such as J I Case motorcars and Oldsmobile farm trucks soon were forgotten. But the impact of the gasoline engine was falling full-force upon rural America; motor-powered vehicles offered hope that the isolation of farm families might one day be overcome.

Farm women, not always welcomed into full equality on all fronts, apparently were expected from the outset to learn to drive right along with the men. "A woman driving her own motorcar is no extraordinary sight at the present time and creates scarcely passing attention," wrote a *Successful Farming* columnist in March, 1913.

But the country magazine editors understood the importance of their women readers. *The Farmer's Wife* was aimed exclusively at women readers, as its title suggests, while more general rural magazines developed women's sections such as the "Women and the Home" pages of the sophisticated *Rural New Yorker* and the "Home and Household" columns of *The Orange Judd Farmer*. But beyond the shared goal of attracting women readers, there was little consistency in the positions on women's roles expressed by the magazines. And readers' opinions seemed just as diverse. Many editors gave prominent space to readers' letters; exchanges on topics involving attitudes as strongly held as those on women's rights could run on for months.

An *Indiana Farmer* "Ladies' Department" column in 1913 held that the "womanly woman" was the one "given over to many little feminine vanities" and concluded: "The woman who can make her home bright and attractive, who can be the model hostess as well as wife and mother, who is well informed and able to talk intelligently, yet who is wise enough to realize that woman's privileges are preferable to woman's rights, is the girl or woman we must all admire, and the one fit to be taken to any honorable man's heart." The *Ohio Farmer* was more flexible. It frequently carried short-story fiction about farm wives rebelling against stingy husbands who put crops and livestock ahead of home improvements, a common story line in many of the farm magazines of the day. These usually achieved a happy ending by having the farmer see the error of his ways. Women's issues were kept alive in the magazine's non-fiction articles, too. Reporting on Colorado's experience with women's suffrage after twenty years, the *Ohio Farmer* told women in 1913 that the right to vote would give them "a hand in making human society more human, and in making this country a true democracy."

An *Illinois Farmer* writer in May, 1915, viewed the role of farm wives strictly in terms of their relationship to their husbands and the farm. "Point to a good and successful farmer," he wrote, "and you will generally find that he has a good wife. . . . Every man owes it to himself as well as his wife to see that she gets a fair share of the good and enjoyable things in life. And it does not do to wait until you have bought all the land you want or put up and paid for all the farm buildings before you begin." During the same year, discussions of "feminism" were common in the "Home Circle" section of the *Nebraska Farmer*. "It is well and right for a woman to strive earnestly to be 'a help mate' for her husband," the editor wrote in a January column, "but that word holds no hint of inequality or of serfdom." In June, a reader claimed that with the coming of the typewriter, "The old-fashioned feminist and the machine of metal were responsible for many tender plants that flourished and grew strong and multiplied." A contributor in September offered a satirical narrative in which a farmer complained that the "Home Circle" put "fool ideas" in women's heads. "I'd stop the dum thing [*Nebraska Farmer*]," he threatened, "if there wasn't so blamed much in it I want to read myself."

Regardless of their views on feminism, suffrage, or women's roles in general, and whether or not it was intended, the magazines collectively painted a picture of life for rural women as a life of hardship. The bitter loneliness of a country wife was described poignantly in a Helen Cowles Le Cron poem in the *Rural New Yorker* in January, 1913:

Will you always frown upon me through the weary, weary years
Till my dream home fades to silence and to night?
I was gay, O brooding mountains, til you taught me pain and tears.
I am alien to your solitude and might.

But the country magazines were virtually unanimous in their efforts to educate, enlighten, and entertain the children in rural families. Most of them included children's sections and many used short stories specifically written for young readers. *Progressive Farmer*, by this time a mainstay among farm and rural readers in the South, in 1915 urged farm boys not to smoke cigarettes. Reporting on a crusade against smoking by youngsters recently launched by Henry Ford and Thomas A. Edison, the magazine quoted Ford: "If you will study the history of almost any criminal, you will find that he is an inveterate cigarette smoker. Boys, through cigarettes, train with bad company. They go with other smokers to the pool room and saloons. The cigarettes drag them down."

The *Southern Farmer* was less moralistic, but favored short stories aimed at young readers, especially during holiday seasons. Publications such as *Twentieth Century Farmer* specialized in children's stories and poetry, while a number included games and puzzles to entertain young readers. *Successful Farming* used bedtime stories to be read by parents, while the *Practical Farmer* and a few others even tried serialized children's stories. The *Idaho Farmer* carried a rich "Children's Corner" section that made generous use of poetry.

If some farm magazine editors were short-sighted on such issues as the roles of women, most of them showed total disregard for problems of ethnic and race relations. Insulting images of black Americans and "foreigners" frequently turned up in the fiction, editorial columns, general articles, and especially the jokes and cartoons that filled their pages. Editor Clarence Poe campaigned endlessly in the pages of his *Progressive Farmer* for separation of the races, using a January, 1915, opinion piece to call on white farmers to support a segregated land-ownership policy. He wanted a law that would permit white communities to prohibit the sale of property to non-whites, "for the protection of their social life, for promoting better schools and churches, for business cooperation, and for the protection of their wives and children."

Not all editors were as conservative as Poe, of course. The *New England Homestead* supported what it called "socialism" in a proposed new Massachusetts state constitution. In a July, 1917, editorial it suggested that delegates to a state constitutional convention approve a provision empowering communities to buy and sell food, fuel, and "other necessaries" in time of emergency. It also called, in November of the same year, for the mobilization of "all persons from 14 to 70 of both sexes" for national service in the war effort. A comprehensive national service plan also was called for, a few years later, by the *Farm Journal*.

United States entry into World War I in 1917 had swift and dramatic impact on the farm and rural interest magazines. As the nation turned to full-scale mobilization for war, they voiced universal pride in the contributions the farms and rural communities had to offer. Magazine issues became markedly thinner in the face of wartime shortages. One result—and it fit their serious approach to the times—was a significant scaling back of entertainment-oriented content. There were fewer poems and short stories, and those that did appear were likely to have patriotic themes. Even the venerable Illinois *Prairie Farmer*, which gave precious little space to entertaining reading material, found room in January, 1918, for a poetic tribute to American forces "On the way to France." Editorially, the magazines generally supported such wartime developments as government price and production controls affecting much of agriculture as well as government control of the railroads. They were uneasy about government regulation, but in the case of the railroads many editors said action to bring the railroads into line was something long overdue.

The rural American economy benefited from the war, but it soon was brought back to earth. The immediate post-war period was marked by high inflation, unemployment and labor conflicts, isolationism, and the "Red scare." These were accompanied by prohibitive tariffs on farm commodities that discouraged European purchase of American farm surpluses. The rural economy slumped. And even as farm prices recovered in the next few years, farm families were left with high interest rates on their mortgages and high taxes on their land. They also faced, to a greater extent than ever before, the threat of over-production. Technology, particularly in the form of the tractor, had revolutionized American agriculture.

Although magazines as diverse as *Farm and Fireside* and *The Field Illustrated* had carried columns on tractors for several years, not all editors had been convinced that the tractor was of practical advantage on the average farm. But *Farm Life*, in a July, 1922, column titled "Tractors go over the top," made clear the extent to which tractors had become a permanent fixture on the rural American landscape:

> The tractor has just passed the stage of skeptical antagonism in its development and now most farmers who were doubtful in their attitude toward the "iron horse" have been converted.
>
> Perhaps there has never been a better opportunity for the tractor to substantiate the claims of the manufacturer than was offered in Indiana and adjacent states last spring. Farmers were delayed by heavy rains and flooded fields until it would have been difficult in the case of many farmers to prepare the ground and plant the corn

in time for a normal crop if horse power had been relied upon.

Many men who had always sworn by horses and had declared that they would have none of the tractors had the alternative of being short of corn next winter or purchasing an "iron horse." With the help of the tractor and by employing a night and day shift in some instances, the corn acreage planted at the present time is reasonably near the acreage for last year, even though many farmers were almost ready to give up in despair after the long flood season.

As had been the case with automobiles a few years earlier, tractors now appeared in rural magazine advertising in a complex assortment of different makes and sizes. It was clear that farmers could afford to mechanize; the 1925 Fordson tractor, as advertised in *Capper's Farmer*, carried a list price of $495. Fenders were $35 extra. (For many editors, the explosion of tractors onto the farm scene also brought an ethics challenge they had not faced before: How could they be specific in articles about the advantages of tractor-power and show photographs of tractors at work in the field and not appear to favor particular makes and models? That dilemma would persist for years to come.)

And even as the tractor brought hope of easing field labor, new products on a smaller scale offered exciting promise for improving the lot of farm wives. Gasoline-powered washing machines were available to help relieve the drudgery of the weekly laundry, while full-page advertisements for phonographs assured that these instruments would bring the music of the city ballroom into the country parlor. Water systems and other conveniences became realistic ambitions in the country home equipped with electricity; these prospects were vastly improved with the new gasoline-powered generators. Oil-fueled cooking ranges and heating stoves could eliminate the need for chopping and carrying firewood and kindling.

Travel articles encouraged rural families to visit other regions of the country, particularly the scenic West. The *California Cultivator* reported in 1920 that 7.5 million motorcars were registered in the United States, an increase of nearly a million and a half in just two years. This rapid growth in the number of automobiles had been accompanied by highway and bridge construction that made travel easier. Midwest country magazines printed comprehensive articles on the diversity of people and places within their own areas, encouraging "local" travel to communities with rich European ethnic heritages. Regional publications such as the *Wisconsin Agriculturist*, *Michigan Farmer*, the *Missouri Ruralist*, Iowa's *Wallaces' Farmer*, and Colorado's *Western Farm Life* paid a great deal of attention to the need for better rural roads and highways. The *Dakota Farmer* brought attention to native Americans in its region with a comprehensive article in May, 1922, on the Sioux Indians as farmers. *Farm and Fireside*, in a February, 1920, article, told its readers about a special farm in Iowa that they might find interesting enough to visit: It once had been owned by Abraham Lincoln.

People in the United States also were made better acquainted with their neighbors to the north. In December, 1923, *Farm and Fireside* carried a full-page advertisement with a bold appeal to "Come to Canada." The Canadian Department of Immigration and Colonization placed this and other advertising in a direct appeal for new citizens, using the theme, "A New Nation Calls for People."

If the farm and rural interest magazines felt threatened by the coming of radio in the early 1920s, they gave little sign of it. Radio columns soon began to appear as regular features. Most of these, like the "Radio Questions" column in the *Farm Journal*, dealt with technical concerns and were designed to help rural families get the best broadcast signals possible in this early period. But *Farm Journal* editors were less enthusiastic about the movies, warning through a series of articles in 1922 that motion pictures posed grave dangers to the morals of children.

The Country Gentleman, meanwhile, had other complaints about the movies. In a March, 1921, article, "Movie Farmers and Stage Hicks," it complained about the stereotypical images of rural Americans projected in movies and plays by actors far removed from the real people they portrayed. A follow-up article in July, "What a Farmer Really Looks Like," was a critical look at the way farmers were depicted in cartoons. It assumed that urban residents would have a stereotyped notion of what farmers looked like "for the next thousand years," but concluded that farmers might not care all that much, "provided the man who drew the picture knows the soul of farm folks and works with humorous good will." After all, it suggested, farmers generally had stereotyped images of city residents, too.

But indignation over their image was just one symptom of a larger problem faced by rural Americans. Casting wary eyes on the rapidly expanding urban population, farm families and residents of declining country towns and villages felt increasingly alienated from the cities. Their resentment in many instances degenerated into dogged fundamentalism that was marked by open hostility to urban culture and surfaced in movements such as anti-science and anti-alcohol campaigns. The widening gulf between rural and urban America would not prove easy to bridge.

Like many other writers, Clarence Poe, the *Progressive Farmer* editor, recognized that there were serious problems facing rural America. He outlined some of them in a perceptive guest editorial appearing in *Wallaces' Farmer* in November, 1924. Rural life needed to be made both financially and socially satisfying, Poe wrote, as neither "large profits alone nor a richer community life alone will prevail." But he emphasized that "country life in America has not yet been adequately organized in recognition that man is 'a social animal'." A harmonious life, Poe asserted, is one "which fully improves upon all the rich possibilities of comradeship and of cooperative action with his fellows, industrial, civic, and social; and he goes to the city largely because he feels we have not yet provided for the development of these relations in our country districts." The very large task facing rural reformers, he said, was the creation of rural communities that involved scientific farming and business cooperation coupled with an adequate social life. He called for an organized effort to develop such communities, and voiced optimism that the goals he set could be accomplished. Poe believed that rural America already had two of the fundamental prerequisites for strong communities: education and home-ownership. Echoing Thomas Jefferson, he said his confidence was strengthened by his faith that the strong rural community he envisioned "will have as its basis a people of sturdy virtue and that strong religious

K. R. WIRE...

faith that has always characterized those who live nearest to nature and to nature's God."

But Poe and other rural magazine editors were not about to give up on what they saw as the advantages of life in the country. The *Wisconsin Farmer*, in its first issue of 1924, asked young people to consider the benefits of country living. The opportunity to see a field of daisies, the pleasure of roaming at will through the woods, the fun of barnyard pets—all these things, it suggested, might be taken for granted by boys and girls in the country but were opportunities denied urban children. "Your farm home would be a paradise to a city child," it concluded.

To their credit, the editors seldom pointed fingers at problems uniquely urban, though the superiority of rural life was a common theme in many of the articles and short stories they published. At the same time, they did not shy away from universal social concerns. In a perceptive opinion column in March, 1925, *The Farmer's Wife* railed at the easy availability of handguns to minors. "There is hardly any foolishness that we practice, as a civilized people, worse than that of allowing boys and minors free privilege in buying and carrying revolvers," the column said. It suggested that young people were prone to want to imitate "the movie swash-buckler who kills villains with paper bullets," and suggested that the streets of European cities were safer than those of America because of European nations' laws restricting the availability of guns. It called for similar controls in the United States:

> Why not move in the direction of the curtailment of the manufacture and sale of pistols for boys and minors? The illicit sale of habit-forming dopes and drugs is under the ban. City ordinances set the distance which the garbage can must be from the door. We arrest men for spitting in public places. We compel the killers of meats and the merchants in eggs and groceries to submit to inspection of their products. Then, why in the name of high heaven, do we go to sleep and allow our boys and young men to procure death-dealing weapons?

It went on the say that the problem was nation-wide and needed Congressional action, and called for Congress to "be petitioned from all over the United States" in an effort to obtain gun control legislation.

The horizons of rural America had been broadened significantly since the turn of the century. The farm and rural interest magazines could take a large share of the credit. They were widely read (the *Farm Journal*, for example, claimed four million readers by 1919) and influential. And among their best accomplishments had been their success in bringing their readers quality literature.

By 1925, country magazine readers had been exposed to many of the most popular writers and poets of the period. The poetry of Eugene Field and Elizabeth Barrett Browning had appeared in *Twentieth Century Farmer* and *Progressive Farmer*, respectively. *Farm and Fireside* not only had carried the poetry of Robert Frost, but also had reported extensively on the life of this favored "farmer poet." In like manner, it had made James Whitcomb Riley and his poems common fare in its pages. *Progressive Farmer* had serialized Anthony Hope's dramatic *Prisoner of Zenda* and the work of Mary Roberts Rinehart and introduced its readers to Eleanor H. Porter's popular "Pollyanna." Rinehart's *The Circular Staircase* appeared in serial form in the *Southern Ruralist*; her short stories were published by *Capper's Farmer*, and *Farm Life* published stories by both Rinehart and O. Henry. *Wallaces' Farmer* serialized Willa Cather's acclaimed *O Pioneers*. Edgar Rice Burroughs, creator of "Tarzan," contributed serialized fiction to *Western Farm Life*, while Max Brand was serialized by *The Country Gentleman*. Irving Bacheller's fine novel, *A Light in the Clearing*, appeared by installments in the *Practical Farmer*. Erle Stanley Gardner's work was serialized in *The Farmer's Wife*, while the *Ohio Farmer* enticed its readers through installments of Gene Stratton-Porter.

Both short-story fiction and novels sometimes were published in more than one magazine, often some years apart. The heroic novel about life in the Kentucky hills, *The Little Shepherd of Kingdom Come* by James Fox, Jr., was published by *Progressive Farmer* in 1915 and again by the *Ohio Farmer* in 1924.

Two of the most prolific and popular writers of the time were Zane Grey and Albert Payson Terhune. *The Country Gentleman* published a number of Zane Grey novels, including *Wildfire* and *To The Last Man*, and for a time ran Terhune short stories almost as a regular feature. Terhune, later to gain fame as "Lassie" creator, also contributed to *Farm and Fireside*. The popularity of these writers was amply demonstrated by *The Country Gentleman*, which offered free Zane Grey books as subscription premiums. "No other writer has succeeded in crystallizing the big, free spirit of America as has this master novelist of the unspoiled West," the magazine proclaimed in a December, 1921, promotion promising free sets of novels with the purchase of two $1 annual subscriptions.

The editors knew they would be alternately praised and damned for their literary selections. But hearing from readers was among the joys of an editor, the *Farm Journal* reported in a page-one brief in June, 1923, that included samples of reader response—letters of both gratitude and condemnation—to a recently finished serial. The editor promised that the magazine would go on as it always had, making its best judgments in line with its avowed purpose "to ever help and never harm our readers."

That editor clearly believed that his magazine, by presenting subscribers with good stories to read, was giving them something of value. Examples of the kinds of stories he may have had in mind—chosen not only because they are good reading but also because they reveal much about that period of rural American history—make up the rest of this book.

EARLY STORIES
FROM THE LAND

1

CHAPTER

STORIES TOLD WITH HUMOR

"**N**OT infrequently, a good laugh is worth more than a doctor's prescription, and often reveals a rift in the clouds when the sky of our life is murky and gloomy."

—The Nebraska Farmer, March 1922

Generous helpings of humor were standard fare in many of the American farm and rural interest magazines during the first quarter of the twentieth century. Readers came to expect humor columns, amusement pages, and general family-oriented entertainment sections. Jokes and cartoons enlivened the pages of even the dullest publications.

Humor was used less frequently in fiction, though most editors tried it from time to time. They treated it with caution. Farm families were proud—likely to be unforgiving if they suspected a writer of ridicule or felt a story belittled rural life. So the editors chose safe ground, printing stories that drew upon universal human foibles. Farmers could laugh at themselves, or they could laugh at urban cousins in predicaments they could identify with. But farmers would not countenance city dwellers laughing at farmers.

Characters who were intended to be funny ofttimes were offensive, especially if viewed by today's standards. Parodies of black people and "foreigners" almost invariably included stereotypical dialect and mannerisms. Fortunately, such characters appeared less frequently in the works of fiction than they did in the jokes and cartoons on humor pages. There probably were very few black Americans and others of "different" national and ethnic backgrounds among the magazines' readers, and we find no evidence that readers complained.

Had the writers and editors been forced to defend themselves, they might have pointed out that they often used an exaggerated rural dialect in dialogue among other characters, too. Surely not all farmers used "I'll be jiggered" and "be gorry" that often in everyday conversation!

But on the whole, the farm magazine humor was entertaining, rarely biting or vicious. Farmers and their families, hired hands, and neighbors both rural and urban who were the most familiar subjects always had redeeming qualities. Mistakes were born of innocence or acceptable character flaws. In the case of the latter, guilty parties usually saw the error of their ways and therefore gained redemption in the end. This was humor with a soft and gentle touch, humor readers could relate to comfortably. It could be witty or sarcastic, it might gain its vigor from situation or colorful character, but it always was topical in some way that rural readers would recognize and understand.

3

At times the rural magazine humor missed the qualifying standard for exceptional literature precisely because its writers refused to accept Mark Twain's premise that the secret source of humor is not joy, but sorrow. "There is no humor in heaven," Twain wrote. The farm and rural interest magazine editors (and, it seems likely, their readers) might have disagreed.

On the other hand, the stories in their favorite magazines perhaps proved most entertaining to those readers desperately seeking a respite from the daily rigors of farm life. If farm families did not live in sorrow, they certainly knew hardship. We can understand those hardships better by viewing the circumstances that farm families found so easy to identify with: The remoteness of farm life that made even difficult days at the fair preferable to another day at home, the drudgery of a washday the farm wife began by drawing water with a pail from an open cistern, the loneliness that left a bachelor farmer susceptible to any promise for romance, or the stinginess of a farmer who remembered hard times. Even in situations designed to poke fun at city cousins, there is some insinuated acknowledgment of the stark contrast between country life and the sophisticated lifestyle available to people in the city. And imagine the limitations inherent in travel by horse and mule! These are among subtle elements in the stories that follow.

MRS. CLOONAN'S WASHDAY

Anna C. Chamberlain
Successful Farming, April 1915

"BE advised," urged Mr. Cloonan. "It thunders. How can you wash today?" But every hair on Mrs. Cloonan's head, not included in the compact little knot at the back, repudiated the thought of taking advice on this subject from any man.

It was Mrs. Cloonan's invariable custom to wash on Monday and she proposed to make no exception to her usual custom on this occasion, even though dark storm clouds lowered in the sky. She hustled breakfast on the table with extra speed to make up for an unusually late start.

The cattle had broken out in the early morning, so that Mr. Cloonan and his hired man, being under the necessity of getting them back, had much delayed the morning meal. They were at the table now, doing their best to make up for lost time as the diminishing pile of pancakes showed.

"Sure it's little help we can give you," continued Mr. Cloonan, returning to the subject when the several mountains of pancakes had been reduced to a level plain, "with all them fences a waitin' to be fixed—"

"Don't you be worryin'," returned Mrs. Cloonan, restoring the altitude of one of the mountains and setting back the griddle. "It's little help I'll be wanting out of either of you, but the rinse water. I filled the boiler and the tubs while I was waitin' an' I left the cistern open so's ye could draw the rest in no time."

"Ye did what?" demanded Mr. Cloonan, desisting from his pancakes in alarm. "Ye left the cistern open! Ye left the cistern—! Oh glory be!" as a crash was heard from without followed by a smothered bellow. "Ye left the cistern open, ye say?"

"There's the big steer now, I'll be bound!" exclaimed the hired man, making a rapid disposal of his last pancake, "an' he's a getting the rinse water hisself, the way it sounds."

With that he rose with a precipitancy quite unusual and he and Mr. Cloonan hurried out to find that his surmise was quite correct. The red steer had indeed gone down through the wide open neck of the big cistern and now stood below in about three feet of water, his great eyes rolling with fright and the spunk all gone out of him.

In the presence of this disaster Mr. Cloonan gave way to a flurry of agitation which manifested itself in a spouting geyser of excited orders. So numerous were these and so complicated, that had his hired man been a centipede or even a myriapod he could not have executed the half of them.

"Bring a r-r-ope," commanded Mr. Cloonan, circling excitedly back and forth around the open neck of the cistern. "Get the big one off the hay fork and all the others there are. Fetch both sets of lines from the harness. Bring the three big poles we use in stacking and set them up right over the cistern. Don't forget the ladder, the sixteen-foot one. Get the—"

The last of these orders were hurled in vigorous tones after the rapidly retreating back of his servitor, who presently disappeared into the barn from which he promptly emerged riding the roan mare, sans rope, sans ladder, sans everything which Mr. Cloonan had demanded.

The downtrodden son of toil, finding the burden of his master's commands oppressive, had arranged for a division of labor.

"I'm going to get Jack Weston and Tim Morley to help," he called as his horse started down the road back of the barn; "we can't never git that critter out alone. You'll find the rope in the hay mow and the ladder out by the stack. Them hay poles is—" But his voice, tossed about by the fitful morning breeze, died away on a turn of the road.

"Well, I swan!" ejaculated Mr. Cloonan, who had planned to linger next to the open cistern and lend sympathy to the prisoner below, while the materials for the rescue were being collected. "By gorry!" was his next expression of disappointment, for now he must bend his proud back to take up the tasks he had designed to lay upon the neck of oppressed labor.

Long before he had finished, the clatter of hoofs behind the barn announced the return of his aide and presently the roan Rosinante arrived breathless upon the scene.

"Humph!" remarked downtrodden labor in the person of Jim Horton, "Hain't you finished gettin' them things over yet? Reckon we'd better git a move on, for when Jack and Tim comes along, things will begin to go some."

The swift arrival of the two neighbors failed to hurry matters much since their combined opinions as to methods varied so greatly.

"There ain't but one way to git him out," declared Jack Weston, his teeth working gingerly over a long stalk of timothy, "and that is to pitch down hay, one forkful at a time, for the critter to stan on. When he gits one trampled under his feet, put down another and another till you fetch him plumb up to the mouth of the cistern. Then ye can lead him right out."

"You'd be more apt to bury him right under the stuff complete, afore you could git him to climbing up like that," derided Timothy Morley, swinging his cud of fine cut into the other cheek with a dexterous twist of his tongue. "Moreover you could never make him tramp the hay into an incline that would fetch him head fore up into the neck of the cistern. Now my idee would be to open it out on one side kind of slopin' like an' let the critter walk out hisself."

"Either of you fellers got time and money to turn in and help me make a new cistern right now at the beginning of spring work?" glowered Mr. Cloonan wrathfully in response to the well meant schemes for the rescue of his property. "My idee is to strap him tight fore and aft. Then rig up a derrick and pulley overhead, hitch the horse on for power and up she comes."

There was no response to this save an exchange of pitying glances between the neighbors and the hired man, as commiserating the feeble intellect which could originate such a plan.

Neighbor Morley spat copiously under the stimulus of a new idea.

"How about butchering the critter right whar he is?" he hazarded. "That way you could save the meat, hide, and the cistern, too. There ain't no other way you could keep all three as I can see."

"How about saving the rinse water that Mis' Cloonan is a waitin' on?" put in the hired man, blocking this scheme with an unsurmountable obstacle.

This consideration spurred Mr. Cloonan to fresh action. The poles were rapidly set and the pulleys fixed in place despite the fire of objections from each of his assistants.

"Now," vouchsafed Mr. Cloonan, when these arrangements were complete, "we'll set the ladder down into the cistern and one of you fellows can go down and tie that steer ready to bring up. I'll hand down the ropes and tell you just how it should be done."

Neighbor Weston looked at neighbor Morley, then both of them glanced at the hired man, whose gaze was fixed on Mr. Cloonan.

"My idee," remarked the humble son of toil with thoughtful deliberation, "is that as long as Mr. Cloonan originated this here plan, he's the one to go down and do the ropin'."

"Nothing of the kind," protested Mr. Cloonan hastily. "In a job like this, the inventor, the master mind, has to overlook things. Stands to reason I'll have to stay up above."

"Weston's had a lot of experience handling ropes and such," suggested the hired man, attempting to elect some other than himself to the post of honor and responsibility.

"Knowledge and understandin' of animals is the real necessity in doin' this business," responded Jack Weston, handing along the chaplet of laurel, "and for them things Tim Morley can give the rest of us the walk away."

"In every job of this sort that I ever heard of," gainsaid Tim promptly, "it was always undertaken by the youngest man. Unless," he added, freezing the protest which could be read on the lips of the Cloonan servitor with an intonation of questioning scorn, "unless the feller was afraid."

"Of course in that case you couldn't expect it," rallied Weston to the aid of Morley in averting common danger, which left Jim without a return shot in his locker.

"Get busy then, you fellers," he ordered, determined not to depart for the danger line without making the conditions as difficult as possible for those who had evaded this duty. "Open out the neck of that there cistern so's we can git the critter through. Two feet each way will about make it."

"Let be! Let be!" insisted Mr. Cloonan, coming to the front again now that a victim had been procured. "Don't you lay hands on a brick. The beast went down through that opening and, begorrah, he'll come out of it."

"You're loony, man!" exclaimed Weston.

"The critter's not an inch less than five feet," contended Morley excitedly, "How'll he come out through a three feet aperture?"

"Will I break him up, was yer meanin'?" gibed the hired man with heavy scorn.

"We'll bring him up head fir-rst," maintained Mr. Cloonan above the babel of voices. "He ain't no bigger'n when he went down, I don't reckon."

"Head fir-rst!"

"Hear reason, man!"

"Ye don't know what ye're undertakin'!" groaned the auditors each and severally.

Above the din of masculine dissension rose the shrill voice of feminine authority. An authority backed, it would seem, by the faraway remembrance of the maternal slipper, so marked and so swift was the response.

"Jim Horton," it commanded, "that's Mr. Cloonan's steer and you're his help. If he was a wantin' you to fetch that animal up by the tail, it would be your business to do it."

Dead silence settled over the noisy group. The expression of opposition and hostility in the eyes of neighbors Weston and Morley changed to one of fraternal sympathy.

"We know how it is, brother," their sympathetic looks proclaimed, "we've got one just like that at home."

"As soon as that dinged ladder is in place," remarked Jim, the first to recover his presence of mind, "I might as well begin."

The ladder being lowered with great promptness, Jim proceeded to descend into the bowels of the earth. He did this warily, not knowing how the prisoner for whose rescue they labored might receive their proffered mercy.

No precautions were necessary, he found. The red steer, lonely and forlorn, seemed to welcome his arrival and made no objections to the numerous loops and coils of rope with which the newcomer proceeded to invest his carcass.

In fact, as Jim conveyed in hollow tones to those who looked down at him from a brighter world above, it was so blamed cold down there that wrappings of any sort were a real comfort.

The hired man set about his task with enthusiasm and proceeded to multiply loops and hitches of rope until their numerous strands began to suggest that the animal had become enmeshed in a gigantic cocoon.

Mr. Cloonan, looking impatiently into the depths, said as much. He likewise added that when Jim was tired of his tatting and crochet work down there, the folks overhead were ready to begin some real work. To which Jim retorted in sonorous tones that when he undertook to do a piece of work, he did it, and if they did not like his style he was ready to come up at any time and give them the privilege of finishing the job.

This proposition hushed the last breath of criticism, and silence reigned until the servitor, knotting the last foot of rope, announced the work securely finished. Then Mr. Cloonan, the master mind, passed down the big cable.

"Double hitch it, Jim," he commanded, "in the heaviest coils about the critter's shoulders. We'll be takin' up the ladder now and begin raisin'."

"Not till I'm out of this," rose the voice of the hired man in frenzied reverberations. "You pass your word to leave that ladder till I climb out, or I don't tie another darned hitch for you."

"Why, Jim," soothed Mr. Cloonan as a conclave of heads at the mouth of Jim's dungeon cut off his slender supply of light, "the hitches may not hold. We'll raise him a ways to make sure. If they give, you'll be there to tighten'em up."

"If they give," boomed Jim in the hollow depths, "I'll be here to catch the critter in my arms and break his fall, I suppose."

Jim's determination to make his exit in advance of the steer being firm, his co-workers reluctantly promised, but even then the Cloonan aide completed his work with one foot on the ladder and made his ascent with the swiftness of one who lacks full confidence in his fellow man.

In the searching light of the upper regions it became apparent that the dampness below had exerted a depressing effect on his disposition as well as his wardrobe.

"Will I take up the ladder and lend a hand with the raisin'?" demanded the op-pressed son of toil in answer to the voice of authority. "I will not. I been a workin' down there in the water while you folks was a restin' your hocks up here. Now you can hitch old Rosy to the pulley yerself and try how it goes to be drivin' sunthin' else sides me."

This suggestion was acted upon, and in a few minutes the creak of the rope and the whine of the pulleys attested the strenuous efforts of the horse, also the heft of the animal on the cable.

"Steady there!" shouted master mind from the cistern's mouth. "Forward! For-ward! Easy! Easy! Steady! Forward! Up she comes."

By dint of these vociferations and the steady efforts of the horse, the weight was drawn higher and higher. Presently the anxious head of the steer appeared at the open-ing. More vociferations and pulling, combined with dexterous handling of the cable and the body followed, after which, by means of the united efforts of Messrs. Cloonan, Morley, and Jim, now restored as to temper and temperature, the suspended animal was swung sideways, pendulum-like, and carefully let down upon his rather wobbly legs.

"Look out, Jim," warned neighbor Morley as the large cable was unloosed and the creature led away to a safer distance, "steers sometimes act a bit sassy after being in trouble like that."

"I ain't afeared," boasted Jim, setting himself with vigor to the task of unwinding the cocoon. "Buster knows his friends. Don't you, old scout?"

Buster, still shivering from his prolonged immersion, showed the whites of his large rolling eyes and reserved his decision.

"You remember who helped you out of trouble, don't you, boy?" continued Jim coaxingly as the last loop was removed.

"Bar-r-rh!" dissented Buster, in whose bovine mind lurked the conviction that some great indignity had been offered him.

"Get along to your pasture!" Jim concluded the disrobing process by thwacking the coils of the rope across the creature's flanks.

This completed in Buster's mind the connection between this flippant and presum-ing human and his recent humiliating experience.

"Bar-r-rh!" he remarked a second time, this time emphasizing his displeasure by charging, horns down, in the direction of his rescuer.

"Hey, there!" yelled Jim, taking refuge behind a sapling. "Head him off, somebody. Hey!"

Buster was limbering up from the chill and could dodge a tree as readily as anyone.

"Head him! Head him!" shouted the quarry desperately, but the neighbors had taken French leave and Mr. Cloonan was leading the horse to the barn.

"Hey! Hey!" Jim took chances on being able to reach the back porch and dashed up the steps a few feet ahead of the pursuing horns.

"Bar-r-rh!" insisted Buster, following close on the same track.

"Shoo! Shoo! Get out!" shrilled the feminine guardian of the precincts, to the rescue with a valiant broom. "Get down from my steps with those dirty hoofs."

Out of respect either for the broom or the petticoats, Buster beat a hasty retreat, and still rumbling displeasure and defiance, retired in the direction of the barnyard.

"You've come just in time," announced Mrs. Cloonan, returning the broom to its corner. "I'm needing the rinse water bad."

"The steer was jest a bringin' you a part of it," sniggered Jim, trying to recover his usual jauntiness, "and I've got a good bit of the rest in my shoes this minute."

Mrs. Cloonan glanced sharply from the dripping nether garments of the family servitor to the disheveled flanks of the departing steer.

"And have both of ye been disportin' yer dirty selves in my clean rain water?" she demanded indignantly.

"I haven't a notion that Buster stopped to wash hisself," returned the hired man flippantly, "and I know Mr. Cloonan didn't give me time."

Mrs. Cloonan turned to front her husband, who, his hat thrust back from a troubled, perspiring brow, was hurrying into the house.

"You'll have to send Jim over to Blackburn's for the rinse water," she declared with emphasis. "I'll not be usin' the steer's foot bath for my nice sheets and things."

Her husband waved dramatically in the direction of the darkening east.

"The hivens are sinding you rinse water, ma'am," he announced impressively. "It'll be here long before Jim could git on dry clothes to go after any other."

THE BOOMERANG

Merritt P. Allen
Farm and Fireside, July 1917

ELIHU Arnold was of medium height, but as he leaned against the picket fence thoughtfully stroking his stubby gray beard and waiting for the afternoon mail, the sun threw a long shadow behind him almost to the steps where his wife sat culling dandelion greens.

"Mary," he remarked after a while without turning around, "I'm gittin' uneasy for a hoss trade."

"I should think you would, seein' how well you done in that last one," she returned sarcastically.

"That wasn't so bad," Elihu defended, straightening up. "Of course, I didn't make much, but I got out of it."

"So'd Jonah git out of the whale, but he got everlastin'ly took in first," his wife retorted.

Elihu sighed. Mary was stout and red-faced, and in most respects an admirable helpmate, but she was too prudent, for she would play on the safe side or not at all and, as everyone knows, there is no safe side in a horse trade. For this reason she was adverse to such transactions, and right there she and Elihu clashed. He read about horses, thought about horses, talked about horses, and smelled of horses the whole year round. To him the attack and defense of a horse trade were the nectar and ambrosia on which he could thrive forever.

So he sighed again and leaned back on the fence, from where he was removed by the sound of the carrier's wagon rattling down the road. He came back presently, walking slowly and reading a letter.

"I've heered from what'sname," he announced at the foot of the steps.

"I suppose he's brother to whatyoucallit," Mary remarked, still thinking of that horse trade.

But Elihu was too engrossed in the letter to notice this shot.

"He's got our price for the land," he exclaimed after reading further.

"Oh," Mary was suddenly interested. "It's the real estate man from St. Albans?"

"Yep; he says he had to hang on like a puppy to a root to git it—not them exact words, but somethin' to that effect."

"That's three hundred dollars clear," Mary calculated aloud. "Show me where you ever made that much with your horse-swappin'."

She had been instrumental in buying the land in question, so she felt justified in this remark. Elihu, to whom such questions were a bore, handed her the letter to postpone more words of this kind, and waited.

"Well," she commented at length, "you're to draw writin's Thursday. Today's Monday. I'll have your white shirt washed and ironed and your Sunday suit cleaned by then. You won't have to start till Thursday mornin'.''

Elihu sat down on the steps.

"I thought I'd start tomorrow," he ventured.

"Tomorrow?"

"Yes; I thought perhaps I'd drive."

"Drive, when the train goes right there?"

"Yes," he answered slowly, "I thought that perhaps your cousin George, who's boardin' at the hotel, might like the ride. The country's so beautiful this time of year and the scenery is—"

"Cousin George! Beautiful country! Scenery!" Mary ejaculated energetically. "Elihu Arnold, you don't fool me. You're goin' to drive so you can trade horses on the way."

Elihu grinned sheepishly.

"Of course, Mary," he said, "all I thought of was givin' George a little ride, but now that you've spoke of hoss-tradin', mebbe I will look around a little." And without more comment he went out to the barn and hitched up the black colt behind which he proceeded to town in quest of Cousin George.

George H. Winter, who, save for a month each summer, dwelt in the city of New York as a lawyer, was not unfavorable to the proposition which Elihu advanced to him. For many years this hearty little man, whose round, shining face and stubby beard reminded him of a whisk broom on a harvest moon, had held a warm place in his heart, and the prospect of a four-day drive with him through Vermont in her best attire was a very pleasant one indeed. So arrangements were completed without delay.

It is eighty miles from Burley to the little town just outside St. Albans where the land was situated, and Elihu and Winter left early Tuesday morning behind the black four-year-old in high spirits. They passed the first night on the road, the next in the city, and, after transacting their business on Thursday, started on their return Friday morning shortly after sunrise. It was a beautiful morning, and to get the full benefit of it they took the lake-shore road instead of turning inland the way they came. The four-year-old, now that he was turning homeward, broke into a long swinging trot and scarcely slackened his pace for two miles, when was brought to a walk by a hard hill.

"Well, old feller," Elihu remarked to him, "I ain't seen a hoss that I'd give you for yit, and I reckon I've sized up every one I've seen."

At the top of the hill the colt was breaking into a trot again when Elihu pulled him up short.

"By time, George," he exclaimed, "look there!"

Winter looked and saw, just over the fence in a pasture, a tall bay horse whose coal black mane and tail and sleek sides shone in the morning sunlight. Before he had taken in these details, Elihu had handed him the reins and was out of the wagon.

"That's a fine hoss," he was saying. "A *mighty* fine hoss. He must stand all of fifteen hands and weigh round 'leven-fifty. I'm going to look him over." And he climbed the pasture fence.

All horses seemed to know Elihu Arnold. Mary said it was because he was such a jackass himself, but then Mary was always saying things that she did not mean. Whatever the reason was, this horse was no exception and came nickering up to him. Elihu stroked his soft nose, ran his hands along his straight back and down his smooth legs, looked in his mouth, lifted his feet one by one, and stepped back to eye him admiringly.

"He ain't more'n seven," he called back to Winter, "and he's wuth three hundred if he's wuth a cent."

They were both so engrossed in the animal that they had not noticed a man coming up the road. He was a young man, a tall, loosely put together fellow, carelessly dressed, and now he took part in the conversation.

"He is a pretty good horse," he remarked, stopping by the fence. "I own him."

Elihu turned quickly, and walked slowly toward the fence.

"Why, he's a fairly good-lookin' hoss," he admitted. "I was jest lookin' him over to see if he'd match up with one I've got at home. Be he ain't more'n fourteen hands high, is he?"

"Fifteen," the stranger answered with an easy smile.

"Does he!" exclaimed Elihu in evident surprise. "But, then, he's so fat it makes him look shorter. Must weigh round thirteen hundred?"

"Eleven-sixty a year ago," the younger man answered.

Elihu feigned surprise again, and remarked as he climbed up on the fence, "I ain't much of a hoss jockey myself, anyway. You don't use him much, do you?"

"No," was the frank answer, "I don't. Fact is, I haven't had a harness on him but twice this summer. I hoped to enjoy him, but my wife's been sick and I haven't had any time." His face took on a careworn expression that spoke of more troubles than he cared to mention to strangers. "I got him for her," he added. "I don't need him, but a party owed me a debt so I took him."

Elihu balanced himself on the top rail and commenced whittling on a sliver.

"I dunno," he mused, "as he'd be such a bad mate for my hoss. What'll you take for him?"

"Two hundred," was the answer, after a moment's hesitation.

"Mebbe that's cheap enough," Elihu said, "but I guess I've got hosses enough without him anyway."

"Where do you live?" the young man questioned.

"Burley."

"York State?" asked the other, for from where they were Burley, New York, and Burley, Vermont, were about equal distance.

Elihu was about to tell him that it was Burley, Vermont, when a thought seemed to strike him suddenly.

"Say," he asked, apparently thinking of it for the first time, "you wouldn't *trade* hosses would you?"

The stranger smiled faintly.

"I'd have just as many horses then," he said, "and I want less."

"Well," Elihu suggested, "you wouldn't be any wuss off."

17

"No," he agreed, "I wouldn't be any worse off." He said it with another easy smile that Winter remembered afterward.

"How'll you trade?" Elihu persisted.

The young man did not reply. Instead, he went over and examined the black colt and then looked across at the handsome bay.

"What do you call your horse worth?" he finally asked.

"Two and a quarter," Elihu valued him.

"On account of the war, horses are pretty high," the other answered, "but I don't believe I want to trade."

"Is he sound?" Elihu asked.

"Sound as a nut."

"Good roader?"

"Excellent."

"Kick?"

"I won't warrant him. I tell you I haven't driven him enough to know him."

Elihu climbed slowly into the buggy before delivering his ultimatum.

"I'll give you twenty-five dollars to boot," he declared, looking hard at the man by the roadside.

The young man thought for some time.

"You can have him," he said at length, "but I tell you again that I won't absolutely warrant him. Do you want to try him?"

Elihu looked at his watch; the forenoon was wearing away and they had a long drive before them.

"No," he said, "I'll resk him. If I git beat it won't be the fust time."

He began counting out the money as he spoke and within ten minutes the horses were changed. Once more they climbed into the wagon and were away. The stranger watched them out of sight with the same easy smile on his face and then turned the black colt into the pasture.

For perhaps two miles the bay drove beautifully; his long, rapid strides were a delight to see and Elihu chuckled aloud.

"George," he exclaimed delightedly, "I guess I've made a trade this time that Mary can't pick to pieces. I never see a handsomer hoss or a better driver. Giddap, there!" and the horse redoubled his pace, apparently without an effort.

"Still," Elihu continued after a while, "there may be somethin' mean about him. I half suspect there is, but we'll find it out quick enough."

They did. Within half a mile the bay stopped. "Giddap!" said Elihu, slapping him with the reins. But there was no move; instead, he turned his head on one side and rolled the white of one eye at his new owner. Elihu swore aloud. He was not ordinarily a profane man, but there were times with him when profanity seemed entirely appropriate to the occasion. This was one of them.

"What's the matter?" Winter inquired innocently, for he was uninitiated in equine mysteries.

"Matter!" snapped Elihu. "He's balked; that's what's the matter."

18

"Perhaps not," Winter encouraged, taking the reins which his companion had dropped in disgust and slapping and clucking in vain. They both got out and Elihu took the horse by the bridle, but he would not be led; neither would he be backed. He seemed perfectly satisfied with his present position in life.

"I've read," ventured Winter, "that a balky horse would start if you put dirt inside his under lip."

Elihu grinned.

"Mebbe," he said. "You might try it."

He tried it, with the result that he was soon the possessor of an appearance suggestive of having embraced a mud puddle with fervor. Elihu laughed and Winter swore and reached for the whip.

"Git in here," Elihu cried sharply five minutes later. "Here comes a team."

Winter got in silently and the team approached slowly. It proved to be a genial-looking old man with a peaked hat and a load of milk cans. He drew up opposite them and grinned broadly.

"Nice day," he remarked.

"Great," said Elihu.

"Fine scenery around here," he of the hat and cans continued.

"Greatest we've seen anywhere," Elihu replied enthusiastically. "My friend here," nodding toward Winter, "is an artist and we jest had to stop so he could drink it in, as he says."

"Wal," observed the old man with a broader grin, "he'll have a chance to git a good big drink."

"Probably," Elihu answered, "you'll see this landscape on the cover of some magazine sometime if you ever see the up-to-date literature up here."

The old man took a generous chew of tobacco.

"By gol," he exclaimed with well feigned surprise, "if it ain't Congress!"

"His name is Nebuchadrezzar Sennacherib Jones," Elihu corrected, indicating Winter again.

"I mean the hoss," the other explained.

"Do you know him?"

"Some. I sold him to John Hodges, the man you bought him of. We named him Congress 'cause he never goes very far without stoppin' and considerin' quite a spell. Well," he called over his shoulder as he drove on, "I hope you ain't got fer to go. I'll be lookin' for that magazine cover."

Elihu took out his pipe and looked at the horse thoughtfully.

"So Congress is your name, is it?" he said. "Well, Congress, when you are ready to act the people will be with you."

All that day they traveled "steady by jerks," as Elihu said, and Winter, after the first anger had worn off, began to enjoy the trip again. They spent the night ten miles short of where they expected to, and the second night they were fifteen miles from home. They crossed the Burley town line the next morning just as the church bells were ringing in the village a mile distant. Elihu was uneasy.

"It's just our luck," he complained, "to have him balk in the village. We've got to watch his tail close." For that was the only sign by which they could judge the bay's intentions—the violent switching of his tail a few seconds previous to stopping, and a tendency to paw before starting.

"There's Walsh Daniels comin' to meetin' now," Elihu broke out a minute later. "He's allus round when he ain't wanted."

Winter looked ahead and saw the Daniels carryall coming leisurely down a cross-road so as to intercept them at the corner. It was full, every crack and cranny being wedged tight with three generations of Danielses. When Elihu's eyes came back from them to the tail of Congress, he swore again.

"There he goes, George, there he goes," he whispered. "Git out and take him by the bits and hang on for dear life."

As he spoke, Congress stopped with a jerk and Winter, taking his cue, jumped down and seized him by the bridle. But Elihu was out first and, taking a wrench from under the seat, dropped on his back beneath the wagon just as the Daniels rig drove up.

"Mornin', Mr. Winter," Daniels called. "Hello, El, what's the matter?"

No reply, but a prodigious rattling beneath the wagon.

"Busted somethin', El?"

Elihu stuck his head out beneath the wheels.

"Oh, it's you, Walsh," he said. "Say, you ain't got a piece of wire, have you? Whoa there!" He dodged back fearfully. "George," he cried, "don't you let that fool hoss start and break my old neck!"

Winter sidled around behind Congress before he answered: "Be as spry as you can. He seems to be getting impatient."

"Drat him," Elihu muttered, "he must be made of whalebone. He's had road enough now to kill a common hoss."

The deacon did not have any wire with him, but he had a piece of leather string which Elihu, coming from beneath the wagon, accepted thankfully.

"Been tradin' horses, El?" Daniels asked.

"Eup," Elihu answered, getting down once more to adjust the string.

"Good-lookin' horse," was the deacon's comment, and he would have said more had not his wife reminded him by a punch in the short ribs with her umbrella that it was past church time. So he contented himself by leaning out of the surrey and looking backward until they rounded a bend in the road.

When the carryall was out of sight, Elihu came from under the buggy once more. "That wagon busted mighty quick, didn't it George?" was all he said.

Winter laughed uproariously.

"If I had some of your ingenuity," he said admiringly, "I would win more cases than I do."

A few minutes later they drove into the village. Congress, head and tail erect, swept through the streets, his feet falling as lightly as though treading on eggs. They met several teams and passed some, and as they whirled past the church Winter caught a glimpse of Deacon Daniels' face pressed tight against the window of his pew. Without another stop they reached home, and as quickly as possible Congress was unhitched and turned into the back pasture.

Time passed. George Winter returned to the city, and September commenced pointing with a crimson finger toward October, but still Congress ran in the pasture, growing fat and handsome every day. The fact that Elihu did not drive his beautiful bay provoked some comment, but he was ever ready with satisfying answers, so no one learned the truth—and you may be assured that he forgot to tell anyone.

For some reason he had been unable to find anyone who cared either to buy or trade for Congress; probably because he never showed him. It did not appear as suspicious so long as the horse could be at pasture, but when winter came there would be no excuse, and in vain did Elihu scratch his head and try to find a way out. As autumn came on, he could think of nothing else, for the time was fast coming when he must show his hand. Tired of practicing deceit any longer, he had about decided to tell the truth and run the chances when, on a bright September morning, Deacon Daniels changed the whole face of the situation.

The deacon had had his eye, privately, of course, on Congress ever since that Sunday morning. A fancier of horses himself, the picture of the beautiful bay would not leave his mind. Often during the summer, with a berry pail on his arm to allay suspicion, he had journeyed to the back pasture and there at his leisure had sized up the horse and returned each time more enthusiastic. This morning as he drove up the road he was deep in thought.

"Mornin', El," he called heartily, driving up to the barn. "Nice mornin', ain't it?"

"Eup," said Elihu, "pretty fair."

"Goin' to have an early fall, you think?"

"Mebbe."

"Got your corn all cut?"

"Eup."

"Say," abruptly, "what you got for horses, El?"

"Nothin' that would suit you."

"I'm lookin' for a friend," the deacon informed. "Cousin of mine. Jim Hodges is his name."

Elihu drew in his breath with a gasp. "Lives 'bout two miles this side of St. Albans?" he asked quickly.

"Yes. Do you know him?"

Elihu laughed. "I guess I do," he said. "I traded horses with him once." He spoke in a vague manner which conveyed the impression that the transaction took place years before.

The deacon smiled.

"If you traded with Jim you got beat," he ventured.

"I got a pretty good-lookin' hoss," Elihu returned, "but I'll admit that he's a good trader."

"I guess he is," the deacon agreed. "He wrote me a while ago about tradin' a good-for-nothin' onto a couple of fellers from York State last summer. What about your

21

horse, do you want to sell him?"

"Why, yes, if I can git my price—three hundred cash."

The deacon whistled.

"It's a good price," Elihu admitted, "but you don't find hosses like him every day."

"Is he safe in the harness?" the deacon asked. "Jim wants something his wife can drive."

"Now, look here at the start," Elihu announced. "I ain't goin' to ironclad this hoss to you or anybody else. I don't like the idee of a man's not buyin' his own hoss, for there's likely to be more of a kick comin' if everythin' ain't right afterwards."

"Oh, that's all right," Daniels hastened to assure him. "I'll stand back of you."

"All right," Elihu agreed. "But remember I don't blanket warrant him. I ain't drove him enough to git acquainted with him, but as fer as I know he is perfectly safe. He's seven years old, sound as a nut, and can road better'n most of 'em."

"Hitch him up and let me try him?"

"Sure," Elihu agreed. "Nobody ought to buy a hoss without tryin' him."

He had expected this and was prepared to risk it, for the stake was great—he was willing to chance anything for the sake of evening up with Jim Hodges. So he started briskly toward the pasture and returned in a few minutes with Congress.

The deacon watched him harness and noted the horse's docility with approval. "Jim's wife could handle him all right," he remarked.

"Sure," Elihu agreed, buckling the last strap.

They got in and left the barn with a flourish. Elihu drove and speeded up the bay so that the deacon was obliged to hold onto his hat and catch his breath. "Well," he gasped, "he can go, I should say." They reached the corner half a mile away and Elihu was preparing to return when the deacon interposed.

"Go round the square," he commanded. Elihu's heart fell, for it was two miles around the square. But he was a sport, and would play the game to a finish now that it was started.

They started off again at a brisk pace, Elihu talking horse as usual, but keeping a sharp eye on Congress. They had gone scarcely fifty yards when the bay switched his tail violently. Elihu cast about helplessly. Though the land was his on both sides of the road, he could not command it to open up and swallow either the deacon or the horse, much as he would have liked to. Then, with a sudden jerk, he reigned Congress to the side of the road. "Whoa!" he cried, tugging at the reins. "Durn ye, won't ye stop?"

"What's the matter?" the deacon asked.

"Come nigh forgittin' it," Elihu explained. "But while we're over this way I want you to see my colt. He's about the neatest colt for his age that I ever see." And pointing over the fence he indicated at the other side of the pasture, beneath some trees, a mare and a colt.

"Of course," the deacon fell beautifully, "I'd like to see him. He's half-brother to mine."

"That's why I wanted you to see him," Elihu explained, "wanted you to compare 'em." And, stepping to the fence, he called the mare to him.

When he had exhausted that topic he found another, and so for half an hour they leaned on the fence and talked.

"He stands well," the deacon observed, nodding toward Congress.

"Eup," said Elihu, with a slight cough, "that's one of his strong points."

Then the bay commenced to paw and Elihu got in. "We'd better be goin'," he said. "It's gittin' near dinner time."

About a week later the deacon met Elihu in the village.

"The horse got there all right," he said. "I wrote Jim that I got him of you, and he answered that he remembered you well, only he thought that you lived in Burley, New York. He said to tell you that he was very much pleased with the horse and that he hoped to trade with you again some time."

"Jim's a sport," Elihu said.

And the deacon wondered what he meant.

AUNT MARIE AT THE FAIR

Leslie Childs
Successful Farming, September 1916

I jist pintidly don't care whether I ever go to another fair or not," declared Aunt Marie Simpson, as she struggled out of her Sunday best and into a wrapper. Mrs. Hawkins, her next door neighbor, had seen the Simpsons drive by on their way home from the fair and had hurried over to hear the news, and incidently borrow a cup of yeast.

"No," continued Aunt Marie, "I would not have gone today, but for the children and Pa pestering me, so I finally agreed to go. I jist felt as if something was going to happen all day. This morning, after we got started, and was down the road about a mile, I remembered I had seen a live coal of fire in the kitchen stove. I had thrown a quart of water in to put the fire out, and intended to pour some more in, but forgot all about it in the hustle and bustle of getting the dinner basket, the children, and Pa into the wagon.

"I told Pa that he must go right back and see if that fire had gone out, and after considerable argument, he did finally go. Some men are so contrary. Jist think—the house might have burned down! Well, we waited there in the road, eating all the dust the people who drove by kicked up, for nigh onto an hour before Pa come back. Some people are so slow. When he did get back, he was all out of wind, and said there wasn't a bit of fire in the stove, and it was stone cold.

"I had counted on enjoying the ride to town, but I didn't, for as we passed Mr. Duke's place, Mr. James, that new man who is clearing for Duke, got in with us to ride. He sat next to the dinner basket, and I jist knew he was mashing them pumpkin pies I had in there. He allowed he wasn't, but I knew he was, and when we got inside the fair grounds I uncovered the basket to see. For a wonder the pies were all right. Still, I don't see how he kept from mashing them, for he went jam up against them every time we hit a rough place.

"When we got the team put up, I took the children and started to go through Floral Hall before the crowd got too thick in there. About ten o'clock, when I was jist beginning to enjoy myself, I heard some mules kicking and squealing down in the direction where we had ours tied. I was certain it was our team broke loose. I didn't want Pa to drive the young mules, but he jist would; said the drive would do them good, so I finally give in.

"Well, I sent Arabella out to hunt up Pa and tell him. After about an hour, time enough for both our mules to be kicked to death in, he come sauntering up with a cheap cigar in his mouth. There was a patent fence man on each side of him, trying to talk him into mortgaging the farm for fencing. I told him to hurry and see if our mules was all right. In about an hour he came back saying our mules was still alive, then made off with them fence men again.

"I worried all day for fear they would coax him into buying a lot of fencing, for Pa is easily persuaded at times. We had our dinner in the shade of a big tree that stood near the wagon. Sally Moffit and her two children, you know her husband died last March, and she moved to town and is taking sewing there, came along and of course I invited them to take dinner with us.

"It's a shame the way some people let their children grow up. That boy of her's, he's five years old and ought to know better, got the stopper out of the honey bottle when I wasn't looking. Before I noticed him, he had honey scattered all over the table cloth; and it was one of my best white ones, too. Then, as if that wasn't enough, he came up behind me a few minutes later and, putting his little hands—all covered with honey—around my neck, began fingering my new black dress. Sally sat there laughing and cried, 'Oh, how cute, ain't he dear?' I felt like spanking him, but of course I couldn't say anything for fear of hurting Sally's feelings, and he is a sweet little fellow.

"Pa went off in the afternoon, and I saw him over by the race track. I was worried to death for fear he'd go and bet on the races. He never did such a thing, to my knowing, but you never can tell what a man will do when out of sight. I sent Arabella over to get him, and we took a walk around the grounds viewing the sights.

"There was a number of shows, and I told Pa I thought we could afford to take the children into one. Pa bought four tickets and we went in and got a good seat, up in front. The music started and a man in a red shirt shouted that Madame some one would now do some kind of a dance. Now, you know, as a working church member I cannot uphold dancing, but being as we had paid for our tickets I felt it would not be wrong to stay and see the show. I intended to close my eyes while the dancing was going on. But land sakes it was such a sight I couldn't.

"A female came out on the stage, dressed in the least clothes I ever seen anyone wear, except when they were going to take a bath. I looked at Pa, and he had his eyes glued on the creature. So taking him firmly by the arm I says, "Pa this is no place for us,' and started to go out."

"Why Ma, I didn't see nothing wrong," exclaimed Pa from the corner of the kitchen, where he was struggling to get out of his Sunday boots.

"Didn't see nothing wrong? I'd like to know where your eyes were, and you a deacon in the church, too. It was jist scandalous, the way she acted. Why, I wouldn't be seen at home by my own folks, in the clothes she wore there before strangers. As we were going out she actually winked at Pa. I saw her.

"We next went and had some lemonade, and Arabella would drink two glasses. I jist felt it would make her sick. About three o'clock the balloon went up, and a man jumped from it in a parachute, but the balloon, all smoking, traveled away. I heard a man say it might travel five or six miles, and I saw it was going in the direction of our place. I felt sure it would drop down in our barnyard, among all the new straw from threshing, and set the place on fire. I never got if off my mind until we got to the hill, on our way home, and looked down here and saw everything was all right.

"Then Zeke Taylor, he used to be our hired hand you know, but is working for

Squire Williams this summer, comes along and tells Pa that he has been cheated out of five dollars, by some one with two shells—I think that's what it was—and ain't got money enough to take him back home. Pa lends him fifty cents. I know we'll never get that back again.

"By five o'clock I was tired out, and told the children we had better be starting for home. Then I missed Pa, and it took an hour to find him. He had gone off with them fence men again, and was talking fence. I guess he would be there yet, talking fence, if we hadn't found him.

"Finally we all got together and started. On the way home a man in an automobile ran right up to us. The mules got scared and almost turned the wagon over into a ditch, but thank goodness here we are all safe and sound at last.

"When did you say the Banks County Fair was to be held? Well, I don't know whether we'll go or not. It's a right smart drive over there, but if Pa and the children want to go, I won't hang back. Better stay and have a bite of supper with us. Yes that yeast is good. Well, goodbye. Pa, you and the children hurry and get ready for supper."

A LOVE STORY WITHOUT AN ENDING

Harriet Lummis Smith
The Farmer's Wife, March 1914

T HE Pikesville *Weekly Banner* came out on Thursday, unless something happened to prevent, and the next morning Cyrus Pettibone was pretty sure to
be at the cross roads awaiting its arrival, via the Rural Free Delivery.

This particular Friday morning justified the superstitious who deem it a day of
ill luck. The mail wagon was half an hour late. "No *Banner?*" he grumbled as only a
slim white envelope was thrust into his extended hands.

"The editor's been to Boston," said the mail carrier. "The paper won't be delivered before Monday, it ain't likely." He clucked to his horse, and drove on, leaving
Cyrus to the solace of the modest white envelope. He studied the address frowningly.
The chirography was modest. The t's, heavily shaded, bespoke a feminine pen. The
postmark was Pikesville. This last discovery whetted Cyrus's curiosity. Little guessing the momentous consequences of an act apparently insignificant, he broke the seal.

A bachelor of forty-odd, Cyrus had preserved a complacency regarding the attitude of the opposite sex toward himself, which is natural to the average male, and
eradicated only by prolonged and painful discipline. He had never, it is true, asked a
woman to marry him, but he took it for granted that any of his feminine acquaintances,
except for obstacles in the nature of a previous and deep-rooted attachment, would
have accepted such an invitation with grateful alacrity. His mother, from his youth up,
suspected every single woman within range of "setting her cap for Cy." Yet while
recognizing himself as the legitimate object of feminine desire, his actual excursions in
the domain of sentiment had been so few and so cautious, that he might legitimately be
called inexperienced. Nothing in his previous career had prepared him for a letter like
the one now in his hands:

> Something is lacking in your home. You cannot deny it. There are days when you are
> lonely, when you feel the need of cheer, of change, of gaiety, and you ask yourself how
> long this sordid grind of toil is to continue unrelieved.
>
> There is a remedy. There is no need of these monotonous days, these lonely
> hours. Do not act hastily. Wait for further word.

"Dod blobbs!" gasped Mr. Pettibone. The oath was original with himself, and uttered
only under stress of great emotion.

The first love letter is a thing of moment, whether the recipient is a blushing pink-
and-white bit of femininity or a bearded bachelor, well past two score. The notes Cyrus
had hitherto received from various lady friends had most of them been written twenty
years earlier. They all opened with "Friend Cyrus," and from that circumspect begin-

ning, took their decorous way through four pages or less of matter not calculated to quicken the pulses. This letter was different: elusive, vague, unsatisfying, mysterious. And are not those things the very life blood of romance?

Cyrus Pettibone had never before realized the lacks in his home life. His mother, despite her sixty-five years, was a housekeeper of renown whose recipes were solicited respectfully by every aspirant for house-wifely honors for miles around. Cyrus was fed, not wisely, but too well, as his increasing girth indicated. He would have been no more surprised to find a centipede in the toe of his sock, than to put one on and be confronted with a hole. But there was a lack! Yes, there was undoubtedly a lack.

"There is a remedy." This statement appealed to Cyrus as a peculiarly delicate way of stating an obvious truth. Of course there was a remedy. He let his imagination dally with it for a moment, investing it now with raven hair, and eyes dark and mysterious as night, and then transforming it without an instant's warning, into a golden-haired blonde. Why go on working hard, eating hard, and going to sleep in his chair after supper till at nine o'clock his mother woke him and sent him off to bed? The "remedy" would soon alter this. Cheer! Change! Gaiety! He munched the words as if they had been sweetmeats.

"Do not act hastily." The caution drew from Cyrus an ironic smile. Well hardly. His eye teeth were cut by now, he guessed. As a matter of fact they were not only cut, but drawn and replaced by the snowy, gleaming substitutes the Pikesville dentist furnished for ten dollars a set.

"Any mail, Cyrus?" Mrs. Pettibone asked as he entered the house.

"Paper didn't come this morning, editor's been to Boston."

"Charley Evans always was a gadder," said Mrs. Pettibone. "And folks can't gad and do their work too. I've never been further from home than the Junction. Ain't never had time, but my wash has been on the line by nine o'clock every Monday morning since before you was born." She changed the subject as certain preparations on her son's part awakened her suspicions. "Not going anywhere this morning, be you?"

"Well, yes. Think I'll drive down to Jimmy Johnston's. There's a few little things I need. Any errands?"

Mrs. Pettibone kneaded her bread, violently. "If I wanted anything, I'd go over to East Jericho and get it at Camp's."

"Camp's ain't half the store that Johnston's is. Jimmy's up-to-date. No back numbers about him."

"He's been to the city, too," said Mrs. Pettibone disparagingly. "'Twas there he learned all this stuff about sales, bargain sales, and fire sales and rummage sales, and I don't know what all. Just because a lot of stuff is dumped together on a counter, and called a sale, some folks think they're going to get more than their money's worth. But I notice that Jimmy Johnston's bought another automobile, and that new wing on his house must have cost him a pretty penny. I guess he ain't losing any money."

The dispute was an old one between them, and Cyrus departed without any attempt to refute his mother's argument. Under the circumstances it was impossible for him to feel the slightest interest in Jimmy Johnston. His thoughts were still busy with his enigmatic letter, with the lacks in his home life, with the "remedy" and how he should set about finding her.

Phoebe Packard was washing windows as Cyrus drove past. The word "spinster" expressed Phoebe to a T. Even in her youth she had seemed estranged from sentiment and her buxom middle age effected no reconciliation. Apparently the most inveterate of the village matchmakers had regarded her case as hopeless from the beginning. Just why this should have been is one of the mysteries in the psychology of love. Phoebe Packard was nothing worse than comfortably plain, with a temper like honey and a county-wide reputation as a cook, yet she had never been favored with an opportunity to exchange single blessedness for the uncertainties of matrimony.

Phoebe's broad back was in view when Cyrus first espied her. She turned her head at the sound of wheels, and then unexpectedly flourished the cloth with which she was polishing the glass and called his name. "Oh, Cyrus! Wait. Cyrus! I've been wanting to see you."

A sudden panic-breeding suspicion took possession of Cyrus. What if Phoebe were the writer of the mysterious letter? It was within the bounds of possibility that she knew the lack in his home life by her own, that she made her loneliness the measure of his. Her sudden excitement at the sight of him was at least suspicious.

Instead of halting, Cyrus took out the whip. "Can't stop now, Phoebe," he shouted. "In a tarnation hurry." He lashed the surprised mare and the dusty buggy rattled on.

Preoccupation did not prevent Cyrus from making his usual hearty meal at the midday dinner. As he helped himself for the third time to the spiced gooseberries, his mother commented. "You seem to like 'em."

"They're the best preserves I've tasted this year."

"Phoebe Packard brought up a jar," explained Mrs. Pettibone, refilling her cup. "She said she'd been laying out to give it to you when you drove by, but you was in a hurry this morning, so she fetched it herself."

Cyrus pushed the delicacy to the side of his plate with a sudden strong distaste. Suspicion was becoming a certainty. Phoebe Packard, whom no man had ever wanted, fancied she could win him by anonymous letters and spiced gooseberries. Phoebe Packard had the effrontery to fancy that she could fill the lack in his heart and home. After his dreams of the morning, the reaction was jarring.

For forty-odd years Cyrus had lived in a state as nearly approaching contentment as any son of Adam can reasonably expect. Now the serpent had entered Eden in the shape of a letter written in a feminine hand. Even his suspicions that his middle-aged neighbor was the writer could not set at rest the uneasy yearnings it had engendered. If he were not careful, his life would be over before he had really lived. The remedy for the lacks he had just begun to realize was rapidly taking a definite outline. In fact it strongly resembled Mattie Whittier, the pretty girl who played the organ in church Sundays and flirted, between hymns, with the tenor of the volunteer choir. "I expect she'd want a piano," Cyrus said to himself, and smiled indulgently. Pianos cost money, but if she wanted one, she should have it. He fancied her playing to him after supper, "Silver Threads Among the Gold," his favorite melody, and looking at him over her shoulder, in the provocative way she looked at the tenor. That would be better than going to sleep over the locals in the Pikesville *Banner*!

When Cyrus came downstairs that evening, his mother could see that he was bound on a sentimental errand. His tan shoes with the narrow pointed toes had not emerged from their seclusion since a dozen years ago when he had worn them to a wedding, and driven home at midnight in his stockinged feet. The hand-painted necktie, white daisies on a pink background, was a souvenir of an even earlier epoch. Taken altogether Cyrus looked uncomfortable, and self-conscious.

"I thought he looked flustered when I told him 'twas Phoebe who brought the gooseberries," thought Mrs. Pettibone with a self-congratulatory chuckle. "He's getting to an age when a woman's knowing how to put up preserves means more to him than her complexion." Blind mother, to suppose that the most venerable son ever reaches a point where feminine accomplishments, or virtues for that matter, can be weighed in the balance against the curve of a pink cheek, or the dimple lurking therein! Deluded woman to deceive herself by fancying that the most dutiful son will ever woo the lady of his mother's choice!

When Cyrus returned at midnight he had become a man of experience. He had proposed and been rejected. For once he had been swept off his feet by impulse. He had begun by inviting Mattie to a drive and then to accompany him to the Mapleville Fair, and when these tentative offers had been refused, he had disdained caution, and come to the point: would she marry him? She knew who he was, and that there wasn't a better farm in the country than his. If she wanted a piano, she could have it, and she could depend on his mother to do the cooking as long as she could get about.

Strange to say, Mattie had seemed more surprised than gratified by his offer. At first she had been inclined to giggle, as if she suspected him of trying to be humorous. Later she had grown quite irritable and repulsed him savagely when he tried to take her hand. Pressed for her reasons, she had explained that she didn't want to marry him, and that she never could nor would want to marry him under any imaginable circumstances. Her plainness of speech was disconcerting to a man who had been taught to look upon himself as a prize. He lingered, repeating his offer and adding such inducements as suggested themselves, till she began to yawn, openly and with a malicious purpose, casting restive glances at the clock. He finally left her in a rage, intensified by the fact that his feet ached in the tight shoes, and that his high collar had painfully rasped his unaccustomed neck. Moreover, beneath his resentment at Mattie's incomprehensible caprice was the thought that the knowledge of his errand and its outcome would gratify the writer of the anonymous letter, presumably Phoebe Packard. Cyrus resolved that he would show 'em.

It is painful to record so protracted a lapse in the history of a man hitherto distinguished by cautious common sense. From his first reckless beginning, Cyrus plunged into a very orgy of courtship. He proposed right and left. The news spread like fire in prairie grass. At his approach young girls turned from pink to crimson, and held their handkerchiefs to their laugh-twisted mouths. The halting of his buggy before a door where there were marriageable daughters was the occasion for reprehensible gaiety.

A.S.Hicks

The girls to whom he had not proposed felt hurt, and racked their brains for reasons for the unaccountable omission

The girls who had been invited to become Mrs. Pettibone compared notes with reminiscent giggles. At Jimmy Johnston's store, Cyrus was greeted with significant glances, and after his departure roars of laughter welcomed such details as the men had gleaned from the conversation of wives and daughters. On the principle that like cures like, Cyrus made each fresh rejection heal the hurt of the last, and went to each new wooing untroubled by any regrets over past denials. His mother was more to be pitied than he. After one or two unavailing attempts to keep her son from making a fool of himself, as she phrased it, Mrs. Pettibone resigned herself to the inevitable, and was waiting grimly for him to announce the name of her future daughter-in-law. "She's bound to be giddy and giggly," thought Mrs. Pettibone. "For that's the kind he's picking. So fer as I know he hasn't asked a widow yet, or a nice settled woman like Phoebe Packard."

But apparently in this new form of hide-and-seek, the game was to keep from being caught. Some girls laughed when he proposed, and some looked as if it would not take much to make them cry, but with singular unanimity all agreed in saying no. Cyrus grew haggard from late hours and blighted hopes, but his mouth took on a new stubbornness. There was a look about him that somehow suggested that he would propose to the whole countryside if need be, but he would find a girl that was willing.

One night he came home late, climbed dejectedly up the creaking stairs, and was transfixed on the landing by the apparition of his mother's night-capped head.

"Cyrus!"

"Yes, ma."

"A letter came for you this afternoon. I stuck it behind the clock and forgot to give it to you. It's on your bureau under the pin cushion, so's not to blow away."

The hero of a score of defeats knew that writing at a glance. What memories it suggested. He was a tyro in love when the first letter reached him. The second found him a man bent nearly double under the accumulated weight of sentimental experiences. For better or for worse, the first letter had started him on a career of love-making rarely equalled. He would not have been human if his hand had not trembled slightly as he broke the seal:

The thoughts of past failure, of disappointed hopes are not pleasant company for your times of solitude. Why not take steps to distract your mind from these painful reminiscences. It is possible. Wait and learn how.

Cyrus sat down heavily on the edge of his bed, the letter in his hand. "She means she's still ready to take up with me," he said, and realized as never before the persistent character of the feminine affections. Something touched that still sensitive kernel at the center of his shriveled heart. For the first time since it had occurred to him that Phoebe wished to marry him, the thought awoke in him no resentment.

Phoebe Packard was not an ugly woman, he reflected, staring absently at the braided rug. She had never been a beauty, to be sure, but sometimes a pretty wife was considerable care to a man. Then, too, Phoebe was a good cook. He would find it hard to

34

reconcile himself to tough pie crust and soggy dumplings. On the whole one might go further than Phoebe and fare worse. He fell asleep promptly that night, and his rest was tranquil.

When he proposed to Phoebe Packard the following evening, that gentle-spirited spinster looked at him commiseratingly, and seemed in no haste to answer. "Good gracious, Cyrus," she said at last. "You don't want to marry me a mite more than I want to marry you."

"Then you—" Cyrus could get no further. His jaw dropped and he sat staring at her dumbly. Phoebe's feminine intuition completed the unfinished sentence, but even then she showed no resentment.

"Oh dear no, Cyrus," she responded, rocking gently. "It seems to me that men folks, even the best of 'em, are considerable of a trial. Now there's my cousin Sally's husband. He will keep his shoes standing in a row under the bed. Every time you go into Sally's room—and she's as good a housekeeper as you'd find in a day's journey— you see that row of toes peeping out at you. I couldn't sleep nights thinking of it. And if it isn't one thing, it's another. I've never been used to putting up with men folks' ways, except the boys that have taken care of my cows and horses, first and last, and I'm free to say they've nearly made me forget that I'm a Christian. It's a good thing to know when you're well off, Cyrus. I ain't a bit inclined to change my lot."

The proposal of Cyrus had not been of the sort to flatter feminine vanity. It was distinctly condescending. The lady's unexpected coyness fanned the flame. His wooing became ardent. Phoebe at length drew her chair to the other side of the round table.

"If you're going to be silly, Cyrus," she said placidly, "I guess I'll read my missionary magazine a spell. For folks of our age, that kind of thing ain't becoming."

When the sullen, disappointed wooer was ready to take his departure, she gave him a cordial hand. "I wish you real good luck, Cyrus," she said. "Of course if you're bound to have a wife you'll get one fast enough; any man can," added Miss Phoebe kindly. "I've heard how hard you've been trying, and I dare say the next one will say yes. Give my regards to your mother, Cyrus."

The third letter came the next morning. Cyrus pounced upon it as a hawk swoops upon its prey. The writer was not Phoebe, that was plain. But she was somebody, and this very letter might contain the clue to her identity. His middle-aged heart thumped with an admirable imitation of youthful sprightliness. Drooping hope revived. Eagerly he began to read, his face changing ludicrously from wonder to wildness:

> Music hath charms, not only to soothe the savage beast, but to make home life happy and satisfying. What is so sure to banish care as sweet melodies? Who can be lonely when at will he may hear the voice of the songster, or the harmonies of great orchestras?
>
> There is a lack in your home life. MacDuffy's Talking Machine will supply the remedy. On sale at Johnston's with full line of records. Stop in when next in town, and hear the people's favorite, Joe Donnovan, sing, "Has Any One Here Seen Kelly?" Easy terms if desired. Give Jimmy Johnston a call.

WE BREAK THE MULES

Lyle Heintz

The Farm Journal, August 1922

UNCLE Judd Hiller owned a fine team of three-year-old mule colts. When they were a few days old, he had bestowed upon them the names, Dick and Dolly. Dolly, at least, ought to have been gentle, but she wasn't. Evidently she believed in equal rights for her sex.

At Uncle Judd's request I went down to his place one day last spring, and he said that the next morning we'd break the mules.

"I've had the harnesses on 'em several times now and they ought to be tolerable gentle," he assured me.

I was in favor of driving both colts together the first time. Uncle Judd was more conservative. He wanted to drive old Dobbin, the family horse, and one colt at a time. "It's too dangerous driving two colts together," he admonished.

"Danger," I replied, "is the spice of life. Without danger life would be tame." Uncle Judd lacked a sufficient array of words to argue with me, so he let me have my way.

Next morning I secured a pair of Uncle Judd's boots, which were so big I could jump into them and then jump right back out. By the time I had assembled the clothes I was going to wear, Uncle Judd was down harnessing the mules.

When I was about three rods from the barn—*whang!* A board flew off from it and a piece nearly hit me in the head. Then I heard Uncle Judd shout, "Whoa, *Dolly!*" I advanced and peered around the corner of the door. "Dolly's feeling a little too good," he explained. "She just about keeps me busy tacking boards on the barn."

I agreed with him that Dolly was feeling good. Dick acted like a gentleman while he was being harnessed, yet I noticed that Uncle Judd didn't give him a chance to act otherwise.

We were hitching the colts to the low wagon when Aunt Sally came out on the porch to watch us. Uncle Judd was holding the mules by the bits while I fastened the traces. I had three hooked and was getting ready to fasten the last one, when Aunt Sally said, "Pshaw! They're just like old horses already." She hadn't any more than said it when Dolly reared forward, and Dick stepped on Uncle Judd's toes. He let go of the bits with a yell and the mules took straight for the barn. Luckily the tongue didn't come down, and the mules, both at once, tried to enter the little barn. They couldn't get in, and there they stuck.

I had already seized the reins and was quieting the mules when Uncle Judd came up, limping decidedly. He was favoring the left foot, on which he had several corns. "Leave 'em in the door until we get the tugs hooked," he exploded. "If I wasn't a deacon of the church I'd swear a little. Phew, but those corns are sore!"

We got the tugs hooked and pried the mules out of the door. They came back with a lunge and my foot, or rather my boot, was under the wheel. The mules backed a few feet and stopped.

"If those boots hadn't been so big you'd have had your foot smashed, young man," Uncle Judd assured me. But I'm not sure whether he was right or not. If the boots hadn't been so big there wouldn't have been anything under the wheel.

Eventually we got the mules started forward and headed toward the public highway. After starting, they went willingly enough—too willingly, in fact. Before they were out of the gate they were on the dead run, in spite of our efforts to hold them. Away went uncle's hat; it lifted from his head like a kite. We covered the first mile in record-breaking time, in spite of the mud.

By leaning forward a little I heard Uncle Judd say: "Blast 'em! They are running away, I guess." I had been aware of the fact for several minutes, but so long as everything hung together we were all right.

"If it wasn't for Sam Higgins makin' fun of me, I'd jump out, but he'd never get over it," I heard Uncle Judd shout.

"Hold on to the rope," I said. "They'll soon tire out."

"Seems to me they're just getting started," Uncle Judd observed.

As we flashed past Sam Higgins' farm I didn't have time to see whether any one was watching us. I suppose we didn't cut a very pretty-looking figure. Mud was flying into the air, Uncle Judd was hatless, his beard was plastered against his vest, and I was almost sitting down I was pulling so hard. Anyway, I hoped Sam Higgins' daughter wasn't watching.

We were a mile up the road past Higgins' when Uncle Judd shouted to me: "Let 'em run, I'm goin' to jump."

"They're running now," I said, trying to be humorous in the face of danger, but Uncle Judd didn't feel like laughing. He had one leg over the box when—*crash*—a front wheel gave way and spun out to the side of the road. The lurch the wagon gave added impetus to Uncle Judd's leap and he landed head first in the mud. I wasn't going to ride that lurching wagon alone, so I scooted for the rear end. The end came before I was ready to go, and to make matters worse the heel of my large boot caught in the scoop-board socket. I fell, but my boot stayed in the wagon. I sat there and watched my boot riding along in the lurching wagon. At last, about eighty rods down the road, it bounced out.

Uncle Judd came over to where I was getting up. He was spitting the mud from his mouth. He was a good sport though; he never once said: "I told you it'd be too blamed dangerous drivin' 'em both together." He did say, however, "If drivin' two mules together is the 'spice of life,' spice tastes a lot like mud to me."

I was considering how to get down the road to my boot when I heard a buggy coming behind us. It proved to be Sam Higgins, and worse, his daughter was with him. As they came up Higgins said: "So you jumped out and let 'em go, did you?"

"Not on your life," replied Uncle Judd, pointing to the broken wagon wheel. "That wheel broke. That's what did it."

"Did the wagon upset?" asked Higgins.

"No, but it tipped so that it threw us out," evaded Uncle Judd.

Higgins asked us to ride along with them, until we found the mules, and Uncle Judd accepted. I looked up at Miss Higgins and found that she was looking at my foot. This was painful for a moment, until I explained how my boot caught in the wagon, and how I only escaped being dragged to death by its slipping off. This was something of a prevarication, but I noticed Uncle Judd nodded approvingly.

"Judd," Higgins said, "If you'll hold this basket of eggs on your lap you can sit in front with me." That detailed me to sit with the girl. Nothing loath, I climbed in, and we started.

Higgins stopped when we came to my boot and when I slipped it on so easily Phoebe (that's Miss Higgins' given name) said that she believed I could slip both feet in one boot. I couldn't decide whether she was making fun of the boots or complimenting me upon having small feet.

Phoebe and I got along splendidly and I'll confess right here that the ride behind Higgins' team was lots pleasanter, even if it wasn't so thrilling, than the ride behind the mules. It was pleasanter for me, at least. I'm not speaking for Uncle Judd.

We soon came to the place where the mules had turned into a farmer's barn-yard. A man had them by the heads holding them.

Uncle Judd thanked the man when he offered us his wagon, but refused it. He guessed we'd "lead 'em home," and I didn't argue any with him.

We found Uncle Judd's hat on a fencepost where it had traveled from his head, but in the meantime some hunter had passed and, making the hat a target, discharged his shotgun at it.

Aunt Sally said she was worried sick, but she wasn't so frightened but what she could take a good laugh at Uncle Judd's hat.

We did break the mule colts, but not both at once. We used Dobbin in the place of Dick and then in the place of Dolly.

I had a letter from Uncle Judd the other day. He said that Dick had tamed down, but that Dolly was just as stubborn as ever.

And, by the way, this may interest some of you folks; I get a letter from Phoebe nearly every day.

INTENSIVE FARMING IN AN INEXPENSIVE FLAT

Robert Wells Richie

The Country Gentleman, March 1913

I t started, as I remember, that day my wife came running in from the kitchenette with a healthy Bermuda onion in her hand and a sympathetic light in her eyes. "Oh, see, Cedric," she chortled with a happy little gasp, "the poor dear onion wants to grow. See all his little rootlets!"

My wife has a most profound sympathy for Nature. I have known her to be mournful for half a day when she saw men in the park trimming the elms—"cutting off all their poor dear arms"—a homeless cat stirs in her strange philanthropic impulses; a crocus pushing up through the last March snow assumes for her the character of a hero. It is a commendable faculty, this kinship with Nature, and one which a man may well admire in his wife.

"Onions, my dear," I remember having answered with the air of preciseness I sometimes assume in conversation with my helpmeet, "all have rootlets. It is characteristic of onions to have rootlets, while carrots, for example, have a taproot."

"Yes, but dear, these rootlets want to grow—and see the nice green sprouts all sticking up from the top of his little head, Cedric. I'd feel like a cannibal—just like a savage Hottentot or one of those things—to eat an onion when it was trying so hard to grow. It's alive and it shall keep on living; yes it shall."

As I look back now upon this modest beginning of our experiment in thumbnail ranching I recall that the incident of the onion's planting did not impress me greatly. Genevieve put it in a small flowerpot which had been tenanted by a later lamented carnation and set it on the sill of our kitchenette window—a window that looks out on the court of the Hallorhan Arms. There are some seventy or a hundred windows set in the four walls of that court; ours is on the highest tier.

"He shall grow up to be a nice big onion, so he shall," Genevieve crooned as she patted the dirt round the top of the big bulb. "And then Dickey shall eat the nice seeds that come—if they don't give him bad breath." Dickey is our canary.

Perhaps three weeks passed and I heard no more of the onion. One night we were playing auction with the Heffrens across the hall on our floor—all four families on the top floor of the Hallorhan Arms are very chummy and clubby, you see—and I think it was Mrs. Heffren who said between deals:

"Did you bring that cactus home from Mexico with you?"

"Cactus—cactus?"

"Yes, that wonderfully spiky cactus you have on the window sill of your kitchenette."

My wife kicked my ankle under the bridge table, her eyes dancing with mischief. I caught the hint.

"Oh—um—yes. You mean that maguey smelliferous. Oh, yes; got it at Vera Cruz, where it is very much prized. Just wait until you see the blossoms."

The Heffrens murmured their polite interest and nothing more was said about our early-blooming Bermuda. Hardly had our own door closed on us, however, when Genevieve, dancing and clapping her hands, propounded the Grand Scheme. We would grow something else on our window sills to fool the Heffrens, that's what we'd do! The Heffrens were city folks, both of them; neither had been east of Patchogue or west of Hoboken; they had never been nearer a cow than the one pictured on the condensed cream can; they didn't know whether a hayfield was shaved or just mowed. My dear wife always asserted a superiority over city-bred folks, born of her early girlhood on Staten Island. Her father had a garden patch.

"I think," she said, "it would be perfectly darling to raise some hay in a window-box or plant a silo in the dining room window. The Heffrens would think they were some sort of decorative plant."

"Silo?" said I. "Silo?"

"Uh-uh; it's a very popular crop with all the farmers in the Middle West," my wife answered with a satisfied air of superior knowledge. "I read just the other day that a farmer in Iowa said his silo netted him two thousand dollars a year. Really, Cedric, you should broaden your knowledge by general reading. I read that in the back of an almanac I got at the druggist's."

I do not believe that at the instant I caught any of my wife's enthusiasm, but shortly after, when I picked up my little limp leather copy of old Quintus Horaitus Flaccus, the page opened to:

> Lest you may question me whether my farm, most excellent Qunictius,
> Feeds its master with grain, or makes him rich with olives,
> Or with its orchards and pastures, or vines that cover the elm trees,
> I, in colloquial fashion, will tell you its shape and position.

And so while my wife was taking down her hair that night I got back to the Sabine Farm—I always snatch at the classics while my wife is taking her hair down—and the odor of clover was in the living room of our apartment; bees hived in the piano. Old Horace Q. got me, even as the echo of Genevieve's desire to raise hay on the window ledge was in my mind. I saw dim visions of boyhood days—the golden desert of wheat on a California ranch; miles of prune trees in blossom; stubble fields flowing about live-oak islands.

"My dear," said I after I had switched out the lights, "your suggestion is a good one, though the motive is defective. Let's have a little window ledge ranch of our own—not to fool the neighbors, but for our own souls' sake. We live false lives here in this New York wilderness of stone and steel. We're as far away from Nature as old Horace was from steam heat and hall-boy service—and he was happier than we. Man should have growing things about him—should always be in touch with the flow of sap and the spring of life through green things. We see nothing grow but skyscrapers and the cost of living; nothing shoots up in our experience but elevators. It would be like—like a sweet burst of symphony music to have all our window ledges springing in living stuff."

"Cedric, you are a poet—not a lawyer," Genevieve murmured and went to sleep.

Our timothy was up a good three inches in the kitchenette ranch—we called it the "lower ranch" because it was, strictly speaking, south of the "home ranch" in the dining room—before the Heffrens began asking questions. We had been itching for the moment when they would inquire what that fine green fuzz in the kitchenette box was. When I answered the Heffrens by a single word, "timothy," they were all attention.

"How delightful!" Mrs. Heffren exclaimed. "One of those old-fashioned plants like sweet william."

But very patiently, having consideration for the ignorance of our neighbors, I explained that timothy was a species of hay, and step by step I unfolded the poetry and the homely glory of our endeavors at getting back to Nature. I really never saw two people embrace an idea so enthusiastically. Horace Heffren declared that he would go round and see a carpenter in the morning and that he'd have a crop of celery growing within a week. He insisted that it must be celery; that was so useful.

"And take it from me," said Heffren as my wife and I lingered at their door in making our adieus, "you may think you are some farmer just because you came from California and I spent my youth on West Thirty-seventh Street, but I'll stake a dinner at Paquin's that I show better results at harvest time than you do."

"You're on." I caught him up with some heat. Heffren is a good fellow, but he is possessed of that New York cocksureness that I have never learned to admire. My Genevieve, catching the challenge that was given and accepted between us, was breathless with excitement.

"Cedric, we must beat him with our crops," she exclaimed when we were behind our door.

"My dear," I replied with assurance, "he is beaten already. We have science on our side and we'll do the thing scientifically; ranching is as exact science as algebra nowadays. I feel sorry for Horace, because I've got him chained to the pile driver at the start; I took a year's course in the cow college at good old Berkeley, you remember—to fill in my science requirements."

When this fellow Heffren put the thing on a competitive basis of course there was nothing to do but to dig to the bottom of things and plot our agricultural strategy. We had then only established the lower ranch outside the kitchenette window in timothy, and the home ranch on the dining room ledge, just having been put in place at the cost of a $3.50 carpenter's bill, was lying fallow, as it were. I immediately got the carpenter busy laying out—I think that's a good agricultural term—a fire-escape quarter-section on the north and two small experimental stations—one outside each bedroom window. Genevieve was for making a mushroom cave behind the piano in the living room, where it was dark; but I told her we must make haste slowly; mushrooms required specialized knowledge and, anyway, they might rust the piano wires.

I suppose our Congressman—Hicks, of the Thirteenth District—got the surprise of his life when I wrote him, asking him to use his influence with the Agricultural Department at Washington to forward me the latest bulletin on intensive farming. Also on soil analysis. Also on dry farming. The latter specialty was particularly necessary to us, I must say parenthetically, because of the New York tenement-house laws which forbid the sprinkling of the neighbors below you instead of the plants you have in a window-box.

I received an ironical letter from Congressman Hicks in reply, saying he had put me on the Agricultural Department's seed list and that he was glad to see that Brooklyn was going to hold her own with the expanding West. And I also received the bulletins—sixty-two of them, from boll weevil to San Jose scale. Genevieve was boiling over with excitement; she had not been so perfectly puffed up about anything, she said, since the burglars took our neighbor Mrs. Stuyvesant Saintly's eight-day clock.

I will frankly confess that at first Genevieve and I found the department bulletins confusing. Our first care, you see, was to pick good crops for the home ranch, the fire-escape quarter-section and the two bedroom plats; only the timothy was planted and growing. Genevieve, who always goes in for the *outre*, thought Egyptian corn would be proper for the home ranch and would not be dissuaded until I read to her from Bulletin No. 3312A that Egyptian corn wanted a sandy, arid soil and dry climate—nothing like that at the Hallorhan Arms, in Brooklyn. I am free to admit that I had a secret partiality to ginseng; but I could not find a word about this profitable product of the Orient in any of the bulletins and I wisely suppressed an adventurous spirit in favor of something less dilettante. Our endeavor was made difficult by the position of our various ranches. Only the ones outside the kitchenette and the dining room windows got the sun; the other three fronted the north and were without sun at all hours. Heffren had the advantage of us in that his apartment across the hall had a southern exposure, but I relied on his ignorance in believing he would not rise to that advantage.

Another thing—soil. I noticed that in all the notes about crops the bulletins carried marked reference to variety of soil contingent upon success in this and that planting. Of course the florist who filled the window-boxes with earth for us did not say where he got the soil or what kind of soil it was—partly because we didn't ask him. However, I assigned Genevieve to stop in at the florist's on her way to the bridge club on a certain Wednesday and take exact notes on what the florist might say concerning the qualities of the soil he had supplied. Her mission was not altogether successful; the florist said he supposed the soil came from somewhere on Long Island—he'd got it from another man and didn't know definitely.

Genevieve was more disturbed on this matter than I. She said she had smelled of the home ranch and it smelt sour. We had Bulletin No. 1114C on "Sour Soils and Their Treatment." I read up on sour soil. Certainly the home ranch didn't look sour. I told Genevieve somebody must have been cooking cabbage in another apartment when she smelled the soil. We let it go at that—for the time being.

Finally, after what Genevieve called "a grange," we sat up over the bulletins until midnight, and we made a decision about our crops. We planted Early Golden pumpkin in the home ranch—it would make a big show and put the Heffrens' eyes out, Genevieve said—Calgary red wheat and Tehama oats in the experiment stations off the bedroom, and citron on the fire-escape quarter-section. It was Genevieve who insisted on the citron; she said she had never seen a citron outside of a plum pudding or a wedding cake and she was just bound she'd get a look at a live citron. Anyway the name had such a sweet and sort of "gooey" sound for her.

I really must give credit to a woman's instinct, even in matters of farming. Genevieve's first suspicion about the sour soil in our home ranch was more than justi-fied when the Early Goldens came up a sickly and anemic greeny-yellow, stems too long and leaves all limp and spiritless. Genevieve and I held a consultation one night shortly after the appearance of the pumpkin plants and I tested some of the soil for potash as per Bulletin No. 7273, Series F. The test was made in the bathroom with two empty medicine bottles for test tubes and a medicine dropper, and if it showed anything it was that the soil in the home ranch was lacking in pretty nearly every element except some traces of broken flowerpot and a "color"—that is a good mining term, at least—

of excelsior. Consequently I went to the druggist's to have him put up a prescription of potash and phosphorus. Genevieve insisted on the latter infusion, because she said that she knew perfectly well the phosphorus would combine with something or other to make phosphates, and how did we know there were enough phosphates in Long Island soil.

The druggist asked if what I wanted was a dog-wash for mange; he had something better than my recipe.

"Too much potash in the soil is a far greater handicap than too little" was what the bulletin on soil analysis said.

"We'll simply have to turn to the horrid old tables and work it out," my quick-witted wife suggested when I brought back the potash and phosphorus. So she got pencil and paper and turned back to the table of logarithms or quadratic equations in the back of the bulletin, which told what percentage of potash in fertilizer should be used to the acre. Since I have such a wretched head for figuring Genevieve worked out the problem while I computed the number of square inches in the home ranch with a tape measure. Genevieve was three hours at it.

Her results were: 1/37289 of a ton of potash to 1/47691.09 of an acre.

We had 1/5785 of an acre in our sour home ranch and I put the potash in with a spoon—also the phosphorus, which smoked.

If truth be told the home ranch did not flourish so luxuriantly as we might have desired, though the timothy was soon screening the kitchenette window and people in the houses to the north of us were scanning our Tehama oats and Calgary wheat with opera glasses every Sunday. This was a great grief to both of us, especially Genevieve. For those Early Goldens were counted on to put the Heffrens' eyes out; instead they had cucumbers in their dining room window that were a flaunting exasperation. We tried injecting the home ranch with a solution of cockroach spray—Genevieve insisted there must be angle worms in the soil which gnawed the roots of the baby pumpkins—and I smoked myself into heartburn to provide cigar ash as a top covering; but to no purpose.

My resourceful little partner was called to her mother's home by illness in the family, and through a terrible oversight, for which I can never forgive myself, Dickey, the canary, was not fed. The following telegrams were exchanged between myself and Genevieve:

"Dickey passed away today. Can you forgive?"

"Bury Dickey home ranch. It affects pumpkins favorably. Forgiveness."

Dickey did affect the pumpkins favorably—tremendously. Never did a blithe little songbird leave behind him such a monument to his worth as did Dickey in those sturdy, almost pugnacious, vines that instantly leaped the edge of the home ranch and went reaching down into the court of the Hallorhan Arms. Genevieve said that when the vines bore fruit she would preserve some of the pumpkins; that would be providing a mortuary urn for our little pet in a very true, yet poetical, sense.

I think I may say with all the conservatism of a bulletin on "The Unknown Quantity in the Culture of the Legume"—that being the most Toryish screed in all our agricultural library—that the demise of Dickey and the conversion of him to the uses of soil doctoring marked a turning point in our happy experiment. Thereafter all the earlier portion of Joseph's dream translation relating to the fat kine and the abundant years worked out in our modest five-rooms-and-bath. Worked out, did I say? Ex-

45

ploded! Where we had been nursing pale and bloodless Early Golden orphans we now had a jungle fighting for place at the dinner table. The citron, after exhibiting vague and disturbing misdoubts of life on a fire escape, now made the north exposure of our apartment resemble the Ivy Tower of Kenilworth Castle. Genevieve said with a little catch in her voice that it was the song of the departed Dickey translated into terms of vegetable lyrics that was thus filling our hearts and our window ledges with gladness.

"Now remember, Cedric," my wife cautioned over the telephone as I was about to leave my office on one of these halcyon days, "remember and get that whaleoil soap for the citron. If Snigle-Snoopers don't carry it in their toilet articles department you might try—a poultry store. And Cedric!"—this in a scream of anxiety—"call on the bug man on the way home and tell him he'll just have to come up here immediately. Tehama and Calgary were simply covered with ladybugs all day. I wouldn't for the world have the neighbors know we had the bug man in our apartment; but I've been reading bulletins on wheat and ladybugs; and Tehama and Calgary are just—shocking!"

Catching Genevieve's spirit of acute anxiety, I requisitioned the immediate services of that bug man as a panicky father summons the family physician to a croup case in the nursery. I didn't tell him any of the symptomatic conditions; simply gave him our address and said the case was urgent. He came that night, carrying his kit.

It would be beneath my dignity, I conceive it, to record any but the barest details of the boorish conduct displayed by the bug man; I will not dignify him by chronicling more than a phrase or two of his conversation.

"So this is what I missed a lodge meeting for!" he asserted when Genevieve opened the bedroom windows and pointed to a row of sleeping ladybugs on a straw of the Tehama oats. "Ladybugs, is it?"

"I take it that ladybugs are nevertheless bugs," I replied with some dignity, "and that you are a bug man by profession; hence—"

"Cockroaches—yes," the bug man answered in a hoarse roar, "and the little fellers—yes; and ants in season; also mice when them that has 'em has 'em. But—ladybugs! Say, what you want to do is to call the city dog catcher!"

It was my ingenious little wife who discovered the next day that my violet shaving water would drive away the ladybugs; so that problem was settled despite the bug man.

However, just about the time Horace Heffren poured carbolic acid on his alfalfa field, thinking it was a fertilizer, and practically putting himself out of the running by the resultant loss of his entire crop, the enigma which finally proved the undoing of our whole scheme presented itself. It lay again with those cantankerous Early Goldens. The intelligent creatures had grown so rapidly on Dickey's hypophosphates that the burgeoning fruit would not stay on the ranch, but hung about ten feet below the window sill, so that when the south wind blew it would tap in ghostly fashion upon the dining room window of the T. Stanford Lelands below us. Of course this enthusiasm on the part of the vines entailed early difficulties—Genevieve would have to take in six or eight feet of slack on the vines every time she wanted to exhibit the young pumpkins. Also a very evident strain on the roots exhibited itself.

When the soil about the base of the home-ranch crop began to crack and the roots appeared to be dragging out of the ground Genevieve and I attempted to anchor the vines at their base. By using three of our four napkin rings as tee-blocks—if that is the proper nautical appellation—and running heavy twine cables through those rings to a full hitch about the waist of each plant, we relieved the strain in some measure. But even at that the yellowing pumpkins continued to drag on the vines to such an extent that we were forced to another expedient. Once more my wife's inventiveness had full play. She got out of the trunk our last summer's hammock—a rather saggy and uncomfortable hammock it was, too—and with my aid she gathered all the pumpkins and supporting vines into the hammock and let the mass swing in riotous disarray a few feet below the window ledge. It gave a hanging basket effect, Genevieve said.

However, fate—or perhaps it was the Nemesis of an outraged canary—pursued. Mrs. T. Stanford Leland is a very flighty woman and capricious. One night when she was alone in her apartment one of the pumpkins fell out of the hammock and crashed squdgily against her dining room window like some obese ghost. She immediately suffered—or at least she subsequently deposed and said she suffered—a fit of nervous hysteria, and her husband came to see me the next night.

"As long as one is forced by the terms of his lease to live under an insane family and his rights are not traversed or his peace broken," said this T. Stanford Leland person, "one endures and says nothing. But when the idiot upstairs in an apartment house—an apartment house, mind you—raises pumpkins and those pumpkins try to climb into one's window, that is the finish."

I remember with pride my Genevieve's instant rejoinder to the effect that at least a pumpkin kept its mouth shut and some people's parrots didn't; moreover it was remarkable how an ignorant bird unconsciously reflected the mental processes of its owners.

Of course the fat was in the fire then. Leland said he would have the Board of Health and the tenement house inspectors and the burglar insurance adjusters on me. Straightway his wife went next day before a police magistrate and swore to a complaint with the rank affidavit already alluded to accompanying. She made the complaint cover Heffren's cucumbers as well, which gave a grain of comfort to Genevieve and myself. Though I am a lawyer I confine my practice to the handling of estates and do not mix in police court cases. However, I knew enough to realize that the Lelands could make it unpleasant for me if they wished. Consequently when we—Genevieve and I—appeared in court the next morning to answer to a summons we were prepared to put into execution a brilliant coup which had been planned by my wife in the dark hours.

"I am ready to plead guilty to the charge," I answered calmly when the magistrate turned an inquiring eye toward me after the reading of Mrs. Leland's outrageous affidavit, "and as my own counsel for the defense I will now produce before the court the corpus delicti."

Whereupon two piano movers whom I had hired and secretly coached staggered into the courtroom bearing between them the largest clothes hamper I could buy. They set it down before the magistrate's desk and then Genevieve and I, with loving caresses and tender care, unreeled from that basket about sixty feet of pumpkin vine, interspersed at frequent intervals with gorgeous golden fruit, like mortar shells gilded.

The magistrate struggled for an instant with incipient epilepsy and then spoke to the clerk:

"The complaint in this case, alleging nuisance, is changed to assault with a deadly weapon. Prisoners discharged on their own recognizance—and the weapons are confiscated by the state."

47

THE BELL STRIKE

Leilia M. Ellefson
Successful Farming, August, 1912

T HE horses and cows were leisurely wandering toward the barnyard, and the pigs begging for supper as Silas Bell drove up the lane to the farmhouse. "Hungry, be you?" he muttered, chirping to his tired horses. "Well, I reckon Mary's cookin' will come in right handy fer me too." He drove around to the back of the house and hollered for one of the boys to come take the team. He called several times but there was no response.

"Well, I'll be jiggered!" he growled, climbing out of the wagon and opening the kitchen door. Instead of the delicious odor of cooking that always greeted him, the great silence of the empty room seemed like a sharp blow in the face. Not even a fire in the cook stove. "Jig me! If this ain't queer!" he muttered, going past the shining pans and bare kitchen table into the dining room. There his attention was at once caught by a large sheet of cardboard dangling from the hanging lamp. It reminded him of the big sign that he had found one day, many years ago, nailed to his front gate: BELL'S BEST BEER ALWAYS SOLD HERE.

Hallowe'en night had never seemed to him a sufficient excuse for such an insult to a deacon of the church. With several indignant, reminiscent snorts he fumbled for his glasses and went nearer to read:

STRIKE NOTICE! Whereas, after years of reasoning, asking and begging, it is impossible to get justice from the Master of this House, we have gone out on a strike. Said strike not to be called off until our demands are allowed.

TERMS:

1st. An allowance for Mother which will place her a little above the inmates of the county farm. She would be grateful for enough money to buy herself a Sunday dress once every ten years without the usual growls of extravagance.

2d. Monthly wages for John and Frank. At least a tenth of the amount the neighbors pay their hired help.

3d. Sue would like to have a piano and music lessons, but she will be satisfied with a new dress every three years, and ten cents a month to buy girl fixings.

4th. A set of marbles, a sled and a toy engine for Ted, and enough time allowed from work to get acquainted with them.

5th. Baby Marjorie asks only for a real curly-haired doll baby. She is tired of rags. Signed, The Bells P.S. When you are ready to settle according to above terms, you will find us camping on Hunter's Island.

No arbitration will be considered!

Only a signed surrender accepted!

No settlement after fourth week!

THE BELLS.

49

Mr. Bell's mouth sagged and his eyes bulged out like a frog's as he read and reread this notice of rebellion.

"Well, I'll be dum-jiggered!" he finally mumbled weakly, as he sank down on the nearest chair, pulled a big red bandanna from his pocket and wiped the beads of moisture from his bewildered head. When he rallied sufficiently from the shock to roam over the deserted house and note the signs of a hasty departure, his stunned brain awakened to the fact that the strike was a genuine affair, and his temper blazed up like kerosene-soaked kindling wood. His stubby beard stood out from his chin so stiff and yellow it could easily have been mistaken for a whisk broom—that is if one did not see the grotesque contortions of the attached face. To say the least, for a deacon of the church his actions were certainly unorthodox.

And they had not even left the cat for him to kick.

"I'll bust this strike dum quick," he told himself quickly. "It'll be the shortest one yit."

He strode heavily through the fields toward the retreat of the strikers. As he came suddenly out of the woods he saw, across the water, his entire family sitting around a well-filled supper table.

The creek was far too deep to wade, too wide to jump, and the only boat possessed by the entire neighborhood was securely tied to a tree on the opposite bank.

Mr. Bell clawed his beard and gulped angrily a few seconds before his voice came.

"Hi, there!" he roared savagely. "All o' you git fer home now, double quick! What d' you mean by sich dum-foolishness?"

His arrival caused a ripple of excitement among the strikers. Mrs. Bell nervously plucked at the tablecloth; but when John looked at her for assurance of loyalty she set her lips firmly and nodded encouragement.

"Did you bring a signed surrender?" John asked, not leaving the table.

"Signed fiddlesticks! You git fer home!"

"Well, I'm sorry," John replied, calmly returning to his supper. "There's nothing to be said then."

"Nothin' ter be said?" yelled his father. "You young jack-a-snipe! I've got somethin' ter be said!"

The family continued eating and ignored him, which added fuel to his wrath.

"Mary, I'm 'shamed o' you fer takin' hand in sich er fool trick!"

Mrs. Bell glanced around over the coffee pot and answered mildly: "I'm very sorry, Silas, but when things come to a point that the children are driven from home by your miserly ways, why—I go with them."

Half stunned, Mr. Bell muttered a few incoherent words. Could that really be Mary? After a few moments Mr. Bell recovered his equilibrium, and his anger blazed out again. "Sue! Git in that boat an' come git my supper. Now march—quick!"

Sue carefully buttered a piece of bread before replying:

"I can't, Pa. I've joined the union; and you know the rules of a union, don't you, Pa? All go back or—"

"Union be jiggered!" Mr. Bell broke in fiercely. "I think you've gone stark, starin' mad!"

He paced back and forth on the beach, the pebbles flying in all directions from under his feet.

"Better take off your shoes, Pa," Ted advised. "You'll cut holes in 'em; and shoes cost money!"

"Ted, be quiet," Mrs. Bell reproved, suppressing a smile.

Ted could mimic his father so perfectly.

"None o' your imperdance, you young scamp!" snorted Mr. Bell. "If I could git 'cross this dum creek I'd whale you good!"

"Gee, I guess!" Ted giggled. "But you can't get across."

"Frank! Ain't you got no sense nuther!" Mr. Bell blustered. "You hustle fer home an' do the chores."

"Can't, Pa," Frank laughed. "I've joined the union, too."

Mr. Bell took a few more angry strides back and forth before trying the youngest member of the family.

"Margy," he said, trying to make his voice persuasive, "don't you want-er go home with Pa?"

"'Cuse me, I think not, Pa," she replied, trying to be courteous, but shaking her curls decidedly. "Nobody's coss or 'tingy ever here."

It was quite a while before Mr. Bell again opened communications with the opposite side:

"Mary, do you think it's smart galivantin' off an lettin' me starve?"

Mrs. Bell looked at her angry spouse a few moments, then replied sweetly:

"Why, Silas, you know you have always said that any lazy goose could do a woman's work: that it was only play. Of course it won't be any trouble for you to get along."

Mr. Bell's mouth opened and shut a few times, but no sound came forth. Savagely pulling at his beard, he hopped from one foot to the other and glared at the cat sitting on a rock contentedly washing its face.

After a few moments he asked in sort of a repressed-volcano voice:

"So you all inten' ter be idgits 'til I come ter terms, d' you?"

"You have the notice," John reminded him.

"Well, dum it!" he exploded. "You'd better build you er house! Campin' will be cold livin' next winter!"

"Thank you," returned John calmly. "We know of a farm with a good house we can rent before cold weather."

"I'll not be bossed by no sich er lot o' family fools!" roared Mr. Bell. "I'll git help an' let all you idgits go ter the lunertic 'sylum; that's the house you'll land in fer winter quarters!"

"Hired help will cost you more, Pa," John said. "You'd better pay us."

"Not by er dum sight!" his father snorted. "I'll show you who's what in my family!"

With a final ferocious glare at the strikers he stamped across the beach and disappeared among the trees.

Three weeks passed and no settlement was in sight. Mr. Bell had driven all over the country searching for bargains in the help line, but had failed to find any. Men demanded three dollars a day and board. He could not get one girl to do all the house-work, and two cost him six dollars a week, besides board, to say nothing of the amount they would waste.

"Dum it," he fumed over and over again. "It's er pretty pass when one has ter give away his farm to run it!"

Several times he went over to the edge of the woods and covertly watched the strikers, hoping to see some sign of surrender, but each time he found them enjoying themselves so much he returned home in a fury of disappointment and stubbornness.

Strategy he tried only once. That was the time he went to bed and hired a boy to go tell his family that he was very sick. But as John cross-examined the boy and found out the facts of the case, Mr. Bell gained nothing except the information that for twenty-five dollars a week he could get a trained nurse from the city; and that a cook, two maids and an errand boy would, perhaps, be all the assistance she would demand. This mes-sage shot Silas out of bed like a sky-rocket. He dum-jigged everything so lively the frightened boy dodged behind a chair and escaped through the window.

Things continued to go from bad to worse. The commotion raised by the new servants coming and the discharged ones going was fast approaching a continuous performance. Almost distracted by the demands, waste, and independence of these descendants of several nationalities, Silas told himself many times, and each one of them once, at least, that "All the dum-imperdent-trash-idgits in the whole world muster immigrated ter this neck-o-woods!"

He had at last come to the point of trying a man with a cue; but when Silas caught him testing the temperature of the frying pan in typical Oriental fashion, there was a noisy difference of opinion: and the Chinaman, somewhat disheveled, his almond-shaped eyes throwing back disgusted glances, went trotting down the path muttering "Melican man dam-fool."

After a final threatening kick, Silas sat down on the porch to cool off. He mopped the perspiration from his red face and assured himself grimly that he was a deacon of the church and believed in foreign missions, but he'd be dummed if he was going to give all he made to the heathens—and board 'em besides.

As he thought about the strenuous work of the last three weeks, and the money he had paid out for help, his eyes bulged wildly and his beard grew stiffer and stiffer as his mouth clinched together tighter and tighter with indignation. Finally he jumped up with an angry snort:

"If I warn't a deacon I'd swar!"

In desperation Silas had written to his sister-in-law asking her to come visit, but not explaining the state of affairs.

"If only I can git Marthy here, I'll show 'em!" he consoled himself. "She's got sense, Marthy has, and will help a man that's pestered by sich 'er family o' dum idgits."
He was anxiously looking for a letter, hoping she would set a date for her arrival; so now when he heard a wagon rumble up to the gate he peered eagerly down the path

with the hope some neighbor had brought his mail. But a shout of joy escaped him as he recognized the substantial form of the woman climbing over the wagon wheel.

"Marthy Bell!" he cried, hurrying down to the gate. "Jig me if I ain't glad to see you!"

"Howdy, Silas," Martha returned, straightening her bonnet and brushing off the streak of dust the wagon wheel had printed on her black alpaca dress before holding out her hand to Silas.

"I got your letter and I started right off. Air Mary or the children sick?"

Silas straightened up and answered stiffly: "Guess they're well; they ain't ter home."

"Fer land's sake, Silas. What's the matter with you?" Martha cried in surprise, as she took her first good look at him. "You look like a mad turkey gobbler that's been fightin'."

Silas hastily put his hand to his bristly red hair and tried to smooth down its indignant uprising. He was startled to find his forehead wet with blood oozing from a scratch the Chinaman had given him as a farewell token. His shirt was torn in several places, showing the red flannel underwear he wore, winter and summer, as a scarecrow for rheumatism. The black satin necktie he considered an outward symbol daily due— collar or no collar—his office as deacon of the church was sprawling like the arms of a Dutch windmill under one ear, this happening to be one of the days there was no collar to restrain its religious liberty. His face grew redder, if possible, under the astonished gaze from Martha's eyes. He hemmed and hawed as they went up the steps and he brought out a chair for her.

"This beats me!" Martha said, sitting down with a tired thud. "You look an' act sort of luny, Silas Bell; an' I never heard o' Mary bein' away from home 'cept to meetin's Sundays. Where air they?"

"Well, Marthy," Silas began slowly, taking time between words to take a chew of tobacco, "we air havin' er little family trouble and they're left."

"My stars!" Martha gasped. "Fer land's sake, what kind o' trouble?"

"Now, Marthy," Silas spoke in a whealing tone, "you're my brother's widder an' I allers thougt er heap o' your managin', an' I know you'll see this er—er trouble as I do: Mary an' the children think I ain't give 'em ernough gew-gaws an' they're gone on er—er strike."

"A what?" Martha squealed.

"Er strike," Silas repeated, looking foolish. "You know what er strike is, don't you, Marthy?"

"Yes," Martha said. "But, my stars, I never heard o' that disease tackling a whole family before."

"Nuther did I," Silas agreed quickly, thinking he read sympathy in her amazed face. "Course it's ridiclus, an," his lips tightened, "mighty dum hard on me." Martha's keen eyes searched his stubborn face a few minutes before she spoke.

"What do they want?" she asked directly.

"They left er—er bill," Silas stammered.

"Fer land's sake!" Martha persisted. "Let me see it."

Being so desperate for sympathy, Silas did not pause to think that he was about to expose the skeleton in the family closet, but hurried into the house and brought out the notice. While Martha was fishing her glasses from her handbag he fastened the cardboard against the house.

"Read it!" he cried indignantly. "It's the biggest lot er dum foolishness you ever heard tell of!"

Martha's face was a study as she slowly read. When she reached the end she leaned back in her chair and laughed until her fat body shook like a jelly fish and the tears ran down her cheeks.

Silas stood pulling his beard and chewing his tobacco with quick, vicious snaps. He looked at Martha reproachfully when she gave way to mirth, but her laughter was so hearty and contagious that finally a sheepish grin stole over his face.

"Dum hard on a man, ain't it?" he asked plaintively.

Martha sat up with a sudden jerk; her laughter fled so quickly that a big tear, half-way down her nose, halted in confusion.

"My stars! Hard on a *man*!" she cried sharply, shaking her finger at the card. "Is it true, Silas Bell, that you wouldn't buy that baby a doll?"

Stunned by this sudden change, Silas stared at her stupidly, the grin frozen to his face.

"Fer land's sake, man! What air you grinnin' like an idgit fer? It ain't nuthin' funny."

The grin slowly changed to a half-shamed look and Silas answered sullenly:

"Mary made nice rag dolls."

"Huh!"

"Now see here, Marthy," he said querulously, "you ain't er goin' to turn against me, air you? I think it's er dum mean way fer 'em ter treat me."

"Lord help your persimmons of a soul, Silas Bell!" Martha exploded. "My stars! If I'd been in Mary's place I'd helped time make that bald spot o' yourn so big your head wouldn't look so much like a fat doughnut!"

"Why, Marthy!" gasped Mr. Bell.

"You needn't 'Marthy' me, Silas Bell; you're goin' to hear the truth about yourself fer once."

Martha's face settled into firm lines, showing she had the courage of her convictions. "You jes' set right down in that chair," she went on firmly, "an' listen 'til I git done."

Mr. Bell was too surprised to rebel, so sank down in the chair limply.

"I allers knowed you was most stingy 'nough to save the hide off a flea's back—if you could ketch it—Silas Bell," Martha began, looking over the top of her glasses, "but I never knowed before you was a sneakin' thief!"

"Marthy!"

"I said a sneakin' thief!" Martha repeated, her plump hand coming down with a firm thud on the arm of her chair. "That's what a man is when he keeps what belongs to others jes' because he can an' knows he won't be put in jail fer it. That's you, Silas. Mary an' the children has worked like slaves fer you an' 'pears like," pointing at the card scornfully, "they've got starvation rations an' had to beg fer 'em at that."

"Marthy, I—"

"Keep still! I ain't done yit," Martha cut him off. "Tain't as if you was a poor man, Silas Bell. Look at them big fields o' grain; all the land in sight most is yourn; an' look at them big herds o' cattle stuffin' theirselves with clover 'til they're most bustin'. Seems if some men air a heap better to their stock than they air to their own flesh and blood kin."

Mr. Bell opened his mouth to speak but was silenced by Martha jumping to her feet and shaking her finger in unaccustomed rage before his blinking eyes.

"You don' deserve sich a wife as Mary, nor sich children, nuther; they'd treated you right if they'd left you years ago an' gone to work where the hours were shorter an' the pay better—an' surer. A nice man you air to be a deacon o' the church an' posin' as a good religious man! What kind of religion have you got that don't teach you to take care of an' appreciate them the good Lord sends you?"

Martha paused a moment to get her breath but Mr. Bell had at last been stunned into silence. He just kept blinking at the threatening finger before his face.

"An' tell me this, Silas Bell," she demanded sternly: "What'd you 'a had if it hadn't been fer Mary? You was poor as Job's turkey when she married you; an' the first piece o' land you ever owned was bought with the money Mary's father give her. An' now seems if she can't git 'nough money out o' you to buy herself decent clothes—let alone feathers and fixin's thats rightfully hers, an' none o' your business, if she wants 'em."

Martha straightened up and tied her bonnet strings with such a jerk that the posies stood up like bristles.

"I guess I'm done, Silas," she said, going down the steps but pausing a moment to add:

"My stars! If I was you I'd be 'shamed to look an honest well-meanin' pig in the face. Think about it for a while, Silas Bell. Goodbye. I'm goin' to join the strikers."

She waddled down the path with her head high in the air, never looking back at the poor man she had reduced to a state of collapse.

He gazed after her until she finally disappeared into the woods leading down to the water. Then he roused himself and threw his old straw hat over the porch railing at the hens, who seemed to his imagination to be taunting him mockingly:

"Thief—thief, sneakin' thief!"

The camp of the strikers was thrown into confusion early the next morning by Ted turning handsprings from one end of the tent to the other, and yelling for everybody to come out and see the sight. Not knowing what might have happened, they all rushed out in various stages of their toilet. Martha rolled out of bed in excitement, hastily tied on her beflowered bonnet and, as fast as her bare feet could carry her over the pebbly beach, followed the others to the water's edge. On the other side, fastened between two trees, there was a big sheet painted in staring black letters:

Cooperashun for all dum it! Com hom!
Silas Bell

2
CHAPTER

STORIES OF ADVENTURE WITH MACHINES

"HELP is scarce in all our rural districts and whenever farmers can overcome the handicap through the purchase of labor-saving devices, they are doing so. With a small tractor one man will plow from five to eight acres per day, whereas with a team this same man could plow not much over two acres. Other work could be accomplished in about the same proportion. Thus for doing the regular field work it would be found that the tractor would cut down the man days required, perhaps from 50 to 75 percent."

—*The Michigan Farmer,* August 1916

Edwin Markham's famous poem, "The Man with the Hoe," published just before the turn of the century, won wide condemnation in rural America. It reflected poorly on farmers, many believed; they pursued its creator with a vengeance. But Markham himself claimed his poem was not meant as a reflection on American farmers, but rather was about a French peasant left by circumstance with little hope in life.

Wallaces' Farmer reported in April, 1919, on an appearance by Markham in Des Moines, Iowa. The poet told his audience that his most famous poem had become something of a "Frankenstein" to him because it had been so widely misunderstood. Unlike the American farmer, "riding rosily on a reaper," Markham said, the subject of his poem lived a life of menial labor. The poem was intended as a protest against drudgery. Labor is the common man's art, Markham told his Iowa audience that day, but drudgery leads to despondency, which is fatal to the ideal life to which man should ascribe.

Markham overstated the case for American farmers, of course. But it was true that machines had done much to alleviate the work load in the fields and around the barnyard, even though farm mechanization still had a long way to go. Horse-drawn machines had had great impact on farm work by the turn of the century. By the time Markham's famous poem was published, the mechanical reaper had been in the field for several decades. Steam power had led to awesome tractors, but these were too expensive and too hard to maneuver to be useful in most farm settings. The real revolution came with the gasoline engine.

Every new labor-saving machine was welcomed by farm families, not only because it might lighten the physical load but also because it promised more time to enjoy the pleasant things of life. Thus the farm and rural interest magazines were filled with articles and advertisements that introduced new machines, new uses for old machines, and practical improvements to familiar machines that had been around for a long time. Given the general level of interest, it is not surprising that machines proved to be popular topics in the rural magazines' short-story fiction.

The machines themselves often were treated as major characters, essential to plot and setting. In the hands of skilled writers they became animate objects. At times they were endowed with human characteristics. Clearly it was intended that there be strong bonds between men and their machines.

Most common were stories about railroads. The railroad was important to most rural communities, and had been around for a long time. Railroad stories therefore required little imagination and usually followed something of a basic formula. They typically were dramatic, masculine adventures involving fast and powerful steam locomotives. Stories about automobiles on the farm began to show up more frequently after 1910. World War I acquainted most Americans with the flying machine, but writers were largely unsuccessful in attempts to bring the airplane into stories with rural settings. Large farm equipment such as the steam engines and their companion threshing machines that moved about the countryside for custom grain harvests seldom turned up in stories published through 1925, and stories about small, unusual machines such as outboard motors were very rare. But each of these is the subject of a story in this collection. Each demonstrates, in its own way, the true romance of the machine in rural American literature.

THE LAST RUN OF "93"

Helen E. Haskell

The Ohio Farmer, March 1916

TOM Walsh, lurching along the tracks of the B. & W., stopped with a jerk that almost upset him.

"Glor'usly drunk," he muttered, "Whoop—ee!"

Having relieved himself of his pent up feelings, he bolted forward again, staggered from one side of the tracks to the other, and came to a stop against the roundhouse. He fumbled in his pockets, produced a key ring, then, propped by the wet and slippery sides of the house, managed to get to its doors and, after some futile jabbing, find the keyhole. He shoved the doors apart, passed through them uncertainly, pulled them partly together after him, made some ineffectual attempts to light a match on his rainsoaked trousers, gave it up and came to rest against the cold boiler of a locomotive.

"Old nine'y-three," he muttered and leaned his head against the side of the engine. "Good ol' girl—nine-'y-three. Did'r best."

This delivered, Tom reached around for his whisky flask, took another drink and then let out a long stream of soft-spoken, maudlin curses upon the head of Daniel Wolcott, the new superintendent of the Delhi branch of the B. & W., only son of a millionaire father, and president of the Penfield bank, an institution owned and controlled by the railroad.

Tom had been with the B. & W. for twenty-five years, driving engine No. 93 back and forth on the sixty-five miles of track that joined Penfield, the small town at the end of the branch, with Delhi, the junction where the branch connected with the main line. For twenty-five years he had kept sober, making his runs on schedule time. Then the B. & W. had built an extension of its line to Waycote, a flourishing milling town ten miles beyond Penfield, had fired the old superintendent and put the division into the hand of Daniel Wolcott who, with the heartless zeal of youth, had raked through its equipment, ruthlessly consigning to the scrap heap whatever he found behind the times either in the matter of locomotives or men.

Tom's engine had failed to pass muster with the boiler inspector and she had been thrown into the discard. With her had gone Tom Walsh, the man who had driven and coaxed and coddled her for twenty-five years. Tomorrow a new locomotive would roar through Penfield, driven by another and younger man.

Tom patted the sides of his inanimate old companion.

"Good ol' girl," he muttered plaintively.

He leaned against her, slipping down gradually to the floor, where he presently dropped into a fitful slumber from which he awakened a couple of hours later, shaking with cold.

Outside, the rain had ceased; but a north wind had come up, driving an icy blast through the half-open doors of the roundhouse.

"Ought to have a fire," chattered Tom, getting to his feet. "Catch my death of dampness." Again his hands came into contact with the boiler of the engine. "Nine'y-three cold, too. Poor old girl!"

With some difficulty, he climbed into the cab, found the door of the firebox, pulled it open, and felt inside. Then, scrambling down, he made his way on capricious legs to the kindling pile and gathered up an armful of wood and shavings.

Five minutes later the roundhouse was filled with the scent of burning pine and Tom, force of habit proving stronger than the brain-befogging whiskey, was examining the water gauge. Having satisfied himself that there was plenty of water in the boiler, he threw several scoops of coal upon the fire he had made and settled himself into the driver's seat of the cab.

"Old nine'y-three warm me up in jiffy," he muttered, sliding down on the small of his back. "Stick together—Tom and nine'y-three. Always have, always will."

He slipped still farther into the seat and was presently snoring sonorously.

It was an explosion outside the roundhouse that brought Tom to his senses with an uncomfortable shock half an hour later. He sat up, rubbed his eyes and stretched himself, then, his hand striking a lever, realized that he was in the cab of his engine.

He got to his feet and looked around dazedly. Then he pulled the chain that opened the door of the firebox. The glow from the coals within lighted up the walls of the roundhouse. His memory came back with a rush. He had been drunk. He was still weak, and he had an unpleasant, gone feeling under his belt. Nearby, somewhere, an automobile engine was pounding. The explosion that had awakened him must have been caused by a bursting tire. Tom pulled out his watch and looked at it by the light of the fire. It was almost three o'clock. He climbed down from the cab with a vague idea of going out and asking the automobilist to take him home. He had difficulty in reaching the doors. His legs were uncertain. He felt ill, ugly. Little hammers seemed beating against his temples.

The doors were still open a crack. Through them he could see the sky, starry, with scudding clouds, and nearby, in the road, the automobile which had come to a stop. There were no lights on it, but the fitful glare from a flashlight showed an exploded tire.

Shadowy figures moved back and forth, talking in voices subdued to a murmur. Suddenly the torch lighted up a face and, recognizing it, Tom shrank back into the blackness of the roundhouse, seized with a suspicion that sobered him.

Outside somebody snarled an order. "Shut off that engine! Are you trying to wake up the neighborhood?"

The throbbing of the engine ceased. Again the flashlight glared upon a face—white, ill-looking, under its wide-brimmed Fedora.

"We've got to get a move on if we make the five o'clock out of Delhi," somebody grunted. "Where's the pump?"

"S-sh! Not so loud."

Again the light flashed. This time it showed a man, strange to Tom, burly, the lower part of his face covered with a black handkerchief. He was standing in the tonneau of the car. In one hand he held the seat cushion, in the other a dark leather satchel.

As the flashlight picked him out he cursed softly.

"Turn off that search-light, you idiot." And then, "Here, Olmstead, take the swag while I get the pump."

There followed a silence which to Tom, crouching in the shadows, seemed more articulate than words. Presently there were low grunts as the new tire was pulled into place and afterwards there was the squeak of the pump as the tube was inflated. The men worked swiftly and in darkness. When at last the car whirled down the road its lamps were still unlighted.

After it had gone Tom stood for some time, motionless, trying to figure out what it meant. But he had difficulty in marshalling his thoughts. As if to help himself think, he began muttering aloud.

"Going to catch the five o'clock out of Delhi! Will Olmstead with them—and a bag full of swag!" He pulled out his watch, struck a match and looked at it. "Three fifteen," he mumbled. "They'll have to push right through." The flame of the match crept up and burned his fingers. He snapped it out. "Suppose I ought to crawl down to the village and give the alarm. Too shaky on my pins to make it." He scratched his head. "And if I could make it what 'ud be the good. No night operators on duty either at Penfield or Delhi." He laughed disagreeably. "What do I care anyway? Young Wolcott's given me the sack. Now let 'em loot his bank. It ain't for Tom Walsh to interfere."

He climbed back into the cab of his engine, threw more coal upon the fire, reached around for his flask, and took a drink. Then he settled down to finish the work of sleeping off the effects of the liquor.

But now the old engine began to make strange, disturbing noises. She shook herself, bubbled, rumbled, awakened Tom again and again, until he began to fancy that she was remonstrating at his inactivity.

He pressed his fingers against his temples where the little hammers seemed to be pounding.

"Go to sleep ol' girl," he muttered. You'n I don't owe Dan Wolcott anything."

But for once the old locomotive was fractious. She impinged her dissatisfaction upon Tom's consciousness. It seemed to him that she was begging with him for a chance to show the stuff she still had in her. He tried to soothe her as if she were an animate thing. But it was useless. Over and over again she seemed to speak to him, to plead, until at last, as if to convince her, he pulled out his watch.

"It lacks only five minutes of four, old girl," he said. "You never could make it."

And then, almost before the words were finished, he jerked open the door of the firebox, grabbed up the scoop and began throwing coal upon the glowing mass inside. His teeth were gritted together, his face set.

"I'll give you your chance, partner," he growled, opening the draft. "Maybe we can show 'em, you and me, that we're not quite ready for the discard."

He climbed down from the cab, groaning with the pains that shot through his temples, pushed open the doors of the roundhouse, lighted the pilot light, and got back into his seat. Then he glanced at the steam gauge, nodded, and grasped the lever. A moment later, with a wheezing and coughing of the open exhaust, the engine rolled out of the roundhouse and stopped on the turntable. Again Tom climbed down, grunting as he released the bolt and tried ineffectually to move the table; tried a second time, started it, and pushed it around until his engine was headed right.

The exertion seemed to clear his brain. As he climbed back into his cab he glanced at the steam gauge, nodded, chuckled and muttered something about sixty-five miles and a clear track. Then he opened his throttle and with a shriek the engine started in the direction of Delhi.

She had less than an hour in which to make the run. She had never, even in her palmiest days, made it in less than an hour and twenty minutes. And now she was old, her boilers were weak. As she roared down the track and rushed around the first curve with her flanges almost riding the rails, her whole body shuddered a protest.

But in the engine cab, Tom Walsh, his hand on the lever, his eyes on the ribbon of track that the headlight picked out for him, never doubted her for a moment. She was like the other half of him, responsive to his will. He knew her from smoke stack to tender; knew her strength and her weakness. He loved every shining inch of her. And he was giving her a chance.

Clankety-clank she rushed over the track, smoke and flame pouring from her stack, pistons pounding, steam hissing, her suction pulling up and leaving dust and cinders in her wake.

Tom had made the run ten thousand times; he knew every foot of the road, but never before had it seemed like this. Trees and houses rushed by, blended in unfamiliar masses. The way stations, dark and silent, were like strange blots against the sky, appearing for an instant and then roaring past him. As the miles were left behind he felt an exhilaration that was like the intoxication of the evening before. His eyes were like two blazing coals. Under the soot that grimed his face, his cheeks were burning. He shoveled coal into the firebox, furiously, exulting as the needle crept up in the steam gauge, while the locomotive picked up speed with every mile.

Now and again, as day broke, heads were thrust from windows of houses along the tracks. There were shouts in men's voices, but before they reached Tom Walsh's ears they had grown faint, far away.

At 4:35 Tom had covered forty-two of the sixty-five miles between Penfield and Delhi. He had pushed the old engine through at a little better than seventy miles an hour. But over a third of the way lay before him. Would she last through it? He asked himself the question, then opened the throttle wider than ever. Five miles of level track stretched before him. The engine leaped forward at a speed so terrific that the rails seemed to be pouring into its throat. In the graying dawn the telegraph poles at the side of the track looked blurred, run together like spokes in a revolving wheel.

Two miles farther on a freight agent rushed from the station house, shouting and waving his arms. But "93" roared by him, leaving him staggered, covered with cinders and dust. The man went back to the station, called Delhi and reported the passing of an engine with a madman in the cab. He declared that it was running a hundred miles an hour when it had gone by his station.

Ten miles from Delhi Tom Walsh discerned a handcar running leisurely before him. He did not slacken speed but pulled furiously at the whistle. Its crew heard and looked around. They had had barely time to throw their car from the track when Tom was abreast of them. An instant later and he had passed them, his whistle shrieking, the old engine roaring on her way like a mad tornado. And in the cab, his eyes red, his face covered with soot, sweat dripping from his forehead, coatless and collarless, Tom Walsh, looking neither to the right nor the left, pitched more coal into the firebox. For a moment the men with the handcar stared after him in speechless astonishment, then tipped their car back upon the track and went pounding after him.

Five miles from Delhi, in spite of a white hot fire, the old engine began losing speed. Tom looked at the steam gauge. Something had happened. The needle was dropping. Her steam was going down. There was a leak! But there was no time to stop and determine where. In seven minutes the Chicago express was due in Delhi. Five minutes later and it would be rushing out again. Thank heaven, there was a mile of down grade just ahead. Once on that "93" could get her breath. Tom called her his babe and his partner; fancied she had understood and responded when the gauge showed that the steam was creeping up again.

"You've got a chance yet, old girl," he shouted and heaved on more coal. "Got a chance to make a record that'll shame 'em! Go to it, babe! We'll show 'em, you and me! We'll show 'em!"

And in answer "93" rushed on, thumping, pounding, groaning in protest, but eating up the miles while Tom talked, coaxed, implored her.

"It's more'n your utmost, old one, more'n your best, I'm asking. But you've got to make it, my beauty! Got to put over a miracle! You and old Tom, together," he pleaded, talking to the great, inanimate monster as if it were some favorite horse.

And somehow the miracle was performed; old "93" came slipping into the Delhi station three full minutes before it was time for the Chicago express to pull out. Her boilers were leaking. Somewhere a journal shrieked for oil. And there wasn't an ounce of power left in her when Tom Walsh jumped from his cab and, dashing through the crowd that had gathered to watch for the wild engine that had been reported no less than a dozen times in the past five minutes, hurled himself upon a slim, pale faced young man in a wide Fedora hat who was about to board the outgoing train.

The man tried to shake him off, but Tom clung, one hand on the youth's coat collar, the other on the black satchel he carried. And while he clung he yelled at the top of his lungs for help. Somebody heard and rushed toward the squabbling men. An instant later Tom got a staggering blow between the eyes and the satchel was almost wrenched from his hand. But he clung to it desperately, with both hands now, while three men tried for a moment to loosen his grip, beating and kicking him unmercifully. And then the crowd pressed around him.

In spite of his battered condition and the blood and soot that covered him, somebody recognized Tom Walsh and called him by name. He couldn't make out who it was, for he was blind with pain. And he no longer remembered why he was clinging to the satchel. His senses were reeling. He seemed conscious of only one thing—that he must hang on for the sake of old "93." He muttered something that sounded like "good old girl," and then consciousness slipped away.

They picked Tom up and carried him into the station. Somebody went for a doctor. Somebody else opened the black satchel from which the handle had been torn almost away. It was stuffed with gold and bank notes. The baggage agent recalled having seen young Olmstead, teller of the Penfield bank, in the mix-up with Tom. But when they looked for him he had disappeared. The doctor came and Tom was bathed, bandaged, and taken to the hotel, since Delhi had no hospital.

Meantime, the news that there had been an attempt to rob Penfield's bank spread. It reached the ears of its president, Dan Wolcott, who lived just out of Delhi, and ten minutes after Tom Walsh had been comfortably put to bed young Wolcott, who had learned all that anybody knew about old "93's" mad run, appeared at the hotel asking for Tom.

He entered Tom's room, jauntily. He had gone through the black satchel. The vaults of the bank at Penfield had been gutted. He felt bountifully grateful to the man lying in the bed, his face stiff with plasters, one eye covered with a bandage.

"You pulled off a big thing, Walsh," he said, holding out his hand, "and I want to thank you and to say that you'll not regret it. I'll see that you are handsomely rewarded—"

Tom Walsh rose on one elbow, looked at the outstretched hand, and shrugged his shoulders. Then he cursed softly under his breath.

"You've been in the service of the B. & W. for a good many years, Walsh," went on the young man, ignoring the curses and still holding out his hand. "It may be that we can arrange a pension—"

"Dang blast your impertinence, Wolcott," snapped Tom. "I'm not looking for a pension. I've got a wad soaked away." Again he swore softly.

Daniel Wolcott's hand fell to his side.

"I—I want to do something for you, Walsh, after all you've done for me and the B. & W."

Tom sat up, striking the bed with his clenched fist. "So you think I did it for you, do you?" he growled. "Well, you've got another guess coming. I'd have seen you blown to blazes without raising a hand to prevent it. That's the way I feel about you. Understand?"

Young Wolcott drew back, amazed.

"But you saved the bank. Kept Olmstead from making a getaway with fifty thousand—"

"Forget it," interrupted Tom, then leaned back, his unbandaged eye blazing.

"It wasn't for the bank I made the run this morning. It wasn't for you, Wolcott, nor for the B. & W. It was for old '93.' To give her a chance! To show you that she still had the goods! There's not another engine on the road could have done it. Seventy miles an hour is what she made and then her old heart stopped beating. And now she deserves something better'n the scrap heap. It was she who saved the bank." He drew his sleeve across his eye. "I don't want your rewards and your pensions, Wolcott. I'm fixed. But if you're inclined to do something decent to show that you've a man's heart in your breast—take the old girl back home, keep her polished and oiled as she's always been. Fill up her tender like she was going on a run tomorrow or the day after, so she can keep her self-respect."

Dan Wolcott swallowed ineffectually—tried to speak—couldn't—and again thrust out his hand.

This time Tom Walsh gripped it.

"Thank you, Wolcott," he said and sank back upon his pillow.

THE FIRST RIG IN

N. Gregory
Wallaces' Farmer, August 1923

THE blazing August sun transformed the wet, heavy atmosphere of southern Dakota into a steaming, oppressive, smothering medium of heat. Rance Holiday, 18-year-old engineer, heaved coal into the firebox of the snorting, straining Mitt-Stormer engine which spun the big cylinder of the 48-inch Wildcat Special separator into which wet, soggy bundles of wheat were being hurled by four sweating pitchers.

Rance wiped sweat strenuously with his crooked arm and thought hard words when the needle on the steam gauge stubbornly refused to climb past eighty.

At the back end of the separator Jasper Gattling also wiped sweat and listened to the deep *br-r-r* of the big blower and guardedly watched for a muffling of the tone which would forecast a choke down. He was a year Rance's junior but a better separator hand never looked into a blower drum.

Up on top, Eph Bixler, owner of the rig, big, grizzled and dust coated, stood watching the whirring teeth of the cylinder. Eph was a good natured man as men go, but a wet threshing season with numerous breakdowns, a heavy payment due on the rig, together with a set of pitchers now hurling wet bundles crossways, butt-endways and every other way but rightways into the chute brought a heavy scowl to his face.

"Hey, you spike pitcher!" he shouted finally, "see if you can pitch one bundle into the chute, straight, out of a load!"

The spike pitcher thus addressed was hard worked; his buddy was lying down on him and he was hot and tired and mad. At Eph's injunction he blew up completely. He paused, glared up at the big man above him, rammed his fork deep into the load, sat down on the handle and heaved a great bunch of bundles into the feeder in a wad.

Eph knew it would choke the machine if it all went in so he leaned over to pull off a few of the bundles, slipped, lost his balance and pitched forward into the feeder, turning completely over in the fall. One arm went in under the slashing band knives and the cylinder caught it. Eph's face grew ashen and he caught the side of the feeder with his free hand to arrest his movement, but the cylinder was slowly pulling his arm down, eating it as it pulled.

Down at the engine Rance was still heaving in coal; he felt the engine pick up as the separator emptied, glanced up and saw Eph lying in the feeder with his arm inside the machine almost up to his shoulder. Lightning-like, he reversed the engine to a stop and was on the ground running for the separator before the stupefied pitchers recovered themselves.

Eph pulled the remnant of his arm from the cylinder, held the stub up, spurting blood all over him, looked at it in a dazed manner, then tumbled limp to the ground.

"Call a doctor! Call a doctor!" shouted Rance as he reached Eph. "Here, Jasp, get me a short stick."

Working swiftly, he bent a tourniquet on the arm, stopping the blood. The doctor arrived shortly and Eph was removed to the house.

After supper Rance and Jasper were sitting on the coal lockers of the engine discussing the accident when Humpy Shanner appeared in the offing. Humpy was a big, awkward fellow of about thirty or thirty-five—the water hauler for the rig. He derived his name of "Humpy" because he was hump-backed. He also talked with a gargle in his throat, always was trying to clear his throat and never quite succeeding, but he was a diamond in the rough, of the purest water, too.

The boys heard him clearing his throat and talking to himself as he came up, shaking his head, too, slowly. "Pore old Eph," they heard him say; "arm's gone; wheat no good; in debt deep; and a better fellow never lived—"

"Nor never will," called out Jasper.

Humpy stopped, cleared his throat, then came up to them. "Eph wants to see you boys," he said. "Better go right in."

"We're gone!" exclaimed Rance, jumping down. Jasper followed him into the house, where they found Eph propped up in bed, weak and wan from the amputation but smiling gamely.

"Doc says if you hadn't tied up this stub that I'd been cold when he got to me," he said. "Much obliged."

"Say!" exclaimed Rance, "did you call us in to tell us that? Because—"

"Hold on! Hold on! Don't go off half-cocked, Rance. Your worst fault, though I wish nobody had a worse—I called you in to talk business. I've went in the hole every day I've run this season. Owe two thousand on the rig, lose it if I don't make a payment this fall. Now keep still!" he said as they both started to speak. "I've got a cousin up in the hills, was down to see me this afternoon. Says there's thirty or forty thousand bushels up there in his locality all stacked and dry. But it's a hard place to get into and hard to get around after you do get in. Bad roads, bad hills and so on. All the rigs up there always pass them up as long as there's anything to thresh in the valley. Reckon you boys could take the rig up there and thresh 'em out?"

"You tell 'um!" said Rance.

"Boy, howdy!" exclaimed Jasper.

"Give you half," went on Eph. "You—"

"Nothing doing!" exclaimed Rance, jumping up. "We'll take our regular wages, nothing more."

"Not a cent," seconded Jasper. "Not a berry more."

"—thirty mile pull. Didn't promise Levi we'd come sure—Levi Reeves is his name. Reckon you can start in the morning? There's a bad bridge at the Highbank Crossing and the river's still coming up—"

"We'll work all night to get ready," affirmed Rance. "Come on, Jasp, let's get busy," and out they ran in spite of Eph's orders to wait a while, that he had something more to say.

Day broke with them well on the way, the old Mitt-Stormer churning along at a famous rate, belching great clouds of black smoke. She was a high wheeler, fast on the road, thirty horsepower on the draw bar, seventy on the belt. Behind, Humpy was obliged to push his team into an occasional trot to keep up.

Their route lay in this manner: Fifteen miles through the valley to the Highbank Crossing bridge, a weak, faulty structure, never safe, and now with the river high a precarious crossing with a big engine and a 48-inch separator.

"I'm leery of that bridge," said Jasper.

"So'm I," admitted Rance. "But it's a lead pipe cinch if it's there when we get there we're going to drive on."

"You tell 'm!" grunted Jasper. "We'll drive across or drive her to the bottom!"

The roads were slippery and the Mitt-Stormer skidded and slewed all over the road, groaned and snorted, but kept going steadily onward. Along about the middle of the afternoon they approached the bottoms. As they topped the last rise and the Mitt-Stormer stuck her nose downward, a wide expanse of water met their eyes. The road was covered for a quarter of a mile and on a little knoll below them, surrounded by water, a man was working to replace the tops on two huge wheat ricks which the wind had removed.

"It'll be all over that knoll before morning and those ricks will be twenty miles down the river," said Rance soberly. "Paper reports the river is coming up fast fifty miles above here."

"He's wasting time," admitted Jasper, and jerked the whistle cord. At the sound of the Mitt-Stormer's clear, high yell, the man's bent back straightened with a jerk. Hurriedly he dumped the few remaining bundles from the wagon and came for the road in a trot.

"What rig is this?" he asked.

"Gattling and Holiday," replied Jasper.

"Looking for wheat to thresh?"

"Not here," said Jasper.

"Say," the man adopted a pleading tone. "I'll give you twenty cents a bushel to thresh this set. River'll have it by morning if I don't get it out."

"But we've got to cross that bridge before night," said Rance. "According to the weather reports a foot more rise and it will go out. We've got to cross this afternoon."

The man threw up his hands silently. It required no mind-reader to see that his need was desperate. The boys eyed each other.

"What will we do, Jasp?" asked Rance in a low tone.

"We've got about three hours of daylight to cross that bridge. It's a cinch if we don't cross today, we won't tomorrow. We won't be able to even get to the bridge."

"Yes, but we can't see the river take that man's wheat. Can't do it, that's all!"

"Well?"

Rance turned to the man. "Is the ground solid between here and the knoll?"

"Think so," the man's eyes lighted.

"Get a crew here, as quick as you can. Turn her, Jasp."

They pulled out to the knoll and set and the crew began to appear. In half an hour the rig was surrounded by men and wagons.

Rance jerked the whistle cord twice and opened the throttle. *Ch-choo! ch-cho! ch-cho-oooo!* snorted the exhaust; *hum-mmmm!* droned the cylinder, like a giant bee; *br-rrrr!* roared the big blower, and *wheee-ing!* rang the first bundle as the cylinder snatched it down. They were off!

No man loafed on that job. Jasper took out the dividing board and Rance wired down the safety valve and fired the old Mitt-Stormer to her limit. Wheat spouted in a great welling stream into the grain boxes, the weigher opened and shut as regularly as a clock ticks and almost as rapidly.

While the work stormed on, the sun sank, sank, and sank until it touched the distant tree tops, then seemed to fairly plunge beneath the horizon. Darkness fell before the cylinder sucked the last bundle down and Jasper threw off the slipping belt.

The farmer ran up to the engine. "No use for me to try to tell you boys how much this means to me," he began, "and I won't try. But if the time ever comes when you need help you won't have to ask me twice. Ed Strayley, that's my name."

"Got a good lantern?" asked Rance, his mind busy on the situation before them.

"Sure. But you boys gotta come up to the house and get some supper."

"Nothing doing," said Rance shortly. "We're going to hit that bridge, in mighty short order."

"What!" shouted Mr. Strayley. "Boy, the river's over it in the center! I wouldn't cross it for a thousand dollars tonight."

"Don't suppose I would either, but it is for a bigger consideration than that. Ready with that coupling pin, Jasp?"

"Ready," said Jasper.

They coupled up and the old Mitt-Stormer pointed her nose resolutely for the bridge, Humpy on the water wagon trailing them closely. Just as the front wheels of the engine struck the floor of the bridge Strayley came running up carrying a lantern and a basket.

"I'm scared green," he confessed, "but danged if I ain't goin' across with you. Might help out a little."

"You're not the only one that's scared," said Rance through set teeth.

"Not by a blame sight!" seconded Jasper.

"There's plenty other people," came Humpy's gargle, which brought a laugh and cleared the tense atmosphere.

"Let's hit it," said Rance. He opened the throttle and the Stormer lumbered out on the bridge, the sinister swish, swish of water, much water, persisting over the sound of the exhaust.

The night closed in dark, black as a coal mine a mile deep, and close—smothering. Not a star was visible, not a ray's reflection from the murky flood sweeping so close beneath them. The bridge was a long one with a high framework which the rays from the lantern lit up ghostily.

On lumbered the engine, until the drivers began churning in constantly deepening water as they advanced.

"Must be near the center," Ed Strayley broke the long silence. "This floor ain't nailed and some of the planks may have floated away. Reckon we'd better stop and look ahead a little?"

"Good idea," agreed Rance, and taking the lantern from Ed's hand he stepped down into the water that came half way to his knees. Ten feet ahead of the engine he paused. Directly in front of him the water was boiling up in an ugly looking swell. Cautiously he explored it with his foot. No bottom! The planks were gone.

"Jasp!" he called in a guarded tone, trying to keep the apprehension out of his voice, but that he failed was evidenced by the haste in which Jasper leaped from the engine and splashed up to him.

"What is it, Rance?" he asked.

"Floor's gone," briefly.

They both stood silent, listening to the swish and suck of the river; stood until a blazing flash of lightning cleft the night and a roar of thunder shook the bridge. Then as the echoes went grumbling, tumbling, rumbling away down the river big drops of rain began to fall.

"Boy, howdy!" exclaimed Jasper. "We're in it!"

"Can't back out," said Rance.

"Can't go ahead," said Jasper.

"Got to!" Rance spoke fiercely. "Wait here."

Back at the engine he seized a 15-foot flue swab and hurried back. With it he explored the space before them and eight feet out the swab struck the floor again.

"There!" he exclaimed, a world of relief in his tone. "I was afraid there was a lot gone. All we've got to do is to take up some plank back of us and lay 'em down here."

"How'll we keep 'em there?" asked Jasper. "They'll float away as fast as we lay them. The sleepers are iron. We can't nail to them."

"We'll lay them endways the bridge and nail to the other planks. Let's get a move on. The river's rose an inch or more while we've stood here."

Ed Strayley once in action became steady as a clock. Humpy was worth three ordinary men. He heaved up one of the great water-soaked planks, sixteen inches wide, two inches thick and fourteen feet long, weighing upward of three hundred pounds, like a toy.

"Come on," he rattled. "Hop to it." Between them the boys lifted another.

"She's caving my knees in!" panted Jasper. "Must weigh ten ton!" Ed carried the lantern, ax, and nails. Back at the open space he spoke.

"It won't do to cover this whole space. The pressure of the water from beneath will lift everything we nail to. Better lay two plank on each side for the wheels to run on and leave the center open."

"Good idea," agreed Rance. "Somebody'll have to get across to catch the ends else they'll float down."

"Wait," gargled Humpy. He explored the water with his foot until he found a sleeper, inched out a few feet with the plank he still held, then lowered it and put his weight on it. "Nail it!" he grunted.

Did you ever try to drive a nail in a foot of water, through two inches of seasoned oak? Ed Strayley worked and sweated and bent nails for full five minutes before he secured the ends. Almost an hour passed before the four planks were laid and nailed and the water had risen to their knees.

"Ready!" panted Rance. "Ed, you stand on the other side of the gap, in the center, and hold the lantern on your head. We'll point the old Stormer's nose at you. 'Twon't do to miss the planks."

Ed took up the position and as the boys climbed aboard the engine he turned to Humpy.

"Guess it's no use for me to tell you that it's ten times as risky to drive the team across as this rig. Maybe you'd better unhitch the horses and take them back to the other side."

"Not on your life!" Humpy's gargle was loud and pronounced. "The water wagon follers the engine, Rancie, boy."

"No use to try to talk him out of the notion," said Jasper. "Open her up."

Rance opened the throttle and the Mitt-Stormer surged toward that narrow crossing, forty feet of swirling water underneath. The lantern gleamed dimly through the sheets of rain now falling.

Thump! The front wheels struck the ends of the planks, climbed up; the rear ones followed. Out they crept.

At once they felt it—a sinking sensation.

"Boy, howdy! Boy, howdy!" shouted Jasper. "The planks are bending, Rance! Give her the gun! Give it to her!"

Frantically Rance snatched the throttle wide open and the Mitt-Stormer's exhaust almost tore off the smoke stack. There was a hiss as the water entered the ashpit.

"If it gets into the firebox, good night!" said Rance. Then they felt the rise as the engine left the planks.

Jasper drew a deep, gasping breath. "First one I've had since we started," he said.

"Go ahead of us, Ed," called Rance, "and feel for missing planks. We've got to get out of here!"

"How about Humpy?" asked Jasper.

"We can't help him any. He'll have to trust the horses. They're trusty."

And those horses brought the wagon across, although they snorted gustily when they felt the planks give beneath them. Up on the seat Humpy sat steady as a rock, gripping the lines convulsively in his big fists and talking to the horses in a soothing tone that gave no hint of the fear that gripped him. Closely he followed the rig, which in turn closely followed the bobbing lantern ahead.

"He's stopped—no, he's going on!" exclaimed Jasper. "Lord, if he only keeps going!"

On crept the light, on until the boys saw it stop, describe a wild circle as Ed whirled it about his head and sounded a wild, wild yell of relief. Then Rance jerked the throttle wide, and Jasper yanked on the whistle cord until it almost broke while back of them Humpy's weird, gargling yell joined the bedlam. They were across!

"There's a bad hill ahead where we leave these bottoms," said Ed. "Be foolish to try it tonight. Doubt if we even make it in daylight. I've got a basket of grub on the water wagon. Figured you'd need it."

"Boy, howdy!" exclaimed Jasper. "Let me shake you by the hand. It's a life saver, that's what it is!"

Rance opened the firebox door and by its cheery gleam they ate the belated and well-earned supper. Never before in all their lives had food tasted so good. The canopy over the engine broke the rain and there they dozed off—Rance on a coal locker, Jasper on the water tank, and Ed and Humpy sitting back to back against each other. They slept fitfully. Jasper rolled off the water tank and awoke yelling, "Boy, howdy! Boy, howdy! The planks are bending, Rance. Giver her the gun! Give it to her!" which woke them all, so they sat and gossiped until almost daylight.

"Well," Rance arose and stretched mightily. "Wonder how far it is from here?"

"Were to?" asked Ed.

"What was that fellow's name, Jasper?"

"Reeves, I think. Levi Reeves. Know him?"

"Ought to. He's my brother-in-law. It's ten miles from the top of the hill. They've got some fine grain up there. All stacked, too. They stack every season up there."

Rance had up steam by daylight and they started. The roads were bad and the grade increased constantly. The big drivers slewed and skidded; a worried pucker grew between Rance's eyes, then the hill loomed before them.

"Dead Man's Hill," said Mr. Strayley, almost dramatically. "A holy terror, worst in the county."

"I believe you," said Rance as he surveyed it. He stopped and filled the boiler as full as possible without danger of knocking out a cylinder head. Then he crowded on steam until the safety valve lifted with a great *whoooisssh!* of pent up steam, then they hit the hill.

Up the Stormer climbed valiantly, the exhaust growing slower and more terrific. Near the center of the hill was a sharp curve, such as most bad hills have, flanked by deep ditches. When the engine struck this turn the drivers skidded and slewed towards the ditch.

"Shut off! Shut off!" yelled Jasper. "I can't hold her in the road!"

"She'll drop back if I do," said Rance. "Get the chock blocks ready."

Down leaped Jasper and Ed, blocks in hand.

"Ready?" asked Rance sharply.

"Ready!" they sang out.

"Watch your fingers!" shouted Rance, and shut off.

Ker-chunk! sounded the wheels as they dropped back against the blocks. A half-stifled yell came from Ed and he held aloft a streaming hand.

"Did it catch you?" asked Rance, leaping down.

"Got my front finger." Ed's face contracted in a spasm of pain and he waved the hand wildly, splattering Rance with blood.

Rance caught the hand, tore a fragment from his shirt and bound it deftly. He was handy about such matters, having taken first aid in school. "Where's the nearest doctor?" he asked.

"About four miles up the road."

"Well, you beat it on up there and have that hand dressed properly."

"No," protested Ed, "you need me here."

"Go on!" commanded Rance. "If that finger becomes infected you'll lose your arm, or worse. We'll manage."

"All right. But I'll be back right away." And he took off.

In the meanwhile Humpy had unhitched the horses and brought them up. He now swung them into a position in front of the engine and hitched on.

"Ready?" he called.

"Let 'em go!" said Rance, and opened the throttle.

"Git in the collar!" yelled Humpy, and those horses crouched and pulled until you could scarce have thrown your hat under their bellies. The engine labored fiercely, and slowly they forged ahead, foot by foot, until they swung into the straightaway and stopped to rest the team.

From there on the going was steadier. The hill was long and it was a fight all the way up, but near noon they topped the summit, water low, team panting and exhausted, the boys and Humpy but little better off.

Below them the country stretched invitingly. Off to their right, some three or four miles, a pillar of black smoke climbed upward; approximately the same distance to their left another similar column showed.

"What do you reckon that is?" asked Jasper, glancing at Rance.

"Don't know," Rance spoke in an odd tone.

"Yes you do," gargled Humpy. "You both know as well as I do that both them smokes are threshing rigs."

"But they're not pulling," said Jasper, "or if they are they're not pulling the way we are."

"No use to kid ourselves, Jasp," said Rance quietly. "We know they're pulling for the same place we're headed and if they beat us in our goose is cooked."

"They hain't beat us in yit!" rattled Humpy, leaping for the team. "Be ready to take on water." Down the hill he drove at a stiff trot.

Below them a horseman appeared on the road.

"Watch 'im come!" marveled Rance.

"He's sure burning the wind," agreed Jasper.

"It's Ed. Bet I can guess what he's in such a tearing up hurry about."

"Anybody could," said Jasper as Ed came fogging up and swung down from his panting horse.

"Two rigs pulling for the Reeves settlement," he said. "If either of them beats you in you know what it means. Them fellows have always made it a rule to thresh with the first rig in, all of 'em."

"How far have they to pull?" Rance shot at him.

"That smoke," Ed pointed to the left, "is Smeltzer. He's got less than five miles but his engine is old, low geared and slow. That smoke," he pointed to the right, "is Stirling. He's got nine miles and he's got a fast engine. He's a crooked son-of-a-gun. If we beat him we'll know we've done something. Here's how the roads run," he said as he knelt and drew a diagram showing the relative position of the three rigs. "We're on the straight road, this X is us. This X on the left is Smeltzer, and this one on the right is Stirling. This X, a little above where the roads come together, is Levi's place, first set. The first rig to get to the place here, where the roads meet, is the first rig in."

Rance set his jaw. "We'll beat them or tear the gears out of her. Eph ought to have told us about this. Here's the water."

Quickly they took on water, then Rance climbed over on top of the boiler and wired down the safety valve, climbed back and jerked open the throttle.

"Keep her in the road, Jasp," he said. "She's wide open and she stays wide open clear in!"

The manner in which the old Mitt-Stormer rolled down that hill with the Wildcat lumbering behind would have given a thrill to the most slow-minded person alive. And the pace slowed up mighty little when they flattened out on the level stretch below. Then it was up hill and down, up hill and down. The old Stormer ate coal like a railroad locomotive. At the end of the sixth mile Rance's shovel rang sharply on the bottom of the coal locker.

"Jasp!" he exclaimed, "we're done unless we get some coal right away!"

"There's a coal shed where the roads meet," said Ed. "I'll ride ahead and bring a couple of sacks back on the horse."

"Wait," said Rance. "Suppose you take the wagon and let Humpy go. If Stirling is the kind of a fellow they say he is you might have a run-in with him and you wouldn't be in very good shape to take care of yourself with a crippled hand. 'Twouldn't be fair for you to run the risk for us."

"I'm more than willing to run any risk," said Ed. "It's because you stopped to thresh my wheat that your rig is behind; but if you'd rather Humpy went, I'll drive the wagon."

"Like to have you along with us," said Rance. "You know the road and we don't."

So Humpy forked the horse and rode off at a gallop. A couple of miles up the road the two roads on which the Smeltzer and Stirling rigs were traveling swung close in to the boys' road. As Humpy rode up he could see the smoke from the Smeltzer rig plainly. Reaching the coal shed, he bought a couple of sacks of coal, and since each of the sacks held about a hundred pounds he tied them on the saddle, walked and led the horse on the way back.

Two miles down the road he obtained a good view of the Smeltzer rig, churning along on its low drivers, the exhaust irregular and erratic, indicating an off eccentric. With two miles to pull there was little danger of Smeltzer beating them in because they had pulled about seven miles while he had pulled three, leaving them but three miles to pull to his two. But just about a mile farther on, just before the road on which Stirling was traveling made a wide sweep away from their road, a cloud of steam appeared above the tree tops and the clear, sharp exhaust of a smoothly running, powerful engine sounded clearly.

Humpy halted his horse and watched the rig round the curve. It was a big, new, shiny, cross-compound Steeves and Humpy could plainly see the big, black-whiskered man driving because the distance that separated them was considerably less than a quarter of a mile.

"Goin' to have to do some tall steppin' to beat him," he said aloud. "He's traveled mile for mile with us and has a mile the advantage now, but his steam's low; guess his coal must be short, too." As he started on Stirling looked across the intervening space and saw him, turned and spoke to his fireman, then shut off and swung down.

A hail from Stirling halted Humpy. It was useless to try to run away; besides, Humpy had never learned to run from trouble. So he waited quietly until Stirling strode up.

"Hello," said Stirling. He was even bigger than Humpy and Humpy was over six feet when he straightened his back—a whale of a man. "What are y'u packin'?"

"Coal," said Humpy briefly, eyeing the big man closely.

"Give you a dollar a sack for it."

"Come again," gargled Humpy.

Stirling's eyes narrowed. "How much?" he asked.

"Bout the only thing you've got that would buy it is that rig of your'n," said Humpy.

Stirling took a step forward, an ugly light in his eyes. "Think so, Mr. Hump Back?" he sneered. "Well I happen to be needin' a couple sacks of coal bad, right now, and I aim to have it. What are you aimin' to do with it that makes it so darned valuable?"

Humpy pointed down the road where the Stormer's smoke was now visible.

"Burnin' it," he said. "That's Gattling and Holiday's smoke and if you're out of coal you'd better hike after some. Only two, three miles down the road."

"Think so?" said Stirling again, coming closer. "This'll suit me best."

He moved with astonishing quickness for so big a man and his great ham of a fist caught Humpy square between the eyes. Now Humpy was a tough customer in a fist fight, strong as a bull and tougher, yet he went down before that buffet—anybody would. But he came up with a spring, head first, and rammed Stirling in the belly, full force.

It was funny to see Stirling's face. His eyes popped out, his mouth flew open, he gasped like a fish out of water, then melted into a heap in the road. Humpy took up the reins and moved on down the road muttering and shaking his head.

On the Mitt-Stormer both steam and spirits were low. Humpy's arrival with the two sacks of precious coal raised both. With a new fire roaring in the grate they quickened their speed.

"Stirling's ahead," said Humpy. "Think he's out of coal."

"Did he give you them black eyes?" asked Jasper.

Humpy nodded.

"What was he doing when you last saw him?" went on Jasper.

"Tryin to git up," said Humpy with a rare grin

When they came in sight of the Stirling rig black smoke was poiuring from the stack and the rig was picking up speed steadily. Up, up, until the rigs were runningalmost parallel. Almost, but not quite. Vainly did Rance struggle to get the throttle a little wider. No use; and slowly, ever so slowly, the big new rig began to gain.

"'e's got the heels of us Rance!" gasped Jasper. "Is she wide open?"

"Never been any other way," said Rance, his lower jaw sticking way out, clenched tight as iron.

Across the narrowing space between the rigs they could see Stirling's insolent grin. He even reached up and jerked the whistle cord twice as he pounded ahead.

Humpy climbed up on the engine, madder than fire. "Say!" he gargled awfully, "shall I go and take him off?" He jerked his thumb towards Stirling.

"No!" Rance spoke sharply. "No dirty work."

"He tried it on me," defended Humpy. "Turn about is fair play."

"No," said Rance again; "two wrongs don't make a right."

"Then for the Lord's sake do something, Rance!" prayed Jasper. "Do something! He's leaving us clean!"

"Gimme your knife!" said Rance. Taking it he climbed up over the hot, lurching boiler. "Keep your hands on that wheel!" he warned, and slashed the governor belt.

The old Mitt-Stormer seemed to hump herself and jump. The engine raced at an awful speed, the gears whined and the big clogs on the drivers began to pour past their eyes at a furious rate.

"We're coming up!" shouted Jasper. "Look at him scoop!"

They were coming up fast. Ahead on the left Smeltzer was pounding along and the Mitt-Stormer passed him at the same time she resolutely stuck her nose ahead of

Stirling's big cross-compound monster.

Then, with victory in sight, fate played them a mean trick, as she often does.

A woman driving a high-headed horse top buggy appeared on the straight road ahead.

"Oh, Lord!" groaned Jasper. "I do hope she don't come this way!"

But she did, and as the high-strung horse sighted the Mitt-Stormer roaring down on him he sat down in the shafts and pawed the air.

There was no time to deliberate. To shut down would give Stirling the lead. But Rance did not hesitate. He shut down.

Before the Stormer stopped rolling Jasper was on the ground, dashing for the horse. He seized the bits. "Get out, ma'am; please hurry!"

The woman lost no time in tumbling out and Jasper whirled the horse around, leaped in the buggy and dashed down the road, the wild clamor of the Stormer's exhaust coming to his ears as Rance again opened the throttle.

Humpy was steering, a wild light in his eyes. Rance's jaw was set harder than ever. Stirling had secured the lead. He had fifty yards to go, Rance seventy-five, the Mitt-Stormer gaining rapidly. Oh, it was a race! Up, up, again up they came.

"Be a tie!" gargled Humpy excitedly.

"No tie!" flashed Rance. "There's not room for two rigs on that road!" Which was true. The road into which the two converging roads led was graded high and narrow, flanked by deep ditches on each side. "The rig that stays on the road when we come together will be the rig that threshes this wheat."

"He's got the biggest rig," said Humpy.

"Then he'll hit the ditch the hardest!" flashed Rance. "I won't shut down if I break this engine into scrap iron!"

Stirling saw that a collision was coming. He reached for the whistle cord and sounded his warning. Rance did likewise and kept coming.

"Better jump, Humpy," warned Rance. "We'll be together in five seconds!"

"Not me!" rattled Humpy. "He's weakening! He ain't got the nerve to drive into us!"

It was true. Stirling weakened at the last moment and shut down while the old Stormer swung into the turn, whistle cord tied clear back, Humpy grinning the widest grin in his life and Ed Strayley trying to dance a jubilant jig on top of the water wagon!

Up ran Jasper, mounted the separator, faced Stirling's rig and formed a trumpet with his hand.

"Gattling and Holiday!" he shouted. "First rig in!"

MANDY PETTENGILL'S "JAZZ"

C. B. Horace

The Farm Journal, September 1919

"MANDY," said Uncle Zeke Pettengill, grasping his newspaper and letting his specs almost bob off his nose, "what is that?"

"Land sakes, what *is* that?" repeated his wife, throwing her dishrag into the pan and starting for the door.

Somewhere down across the fields beyond the orchard was the roar of a powerful motor. No such sound had ever reverberated in that hilly farm country of Northern New England. On the faces of the two elderly people, as they rushed from the house, was a look of wonder and astonishment.

Up the road panted a neighbor. "Right down there in your pasture, Zeke, I saw it as plain as day; one of them dadbusted flying-machines, cahooting down into your pasture like a jayhawk!"

Two convulsive bursts of noise, a sputter, and all was still. As the three trooped down across the fields, a helmeted, leather-coated figure climbed over the stone fence from the lower side.

"Good evening; a little engine trouble; had to come down. On the way from Boston to Montreal; new route-marking service," vouchsafed the aviator, taking off his goggles and rubbing a smooch of oil from his cheek. "Can you give me a bite of supper and a place to sleep? I'll get the old bus working in the morning."

"Well, I declare if we can't," said Uncle Zeke hospitably. "I reckon you aren't hurt, to look at you, and we just got up from supper. Mandy will fix you up. Eph and I will just go down and fetch up the cows, and maybe have a look at that hoss of yours, if you don't mind."

"Not at all. Don't touch anything, if you please. You will find the cows in this end of the pasture. I'll be back in a little while to stake down the ship and cover up the engine."

Thus it happened—Mandy Pettengill's ride in an airship. What she put into that young sky-rider's stomach took effect close to his heart. It had been a long time since he had been urged through such a joyful riot of spareribs, cold chicken, apple sauce, fried potatoes, baked squash, chow-chow, hot biscuits, maple syrup, sugar cookies, pumpkin pie, and milk.

"I sat there," said Mandy to her open-mouthed auditors at the next meeting of the Ladies' Aid Society, "admiring the way he seemed to like my cooking, when he looked up and saw that talking-machine that Zeke bought last Christmas, and up he jumped and clapped on a record.

" 'Nothing like having a harp when you are in heaven,' he said.

"And there we were, just as sociable as you please. He told me about his ma and

85

pa out West in New York State and I told him about Sam being drafted and still over in France, and how Sam had written about seeing the airplanes, common like, most every day. Then I said I had never expected to see one, much less down in our back pasture. From that, we got to talking about what it seemed like up in the air looking down. And finally I said, 'Well, I have something to write Sam about this week.' And he up that quick and said: 'You go up for a jazz,'—that's the word he used—'you go up for a jazz with me tomorrow morning and you will really have something to write about.' Well, sakes alive! When he said that, I nearly fainted.

"'Young man,' said I, when I had caught my breath, 'you couldn't hoist me into one of those things with a derrick. I was made on land, and on land I stay."

"'Ma,' he said, looking me right in the eyes and grinning, 'a woman that can cook as good as you can has just got to get up on top where people can see her.' Then he got up and went off down to the pasture to see to his airplane, and I sat there, forgetting all about clearing off the dishes till Zeke came in with the milk and asked: 'What ails you, Mandy? You're as white as a sheet!'

"'Zeke,' said I, 'if you're through separating the milk, you come along with me down to the pasture till I see that airplane; and don't go to worrying about my health, for I've never felt better in my life.'

"With that we went down and looked over that flying-machine and saw what it was like inside and out. Before we were half through, the neighbors began to arrive, and by the time it was dark, about half the men in town were there, and most of the folks from Burdin's Corners. It seemed like 'most everybody had been listening on the telephone line, and everybody knew all there was to know without seeing with their own eyes. And they had come to attend to that and no mistake.

"Finally, Len Barrett, that game warden from up Wellington way, came along, and he, being the nearest thing to an arm of the law, said he considered it his duty to establish a guard over government property. So he appointed Hen Willis and Gus Herrick and Josh Davis as deputies, and they all went to guarding alongside a campfire they built near Hen's buckboard. We went home after that and put the Lieutenant in the spare room, after talking a while and playing the phonograph. The last thing the Lieutenant said was: 'Good-night, ma; don't get your wind up.'

"'What did he mean by that, Mandy?' said Zeke. 'He doesn't expect you're going to have colic, does he?'

"I went in and sat down on the bed, feeling kind of queer. Every time I thought of going up in the air higher than a barn I just couldn't seem to get my breath. I just had the fidgets. So I got a drink of water and put some on my forehead, but it didn't do any good. I went out to the back door for a minute, but I couldn't seem to think of anything but looking down from the top of a building. And at last it struck me what the Lieutenant meant by 'getting your wind up.' My wind was so high up it fairly choked me.

"By the time I got into bed Zeke was breathing easy. I just closed my eyes and thought of Sam off there in France, and I made up my mind that if Sam had done all he had done, I could go flying once without showing the white feather, or my name wasn't Mandy Pettengill. So I said my prayers a little mite longer than usual, and turned over and went to sleep.

"It wasn't sleep, either; not what *you* might call sleep. Once I was swooping over our barn and run plump into the windmill—which was Zeke's back.

"'Mandy, are you sleeping or playing football,' he said. And I answered, dry like: 'I'm running for the Legislature,' which is a sore spot with Zeke. Another time, I was chasing around in the air after a duck. The duck kept getting bigger and bigger and finally turned around and opened its mouth to gobble me. I struck at it with all my might, and screamed. Zeke sat up and rubbed his ear and said: 'Mandy, if you think I'm a punching bag, I'm going to get up.'

"He scratched a match and looked at his watch. It was a quarter past four. When I heard him take down the milk pails, I got up, too. It was too early to get breakfast, but I wanted to get some woolen petticoats out of the cedar closet. When Zeke came in with the milk and started the separator, that brought the Lieutenant out of bed.

"At breakfast the Lieutenant got up and put a record on the phonograph. I never saw such a fellow to have music with his meals. Zeke said he had found the guards all sound asleep on a horse blanket under the buckboard, but the airplane was all right.

"After breakfast I put on my knit wool hood and sweater, and we all went down to the pasture. I kept trying to be natural, but my heart was going like a triphammer and I could hardly talk. The Lieutenant caught my eye once. I nodded and tried to smile, though it was a sickly attempt. He fussed around the flying-machine for a while and finally said: 'Ah!' Soon after that, while I was trying to ask Hen Willis about their new baby, he caught hold of the whirligig piece of wood out in front of the engine and turned it two or three times. Then he got in and did something, and that engine gave a snort and that whirligig went round till you couldn't see it. He had Len Barrett and Zeke holding down the tail of the machine. Both their hats blew off in the hurricane that struck them, and Zeke must have thought he was going over the top, for he closed his eyes and held on like grim death. Pretty soon the Lieutenant turned off his engine a little, and called out to Zeke and Len to catch hold of the wings and turn him around into the wind. With that he moved along slow on the ground for a little, to a place where it was smooth. Then he looked around and nodded to me like he wanted to say something. I felt myself go pale, but I happened to glance about and there were people coming from every direction. I never knew there were so many boys in Somerset County. Right then I said to myself, 'You're Sam's mother,' and I walked over to that airplane like a general.

"'You are the best in the world,' said the Lieutenant, getting out. 'Put on this pair of goggles and I'll soon have you up where they can all crane their necks at you.'

"I was on the other side of the machine from Zeke. He was rubbing some of the sand out of his eyes from that hurricane, and he didn't see me when the Lieutenant helped me clamber up into the back seat. Leastways, he didn't see me till I had my feet down into the hole and was just going to sit down. Even then he didn't seem to figure out what was going on.

"I sat down, and the Lieutenant climbed up and made me buckle a belt around me that held me to the seat. I looked over toward Zeke; he just waved his hand and shouted something I didn't catch, for the Lieutenant had gotten into his seat and speeded up the engine. In a jiffy we were moving. Zeke shot past, his mouth wide open and his eyes fairly starting out of his head.

"Bless my soul! We were flying. We were way above the trees and the barn, and I could see the village as plain as your face. Then I felt myself tipping, and there I was staring right at the ground underneath. I saw Zeke with his hat off, but he wasn't waving it like the rest. He had his hand up like he was scratching his head, and I knew as well as I want to that he wasn't thinking the right thoughts for a deacon of the Baptist church.

"Now I can't tell you all about that flying, because I was seeing too much and feeling too much all at once. First, I'd be seeing all plain and easy—Moose Pond only a stone's throw this side and Wellington only a stone's throw off in the other direction, and the village right beneath us. Then up and down we would go like a roller coaster. I happened to look up and there was a great smother of gray cloud right above us. The Lieutenant looked around and grinned. I tried to grin too, but all I could do was wrinkle my nose like a sick calf. With that we shot into the cloud. It was just like a fog and that wet it might have been raining. All I could see for a minute was the back of the Lieutenant's head, and then it got lighter. Pretty soon we were above the clouds.

"We sailed around there for a while, and I would just get up enough courage to admire the cloud boiling around beneath us, or look off beyond it where I could see Hartland and Cambridge and Dexter and Pittsfield, with the sun shining on the buildings ever so pretty, when up we'd tip and go scooting off in another direction. Every time we did that, it seemed like I would fall out if it hadn't been for that belt.

"My spine was a whole piano-forte of thrills, but that young fellow in front had saved something in the way of a grand finale that I'm glad I wasn't looking forward to. The Lieutenant shut off the engine, looked around and shouted: 'Hold on tight!'

"Over we turned and pointed for the cloud. I just braced myself and shut my mouth tight, which was a good thing, I guess, or I should have turned inside out. Falling! I've often dreamed of falling, but it wasn't anything like that. I was falling as fast as I could, but that airplane was falling faster and was taking me right along. I closed my eyes when we hit the cloud, but something began to happen. We were not only falling, but whirling round and round. 'Tail spin', the Lieutenant said it was afterward.

"When we shot through that cloud the earth was fairly rushing up at us. I knew in a flash that it was my last look at it alive, but I didn't want to die, and I couldn't think of anything except wanting to see Sam and Zeke. So I prayed real quick, and the Lord answered, for right then we stopped falling and spinning so sudden that I nearly went through the bottom of the seat.

"The Lieutenant looked around and smiled, waving his hand. He seemed to know that he had me to thank for that. But at that he wasn't satisfied. I hadn't more than gotten my mouth open to try and breath again, when up we pointed, and before you could say Jack Robinson, my head was sticking straight down toward the ground. Looping the loop, that was. I'll bet a cookie I'm the only woman in the state of Maine that ever looped the loop in an airplane! All the time we were flying around in a small circle, or rather the world seemed to be going around like a great beautiful millstone, and getting nearer and nearer all the time.

"Then there were a couple of quick explosions in the engine that made me jump. We were going nice and easy, and I looked down. There was our house and barn right beneath, and about a thousand people running for the fences. Our south field fairly jumped up at us. Then we bumped easy—didn't bounce a bit more than going over a thank-you-marm in the road—and stopped.

"I don't know how I managed to get out, but I did. My knees were so weak that I could hardly stand up, and my hands were wet with sweat; yet I was so cold I just shivered. The Lieutenant said 'Goodbye' and flew away soon. Zeke and I came up the back way along the pasture lane to the house. Zeke tried to talk to me, but my head was ringing so I couldn't hear, and I felt pretty queer all over. That was the day before yesterday, and I spent a good part of it in bed. Yesterday I sat down and wrote all about it to Sam. Sam won't get the letter, though, for when Charlie Mack came with the mail this morning, there was one from Sam. He is on the way home and may get here 'most any day.

"I'm sort o' glad Sam doesn't know about my flying, after all. When he gets to telling all about the airplanes over there, Zeke will ask me, casual like: 'Was that your impression, Ma, last time you were up?'

"And I'll say to Sam: 'Sam, that may or may not be so, but for all that, airplaning is a mighty thrilling occupation, and you can take it straight from the only woman in Maine who ever looped the loop.'"

CONVERTING A CONSERVATIVE

Robert Carlton Brown
The Country Gentleman, October 1912

I N the front yard a bench from the old district school did service as a lawn lounge, its gaunt iron arms striking a jarring note in the rustic surroundings.

"But it's jest as good to set on," said Garret Keenan, "as though we'd paid out money for it."

George Keenan agreed, agreeing being chronic with him.

Cal Keenan said with a submissive, conscious giggle, that it was funny and old-fashioned, like everything else they clung to; but Gertie, her sedate elder sister, said she didn't mind it because if you stuffed a handkerchief between the top rail and your backbone it was more restful to sit down in it than to stand up.

Gertie's training had been stoical. She had been born a utilitarian. Old Daniel, her father, had purified his Puritanical soul by exacting from his first-born a rigid, dutiful day as colorless as his own. Garret, the next child and oldest son, followed his father in the field, learning to plow and squeeze a penny as proficiently as Daniel himself. Garret brought up George, who was meek, and Gertie did her best with Cal, who was no feminine Job. The eldest three did not chafe at unimproved, unprogressive surroundings; Cal did.

Daniel and his good but spineless wife had been dead twenty-four years and the Keenan "boys" and "girls" clung to the old homestead still, grinding out their days as methodically as they did their sausage meat.

Gertie, nearly sixty, found comfort in the Mayflower bed of her mother, worn ropes doing service as slats; and Garret and George still slept in the haymow when there was company at the house—which wasn't often—or when they had a hired man—which was still more seldom—who might set fire to the barn with his pipe. Cal, however, had a bedroom that she papered herself, a bower of calendars, chromos of flowers, accurate and exacting etchings of romantic seacoast scenes, wild, rugged mountains and limpid lakes.

And yet the Keenans were wealthy, holding substantial mortgages on all the surrounding possessions of luckless farmers. Toil and thrift were their watchwords, and though their methods were the most old-fashioned and cumbersome, as a result of frugality and self-denial they continued collecting mortgages and churning their own butter.

Late one afternoon in early summer Gertie and Cal Keenan sat in the front yard, their day's work done, with the exception of boiling potatoes for the men's supper. Gertie was sitting on the old school bench sewing, with Cal idle at her side in a low Dutch rocker that might also have come over on the Mayflower.

"There go the Barrys in their new automobile," said Gertie, looking up over her

91

glasses at an approaching dust cloud.

"Oh, I wish Garret would get one!" cried Cal impatiently. "A big red one with shiny brass lamps!"

"Garret, he knows best, Cal," cautioned Gertie, taking advantage of snipping off a thread to glance sidewise at her sister.

"Yes, but Garret's so old-fashioned. It don't seem to me we get half as much fun out of life as we should. It ain't as though we didn't have money to enjoy ourselves." Cal's voice was pleasantly petulant.

"Garret, he says automobiles are riskier an' more complicated than threshing machines. Who'd run it if we did have one?" Gertie quavered doubtingly.

"I would!" cried Cal with spirit, her black eyes snapping defiance.

"That would be womanly, I must say," Gertie reproved over the top of her spectacles.

"Well, you people can do as you like. I ain't going to spend my whole life washin' dishes an' makin' cheese and cookies. I'm going on thirty-four, Gertie, and I'm not going to—Why look!" she broke off in a conscious flutter. "The Barrys are turning in here."

She rose from the rocker, patted down the plaits in her rusty dress, swiftly smoothed her hair and hurried across the lawn, followed by Gertie, who had stopped to put up her needle with trembling fingers and pick up her handkerchief, which had dropped from between the top rail of the bench and her back as she had hastily arisen.

A hale, hearty old fellow with Santa Claus cheeks, sitting in the front seat beside a tanned young man in a chauffeur's duster with businesslike gauntlets, waved his hand and jumped out with the greeting: "Hello, Cal! Hello, Gert! Came to take you folks for a ride. Mother an' the girls have gone into town on the train for the day."

"Take us riding?" beamed Cal, dropping a limp hand into Dr. John Barry's hard, broad palm.

"That's it! Where's George and Garret?" asked the elderly boy with a bursting smile.

"The boys are over in the field there," answered Cal, her eyes dancing. "Shall I run across an' get them? It won't take a minute!"

"No. Jump in! We'll drive over an' pick 'em up. I'll go ahead and open the gate." And Doctor Barry bustled toward the gate, his duster flapping out behind him.

"But our hats!" exclaimed Gertie, squinting up at the sun, and clutching at a thin knot of gray hair twisted into a doughnut on top of her head.

"Come along now! We'll get the boys; don't stop to fix up. There's some veils in the pocket on the door there in the back seat," the doctor turned with a wave of his hand toward the tonneau.

Gertie nervously untied her apron while Cal fumbled with the brass handle of the auto door.

"Here, I'll do that, Miss Keenan," offered the thin, pleasant-faced young farmer at the wheel, leaning over to give the handle an accustomed twist.

"Thank you, Mr. Owen," said Cal, flushing.

"Cal, you sit in front with Bill," ordered the doctor in a commanding tone as he stood beside the gate which he had energetically opened. "I want to sit in back with the boys and Gert. Us old folks'll sit together." He laughed a hearty, healthy laugh, a laugh which had piled firm flesh on his big, bony frame.

Cal hesitated like a timid bird about to leap to a doubtful branch until Gertie gave her a push and she landed with a little stifled cry in the roomy leather seat beside Bill Owen.

Gerty hoisted her lumpy, uncorseted form into the back seat awkwardly, hitting her head on the leather cushion as she sat down and bobbing forward in surprise with the expression of a startled chicken. She folded her apron neatly and sat prim and precise as though in her own stiff, stuffy parlor. The machine started with a jolt and she jerked back against the seat, clutching at her unstable topknot, which was already slipping down.

"Here, Gertie," cried Cal, turning with a triumphant flush and holding down her curled bangs with one hand, "give me that old apron. It's that one of Aunt Martha's, isn't it?" She looked at the threadbare square of cloth, and suddenly snatched it from her sister's lap.

With ruthless abandon she ripped the frayed apron in two and handed back one half to Gertie, who sat blankly astonished at the reckless destruction of a treasured bit of property.

"You shouldn't have done that, Cal," she reproved crossly. "It might have lasted a year yet."

"It wouldn't have lasted another wash," answered Cal, pulling her half of the apron over her head and tying it tight beneath her round chin in a jaunty knot. "Put it on. Your hair'll all blow off and you'll lose your hairpins if you don't."

"I wouldn't want to lose my hairpins," said Gertie plaintively, looking at the faded bit of apron and finally flinging it over her scant hair. "You shouldn't have done it though, Cal."

But Cal, all animation, feeling inspired, had no interest in remorse. She rose part way from her seat and waved her handkerchief to Garret and George, who stood staring stupidly at the spectacle of the approaching auto running right into their field, with Doctor Barry in his flying duster waving his big, hairy, red hand from the running board.

"We're going for a ride! Come on!" shouted Cal.

Barry called out in loud, urgent invitation, and George Keenan, with a conscious grin, dropped a pitchfork and looked up hopefully to Garret.

"We ought to get this alfalfa stacked 'fore night," said Garret, his eyes drifting to the sky, clear and cloudless.

"Oh, come on! You boys work too hard," urged John Barry, holding wide the tonneau door.

George turned his little, red, wrinkled face up to Garret's broad, brown, bullock visage. The beating of George's heart showed plainly in the prominent pulse at his wrists below tightly buttoned denim sleeves, at fitting which Gertie was expert.

Garret looked down at his overalls and pushed his straw hat back on his head in deliberation. George glanced consciously at his attire, eased his hatband a little and looked up at Garret speculatively.

Then Garret accepted, with becoming gravity, at the urging of Cal, and they got in, George adapting himself to a little folding stool between the feet of the others and Garret stretching out between Gertie and Barry, exclaiming with a long-drawn breath as the auto started and he took off his hat: "Well, this is real nice!"

Cal's heart fluttered, George's pounded, and Gertie's leaped at the prompt and unprecedented expression of enjoyment. Like guileless children unexpectedly sustained in a flighty escapade by a stern father, the three dominated Keenans gave themselves up to reserved enjoyment, glancing furtively at Garret occasionally to see if he were still pleased.

Garret was. He lay back in luxurious ease in the tonneau, pointed out farms on which the family held mortgages, remarked on the progress of all the early crops in which he was interested, and talked politics and pigs with the doctor, while Gertie and George sat submissive and silent, breathing in the brisk air stealthily, enjoying their outing like mice flirting with a friendly trap that might clap shut at any second.

Cal, out of range of the household head in the back seat and buoyed up by the excess of oxygen forced into her lungs, talked radiantly to Bill Owen.

"Do you know," she said dreamily, "I'd like nothing better than to sit in a machine all day and ride. We could go to town and buy things; we could have picnics in lovely groves like that"—she pointed to a clump of oaks fringing a ravine, almost as romantic as the etchings in her room.

"Why don't you folks buy a machine?" suggested Bill in a tone diplomatically lowered, for he had left the farm to sell automobiles and was meeting with success. "Couldn't you get Garret to—"

"Bill!" cut in a big, bellowing voice from the back seat, "Garret wants to go up on Sweeny Hill; he ain't been there for thirty years. He says he's heard you can see the new capitol from there."

"Sweeny Hill!" cried Cal excitedly. "Oh, I've heard of that all my life, but I've never been there!"

"It's only eight miles from home," said Owen in a still lower tone as he slowed down to turn into a narrow uphill road. "You see if you had a machine of your own you could go an' see the capitol every day."

"Once would be enough," answered Cal, lingering over her dream. "I'd go on a different road every day and when I ran out of roads I'd begin and go all over them again. It must be a fine business selling automobiles. Like it better than the farm?" she asked, looking straight ahead.

"Yes, you get to see something different every day. It's changed me a lot," he said consciously.

The machine was puffing up the hill and on reaching the top the whole party stood up to gaze across the dim dales to the dome of the capitol, twenty miles away, standing out sharply against the distant Blue Mounds that melted into the sky.

"Funny how distance is deceiving," remarked Garret with a perplexed shake of his great head. "Now them Blue Mounds is thirty mile away and yet they don't look more'n a mile."

"Seems's if you could almost jump there!" George piped awesomely.

"You'd have to make it in two yumps and a half, as the Swede hired man said. Yumps!" repeated Gertie with a cackling laugh.

"*Yumps!*" giggled George irrepressibly, glancing up sharply at Garret, who smiled broadly at the time-honored joke, deliberately dragged out by Gertie to liven gala occasions.

"Well, folks," said Doctor John, "if you've seen enough of the capitol I guess we'd better turn round. I'll take you out again some other day; I got to meet mother and the girls on the four-o'clock train."

They returned by a different road and George was gleeful on recognizing a junction station where, twenty-four years before, when only a boy, he had taken a load of pigs for shipment.

"Hasn't changed much, has it, Garret?" he said in the calm manner of an accustomed traveler.

"Joe Seddings used to have a grain shed on the other side, right close by the track," said Garret critically.

Cal spoke in a quiet, discouraged tone to Bill Owen: "Don't it seem funny we've all lived in this place so long an' never been ten miles from home?"

"You and Garret went to the Farmers' Convention down in Texas, didn't you?" asked Owen.

"Yes, but that's four years ago. Nothing's happened since. I haven't been as far as Milwaukee since then. Oh, I wish we had an automobile!" She lapsed into big-eyed silence, grudging each mile they ticked off toward the farm. She could see herself stepping out on the lawn at home, the machine would whiz away in a cloud of dust; she would be alone again, alone with Garret and Gertie and George, who were as companionable and lifelike as the little old melodeon, the picture of Father Daniel in the parlor, and the teakettle. Yes, she thought she even preferred the teakettle for company. Sometimes it obstinately refused to boil and again it boiled over. It led no such even, eventless life as that of her brothers and her sister.

Vaguely she heard Dr. John Barry in the back seat urging Garret to buy a machine. She listened closely as Garret replied pompously and even a little irritably with a dozen reasons why they didn't need a car. She knew from the restless way George wriggled on his portable seat and bumped into her back that the question displeased Garret.

When they reached home Cal thanked Doctor Barry heartily, asked him in for a cup of tea and some cookies, which he refused because of his hurry. Just as the machine was turning round to start off for the station, the three eldest Keenans hovering about the porch like a group of disappointed children called in from an exciting game of tag, Cal cried in a flutter: "Oh, I've forgot my handkerchief! It must be in the front seat there."

She ran to the machine and Doctor Barry leaned over to help her look for the bit of linen. They exchanged several quick sentences and then Cal, having recovered her kerchief, called out goodbye; and the doctor, with beaming face, stood up to wave his hat about his head in farewell.

When Cal returned, a little flushed, the eyes of all the Keenans were ruefully following the departing machine.

"What funny little brass handles and things it had all over it," giggled Gertie. "I'll bet Bill Owen, he jest let out his speed to try and scare us."

"My, but it was fine!" said Cal a trifle languidly, sinking to the steps. "Garret, we ought to have one."

Garret's wandering eyes turned sharply from the disappearing machine and he covered the guilty look of a truant with a stern frown. "It's all right to have friends to take you out," he said shrewdly, "but it costs more to keep one automobile than two hired men. John Barry needs one in his business. We don't."

"It ain't as though we didn't have the money," responded Cal acidly.

"But there's the future to provide against," sighed Gertie, folding her hands in resignation.

"It's out of the question," said Garret with cold finality. "Why, think how much gasoline it takes jest to run the summer stove alone, and then you'll get an idea what it'd take to run an automobile! Come on, George, we got to get to the chores now. That alfalfa ain't in yet an' the corn'll need cultivatin' tomorrow."

George, whose eyes alone had remained fixed on the machine that was fast becoming a cloud of dust, drew a deep breath. "Gee!" he exclaimed. "I'd like to ride in one of them things from mornin' till night. Lots softer'n sittin' on a plow."

Garret jerked his head impatiently and started for the milk shed. George followed, his head turned like Mrs. Lot's, looking after the speck of dust in the road.

"I think it's mean Garret won't buy one," Cal said hotly, starting up the steps.

"I guess Garret, he's right. They cost such a lot to keep; there's oil and the lights they have at night and a lot of work keepin' all those funny little brass handles polished," remarked Gertie thoughtfully.

"If it was a mortgage he'd buy it quick enough," snapped Cal, stepping through the door. "We've got enough money. We couldn't spend a cent if we tried."

Half an hour later Gertie, who had gone to gather the eggs and put the potatoes to boil, called Cal to supper. Cal answered faintly from her room and Gertie, immediately apprehensive, ran to the door of the small becalendared and betinseled bower, the one bright spot in the house, to find Cal stretched out on the bed, her face very flushed and hot, her eyes heavy and sick.

"Why, why, what's the matter, Cal?" cried Gertie, going over to place her trembling hand on her sister's burning brow with the solicitude of a mother.

"I don't feel well," murmured Cal feebly.

"Couldn't you get up an' eat a little supper? There's the boys coming now. Garret, he'll be worried. Can't you get up?" queried Gertie, hovering about like an agitated mother bird.

"Let him worry!" cried Cal, a little spitefully. "No, I can't get up."

Gertie dutifully went to take out the potatoes and put them on the table with skim milk and bread made with "spook" yeast.

After supper, the "boys" creaked into Cal's room and found her lying with eyes closed, gasping for breath.

"Why, what's the matter, Cal?" asked Garret, who had been anxious about her mild rebellion from his ideas. "Ride do you up?"

"No," she murmured. "I think I'm going to be real sick. I felt it comin' on this afternoon, but the ride made me well again. I can't seem to get enough air. Open that window, will you, George?"

George tiptoed to the window clumsily and opened it awkwardly, for it was seldom that a breath of fresh ozone was permitted to enter the house, it being too cold in winter and too hot in summer.

"There, that's better." Cal tossed uneasily on her pillow and George sat down to rub her head, moving his rough hand over her brow as gently as a masseuse.

Garret strode out of the room to talk over Cal's condition with Gertie, who was doing up the dishes in the kitchen, and when he returned George and Cal both evaded his stern gaze and held their breath until Garret, Gertie hovering at his side, spoke: "You don't think you'll need a doctor, Cal? I suppose it'll be more in the long run if we don't get one. You know, George, we lost them hogs with the cholera last year because we didn't get a veterinary soon enough. You was right about that for once."

"I don't want a doctor," said Cal feebly.

"No, she'll be all right soon. Jest kind of upset," added George in a caressing tone, rubbing Cal's head nervously.

"It ain't what you *want* in a case like this. It's what's best for you," decided Garret with the promptness of judgment that distinguished his father before him.

He stepped out of the room without another word and the three remaining Keenans held their breath as he primed the party phone and finally inquired in his big, bullock-like voice: "Hello! Is this Barry's? That you, John? Well, this is Garret Keenan. Cal, she took cold or somethin' on that ride this afternoon and as long as it was your autermobile I guess you better come over an' tend to her."

He hung up the receiver with a bang and went out to the barns, George following shortly with downcast eyes, neither speaking as they made the straw beds for the stock. Before they had finished, a cheerful toot at the side of the house announced the arrival of Dr. John Barry.

Cal brightened at his appearance and when Garret came in, with George timidly peering over his shoulder, he heard Doctor Barry remarking in the blustering, fatherly, genial tones that made him loved for twenty miles around: "What you need's some fun, Cal! Plenty of fresh air and fun! You and Gertie keep cooped up in the house or yard here all the time like chickens; only drive to town to funerals, and that's bad. Garret," he turned to the head of the household, "you and George work in the fields all day and get plenty of fresh air and exercise. That wouldn't do for the girls. Cal's anemic. What she needs is oxygen and enjoyment. The only way she'll ever be cured is for you to see that she gets out every day. She ought to learn to ride horseback—

something so she could get a lot of fresh air." He looked very solemn and held Cal's wrist meditatively, having inserted his clinical thermometer between her dry lips.

Garret looked worried. "I wouldn't want to see a woman ride horseback. Father never liked it an' I don't like it. But we could spare one of the young grays after we get the hay in an' Gertie, she could take her out drivin' every day."

"That wouldn't do. Too slow. Cal's younger than the rest of you; she needs excitement. Tell you what will do her more good than all the medicine in the world," he said shrewdly, looking as if he had just received an inspiration. "You rent an auto tomorrow mornin'. Bill Owen can get one and drive her out every day for a week. He's through teaching me to run my machine. That's all she needs."

"But that'd cost a good deal," objected Garret, looking from Cal to the doctor, and finally allowing his gaze to settle doggedly on the floor.

"Well," said Doctor Barry, "I guess you could stand the cost of renting one, all right, when even I own one." He drew himself up in a dignified pose. "That's my prescription. Of course if you don't want to follow it you can call in another doctor."

"But that would cost more money, too," said Garret dubiously, turning on George, evidently irritated by his silence. George timorously left the room and Garret asked cautiously, guardedly, like a mouse sniffing the cheese in a trap: "About what would it cost for, say, three days?"

Next morning, Cal, supported on one side by George, stumbling solicitously as he guided her faltering steps, and on the other side by Gertie, tiptoeing along as if she were leading a blind woman, descended the stairs and was helped into the front seat of a big red car with bold brass lamps. Garret stood by the porch, a little aloof, with the air of a man who is footing extravagant bills.

As they reached the car Gertie glanced at Garret timidly and helped settle Cal beside Bill Owen, doing a hundred unnecessary little things and evidently waiting for Garret to speak.

"Gertie, you better come along," said Cal. "I might faint or something."

Gertie glanced at Garret with appealing old eyes.

"Yes. It don't cost no more. Go along, why don't you, Gertie?" he offered, with the condescending practical note of a man of affairs.

George glanced up at the cloudless skies, receiving a dazzling shaft from the hot sun, and, nodding his head sagely, addressed Owen in a voice loud for him: "Looks like rain. Guess we won't be able to do much work today."

Garret glanced quickly at the heavens and stared down in stern reproof at George, who dropped his gaze consciously and muttered: "Course maybe it won't rain at all. All signs fail."

Gertie had produced a faded silk scarf with astounding resource, tied it about her head and hopped into the back seat accustomedly.

Owen turned and remarked casually: "Too bad neither of you boys can go along. It'll be jolty ridin' alone in that back seat, Miss Keenan."

Three furtive pairs of eyes suddenly shot toward Garret. He glanced up at the sun, turned, slammed the front door, rubbed his hands calculatingly and walked down the steps. He pushed George on the shoulder with a rough hand. George jumped.

"Get in," said Garret. "It might rain after all. Anyways there's room for us all and it don't cost any more. We can get the hay in by workin' tonight. Bill, take us up to the Sweeny Hill. Funny about that hill. I'd swear the Blue Mounds don't look more'n a mile away from up there." He settled back luxuriously into the embrace of the loungy leather seat and spread he great legs apart, George timidly squeezing in between him and Gertie.

"George says he could make it in two yumps and a half." Gertie rose to the occasion.

"Yumps!" grinned George, rolling out the word with delicious humor.

The ice was broken. They were off. After half an hour of silent, serene riding Garret leaned over and breathed ecstatically: "Let her out a little, Bill."

Every day after that they went riding, having hired a man to help with the farm work. Cal and Bill Owen sat side by side on the front seat, and often their heads nodded together in intimate conversation.

At the end of ten days, Dr. John Barry pronounced Cal absolutely cured, and Garret a little uneasily drew out his pocketbook.

"John, how much do I own you? You remember your prescription was pretty stiff," he said. "And Cal, she took sick in your auto."

"Oh, my bill wouldn't come to five dollars," said the doctor with a depreciative wave of his broad palm toward Bill Owen, and a hearty laugh. "Just tack that on to Bill's account and I'm satisfied."

"Let's see," said Garret, turning to the auto salesman; "the ten days at nine dollars a day, and the other five dollars—whew!" he whistled, looking at Cal with his mouth stupidly rounded in a big "O." "I didn't realize it was countin' up so fast. I could darn near buy the autermobile for that."

"Why don't you?" suggested Bill Owen cautiously. "It's only eight hundred and eighty dollars all equipped. Subtractin' what you owe me already that machine's only going to cost you seven hundred odd dollars. Just think of the saving."

"Why, that's a good idea!" cried Doctor Barry, clapping his broad hands together as if just struck by another happy inspiration.

"Tell you what I'll do," said Bill Owen. "I'll let that ten days' rent apply on the purchase price of the machine and I'll throw off ten dollars besides and take two hundred of it in hay."

Garret drew out a stubby pencil and figured for a moment on the back of a stock breeder's envelope.

"It comes kind of high," he said slowly, "but it'd be extravagant to pay out nearly a hundred dollars for just rentin' that machine. What'd you say a single-seat machine would cost?"

"Six hundred and fifty," answered Bill Owen. "But I could allow you only fifty dollars off on that. I couldn't take out the whole rent."

"Would you make it sixty dollars off and take a hundred in hay?" asked Garret Keenan shrewdly.

"Don't believe I could. But you don't want a runabout. What you want is this touring car. Only two of you could go out together in the six-fifty machine."

"Well, I'll figure it out," said Garret Keenan slowly, clumping up the steps and going to a lettered old desk in the dining room.

As soon as Garret's hulking form had disappeared through the door, Cal, Bill Owen, the doctor, and George joined hands in a tense bond of successful conspiracy.

Gertie stood looking on a little blankly, until she studied out the meaning behind George's twinkling smile, Bill Owen's triumphant enthusiasm, Cal's glowing blush, and Doctor Barry's broad grin.

"Why, Cal, then you wasn't sick at all!" cried Gertie in sudden understanding.

"S-sh!" warned Doctor Barry. "Garret's comin' out. If he guessed for a second what was up he'd make Bill throw off twenty-five dollars on the touring car and take it all in hay, and Lord knows Bill's worked hard enough to earn his commission on this machine."

At that moment Garret Keenan appeared in the doorway. He had all the manner of a king about to address his subjects on an important royal mandate, or a country school superintendent mounting the rostrum to reprove a group of scholars.

Clearing his throat, he said decisively: "It's blamed expensive, but I find it will be cheaper in the end to pay Bill Owen the machine hire and not buy either of them cars."

George Keenan and the "girls" timidly drew together as if for protection and support. The doctor and Bill Owen looked surprised and deeply disappointed.

"That machine," said Garret, pointing to Owen's auto like a man addressing the devil before putting his devilship behind him, "costs too much and is too expensive to run. The single-seater wouldn't be big enough for four of us, and so we'll do without either."

Cal stepped forward from the circle, flushed to her temples, her eyes burning, Gertie tugging timidly at her sleeve.

"Garret Keenan," she said, addressing the household head boldly, "the man who takes candy from children ain't the meanest man any longer. It's you! You take an automobile from your brothers and sisters who've got as good a right to it as you have!"

She paused and glanced nervously down, her anger spent. Garret stood dazed, bewildered, as if a pail of ice water had been suddenly dashed in his face.

Bill Owen stepped to Cal's side and put his arm tenderly about her.

"Garret," he said simply, "Cal's going to ride in my machine after this. She's not going to be deprived of happiness any longer."

Garret Keenan, from habit and discretion, stared in angry reproof at George, who edged behind Gertie and began critically to inspect the bark of an apple tree.

"Yes, Garret," said Cal, "it's been settled four days, but I didn't say anything, hoping you folks would buy an auto and be happy in spite of yourselves after I left."

"You mean you're going to marry *him*, Bill Owen?" cried Garret. Gertie had dropped limply back against George and George's heart leaped wildly in his secure position between Gertie and the tree.

"Yes, we're engaged. We're going on our honeymoon in Will's new car. It'll be here next week," flashed Cal.

"Well, I'll be beat!" exclaimed Garret. "Say! That fixes it." He grasped Owen's hand in a brotherly clasp. "Bill, we'll take that single-seater now. With Cal gone we'll save enough to pay for the gasoline."

"Hurrah!" cried Doctor Barry, throwing up his hat like a boy.

"But," protested Cal, all blushes as her big brother pressed an approving kiss on her forehead. "But a single-seater won't be big enough."

"Where'll George sit?" put in Gertie, interested in the detail even in her agitation over Cal's surprising announcement.

"I got that all planned—all settled!" cried Garret Keenan radiantly. "Bill, you order that runabout with a rumble seat on behind for George."

"But that will be eighteen dollars extra," said Bill in a businesslike tone.

"Never mind the extry expense. We'll soon make it up now that Cal's off our hands. What's more," said Garret finally, like a generous father, "I'll pay for the machine in cash if I get twenty-five dollars off, and maybe, Bill, your commission will help pay honeymoon expenses."

DONKEYS OF DESTINY

Ben Sutherland
The Farmer's Wife, October 1922

"QUIT it, Tuck, and come here! If you haven't any sense of your own, use your daddy's. When I told you to swing that ax till it got so it would swing itself I was only fooling. Quit it! And come here!"

I was at work at the woodpile. But I can quit work when my dad tells me. He told me to chop till he said I could quit. I was afraid he might forget I was chopping.

Daddy Benson was sitting on the porch. I didn't know he had been watching me work. He always calls me Tucker except when he is in fun or when he thinks I have been "doing something" and then he says, "Tucker Breton Benson!" just as if it was all capital letters.

"What do you know about boats?" Daddy asked, moving over so I could sit by him. My dad is some pal, only you can't peel bark off the shade trees and not chop wood for it afterward.

"What do you know about boats, the kind that ride the water, Tuck?"

I didn't know much about them. Boats don't go scooting over the sandhills of New Mexico. Of course a kid can see boats in the movies, streaking-it across lakes and harbors and places. They push the water ahead of them and it rolls off at both sides, like a bronc's mane. But of course a real boat has got to have real water.

Mr. Wilkie is Daddy's pardner and he says the San Juan is not a real river. He says a river is full of water and the Juan is full of mud. And the Juan is all the river I know anything about, unless you count the La Plata and the Animas that comes into the Juan right close to where we live. So I was wondering if a boat would be any good in a short grass country.

"I was thinking of buying a boat," Daddy said. "I am sick of mules. There are two good months for tripping around before—well, before your school begins; and I thought maybe you would like a ja'nt down the Juan in a boat."

I am as sick about that school I am going to as Daddy is of mules, but I didn't know whether Daddy was joshing about the boat trip or not. I had never seen a boat.

Not long ago, Daddy traded his last mining claim for three little Navajo mules, to get out of the mining business. And then he was in the mule business. Mr. Wilkie said it was just three things after one. Daddy had been having pretty good luck before that and so he said we would take a few months off and enjoy ourselves before he went into business again. We made a few trips around with our mule team, the way Daddy traveled when he was a pioneer. We dug into Aztec ruins and hunted for lost mines and marked the old trails that the settlers made. But those donkeys were so mean that Daddy got tired of them after awhile. He said he liked trouble for breakfast but not for

103

steady board. We couldn't explore the San Juan river with mules, anyway. That was how the boat talk began.

Daddy said that boats, as he remembered them back East, were plumb civilized. You could tie a boat to a tree on the river bank and it wouldn't step over the rope and throw itself, like a mule. He said he had a mind to turn our Kelly mules loose for a spell and work hard at something else. Maybe they would wander off and never come back and we could live white again. You never saw mules get on anybody's nerves as these did on Daddy's.

I guess you can't trade mules for a boat, ever. You have to send back East for a boat and you couldn't send mules like our Kellys back East—you would never be allowed. We called all three of our mules Kelly because they acted that way. Daddy knew a man named Kelly, back in Indiana, who was awful hard to bridle. He was Mamma's daddy. But I never saw that grandpa. Mamma and Papa came West because Grandpa Kelly stayed in Indiana.

Daddy and I got so interested in our boat talk that we didn't know when Mamma came out and sat down by us. Mamma has wanted a car and when we said something about boats she thought we were talking about an auto, because some people call them boats. I asked Daddy how long it would take the boat to come after we ordered it.

"It was just two weeks," Daddy said. "She will be here in the morning. I just got a wire."

I don't know which landed on Daddy first, Mamma or I.

But how could we know what Mamma was thinking? She laughed and patted Daddy's face and said it was just like the boy she married, to get her anything she wanted, and she *never* was so surprised! Then she asked Daddy if it was blue or olive. He said it was galvanized and she looked funny. I guess she would have taken a galvanized car if that was all she could get. She said Daddy ought to have asked her and she hoped it had a starter and not a crank like a tin meal sifter.

Daddy looked hard at Mamma about a minute and then he went into his little office room and brought out a catalog. He turned a few pages over and showed Mamma a picture of a boat. She looked at the boat and then she looked at me a long time, but not once at Daddy. Somehow I hated to see Mamma look like that.

When she went into the house, Daddy forgot about me and got to talking to himself. He looked pretty blue and after awhile he said it would have to be made right. But he didn't go in and tell Mamma.

It is a wonder they have only one train a day in Tactec. People that live in little places want their boats just as soon as anybody. Daddy and I went up to the depot long before train time and the agent got mad because I asked him if there would be any train before train time. When the road-master wants to come down here they run a special, but *we* can wait for our boat.

There was a big truck at the station and Daddy put in the time hiring it to haul our boat to the river. And then the train came.

The boat was in a gondola car. She was all done up in paper and slats. She looked pretty small in the car but when we got her on the truck she was a whopper. Every kid in town helped us load her and Daddy said we owed more boat rides than old Charon, which is a man he knew in Indiana, I guess.

We had to go by our house to the river and Mamma came out to the gate as we went by and waved her hand, all friendly. That made me glad.

Daddy had them take the boat to the Old Trail crossing. There is a big cottonwood on the bank and I saw a chain hanging from the crotch before we got there. Daddy had everything all ready, to surprise us. There was no boathouse, but our boat was going to be too busy to need a boathouse.

Mamma came down by the time we had the boat unloaded. So did everybody else in Tactec and Mamma didn't get much chance to talk to us.

We took the crate off the boat and, sure enough, it was galvanized. There were three oars packed in the boat, along the sides, and then there was a funny crated thing in the middle. Mr. Wilkie said it must be the power or else the invoice. Daddy lifted it out and said it was the motor. But when he unpacked it Mamma began to laugh. She said she had always wanted that thing to wind the clock with. Nearly everybody laughed and Daddy said some people always laughed at great inventions. He was pretty red.

Daddy said five good horses were saddled and bridled in that remarkable little machine. Mamma said they must be as little as our Kelly mules. Daddy called it an outboard motor and he said it was to be fixed on the end of the boat with thumbscrews. And Mamma said, "Or clothespins." Daddy never smiled.

We got her all set up, except gasoline, and then everybody had to go home to dinner. But they all said they would come back and help us launch her. All of our friends bet that she could swim, except one old Navajo. He thought maybe our tin duck would dive and when she came up she would say, "Quack! Quack! Where is my paleface?"

Nathe Miller went home with us to dinner. Nathe is my pal. We always take him with us on our mule trips, because our Navajo donks can't talk Benson and we can't talk Navajo. Nathe would rather talk Navajo than white. He says it is a stronger language than white and just right for mules. Daddy thinks there will be a wild man in town when Nathe grows up but he can't spoil our mules, I guess. They're not the spoilable kind.

At dinner we got to talking about our trip and Mamma said when she went along with us the Juan would be a powder horn; so Daddy said Mr. Wilkie might like to go, and I said I wondered if Nathe would go if Daddy invited him. So Daddy asked Nathe and he said of course he would go if we wanted him.

We said we would take a short trip the first time and get our boat to working good and then maybe Mamma would take a trip and we bet she wouldn't want a car after that. She asked Daddy if he meant to take the mules along.

"No," Daddy said; "a mule is a mule, not a fish." And Mamma laughed as if she was thinking of something. She advised us to stick to our mules and sell the boat for a new wagon. It was the first time Mamma ever advised Daddy to drive mules. She has heard that mules will kick. But she said if a man was going to die in New Mexico he ought to die like a man and a pioneer. Boat riding was no way to die, she said.

When we launched the boat there was a man there who knew just how to shove her into the water. He was Daddy's partner. He said he was raised on the wettest river in America and they called it the Ohio because it was that kind of a river.

Everybody helped us carry the boat down to the water and Daddy fastened the chain to her. Then Mr. Wilkie pushed her down into the water and she never splashed a drop. She danced around a little but nothing like mules.

Daddy took the can of gasoline and stepped into the boat with it but he nearly fell into the Juan. I guess a boat ought to have stirrups, like a mule. He got in just the same and poured some gas into the tank. Then he did something to the engine and she went clickety-click. And when he pulled a little lever the boat sure came alive and all the Navajos that were standing around lit out for the Reservation as if they had heard from home.

The boat swung around in the water whichever way Daddy turned the wheel and when he turned it clear around she pulled backwards like a Kelly mule. She sure was a dandy!

Daddy fooled with her a little while and then he ran her up on the muddy bank and unlocked her.

"All right!" he shouted to us. "I got her gait. Jump in!"

Mr. Wilkie helped Mamma aboard and we all got in. Just at that minute a big sand-roller started up right behind the boat. You could see a new sand bar where the wave broke and sometimes the water is ten feet deep there. That is the kind of a bottom the Juan has got.

Mamma screamed and jumped out of the boat. When she got up on high ground she said that was her first and last boat ride. We tried to coax her back but she said she already had her graveyard picked out on a sandhill.

We went across the river and back before we tied up. As we went over we dodged above a sand-roller and when we came back we just missed a great one by going below it. There was a big log in the last roller, with a broken limb at the middle, and the log rolled so fast that the limb looked like spokes in a wheel. Mr. Wilkie said he could see what would happen to a boat in a breaker like that. It made Mamma cry and she begged us to turn the boat loose and stick to those noble donks that had pulled us through many a tight squeeze. But Daddy said those Navajos acted just like a sand-roller, sometimes, and kicked besides.

We carried everything we meant to take with us on the trip down to the river and camped under the cottonwood that night. We had turned the mules loose. They had always been ready to skip out when we turned them loose before, but this time they followed us down to the camp and tried to eat our things. They hung around camp all night.

Daddy was up before daylight. The first thing I knew was when the smoke from the cookfire blew in my face. Then I heard Mr. Wilkie chasing the mules. He said those donks had caused him more sorrow than a stone bruise and he would be glad to see the last of them.

Mamma came down and ate breakfast with us. Then we folded up our blankets on the seats in the boat; we tied our grub box down in the middle of the boat, so it couldn't slip around, filled the gas tank, and kissed Mamma goodbye.

We didn't notice a thing wrong with the Juan till we had got into the boat. The Juan is always muddy. But when Daddy pulled up the sag in the chain to unlock it, he saw there was lots of trash in the water and he said it must have rained up in Colorado, where the Juan comes from. Just as he said that, we heard thunder in the north. We all looked up towards the mountains and they were covered up in clouds, so we couldn't see a single peak. But nobody here pays any attention to such things, unless he has sheep or a family on the other side or is out of tobacco, and then he hurries across before the water gets too high to ford. Mr. Wilkie said if our boat couldn't swim down stream on a flood she was no good, and as for coming back, he didn't want to come back till those *mules* had gone back to their tribe and wore blankets.

Daddy pushed the boat off with an oar and started the engine. We all waved at Mamma and then we looked out across the river. There was a spruce tree, with all its branches on it, floating past us. It was a live tree and the roots showed that it had been washed out of the mountain side. It reached clear across the deep channel and it was three feet through.

We scooted past the tree and when our boat was in the swift water we went about as fast as a car. It made Nathe and me dizzy. I looked at Mr. Wilkie and he had his eyes shut. I guess it was because he didn't want to see our mules any more. They were standing on the bank braying at us.

Our boat skimmed along like a duck. It felt just like when a bronc throws you, after you are out of the saddle and before you hit the ground. But, jinks! I expected to hit any minute. I could see that Mr. Wilkie was scared. Daddy was too busy to be anything else. Every time we went through a patch of trash our motor acted like an Indiana grandpa.

When we got down near where the La Plata branch comes in and were cluck-clucking along, tending strictly to business because the water was full of trash, we began to notice people on both sides of the river. Some of them waved their arms at us. Right where the river is the widest and not very deep or swift, we passed the Navajo Mission on the Reservation side. The chaplain came out and waved his arms at us and yelled, but we nearly bumped into a log just then and didn't hear what he said. Then we came in sight of the Island. There was a little board cabin lodged on the point. It had floated down the river. Mr. Wilkie said there must have been a cloudburst up the Juan.

We ran the boat close to the Island to see about that cabin, but the water was swifter there and Daddy couldn't hold the boat. All I could see as we shot past was a printed sign on the cabin wall. Mr. Wilkie said it was a Colorado fire warning to campers, and he said the cabin looked like one that used to stand just below the dam at Electra lake, at the Rockwood power plant. That is on a branch of the Juan and I never was up there.

We were just leaving the Island behind when Daddy said maybe we had better turn around and try to get back home, because cloudbursts always come three in a team, like Navajo mules. It was just then that Nathe jumped up and yelled and pointed at the

Island. Mr. Wilkie jerked him down and said a few things but my pal kept pointing and yelling something in Navajo. The boat was bobbing up and down between two big timbers that looked like bridge stringers. Daddy was *busy*. As soon as we passed the timbers, he stopped the engine and looked around to see what Nathe had gone wild about.

There was a Navajo Indian on the Island. He didn't want to stay there either, I guess, as he was acting just like Nathe. We ran the boat up close and Mr. Wilkie asked the Indian if he wanted a drink. He wanted to leave that island. He told Nathe in Navajo that there was going to be a great flood and he wanted to drown with his folks on the Reservation side. He had been digging medicine roots on the Island and his pony had left him and swam ashore. He didn't want a boat ride. He thought our boat walked on the bottom. He said anyone but a paleface could hear the engine stepping on rocks. Of course it stepped pretty fast, he said, but it might not be quite so smart when it struck the quicksand near the shore. He asked us to go over and ask his wife to send him a pony.

All that time, the water was rising. We couldn't wait for Nathe to make the Indian understand; so when the water was nearly over the Island, Mr. Wilkie threw the Indian a rope. He grabbed it but wouldn't touch the boat. We towed him over.

That was a lucky job for us. When we got to the Indians' side we could see about a mile up the river. It was thick with green brush and logs. The Mission was in sight, too, with water all around, and it was made of 'dobe that would melt like sugar as soon as the water was a little higher. Then we remembered the chaplain.

I guess if we had been sailors, we could have gone to the Mission; but you hardly ever see sailors in New Mexico, unless they have quit sailing. Mule drivers could never make it—not in a boat.

Daddy headed our boat for the other side. We could see people on the bank and on both sides of the La Plata. The trash in the water was getting thicker.

We were only four miles from home and we knew Tactec was safe, so Daddy said we would keep out of the channel and watch the flood go by. If it wasn't too bad we would go ahead on our trip; and anyway, we had to take care of our boat and try to get it home again. We didn't know anyone was in danger.

The La Plata is a little creek, but swift. It even goes dry sometimes, but now it was a sight. So we pulled in above, where the water was still and looked shallow. Then Mr. Wilkie took one of the oars and measured the water. It was just as deep as the oar blade but he pushed clear out of sight in soft mud. When he tried to pull it up it wouldn't come. It was quicksand.

Daddy got us out of there in a hurry. We went down about half a mile and got near enough to a ranch house to call the people out. They came running and waving their arms and yelled to us to come ashore, quick. The Rockwood dam had broken, they said, and a wave ten feet high was coming—it was at Tactec that very minute. They were warning everybody they could get on the phone.

It was not quite so easy to go ashore. All down the river the banks are lined with quicksand bars.

"We will stick it out!" Daddy said at last.

Well, we didn't. We stuck in the mud. We found a little hollow in the shore on our side and Daddy made for it. Then we hit! That was what I expected every minute since I noticed how it felt to ride in a boat. The engine stopped too, but we never found out why. We were stuck on a bar of mud almost in reach of a good, safe bank. Daddy tried the bottom and it was quick.

We could rock the boat a little at first but we couldn't get her loose. The engine wouldn't start. It had stepped on quicksand.

There was a strip of willows ten feet high on the bank. Daddy thought the wagon road was just beyond the willows, but we didn't know for sure. Anyway, we all yelled at once. Nobody answered.

After a little while, I told Daddy I heard a wagon rattling down the road. But there was another sound coming down the river louder than all the wagons in the world, only it wasn't so sharp and clattery. You could feel it more than you heard it. We couldn't see up the river because we were in the hollow. That made it worse.

Daddy spread a blanket in the water just ahead of the boat, then he dropped the chuck box in the middle of it but it sank out of sight. He could touch it with an oar but it sank deeper and deeper. Anyway, it was only one step towards the shore. And the roaring sound came nearer and nearer.

Daddy says now that it was about five minutes after we heard the roaring that the flood struck us but it seemed a long time.

Nobody knows how we got out of there. It seemed as if the brush in the water rose and fell as it rolled along. Just before it got to us it dipped. When it came up again we were on top. We were not even trying to do anything—there was no use to try at all. If we got out of the boat, we would surely sink in quicksand. Besides, it all wasn't very long happening.

Well, the brush filled up the little hollow in the shore and twisted the way a whirl-wind twists a shock of hay. Then the flood slid on by and we were spread out on the bank like a lot of old clothes—that is all I know about it. Maybe Daddy could tell but there is no use to ask Mr. Wilkie, for he won't even mention that boat ride.

Our clothes were torn and we were scratched and jabbed by the sharp ends of the brush. As soon as we could, we climbed up higher on the bank. There was a fringe of willows along the shore and Daddy said as well as he could remember the river road it must be just beyond the willows. We worked our way through and found the road, all right, and at that very minute a wagon came clattering down the valley.

There was a dandy lady on the seat and she was whipping her team like sixty and the team was three little mules hitched abreast.

I beat Daddy to her but he took her away from me. Then she took herself away from him and stood up in the wagon.

"Quick!" Mamma said. "We must get out of here. There's a lot more water coming. The valley will all be drowned." Then she looked at us, and said, "Oh! You have been in the water. Did you lose my pieced quilt? Whatever have you done with my aluminum pots? Quick! Or we shall all be drowned!"

We got Mr. Wilkie in the wagon as quick as we could but he was awful sore and fat. Then Mamma licked our Kellys with the lines and talked all the time and us men squatted down in the wagon bed and never offered to help her drive. Anybody who offered to help Mamma drive those mules would be foolish—she didn't need any help.

After just a few jumps, we were splashing through water. The driftwood jammed in the river below us and the water backed up farther and farther. We had to get back across the Plata to be on high ground. You would give two bits to see those Kellys race!

"Where is my pieced quilt?" Mamma said. "*Streak it, you little imps!* I had the awfulest time catching them. *Dig, you poor heathens!* They tried to follow you down the river. We got the warning on the phone not half an hour after you left. *Go it, Indians!* I caught them at the Plata and nobody would help me, so I had to walk back and harness them to the wagon, to go looking for you. What is it Nathe says to them when—when he is bad?"

"*Shush-Buh-Chee!*" Nathe yelled. And the Navajos galloped faster. By the time we got to the Plata bridge our mules were paddling pretty slow. The water was over both ends of the bridge but the middle was humped up on a lot of drift logs. It didn't look as if we could cross. Mamma pulled up the team and just at that minute a log or something broke with a loud pop and it seemed as though the tribe landed square in the middle of that bridge at one jump. If you think they *stopped* there, you have never seen Mamma drive Kellys. Maybe you can drive a car, but—*Shush-b'chee!* Those donkeys just 'vaporated.

We landed on the high ground, all right, but our wagon was smashed up. It must have hit the bridge too hard. About a hundred people came running to us and some came in cars, but the first one that offered to help us was an old Navajo who had lost his team in the flood. All he had left was an old wagon, washed up on the bank.

"You take um," he said. "My team he go take um big swim, he get too much wet."

So we took it. But we are going to get him a new team and wagon.

Mr. Wilkie looked around at the cars, to see what make they were, I guess, but nobody offered him a ride. Then he planked himself down in our old rickety Indian wagon.

"It seems to be destiny!" That was what he said. "Mules, mules, forever!" He said that just like swearing.

Daddy said if those noble donks had webbed feet he would undertake to explore the seven seas with them. And then he squinched over towards Mamma and asked her if she thought thirty-five hundred was too much to pay for a car.

But Mamma just laughed, and asked him whatever had he done with her pieced quilt that was with the bed things when we started on the boat trip. And Daddy said it was wrapped around the chuck box but he didn't say where.

3
CHAPTER

STORIES OF ROMANCE

"THE summer nights are silver nights For skies are tender blue, And every dale and glen and vail Is drenched in fairy dew. And summer nights are heavenly nights. A paradise for two, My sheltering arms ere dawn alarms Shall prove it, dear, to you."

—*New England Homestead,* June 1917

The rural and farm magazine editors used stories of love and romance more often than they used any other kind of fiction. Many editors employed fiction primarily as an appeal to female readers; they assumed, no doubt, that love stories were a sure way to win the interest of farm women.

To our benefit, the romantic situations portrayed in these stories reveal a good deal about the rural American society in the early part of the century. For example, many stories involved summer boarders as principal characters. It was common for rural families to offer summer lodging to city residents who sought a few weeks of fresh air, sunshine, and tranquility in the country and were happy to rent farmhouse bedrooms. Doctors freely prescribed a summer in the country for tired and ailing city folk. (The farm and rural magazines, encouraging farm wives to take advantage of this ready source of extra income, often ran advice columns on how to plan and care for summer boarders.) Imagine the possibilities for romantic plots that involved country youth and vibrant young professionals from the city! The city operator, or "telephone girl," arrived in the country fully equipped with an aura of intrigue the young farmer found irresistible. Young country women readily became enamored of urban writers, bankers, and engineers. But stories of romance did not always center around young people. Sometimes the characters were middle-aged and older men and women. These rarely were glamorous people. Frequently, they were desperate individuals seeking escape from the loneliness and boredom of solitary lives. Their opportunities for romance may have been limited, or they may have out-lived a spouse. Such people made strong, believable characters and hardly could have failed to serve as sympathetic figures for readers who might find themselves in similar situations.

Love stories often demonstrated the dangers pride poses for lasting relationships. "What might have been" was a common theme.

Many of the romance stories were trite and predictable, of course. A common formula made a proposal of marriage the be-all and end-all for young women. Whatever route may have gotten a couple to that point, a happy ending was assured when a man asked a woman to be his wife. And even the richest stories of romance could be expected to end happily. The moral tone was still a strict reflection of the Victorian age; physical contact typically ended when a woman was taken into a man's arms, though sometimes a kiss was permitted. Affection was expressed through tenderness, not passion.

Still, romantic themes allowed writers ample atitude. The better writers took full advantage. Romance could be simple or dramatic, could be woven into adventurous tales or found in familiar surroundings. Personal devotion might germinate slowly and ripen and mature over a period of years or burst forth in wondrous fervor in mere days. Love could be fragile or hardy.

The short stories included here have little in common except the element of love and romance. On the whole, they are light-hearted—as such stories most often were. The characters and settings differ, the time frames vary greatly, and the plots are diverse. Collectively, they proffer a range of fiction that is but faint evidence of the assorted styles of stories of romance provided by the country magazines during that period when reading enjoyed a premier position as a form of entertainment, especially in country homes. At the same time, each story tells something about rural America unique to the time in which it was written and the setting in which it was placed.

LOVE AND ROAST GOOSE

Merritt P. Allen
Wallaces' Farmer, December 1925

I never read a Christmas story that began with a stone bruise, but this one is going to, because it started on a Sunday in June when I stayed home from church because I had a stone bruise on my heel and couldn't wear a shoe. It was a sore thing, but not half as sore as Bill was when he had to doll up and go with Ma. He wanted to stay home and be nurse, but Cash said I was in a dangerous condition, that my foot might go to my heart any minute and then I would need a man's help. So he stayed with me and spent the morning reading on the front porch while I monkeyed with a box trap in the barn.

About the time meeting was over, I started back to the house and was nearly there when I noticed Caleb Howes hitting the high spots on the sidewalk. Caleb is one of those moderate people, and usually skips along like a snail with chilblains, but this time he was hitting on all six, and I don't mean maybe.

"Judas priest!" I heard Cash say. "That you, Cale?"

"Uh-hu!" And Caleb hopped the fence into the yard without bothering to open the gate.

"One more drink of whatever it was you got and you'll stub your toe on the weather vane on the town hall," Cash told him.

"Don't joke, Cassius," said Caleb, and I saw he was as serious as a goat.

"Who's jokin'?" Cash asked. "If you ain't been drinkin', what in blazes have you been up to?"

"I've been— I've seen Casper Stone arrayed like a lily of the field, like Solomon in all his glory, like a rainbow in the sky."

"Come in where it's cooler," Cash said, gently.

"Darn it, I tell you I'm all right," Caleb puffed, for he was about out of breath. "I saw Casper walk right down the aisle—and set in his pew—and he wore a dove-colored suit—and a high collar—and a blue bow tie—and low tan shoes—and blue socks. Honest, Cash, he didn't look more'n thirty-five."

"If you ain't looney," Cash said, scratching his chin, "something's happened to Casper, for he ain't shown a sign of life since his wife died five years ago."

But Caleb hadn't been seeing things, for scarcely had he wheezed off down the street when Ma and Bill blew in with the same story: Casper Stone, who had been looking seedier and seedier every day since his wife's funeral, had of a sudden, without any budding, blossomed out like a sweet wild rose.

"And there's a cause for it," Cash declared. "When a sober-minded, middle-aged, self-respectin' man busts out with sporty clothes, socks, ties, hats and all, he ain't doin' it just to shock the lookin' glass. I tell you, Carrie, there's a cause for such an effect."

"And," Ma said with a smile, "her name is Mrs. Alice Greene."

"Eh?" Cash bugged out his eyes. "Her?"

"None other."

"You think so?"

"I know it. And if you had seen her blush when Casper came into the church this morning, you would know it, too."

"Well, I snum!" Cash said. "Well, there ain't a neater little widow. She's as cute as a bug's ear. But shucks, Carrie, just because she happened to blush ain't any sign—"

"You show me a better sign," Ma called back from the kitchen. "When a 40-year-old widow gets as red as an autumn leaf at sight of a 50-year-old widower, it means that there is something in the wind besides air."

"Time'll tell," was all Cash said.

And it told a lot, soon and often. Inside of a week there wasn't one-tenth of one per cent of a ghost of a glimmering doubt but that Casper Stone thought that Mrs. Greene was the cat's meow. It was plastered all over him from his smile to his new shoes, that squared "Alice! Alice!" every step. He put in full union hours up at her place, once he got going, and Bill and I happened to know about it because we were working for her that summer and were neither blind nor deaf. She had a nice place in the village, with a big lawn and garden, and we worked for her several hours nearly every day, for ten cents an hour and as much pie as she could spare, which was considerable, for she was a good sport. So it wasn't surprising that we knew something about that sparking match.

Mrs. Greene had stuck to mourning fairly close since her husband died, but the second Sunday after Casper turned peacock she came out in a blue and white silk dress, white kid shoes, and a hat that would knock an eye out at a thousand yards. And Casper stepped down the aisle in another new suit and yellow, black-stitched gloves! Swing low sweet chariot and fan me with a lilac! The congregation was sure knocked for a goal. The minister had already given out his text, but when he saw those two pillars of his church blooming like green bay trees he threw his notes under the pulpit and spoke for an hour and twenty minutes on "Vanity, vanity, all is vanity," making it, as Caleb Howes said, "as plain as the string halter on a white hoss that folks who think of show in this world won't have much of a show in the next." A pleasant time was enjoyed by all. And when it was over, Casper saw the widow home and stayed to dinner.

The next day Bill and I were helping her put up some new porch curtains (she said she had begun to feel the need of them), when Casper happened in. He was going to lend a hand, but he stopped and picked up a photograph on the table.

"Who's this?" he asked.

"Oh, that," Mrs. Greene smiled sweetly, "is a friend of mine from Burlington. He is really a jolly man, but he looks sad because the picture was taken soon after his wife died."

She went in the house after a hammer and Casper threw the picture on the table. "Jolly man!" we heard him mutter, not pious-like. "He looks like a puppy-dog."

When the curtains were up, Bill and I went into the kitchen to do a little work on a pie and Mrs. Greene made tea in the sitting room.

"Nice weather for July," we heard Casper say.

"This is June," she told him.

"So it is, so it is. You are always right, Alice."

And a minute later he broke out with, "A handsome dog of yours."

"Why, that is a cat," she said, with a little laugh.

"To be sure, a cat. You are always right, Alice."

She laughed again. "I guess you are the only one that thinks so."

"The only one!" His voice wabbled like a ukelele string. "Alice, let me—"

"Boys," she called to us, "you will find some cheese on the pantry shelf."

It sounded as though Casper swallowed his teacup and saucer; then he asked, "May I call tonight?"

She said she would be out all the evening.

"Then tomorrow?"

"I expect to be automobiling all day with my friend from Burlington. He has a beautiful car. Do you know, I think life isn't complete nowadays without a nice closed car."

"Goodbye," said Casper.

The next afternoon but one, as the minister was crossing Main Street, he had to jump fifteen feet to dodge his funeral expenses as a big coupe whizzed past. The next minute it slid into Mrs. Greene's back yard and Casper hopped out.

Bill and I were cutting grass there and ambled over for a look-see.

When Casper finally came out of the house with the widow he was saying, "I thought the old flivver wasn't good enough for you," saying it in a sort of a coo-ey tone.

"*Oh-h-h-h-h-h!*" she squealed. "A beauty! Two passengers?"

Casper nodded. "I don't intend to run a jitney."

"My friend from Burlington has a sedan," she said.

"Damn your friend!" Casper sizzled under his breath.

"What's that?" she shot at him.

"I said Dammerfen—the name of the fellow I got the car of."

"A very peculiar name."

"Scotch or Russian or something. Let's take a little ride."

With a start like that, the town expected them to be completely married by the first of September, but they were not. Casper worked hard not to disappoint the crowd, but the courting song is a duet that no man can sing alone and Mrs. Greene seemed to be somewhat slow in tuning up. She liked Casper well enough, and she rode thousands of miles in that new car of his, but when it came to a show-down of hearts she didn't show up. Cash says women are that way; when they know they have hooked a poor fish, they play him a while just for the fun of it.

Casper was still flopping a month before Christmas when we began the drive for church repairs. Five hundred dollars was needed to put the old building in shape, and somebody popped the idea of raising it all during the Christmas season. So after about thirty million words had been used up in arguing and discussing the affair, the entire

119

congregation, from four-year-old Calvin Coolidge Jones clear on up to 98-year-old Pop Tucker, was divided into two teams, the Reds and the Blues, and each of the teams was supposed to raise two hundred and fifty dollars in a month. But that wasn't the most important part of the thing, not by a long shot. What kept the kettle boiling, and boiling hard, was the fact that the losing side must put up, within a week after Christmas, a roast goose dinner with all of the trimmings. That put the pep into the whole works, at least as far as Bill and I were concerned. We were Blues.

There is no use hoping to tell how all that money was raised. Every legal scheme for prying loose a penny was given a tryout. You couldn't walk down the street without bumping into a food sale or a rummage sale, and you couldn't get home again without being asked to buy an apron and some homemade candy and postcards and pencils and ticket to a box social and a coat hanger and a subscription to a magazine and flowers for a sick friend and a bottle of wintergreen extract and a framed picture of Plymouth Rock to hang in the hen house. And if you bought or didn't buy, you had a feeling that perhaps you were deciding the fate of that roast goose. Boy! The strain was fierce.

Everyone was so busy trying to do everyone else in a nice, pious way that they forgot all about Casper and Mrs. Greene and their affair. But Casper and Mrs. Greene didn't forget themselves. It was a warm winter so far, with no snow, so day after day they rode in the car and came back to her parlor to sit and talk. Casper had never been very much of a·talker, but he must have gone and got vaccinated with a phonograph needle, as the saying is, because he sat in that room and talked hour after hour and month after month. Perhaps with all that practice, he could talk rings around the widow, but he couldn't talk one onto her finger. She seemed to be having the time of her life, and grew younger and prettier every day; but as Christmas drew near, Casper began to look thin and tired, as though he had a mind to hang up his fiddle and his bow instead of his stocking.

But Casper wasn't the only one who was out of luck. The Blues had him skinned a mile when it came to trouble. The drive was to end on Christmas Eve at the tree, and just the day before that, Deacon Brown, who was chairman of the Reds, flopped his wings and crowed that his side had raised two hundred and sixty dollars. Our side had a hundred and seventy dollars, and, as far as anyone knew, there wasn't another cent in town that could be raised with a derrick. We had just about as much chance of beating that ninety-dollar lead as a fish has of drowning. Bill and I were the bluest of the Blues, and I don't mean maybe. If we had been song writers, you would have heard of "The Roast Goose Blues" before this.

"Just think of having to feed that crowd of bums!" I groaned to Bill. "The deacon and dear little Rupert and Gilly Cabbins and Puggy Bean will all sit down and stuff themselves with roast goose that we gave them. Won't that rattle your rivets!" It was sure going to spoil my Christmas.

Bill didn't say anything. For days and days he had been thinking like a windmill, but his thought well was dry—something that has happened only once or twice since I have known him. We wandered off down the street about as cheerful as two kids ever were not. It was the first stinging cold day of the winter, and at the corner of the park square we stopped to take a running slide on the ice where the water from the watering trough had run over the road. The ice was nice and smooth and we were getting a start to slide back when Casper's car zipped around the corner, struck the ice sideways, spun clear around, hit the watering trough, and turned over.

The next minute, half a dozen men came from nowhere and pulled Casper and Mrs. Greene out of the wreck. There wasn't a scratch on either of them, but they lay on the ground as still as death. Somehow we carried them across the road to the Beans' house and laid Casper on the sitting room sofa and Mrs. Greene on a bed in the back bedroom.

Casper was beginning to revive somewhat before we got there, and after a minute he opened his eyes.

"Speck," he said, in a wabbly voice, for I was the first one he happened to see, "how is Mrs. Greene?"

"Oh, I—I guess she's all right," I lied, for she had looked perfectly dead the last I saw of her.

He drew a long breath. "Please tell her I am not injured, just knocked out a little, and will be with her in a minute."

"Lay still and get your breath back," advised the minister, who had helped carry Casper in.

I started with the news for Mrs. Greene, if she was still on earth, and Bill went along. In the bedroom we found her a thousand miles from dead, sitting on the bed asking Mrs. Bean what had happened to Casper.

"Oh," she cried, when she saw us. "You can tell me."

Bill dug me in the ribs, took a step forward, wrung his hands, and rolled his eyes upstairs.

"Tell me," she panted. "How is Casper?"

"We-w-well," Bill stammered. "He's—"

"Where is he?"

"He's on the couch in the front room," said Bill. "He's white—white and still— and the—the—the minister is—"

"Heavens! He must be dying!" And Mrs. Greene was out of the room in a wink. Casper had also got to his feet and they met in the middle of the room.

"Casper!" she gasped. "I thought you were taken away from—me!"

He looked at her and smiled. "And you didn't want me to leave you quite yet?"

"Oh, I never, never, never want you to leave me."

They clinched, and we tiptoed out and closed the door.

In the evening, on our way to the Christmas tree, we stopped in to inquire for Casper.

"How do I feel?" he laughed. "Why, I am the happiest man in the universe. But look here, Bill, why did you try to frighten Alice by telling her I was dying?"

"I didn't tell her exactly that," Bill replied, and by the tone of his voice I knew he figured he had a hen setting.

"But why did you want to frighten her? I am surprised at you."

Bill grinned. "Yes, happily surprised, I'll say."

Bill nodded in that superior, wise way of his. "She didn't realize how much she thought of you till I sort of let on that you were cashing in. I gave her that jolt to bring her to her senses. Honest, Mr. Stone, I was working for you all the time."

Casper stared at him. "By George!" he cried. "I believe that you are telling the truth. I believe I owe you more than I can ever pay."

"I'll settle for a hundred dollars," Bill said, in a business voice.

"What?" Casper stared harder.

"I mean," said Bill, "that if you want to make a sort of thank offering for what you have received you could give a hundred dollars to the church repair fund, and I'll take it right up to the Christmas tree and have it counted in tonight. That is," and Bill gave me a nudge, "if you think Mrs. Greene is worth that much."

"Worth it!" ejaculated Casper. "Say, you infernal boy. Worth a hundred dollars! But that thank offering is a good idea. I'll do it." And while we waited he wrote a check for a hundred dollars.

"But what do you get out of it?" he asked, as he handed the check to Bill.

"Roast goose," said Bill.

EROS AND THE EAR TRUMPET

Clarence B. Kelland

Farm Life, August 1915

TOBIAS Sampleby was without doubt the most noteworthy citizen in China Township, which lies on the St. Clair River, some miles above Marine City. He stood out above his fellows for reasons.

One reason—which possibly may be regarded as an illogical one—was the fact that he was the shortest man in the township. Moreover, he possessed the only ear trumpet in China; he had operated his own vessel; and he now was proprietor of one of the largest and most remunerative farms along the river. Add to this that he had a collie dog trained to keep women off the place, and a vocabulary which combined the most picturesque marine words with the choicest landman's expletives, and there can be little doubt that he was a personage in the township.

Yet, withal, he was a kindly sort who never chased the boys out of his orchard, who loved his animals, and who would have walked miles to do a service for any male being. He adored youngsters as soon as they reached an age where their garments indicated their sex. Babies he feared, because of the ambiguity arising from this cause, and because he might, all unknowing, be dangling a girl. Also he had a keen discernment for the humorous, even when the keen edge of the joke pointed toward himself— unless there were in it a feminine element. If there were, he became a creature to avoid, or to placate from a distance.

On New Year's Eve he drove down the river road to Marine City for a bit of sociability. He saw to the careful stabling of his horse, and then betook himself to the hotel bar—not for the purpose of falling from grace, for he was not a drinking man, but to foregather with sundry sailormen, companions of his younger days, whom he knew he would find there. They hailed the entry of the captain's short, squat figure with acclaim, and made room for him at the table. He had scarcely seated himself when Clem Boston, old-time shipmate, slapped him resoundingly on the back, reached for the ever-present ear trumpet, and roared into its yawning mouth.

"Leap year's a comin', cap'n! She'll be here in two hours. Then you want to keep your eye peeled, you do. The women has their eye on you, most p'tic'lar they have, and you won't never come through the impendin' twelve months without a consort. Some female craft'll get a hawser aboard of you, and you'll be under a towin' contract for the rest of your life. Happy leap year, cap'n!"

Now, if Clem had been possessed of full discretion, he would not have breathed such a quip in his friend's presence. The stony look in Tobias' eyes made him realize his transgression.

"What was that?" demanded Tobias. "What was you sayin'?"

"I was sayin' happy new year, and hopin' nothin' would come to you for twelve months that wouldn't be shipshape and satisfact'ry for owners and sailormen," stuttered Clem, hoping his friend had not caught the drift of his first remarks.

Tobias pushed back his chair, rose to his feet, and faced Clem with an ominous glint in his eye.

"I calc'late I almost understood better the first time," he said calmly. "Now"—he proceeded to his task without emotion—"you unseaworthy, unswabbed, fog-brained, rotten-timbered son of a longshore freight handler; you rusty b'ilered mudscow with a lyin' compass; you gangle-legged grampus with a conversatian like a ungreased donkey-enjine; if ever you dast to speak to me again, I'm goin' to let go all holts and divide you up 'mong them that don't like you—and there's got to be a lot of pieces!"

All this was uttered without heat or hesitation, but with careful enunciation and evident intention. At the end, Tobias turned his back on the company, stalked out of the room and in five minutes was driving his horse at an unusual pace toward the farm.

Tobias woke up in his own room. He merely opened his eyes, but found he had no desire to get up. Something was not as usual, and he tried to figure out what it was.

There was the unmistakable odor of drugs. He shut his eyes, and tried to remember. His last waking memory was of a wildly careening cutter, a dizzying sense of sudden effort, ending in a fall through space. After that was nothing.

He considered the evidence before him and came to the conclusion that his cutter had overturned, probably hurling him over the high river bank, and that he was hurt and in bed.

Yes, he was hurt—that he could verify. There was a bandage tight around his head, his leg was immovable, his right shoulder was held firmly by something that prevented the slightest change of position. Tobias had seen men hurt before—and mended—so he deduced correctly that his leg and arm were broken and in splints. Then he wondered who had found him, brought him home, and who was looking after him.

The door opened softly, and he turned his head to look. He winked, scowled, winked again, and tried to raise his head. There coming toward him was a woman—a woman, in a dress of some sort of blue stuff, with a big white apron covering most of it—a nurse.

Tobias' eyes snapped angrily, but he could not move. He sank back with a moan of despair, and waited for strength to come; but when it came, it served only for one question.

"Where's Shep?" Shep was the dog that chased women off the place.

"The dog?" said the nurse, bending to put her mouth to the ear trumpet. "He didn't seem to like me, so I shut him in the barn."

Tobias grimaced in a futile effort to make plain his rage.

"Lie still, and don't try to talk," dictated the nurse. "You're all broken to pieces, and you won't mend if you aren't careful."

With that she looked to his bandages, forced a teaspoonful of medicine between his reluctant lips, and disappeared from the room, leaving him in a red haze of helpless anger.

At last came a time when he could restrain himself no longer.

"Ahoy there!" he cried weakly. "Aboard the dining room!"

The nurse heard and stepped quickly through the door. He eyed her in silence, but menacingly. As he glared, he perceived that she was small, firm of chin and ruddy of cheek. As to age, he estimated she was safely past thirty. It was her smallness that struck him and held his attention. She was short, but of pleasing figure, in her stiffly starched dress, giving off an air of capability.

"How—how did you get here?" he asked, almost in a whisper.

She put his trumpet to his ear and replied: "Your friends sent for me. I've been here over a week."

He shut his eyes a moment.

"In this house?" he demanded.

She nodded. "Do you want anything?" she shouted into the trumpet.

"Yes," he growled with sudden energy. "I want you to up anchor and be off— that's what I want. I won't give no wimmin—" His head fell back. His force was expended; he could not go on.

She smoothed his pillow deftly, and withdrew. She was too much accustomed to querulous patients to attach significance to his words.

That afternoon, Tobias opened his eyes to see Clem Boston sitting beside his bed, wearing a self-satisfied and triumphant expression. The injured man scowled darkly. Clem smiled the more triumphantly, and spoke into the ear trumpet.

"I done it!" he explained joyously. "Me! You cussed me out for a little joke, you did, but I returned good for evil. I heaped coals of fire onto your bald head till there ain't no more room." He wagged his head with mock gravity. "I picked you up where you was throwed, and carried you home, and sent to Detroit for a nurse. I did! And she's here!"

"You—you fetched that—that woman into my house?"

Tobias' eyes snapped, and his features worked with rage.

"I done so," boasted Clem, "and furthermore and additionally, I want to tell you you're a goner. Yes, sir, a goner! I knowed the minute I see that nurse that she was a marryin' woman—and she's got her eye on you. What did I say about leap year, eh? What was them observations I made?"

He paused, waiting to see the effect of his words. Tobias was stricken absolutely speechless. He could only glower; but if the expression of a human face could do physical injury, Clem would have been carried away on a shutter.

"She's got you where you can't move," continued Clem, "and she'll land you just like you was a little fish. She'll perpose, that's what she'll do, and there'll be a Misses Tobias Sampleby around the house. And I done it!"

Tobias turned away his head, and as a sole defense, withdrew his ear from the trumpet. At least he would hear no more of Clem's gibes.

Clem sat a while, grinning maliciously, and then rose to go. He walked to the door, turned, gave Tobias a farewell smirk and stamped from the house.

Tobias lay silently pondering the matter. He saw the dangers of his position, weighed his chances for escape, and prepared for a stubborn defense, dubious as to the outcome. What could he do, flat on his back, against the plottings and schemings of a woman bent on having him for her own? She would wear him down, weaken him, overcome his will, and he would surrender miserably. Tobias was distinctly afraid.

He watched apprehensively for the reappearance of his nurse, and when she entered the room he read her every action in the light of Clem's disquieting disclosure and appalling prophecy.

It was plain to the captain that he was this woman's destined quarry; that she was set on possessing him, and worked constantly to that end. If she smoothed his pillow, brought him appetizing morsels, spoke to him cheerfully, gave him medicine, it was all a part of her insidious campaign. He could read it plainly, and he was an ungracious patient.

Clem Boston dropped in frequently, for Clem was not a man to allow any turmoil to subside that he could keep well stirred. He sat by Tobias and predicted a leap year proposal and wedding bells until the sufferer wept tears of impotent wrath and apprehension. Nor was Clem careless as regarded Miss Shaffer. In the parlor he descanted to her of Tobias Sampleby's goodness and kindliness—and loneliness. He related significant incidents; he adduced convincing proof; he made the injured man out to be a very exceptional individual indeed—one deserving both pity and love.

Despite Clem Boston's frequent calls and his own fears and suspicions, Tobias grew stronger and stronger. One day Miss Shaffer took up his ear trumpet, while he watched her with the apprehension that came into his eyes every time she spoke to him, and told him a half-dozen little boys, who had called almost daily to ask after him, were outside, and wanted to see him a moment. Tobias' face changed. It wore an eager look, its lines softened, and he turned his head eagerly. "Fetch 'em in, fetch 'em in! So them leetle fellers remembers the old man! Who'd 'a' thought it? Fetch 'em in!"

As Miss Shaffer went to admit the youngsters, she winked repeatedly to get a mist out of her eyes.

She stood in the doorway, after she had let in the boys, and watched them as they surrounded their friend. She saw how softened was his face, how young were his eyes. She saw another man than the querulous, harsh, scowling curmudgeon she was accustomed to serve. In his stead she saw another, soft of heart, merry—one with eyes that looked into the heart of childhood—one with a heart into which the eyes of childhood could look.

She walked rapidly from the room, and stood for a long time looking out of the window across the bleak reaches of the river.

After that Miss Shaffer was still more patient and gentle with her charge—much to his consternation. She did her full duty by him, and more, and he began to grow accustomed to having her about. She was not obtrusive; she was capable, silent, and efficient.

Tobias was not more cordial, but he scowled at her less frequently, and tried to do her justice. Over him hung always his fear of the power which leap year gave her—and

Clem Boston constantly fanned that fear.

Once, on the nurse's entrance, Tobias looked up and smiled. With that involuntary smile on his mind, the ensuing day was one of terror.

With the coming of spring he improved rapidly. Every day saw him renewing his body and strengthening his grip on life. The bandages were now discarded from his head; his ribs had knit, but the leg and arm, together with the weakness resulting from fever and internal hurts, kept him in bed.

"'Most ready to steam out of dry dock," declared Clem. "Is that towin' contract settled yet? Be you goin' to have nursie for a consort? Has she up and perposed, and got a line fast to you?"

The captain, with his gaining strength, was able to reply fittingly and at some length. He made Clem Boston fidget in his chair.

"Wa-all," said Clem, when Tobias' invective was exhausted, "if she ain't yet, she's a goin' to. Wait till she's near ready to leave. Then's when she'll pop the question, and don't you forgit it!"

Time for her to leave! Tobias had not thought of it for months. Of course, when he was well, she would go, and—so he told himself—what a relief it would be! Of course it would be a relief; the only fear was lest she would overcome him before that day arrived.

From that instant his gruffness and crustiness toward Miss Shaffer increased; but he watched her a great deal as she went in and out about her work. His eyes seldom left her when she was to be seen; and the eyes did not always scowl, especially if her back were turned.

Sometimes he tried to imagine how good it would feel to have his house to himself again, to have the obnoxious feminine element removed from his life; but, somehow, it was hard to shape the picture. And he was growing stronger and stronger. The day of Miss Shaffer's departure could not be long distant. He drummed on the bedclothes with his fingers and gnawed his nether lip. Life was unsatisfactory; it had a disagreeable flavor; there was a vacancy about the future that Tobias could not account for. At length he was able to leave his bed and spend his days on the big carpet-covered sofa in the parlor. Next he was able to hobble about the house—it would be no time before he would be able to resume his old life, as well and strong as ever. The prospect seemed to afford him little pleasurable anticipation.

One Saturday afternoon Miss Shaffer sat down near his sofa and patiently read the newspaper to him through his ear trumpet. Her face was not cheerful, and several times she paused briefly, to wink determinedly or clear a huskiness out of her voice. When the paper was finished, she sat still, looking, as was her custom of late, out of the window.

Tobias half turned his face away and closed his eyes. Something made him discontented; he was a victim of depression; there was that which was not right with him, but he could not diagnose it.

Miss Shaffer reached for the ear trumpet, and Tobias jumped apprehensively. Perhaps it was coming now! What should he do? If she should ask him to marry her, what could he say in reply? How could he escape?

"You won't need a nurse any more," she said, with an effort to keep her voice even. "You're pretty nearly well, and—and I suppose I've got to go. Will you—will you hitch up—and c-carry me to town t-to-morrow, captain?"

His hand clutched the blanket that covered his legs. He caught his breath. It had come, that proposal! It had come at last! Through his ear trumpet he had understood her to say: "Will you marry me in town tomorrow, captain?"

Tomorrow! She had proposed to him—a leap year proposal.

The captain put a hand to his face and seized his chin convulsively. What, what should he say?

For minutes he lay perfectly still. Then he realized that he was not afraid—that the proposal had not terrified him. On the contrary, he was happy; life seemed bright; he wanted to get up that very moment and breathe deep of the spring air.

She would not go away—she would never go away. This thought came unasked, almost unperceived in its significance. It repeated itself joyously, until he became fully aware of it—and then he knew. He reached out, took her hand, and looked up into her face.

"Yes," he said softly, "I'll marry you in town tomorrow."

For a moment she was thunderstruck. What did he mean? Was he asking her to marry him? No, clearly not; he was giving her an answer—answering a proposal which he thought she had made. She could see how it was, for she had already had experience of the misbehavior of the ear trumpet, and guessed that it had made of the simple word the momentous dissyllable "marry."

She could not restrain a little laugh—a laugh of joy, of relief, of contentment. Then she looked down into his eyes.

After a time he spoke again.

"I—I wonder," he said gently, "if you'd kiss me. I ain't never had no woman do that."

She leaned over and pressed her lips to his; and though Tobias did not know it, he was by that symbol accepted as her husband. Never, never, was he to know that he had not been the victim of a leap year proposal!

THE O'BRIEN

William R. Leighton
Farm and Fireside, July 1921

I belong to the tribe of Casey, I'm a sawmill machinist by trade, sober and industrious and with some good money laid by; but single. That's not my disposition; it's just rough luck. I've got the heart of a natural-born Romeo, but the makeup of a clown. Any woman who agreed to marry me, with my mop of brick-colored hair and my grinning mouth and the stout, chunky, healthy shape of me, would do it merely because she couldn't help being fond of a good joke. Besides, everybody calls me "Curly." That makes it hopeless. Why, if the great god of love himself had been called "Curly" by the rest of the immortals it would have ruined him for his role.

So when I set out to tell a great love story you know it's not my own. It's another man's. Just the same, the ridiculous comedy presence God gave me let me help the other man through the rough waters of experience. That's compensation.

The boss called me into the office from the factory shops one day.

"Curly," he said, "those saw rigs for the Arkansas job are being loaded out today. I want you to go down there and help get things ready. You'll have several free days before the stuff gets on the ground. You may need 'em. It's a queer proposition they've got. They're likely to have trouble with the natives squatted on their lands. Maybe you'll see some of it. You won't mind a little scrapping if you happen to run into it?"

"Mind?" I said. "Me? Oh, no!"

"You'll stay till the mills are set," he told me. "But you won't be alone with those natives. There's a fellow who'll meet you at the railroad in the morning. O'Brien, his name is. A good man."

It wasn't all new stuff the boss was telling me. I knew something about it. The lumber company owned a most amazing lot of most amazingly good oak timber down in the White River country. They'd been picking it up for years, getting ready for operations; and now they were going to set up half a dozen sawmills, scattered round through the woods, to cut the stuff for a big finishing plant on the railroad. Helping to build their rigs in the shops had got me interested. I could tell they knew what they were about.

"All right, Curly," the boss said. "Keep me posted. Good luck!"

It was a gray dawn when I tumbled off my train at the little Arkansas woods town— a squalid settlement squatted down in a mess of woodsmen's wreckage. The pine men had been there, had cleaned up, and moved on. Everywhere was a litter of rotting treetops and rotting logs. Down by the track was a mountain of rotting pine sawdust where a mill had once stood, and there were rows of ragged, rotting old stack bottoms that hadn't been worth moving when the mill quit. Along the muddy road was a double row of wooden hovels set up on piling to keep them out of the mire. They made the town. Decay was everywhere; the air was dank with its heavy odor. I didn't like the looks of the place a bit.

And then away up yonder at the head of the road, where the woods crowded close against the town's edge, I saw a man coming.

"That'll be O'Brien, now," I told myself. "God bless the Irish!"

He was coming five miles an hour, with every move a joy to him. I noticed that first, and then I noticed the most uncommon good looks of him. My word, but he was a handsome chap! A six-footer, and big, with every fiber of him strung up tight with the zest of life. He was laughing as he came along toward me; I could see the shine of his strong white teeth; and long before he was close enough to let me make sure, I knew the color his eyes would be—real Irish blue, full of living lights, like clear summer water reflecting summer sky. And the gay, impudent, clean-cut face of him! Oh, he was a man!

"And his name's O'Brien, is it?" I said to myself, watching him. "Well, he's not the runt of the family, that's sure. He's *The O'Brien!*"

He swung up to me with his hand out. "Hello!" he said. Just one word, but I loved him from that minute. It was his voice that did it. It's not often you hear a real bass. He had it—a magnificent voice, rich and full, with a throbbing sort of cathedral-organ undertone.

"Hello! You're Casey. Praise be! If they'd sent down a Schmidt or a Paoli or a Svenson—but you're Casey. And I'll bet I know the rest of your name. I'll bet a dollar it's 'Curly'."

"Well, you win," I said. "I might have known you would. You look like a lucky man."

He tipped back his head and laughed—a deep, booming laugh. Here and there a disheveled figure appeared in a doorway, peering out to see what the trouble was.

"Welcome!" he said. "I hope you're not hungry. It's little you'll be getting for your breakfast. If I had you in one of my camps, now, I could feed you right; but we'll not be there for dinner. One of the owners is coming in on the up-train at ten. I've got to wait here for him."

"Hungry!" I said. "Sure I'm hungry. But I'm not going to eat chunks of lukewarm fatback in that dirty hotel. We'll get something at the store."

We carried an armful of stuff down beside the railroad track and kindled a fire there, tramp-fashion. It was good. Day came on golden, and while we ate we talked. I loved that talk. Maybe it didn't go deep, but it was a perfect revelation of that new friend of mine. Every word he spoke was brimming-full of a great, rollicking Irish temper, equal to anything. The heart of him was big and bold and adventurous. He'd been up and down the world, and he'd seen a lot and done a lot and thought a lot; but with it all he'd kept a quaint sort of gentleness that was better than all the rest. It wasn't womanish; it was most intensely masculine. I don't know but that the finest of all the creatures that walk the earth is the man who's won through a lot of experience and gained a clear-seeing, incorruptible simplicity. O'Brien had it. I wasn't going to care what that job might bring, so long as I'd have him there to share it.

134

Well, and then by and by the train came in from the south, bringing old Peter Bates, the head of the lumber company.

I wasn't going to love old Peter. I knew that from the minute I set eyes on him. He thought he was a great fellow, but there was nothing to him at all. He was just one of the commonest sort of rich men, gray and coarse-grained and beefy. You may count a hundred exactly like him in an hour on any business street in America, any day in the year. Those chaps own most of the money, and they walk their ways insolently and most of us turn meekly out of their paths to give them room; but they're a poor breed just the same.

We went down the platform, O'Brien and I, to meet him. There were a few meaningless words and a couple of flabby handshakes. Then all at once old Peter Bates simply ceased to exist for my friend O'Brien. I happened to be watching him, and I saw him stand suddenly straight, with the light of a living fire flashing into those fine eyes of his. I had a notion of what I'd see when I turned around.

A girl was coming from the car. With her foot on the lower step she stopped dead still, her eyes on O'Brien. For a moment I thought the look she gave him meant recognition; but then I knew better. I don't know how to say it for you, unless you're one of those who believe that there may be meetings like that with destiny stamped on them unmistakably from the first swift instant. I believe it. At that, I'm not a crazy sentimentalist. I declare that what I saw wasn't wild fancy. If ever love between man and woman was full-born in one immaculate moment, it happened just then, right before my eyes.

She was slender and dark, proud, too; but that wasn't the mean pride of vanity. The care and the indulgence that money had bought for her had nothing to do with it. Her pride was just the exquisite quality of cleanliness and fineness. She was clean as a jewel, with a sort of jewel brightness about her. But quiet, wonderfully serene. She'd be hard to move over trifles, proof against the sway of light notions. It was no trifle that held her mind then. I think she knew beyond all doubting that something was to come of that meeting. It was written.

Old Peter's cold voice was sputtering about something or other that didn't please him. It struck him all at once that nobody was paying any attention to what he said. He turned and helped the girl from the step. It wasn't courtesy but just a grudging concession of decency that made him speak.

"My daughter. O'Brien. And Casey—isn't that you're name?"

I happened to be nearest her. She gave me her hand, looking straight at me, letting her eyes kindle with a laugh—just as they all do when they get their first glimpse of me. A small hand, dainty, but firm and strong, too. She didn't let me keep it long, but turned from me to O'Brien, and forgot all about me.

There weren't many words between them. Words weren't needed. The meeting was color and light—flame. Somehow I felt as if I ought to be looking the other way, but I couldn't. It was the old man who interrupted. He was fuming and fidgeting, taking a disapproving look at the town.

"What kind of a forsaken hole is this?" he demanded of O'Brien. "I thought you

135

wrote that I'd have a decent place to stay."

O'Brien attended to him then, gently, kindly.

"Not in town, Mr. Bates. It's a ramshackle relic of a town. I meant to take care of you in my own camp. But you didn't say anything about bringing your daughter. My camp is spick-and-span clean, and there's plenty of room and plenty to eat; but a lady—" The girl cut him short with a gay little laugh.

"Oh, don't! I wanted to come, and I want to see what's here—all of it. Don't make me feel that I'm a nuisance. Take me to your camp, Mr. O'Brien."

Somewhere O'Brien found an old double-seated phaeton and a pair of lean little ponies, and we set off into the woods. An eight-mile ride he said we'd have. That suited me: I love outdoors, and that morning was a wonder, following the twisting road through the coolness and freshness and fragrance of the big timber. It would have been perfect if it hadn't been for the old man back there on the rear seat with his daughter. It wasn't beauty he was seeing; it was just so many dollars' worth of trees for his mills to cut up.

"There's a fine white oak!" he'd say in his hard voice. "Straight and sound. Five hundred feet in a twelve-foot butt cut, and big enough for quartering. That's fifty-dollar stuff, just sawed in flitches. And we've been getting this stumpage for ten and twelve dollars an acre, with the land thrown in. That's money!"

He'd sit and chuckle over it with a sound like an ogre relishing a choice morsel, flicking his cold eyes greedily about at the solid miles of woods that belonged to him. He was full of questions too—brusque little questions of detail aimed at O'Brien. O'Brien had to turn round in his seat to answer. I guess that wasn't a hardship; you'd have judged so by the sound of his voice. So far as the words went, he was talking about saw-milling, and nothing else, and just for the old man's fleshy ears; but between the words and over and under and around them his great voice was singing a love song—singing, singing! I knew! Once in a while, out of the tail of my eye, I caught a glimpse of the girl nestled back in her corner, listening. She knew, too. Take my word for it, a miracle was coming to pass in that rickety, rattling old phaeton—the old original miracle of God. Right under old Peter's eyes—he wasn't even guessing it!

We came to a hill by and by, long and steep. The poor little ponies went at it, but it staggered them. The girl moved in her corner.

"Let me walk," she said. "I'm tired of sitting still so long. I want to feel the earth under my feet—the real earth."

I took the lines from O'Brien's hand as if it was a matter of course, and they two got out and fell behind the carriage. I don't believe the old man noticed; he was still peering ahead, studying the timber on the slope. I touched up the ponies to take us ahead of the loiterers. They didn't need us. Old Peter cleared his fat throat.

"You're a stranger here, Casey?" he said. "Then you don't know what this valley land is selling for, cleared up? It's worth a hundred dollars an acre; it'll sell for that when we get it moving. And it cost us only ten to twelve with the timber on it. That's money!"

It was man's work we had cut out for us there in the deep woods, building our sets for the mills; a huge task to be managed with rude strength and the rudest of means, hewing the great timbers for the foundations, dragging them up into place, and laying the structures with the sheer brute power of backs and arms and legs. It was mighty different work in the shops, where the touch of a finger on a switch would release a hundred horsepower. There was no such thing in the wilderness; the job there was like being thrown back to the very beginnings of things. But it was good! That sort of thing does any man good, once in a while.

The best of it was the dead weariness at the day's end, when we crawled back to the camphouse so fagged that every dragging step was hard labor, but with the appetites of a pack of hunting hounds. My word, there's nothing like that hunger for establishing a man on the solid foundations of life! And then there was the simple, honest animal delight of sleep when we'd eaten our fill—sleep that amounted almost to a passion; and after that the waking in the golden, sweet-scented morning of a new day to live it all over again.

The day's work was enough for me—just the round of things I've told of. I didn't want anything more. But that didn't satisfy O'Brien. For him there was love besides— great love, magnificent love!

Such a commonplace word that is, if you use it for the commonplace, everyday, makeshift sort of sentiment between the common run of lukewarm men and women. Love! They don't know what it is. To them it doesn't seem to mean anything but a convenient way of suiting themselves to some of life's meanest needs. It's only once in a long, long while that you'll find a man who can be kindled into white fire by the sort of love that sets him with the gods on high. If I'm a judge, women of that make are just as rare. Maybe once in a lifetime, if you're lucky, do you stand a chance of seeing such a man and such a woman meet face to face.

That was what I saw, there in the camp. As I think of it, there's just one word that keeps coming back to me as the only fit one—flame. There's flame that smudges and blackens, and there's flame that cleanses and beautifies. The love I was looking at was beautiful.

The strength of it made O'Brien tireless. All day long he worked with the best of us, doing his full share of the roughest of the labor; but when the work was done, and the rest of us worn to the last shaking extremity of utter exhaustion, every fiber in him was quick with eagerness for what the evening at the camp would bring.

No great adventure, no impetuous wooing—nothing like that. Mostly they met only at the table in the mess room, where all the workers in the motley crew, and old Bates, too, sat together for meals, and the few words they exchanged meant nothing in particular to us who listened. A tone, a quick meeting of eyes, a laugh, a flash of subtle understanding—those were all the signs of what was happening. It wasn't much. The old man was missing it altogether. It needed the sixth sense of a natural born lover to discover what was going on. I knew! The high passion of it, held in a heroic sort of restraint, would send O'Brien to his bed singing. Sometimes, waking for a minute in the night, I'd see him sitting in the door of the bunkhouse with his pipe, brooding upon the woods at dusk, thinking his lover's thoughts. Oh, I knew! And when day came, there he'd be at his task again, laboring with limitless strength. And so it went on for a week. I fell to wondering how long it would be before the inevitable thing would happen.

We were making great headway with the mill sets. At the week's end the machinery from the factory was set on the railroad siding for us, and extra crews were put at the work of loading the engines and boilers for the saw rigs on the huge wagon gears that were to carry them to the woods sets. There'd have been work enough, and responsibility enough, if we could have kept the job wholly free from the complications.

But trouble started for us. Old Bates had been chafing over the matter of the squatters on his lands. It didn't seem to me to be a proposition to agonize over. Here and there through the woods a poverty-stricken native had found a spot that pleased him, built a rude shack for his family, deadened the timber on a few acres and scratched round a little with a plow. I don't know what claim of title they had, maybe none at all; but there they were. Having so much, Bates might have let them stay.

But not that man! The sign of a greedy man is that his desires aren't according to his needs; he wants it all. The presence of the squatters was an affliction to Bates' soul. He couldn't rest until he had some of the sheriff's officers serving ejectment notices.

There wasn't any violent explosion over it. The natives hadn't a bit of powdery Irish temper; theirs was the punky sort of disposition that sulks and smolders and nurses its grudges in sullen secret till the time comes for striking swiftly in vengeance. That queer mood may lead you into the mistake of thinking you've got them cowed and beaten. Bates made that mistake. He held the poor chaps in thorough contempt.

Then one evening O'Brien and I sat on the porch of the mess building smoking. Bates and his daughter were a little way off, under the trees, where the old man liked to go to enjoy his cigar while he loafed and reckoned up the day's work.

One of the natives came slouching out of the hills in the dusk. He was an old man, gaunt and gnarled and bearded, with small, fierce eyes hidden under a crag of shaggy brows. In the crook of one arm he carried a long-barreled homemade rifle. He singled out Bates, ignoring the girl. He held out Bates a crumpled paper.

"Thish yere was fotched to me this mawnin'," he said dully. "The deputy, he tol' me hit was your doin'. I want you should tell me the meanin' of it."

Bates glanced at the notice.

"Oh, you're Hollis?" he said with that offensive insolence of his. "You're on our land. That's a notice to get off."

The old man stood staring.

"I hain't aimin' to move off," he said heavily.

Bates gave a scornful snort.

"Suit yourself. You'll move off or be moved when the time of the notice is up."

"I been livin' on that clearin' o' mine seven years," Hollis protested. "I bought that piece o' ground. Hit's mine."

"No, it isn't," Bates retorted. "We've got tax title to that land you're on. You'll have to quit."

Hollis stood irresolute, swinging his long rifle from one arm to the other. The girl got up from her seat beside her father, frightened. Just to make myself handy, I left the porch and walked toward them. I didn't know what the old codger might take a notion to do. But he seemed not yet ready for a fight. He stuffed the paper back in his pocket.

"I hain't aimin' to move off," he said again. "Nor hit won't be best for nobody to try movin' me."

That was all he had to say. He turned, and went ambling off up the hill trail. The girl's eyes caught mine, and she laughed nervously.

"Such a ferocious-looking man!" she said. "Are they as wicked as they look?"

"They couldn't be," I joked. "Wickedness doesn't go by looks, anyway. No man is any wickeder than he acts, if you get down to facts."

Bates grunted.

"They're a poor lot," he said in his stupid arrogance. "The spirit of cattle! We'll be rid of him and all his breed next week."

O'Brien had come up quietly behind me. His deep voice made a queer contrast to Bates' fat wheeze.

"They're not cattle," he said. "They have courage enough. They're fighters, but they fight woods-fashion, just as they have since their stock left Virginia. They can make things expensive for us, Mr. Bates. I've been wondering if it wouldn't be better to compromise. There are only a few of these squatters inside your lines."

"Compromise!" Bates spoke the word as if he were spitting out something nauseous. "Compromise what?"

"These fellows have their rights, in a way," O'Brien said gently.

"Rights? Rubbish!" Bates was getting angry. "Let me tell you, my man, nobody has any rights in this world that I'll recognize except the rights he's able to enforce by law against me. That's my code. It's the only code that I'll tolerate in my affairs."

I suppose he thought that would silence O'Brien. Most likely he was used to silencing folks merely by declaring what he would or wouldn't tolerate. Rich men get into that habit.

But O'Brien laughed lightly.

"My code isn't like yours," he said. "When I'm in doubt about what's mine and what's the other fellow's, I just let him have it."

"Faugh!" Bates scoffed. "Nonsense! Childish!"

"I suppose it is," O'Brien agreed, "but it works."

"It's brought you to where you are empty-handed," Bates argued.

"Yes, sir," O'Brien said. "But if I'm empty-handed, I've got nothing that anybody is coveting. That's a comfort."

It was pretty bold talk, considering. The boldness of it or the rank heresy of it made Bates scowl in resentment.

"That's silly!" he snorted. "Nothing to it! There's just one real difference between a powerful man and a weakling; the powerful man knows how to accumulate the means of power—that's money—and the weakling doesn't. There you are! I haven't got mine by nursing any nice little quibbles. I get what I can and let the other fellow take it away from me if he can prove it's his. But he's got to do the proving."

Of course, he thought that was impregnable doctrine. He hadn't a doubt of it. But his daughter didn't think so. I was watching her while the debate went on. Her eyes were on O'Brien, searching him, looking him through and through—and approving him. She hadn't spoken a syllable. There was no need. It was clear as sunlight to me that she knew the difference between money and a man. Her eyes caught O'Brien's, and I saw the color go over her face in a living tide. O'Brien spoke to her then.

"This funny life is just a sort of witches' caldron—'Bubble, bubble, toil and trouble.' My word, there oughtn't to be any such thing as trouble in a place like this. Look at it! We men must be a lot of sorry blunderers."

The talk had become uninteresting for Bates. He brought a memorandum book from his pocket and fell to his eternal figuring. I went back to the messhouse porch, and sat looking on while O'Brien and the girl loitered along the woods path in the half-dusk. The murmur of a word or a note of light laughter came to me now and then. O'Brien came back after a time in that state of mind that's reserved for Heaven's special favorites. Anything like disaster seemed just then a long way off.

But it broke upon us that night. It was midnight or later. I'd been sleeping the sleep of profound weariness—sunk miles deep in it. Then all at once I found myself sitting on the edge of my bunk, shocked, staring, wide awake, shaking.

Through one of those mysteries of the mind's lightning action I knew I had been waked by the roar of an explosion. Some of the other men were moving, crying out excitedly. O'Brien's voice spoke in the darkness:

"Dynamite! They're wrecking things! That must have been the nearest of the outfits, in Smoky Creek bottom. Get dressed, all of you who want to help."

Another mighty explosion came, and then a third, farther off. Somebody got a lamp burning. Half a dozen of us were scrambling into our clothes. Outside the bunkhouse the camp was roused. We heard old Peter Bates clamoring anxiously, demanding to be told what the matter was. For all his importance his voice sounded shaky and oddly futile. We hurried as fast as we could, and got outside, half-clothed and carrying whatever arms we could find. O'Brien didn't wait for orders from Bates, but took us to the creek road, where one of the wagon crews had halted for the night with its loads of equipment for one of the sawmills.

It was a pretty mess we found there. A heavy charge of dynamite had been exploded in one of the tubes of the big boiler, making a ruin of it; every tube in it would have been wrenched by the strain, loosened in the boiler head. Even if the plates had held, repairs couldn't be made in the woods; we'd have to send the boiler back to the shops. And the hillmen hadn't stopped with that. They'd poured a strong acid over the engine, drenching it on every cylinder rod and bearing. It would leak steam like an old teakettle. Besides, they'd slashed the roll of heavy driving belt to tatters, and done everything else they could manage in a hurry. The men of the wagon crews had slept through it all till the explosion came. They hadn't dreamed of the need for keeping watch.

Quickly O'Brien took account of the damage.

"They'll have played the same trick with the other outfits," he said. "We ought to have expected it. Mr. Bates will be pleased."

He wasn't, then. What we had to tell him when we got back to camp sent him into an apoplectic rage. No wonder. I think the worst of the experience for him was knowing that he'd come up against a situation where his money was absolutely worthless—just as it always is when men get down to the rock bottom of life. He'd been living in the stupid illusion that his millions made the beginning and the end of power, an impregnable buttress against any mischance. His loss in dollars by the wreckage hadn't been so great, but the offense against his swollen money vanity was hard to bear; it hurt him far worse than any physical injury.

"That old hellion who was here last night!" he stormed. "What was his name? Hollis! He made threats. He's at the bottom of this. We'll settle with that fellow!"

There was no more sleep for him that night. He insisted upon having O'Brien sit up with him till morning, nursing his fury, working himself up into a lovely state of mind. By breakfast time his bitterness against the old man Hollis had become an obsession. Nothing would do but to set off headlong for Hollis' place in the hills, to have it out with the old chap. It was Sunday morning. O'Brien tried to dissuade him.

"I think we'd better let it rest over today," O'Brien urged. "Our case will keep till tomorrow. We have no proof. A day will give everyone a chance to cool down."

Cooling down was just what Bates didn't want. He'd gathered a passionate anger that had to have vent. No argument was of any use against him. When there was no help for it, O'Brien ordered some horses saddled. He came to me, laughing, where I stood under the trees talking with the girl, trying to reassure her.

"Casey," he said, "will you come? There'll be nothing bad come of it, please God; but I'd like to have the Irish along. You've a wheedling tongue in your head."

"Of course!" I said. The girl spoke then, quietly:

"Have you a horse for me? I'm going too."

"Oh, no!" O'Brien protested. "You mustn't. This is not for you."

She only laughed at him—a gay little laugh, but with a challenge in it.

"Do you fancy I'm going to stay here?" she said. "I sha'n't. I mean to go with you. I'm not used to being left out of things."

Their eyes met. I think O'Brien was glad. His voice had the note of singing that belonged to it when mind and heart were most aroused.

"It's just an errand of peace," he said, "though there's the making of a good fight in it. I love a good fight, too. The hardest thing I do is to keep out of them. But we'll keep out this time if we can."

It was a great morning in the woods—oh, wonderful! We rode all together for a little way; and then somehow O'Brien and the girl fell behind. That was as it should be, though it left me to bear with old Peter's grouch alone. I didn't mind. I wasn't listening anyway. I was thinking of those two back of us on the trail. The perfection of the day seemed to have been exactly fashioned for great love-making. I was rejoicing with my friend; but I couldn't help feeling a queer little stab of hurt, remembering my own grotesque mockery of a face. It's not good for a man to feel that he's clear out of it.

Then O'Brien surprised me. After a little while I heard them riding fast to over-take us. When they came up, O'Brien rode alongside of me, catching at my horse's bridle, urging me to go with him, and we rode on ahead at a gallop, out of hearing. O'Brien spoke then—not to me, but as though he couldn't help himself.

"What is it I'm doing! Oh, I'm mad—mad!"

His handsome face was gray and pinched, drawn with the tension of his passion. My first wild guess was wrong. I thought he'd asked for love and had it denied him. But then I knew that was impossible, for I'd seen the girl's eyes; I knew well enough that she'd never be one to deny great love, no matter by what strange way it would come to her. I had to guess again, and that time I got it right. It was O'Brien who had drawn back, moved by God knows what crazy lover's judgment of unworthiness.

I held my tongue for a minute or two; but I had to say something before long.

"I know what's ailing you," I told him. "It's an old, old complaint. And there's only one cure that I know of. That's to believe in love. Don't you believe in it, O'Brien?"

He looked at me, startled, amazed. I suppose he thought I was crazy too. He gave a choking sort of laugh, deep in his throat.

"Believe in love?" he said after me. "Can you ask that of me? I don't believe in anything else. It's the whole faith of my life. Anything that's done for less than love's sake is badly done, and not worth the doing. That's what I believe."

"Then what's the trouble?" I asked. "What is it you've done?"

"Done?" he said. "It's nothing I've done. Right this minute I'm standing clean before God."

"There's only one thing left," I said. "Then it's money."

He drew a great sigh at that.

"It's not money," he told me. "Not the dollars. It's what the dollars might mean. You can understand. If it were only money—I've had my chances for making money; plenty of them. But I've passed them up, because I couldn't take them and come clean with the rest of what I wanted to keep. No, it's not just money."

He was looking far ahead on the trail, seeing nothing, struggling with himself.

"Listen, Casey," he said. "It's not easy. I wonder if you've ever thought of it like this. The best of a man's strength is in being able to control it. Do you know that? The greatest fighters are the ones who've learned when to keep from fighting. And some-times the strongest desires a man knows are those he's got to master and keep down. It's true!"

I suppose I didn't get his full meaning then. What he said struck me as over-wrought absurdity.

"That's too fine-drawn for me," I said, "I reckon you'll argue that the most ardent lovers are the men who carefully hold back from loving too much."

He had nothing to say to that, but let me go on with my talk when I got ready.

"I'll tell you one thing," I said after a while. "If it ever happens that love like this is offered to me just for the taking, angels nor devils won't be able to keep me from taking it. Now you hear me! There's no false humility that's ever going to hold me back. I'm going to take it. Out of all this world's mess, love's the only thing that's worth taking. And you'd pass it up!"

I couldn't have hit him harder. He looked at me like a hurt animal.

"Don't!" he said. "Don't!" He caught up his bridle rein and plunged ahead alone. I let him go. I couldn't help him.

He was waiting for us at the next crossing of the trails, and when we caught up with him he went straight to business with old Peter.

"Hollis lives just a little way above here," he said. "I know the place. I know him too, Mr. Bates. He'll not be in the best of tempers."

The old man paid no attention to that. He and O'Brien rode a little way ahead, abreast. I had the girl to take care of. She wouldn't stay behind, though I tried to make her. And so we came in sight of Hollis' home.

Poor enough it was—a mere hovel of rough-hewn logs with a crumbling chimney of mud and sticks running up one wall. The dooryard was a hopeless, unkempt tangle. Some hounds set up a baying, and the old man came to the door, peering down the trail. He stepped back into the house, then came slouching down the path to the gates, carrying his long rifle.

O'Brien called to him.

"All right, Hollis! We've just come for a bit of a talk."

Hollis answered by stepping behind one of the high gate posts, laying his rifle across its top.

"You-all stop right thar whar you be!" he ordered. It didn't sound very menacing; his voice was at the listless dead-level of all those woodsmen's voices, even when their feelings are at the highest tension. Maybe that listlessness deceived old Peter, or maybe the old chap was really game. Anyway, he didn't hesitate, but rode straight on. I saw Hollis' rifle swing and steady at the fine mark old Peter made. I felt it in my bones that he meant to shoot. In a panic I clutched the bridle rein of the girl's horse, trying to force her from the trail and out of range. And then, swift as one of the flashing movements of the cinema, I saw O'Brien lunge ahead and throw himself squarely across old Peter's path, covering him, just in the right moment of time to catch Hollis' bullet in his own body. He rocked in his saddle, tried to steady himself, then sagged down heavily over the horn.

You don't remember things clearly after the shock of an experience like that. I was at O'Brien's side in a few seconds, supporting him, trying to find his hurt, trying to make him speak. The girl was there too, standing with him, silent, her eyes flaming. O'Brien tried to smile at her for reassurance, but he made a poor failure of it. Old Hollis set his rifle against the rail fence and came shambling down the path to join us. He spoke to Peter Bates with an oddly futile simplicity.

"He hadn't ought to've done that. I wasn't wantin' him. It was you I was aimin' to git."

Bates took hold of things then.

"We'll have to get him to the camp. He can't ride back. We'll have to make a litter and carry him somehow. Janet, you ride ahead and send one of the men for a doctor. Ride!"

We had a hard time of it with O'Brien. Did you ever sit by and watch a strong man fighting for his very life with the outcome hanging by a mere spider's thread? That's what I watched then, for ten long days in that wilderness camp. I stayed with him because I loved him, but there was little enough I could do beyond waiting for whatever was to come. More than once—my soul, yes, a hundred times!—I thought we'd got to the end. Stooping over him I'd catch no faintest sound of the breath passing his lips; but then, as if the soul of him held to his body by the power of a very miracle, there'd come the lightest whisper, and I'd thank God for another brief respite.

I was his nurse, but I wasn't alone in the watching. Old Bates was kind, anxious to do all he was able. He wasn't forgetting the lumber business, though. It was his daughter who forgot everything else in the world but the man I tended. I don't know when she slept or found her own rest. Day or night, if I stepped outside the door of the room where O'Brien lay, there she'd be, anxious, distressed, getting thin and white as a ghost, waiting to question me. The Lord knows, it wasn't much I could tell her while those ten days lasted.

But then there came an afternoon when O'Brien's quiet seemed ominous. He'd hardly stirred since early morning, muttering a little now and then, and dropping back into profound lethargy. I didn't like it. But by and by he opened his eyes, looking straight at me. He knew me, too.

"Casey!" he whispered. "Good boy! I don't know—" But that was as far as he could get before he sank back into heavy sleep.

I went out of doors, and there was the girl Janet hovering near. She came to me directly, as she always did.

"How is he?" she asked—the thousandth time she'd asked that question, just so.

I didn't try to answer. Instead, I made her sit down beside me on the edge of the porch.

"Listen!" I said. "There's got to be a little true talk between you and me. Tell me this: Do you think I'm an honest man?"

She looked at me straight with the very soul of her in her beautiful eyes. The look was answer enough to what I'd asked.

"Well, then, tell me this besides," I said: "Which is it, do you think, that makes the safest refuge for a woman in this world—is it money, or is it the love of a good man?"

There wasn't a word from her for a long minute while she searched me through and through. In her heart she knew what I was getting at. Of course she did! She didn't try to dodge me.

"I believe in love above everything else on earth," she said bravely.

"Then I'm talking as an honest man to an honest woman," I told her. "If that man in there could wake next to the sight of your face, with that light in your eyes as I'm seeing it now, it would mean more than life to him."

Oh! I'd give the heart out of my body and count it a royal bargain if, just once before I die, for ever so fleeting a moment I might see that radiance on the face of a true woman and know it was for me! She didn't hesitate. She stood up and gave me her hand.

"Will you come with me?" she asked.

She took her place beside O'Brien's bed, bending over, lifting his hand gently, holding it between her own. The touch roused him. If I'm a judge, it would have brought him back from the dead. For just a moment their eyes met and held; then she stooped closer, and with infinite tenderness touched his lips with hers.

"My dear!" she whispered. "Oh, my dear!"

I went outside then. The rest of it was none of my affair. A little way off I threw myself down beneath the trees and felt for my pipe.

"All right, Casey!" I said. "All right! Old Peter will be pleased—won't he? Oh, Old Peter be damned! And Hollis be damned! No—God bless Hollis! Casey, boy, you've got the face of an ape yourself, but you know what love is. There it is, in there, right now. Love! It's just the one everlasting proof we've got that God's in His heaven and all's well with the world. The only proof we've got! Do you know another, now?"

But I couldn't think of any other. I don't believe there is another.

KATHARINE R WIREMAN

AMELIA MERROWS' FOLDED HANDS

Dorothy Donnell Calhoun
The Farmer's Wife, February 1918

A MELIA Merrows sat in the bay window, her hands folded in her ample lap. The little sitting room was full of gray shadows, stirring noiselessly in tune with the snowfall outside. An exquisite color breathed from the soft polish of old mahogany and the gleam of the brass andirons in the firelight. The red geraniums on the window sill gave out a spicy breath.

"It's 'most time for them to be coming," she murmured distressfully.

She pressed her face to the windowpane, peering out into the gray February dusk. Reassured, she hurried into the kitchen and fumbled on the shelf for matches, striking three in her eagerness before the oil lamp on the table was lighted. Then, holding it aloft, she turned and looked with a silent farewell about the little room.

White scrubbed pine table, cheery yellow painted chairs, shiny tin pans met her gaze like the faces of old friends. She made a little pilgrimage among them, giving them tender pats and prods.

"We're going to miss each other," she told them drearily. "It won't ever be the same again with a hired girl round. I'll have to sit in the other room and listen to her doing things wrong out here. My soul!"

Amelia drew a breath that was like a sob. "Forty-five years I've washed dishes and baked pies in this kitchen, and now I've got to give up and fold my hands for the rest of my life because Abel thinks I'm too old to work any longer."

Down the road sounded a flurry of sleigh bells. Hurriedly Amelia arranged her face in a smile of welcome. Its plump curves readily took on smiles. She had never lamented long over the inevitable. "Abel wanted me to have a girl because he thought the work was too hard," she comforted herself as she hurried to throw open the kitchen door. "Men folks don't set so much store by fiddling round their chores as women do. Bless men folks!"

The hired girl was a tall, gaunt person with sallow cheek bones and a general drabness that matched her cheerless name, Lizzie Gray. Abel Merrows shook his grizzled head dubiously when he surrendered Lizzie to Amelia's care.

"One thing," he consoled himself, "a girl as homely as she is won't have any beaux round coaxing her away. Ma'll get a chance to fold her hands. I guess she deserves folding after all these years!"

In spite of his brave assurance, Abel was secretly appalled at the vision his words evoked. Would he be acquainted with the new Amelia of the unfamiliar hands? A queer panic seized him as he plodded across the drifty yard. It would be strange, at first, not to see Ma bustling around dishing up supper, setting out one of her chocolate cakes, light as a feather, with strawberry jam between the layers.

It was in the nature of a pleasant surprise to find Ma herself stirring a savory saucepan on the stove as though no hired girl had happened. But, being as he was a man, indignation trod closely on the heels of Abel's relief.

"Where's that girl?" he demanded aggressively. "Why isn't she getting supper, I'd like to know?"

Amelia tilted the saucepan of stew over the blue bowl, dipping out the dumplings with a careful spoon. Her cheeks were delicately flushed; her eyes shone with the joy of her reprieve.

"Lizzie's gone to bed," she told him comfortingly. "The poor girl was all worn out traveling so far in the snow so I sent her right upstairs. You sit down and start in on your supper, Father, and I'll be right back. I want to run up with this bowl of stew so she can eat it while it's nice and hot."

The next morning the new hired girl had a stitch in her side and Amelia insisted on her remaining in bed. At intervals throughout the day, Amelia ran upstairs with doses of ginger tea and camomile. Abel's mild protest met with gentle indignation.

"Father! And you a deacon in the church, too! She may be a hired girl but it wouldn't be Christian of us to expect her to work 'round with a pain in her side."

Lizzie's stitch was a reprieve for Abel too. It put off somewhat the disquieting spectacle of Ma with her hands folded in awful unfamiliarity.

One week after her arrival the hired girl appeared in the kitchen, but even then Amelia hovered over her, ready to take the broom and dishcloth out of her hands at the first symptoms of relapse.

To be sure, when Abel came into the house from his afternoon trip to the village for the mail he found her rocking ostentatiously in the sitting room bay window, but there was always something a little breathless and flurried about her as if she had just that instant untied her apron; sometimes there was a dab of flour on her cheek and once he thought he caught a glimpse of the egg beater hastily concealed behind the row of geraniums.

When a chocolate layer cake with strawberry jam made its appearance in Lizzie's bony hands Abel voiced his suspicions.

"You've been doing the cooking ever since Lizzie came, 'Melia," he reproached her. "I'd know one of your layers if I met it in Africa. What's a hired girl for, I'd like to know?"

Amelia nodded serenely. "She seems real interested watching me cook. You can't expect old heads on young shoulders—and that reminds me, Father, I baked an extra cake and boiled a ham for sandwiches and I want you to take Lizzie down to the Methodist box social this evening. She ought to get acquainted with some young folks. We don't want her getting homesick, you know."

Two days after the social, Abel came in from his chores to find the hired girl standing on the table in the sitting room, her gaunt person arrayed in a beruffled white muslin dress, turning slowly while Ma basted up the hem. Scraps of conversation floated out into the kitchen as he hung up his cap and overcoat.

"An' then he ses, 'I'd be pleased to call,' he ses." It was Lizzie's shrill soprano, tuned to the pitch of pride. "He ses it just like that, Mis' Merrows—'I'd be pleased to call.'"

"Ruel Granger's a nice steady boy, Lizzie," Ma commented, evidently around a mouthful of pins. "I shouldn't wonder if he had intentions. There! That hem's ready to run on the machine. You go up and curl your hair and put that ribbon I gave you in the camisole and I'll have this done in a jiffy. Maybe you'd better lie down a spell. Trying on is tiring work. I'll call you, soon's supper's ready."

In the mirror over the sink Abel caught a glimpse of his face. It wore a slightly dazed expression. After supper he and Ma sat on the hard pine chairs in the kitchen listening to the creak of rockers in the next room where Lizzie, in all the glory of the ruffled muslin, was entertaining her caller. Ma listened to the murmur of voices, her lips curving in the little secret smile women wear in the presence of love affairs; but her shoulders had a weary droop. Abel eyed her anxiously.

"You look tuckered, Ma."

Amelia nodded cheerfully. "I am sort of tuckered. I guess I'll go up and go to bed. It's been a full day. That dress Lizzie's got on was one your cousin Emma left hanging in the spare room closet last summer. It was all yellow and I had a sight of trouble doing it up and ironing out the ruffles. I thought she looked nice in it, didn't you, Father, now she's getting a little plumper?"

Whether from the ruffled muslin or the additional plumpness, Ruel Granger soon progressed from the formal status of "calling on" the Merrows' hired girl through the intermediate stage known as "going with," to the pronounced attentions that belong to "keeping company." Lizzie began to crochet yards of lace while Ma, that her work might not be interrupted, washed the dishes and scoured the milk pans happily in the kitchen.

More often than not Abel would come down in the morning to find Ma building the fire and setting the coffeepot on the stove.

"Lizzie was out till eleven at the Ladies' Aid social," she would explain rather guiltily. "Young folks need their sleep."

At other times he would find Ma bent above the sewing machine, joyously working over her store of old clothes for Lizzie's adornment or baking a batch of sugar cookies for her to regale her admirer with when he came to call.

"Having a hired girl would be a good thing," he told himself musingly, "if only it didn't make so much work. Ma isn't really able to stand it. I don't know how folks that have two-three of them get along at all!"

He was still puzzling over the problem that evening when Ma plumped herself down in the rocker across the hearth, determination in every kindly line of her soft old face.

"I been thinking, Abel," she said firmly. "Lizzie's going to be married in the spring and it's natural for a girl to want to buy some things to start housekeeping with. The fifteen a month we pay her doesn't go far these days. There's just one thing it's our bounden duty to do and that's—raise Lizzie's wages! It's as plain as day."

Abel, groping in the mazes of his mind for words meet to express his views of

Ma's guileless plan, found instead a familiar phrase that had done good service in their life together.

"Just as you say, Ma," he nodded feebly. "Just as you say."

Accordingly, the hired girl's wages were raised and the weeks that followed were brimful of preparations for the wedding. Yards of unbleached cotton draped the sitting room; napkins, tablecloths in all stages of hemming, concealed Abel's pipe and farm paper from view. The air was redolent with the spicy fumes of baking fruit cake while Lizzie continued to crochet endless yards of lace to adorn the trousseau Ma was making for her.

Ma was gently radiant. "If our little Ellie had lived, Pa," she told Abel, "we'd have wanted her to have a nice wedding."

In May, Lizzie and Ruel were married. The little farmhouse overflowed with guests. Ma was everywhere, helping Lizzie dress, greeting the guests, arranging great platters of chicken salad and plates of cake on her best damask cloth in the sitting room, a busy, radiant little figure with excitement-pink cheeks and shining eyes.

Abel, jammed submissively into a corner of the bookcase, watched the simple ceremony wonderingly. He had always thought of Lizzie as homely, but today in the dainty white dress Ma had given her she seemed oddly transfigured. Perhaps it was the bride-look that all girls, hired or not, poor or rich, wear on their wedding day; perhaps, he mused dimly, she looked beautiful to him because she was going away!

After Lizzie and Ruel were on their honeymoon trip to Centerville and the last guest had gone, Abel Merrows and his wife stood in the bay window, looking across the fields, the sunset light red on their old faces. The breath of apple blooms crept about them from the jars and pitchers of the pink blossoms clustered in the room. Outside in the soft spring dusk a robin burst into song.

Shyly, Abel's gnarled old hand went out, seeking Amelia's. He drew her toward him and kissed her awkwardly, like a boy.

"Pa!" Amelia cried softly. "Pa! The idea—old as we are!"

But she was blushing like a girl. To cover her confusion she turned from the window and looked about the disordered room; the light of eager planning crept into her gaze.

"After all, I don't know as sixty-five is what you'd call real *old*," she said thoughtfully. "Pa, do you know, I don't believe I'll get me another hired girl—not right away. Now I've had such a nice rest and all, I shouldn't wonder if it would seem real pleasant to have something to do again!"

A VAGRANT VALENTINE

Daisy Wright Field
The Ohio Farmer, February 1916

"IS there anything for Miss Beulah Hoffman?"

Once a week for fifteen years this identical question, without the change of a syllable, had assailed the ears of the postmaster at Henryville. Once a year, perhaps, there had been a letter—certainly not oftener. Only gaudy circulars advertising soaps, breakfast foods, and new-fangled curlers, or stray copies of household and farm papers, were usually handed out through the tiny window in the railed-off corner of Silas Henry's general merchandise store to the slender, faded woman in the spick-and-span print dress and stiff gingham bonnet.

It would have been contrary to Miss Beulah's religion to have desecrated the modest gray cashmere gown and severe little gray velvet toque that she always wore "in meetin'" by putting them on of a week day. Well did Silas Henry know that gingham bonnet and white-and-drab dress, that might have been called Miss Beulah's marketing uniform. He sold her, regularly, once a year, nine yards of print and two yards of pin-checked gingham—of a pattern that scarcely varied. Most women of her height bought ten yards for a dress, but the little spinster had perforce to practice economy, and one yard less in a dress, while it mattered little to one who was not a stickler for fashion, meant a quarter-pound of tea in the little blue canister on the third pantry shelf—which mattered a great deal. Once a year, she bought a blue Dutch calico also, but that was strictly for wear in the seclusion of her own domain, being scarcely dressy enough for calling or marketing.

By some good or ill fortune, as you look at it, Silas himself was not in the office when Miss Beulah entered, having left a visiting nephew in charge of the store and post office. Now, this nephew, who was a college student when in good health, was taking a vacation on account of his eyesight and of course was hardly the person to distribute mail, but no one took any notice of that. He looked hurriedly through the pile of letters on his desk, and tossed out one.

Miss Beulah scarcely glanced at the address on the huge square, creamy envelope, which was of a suggestive heft and thickness, as she pushed it in between the tea and starch in her basket, and hurried out of the store, a heightened color on her thin cheeks that was positively becoming. At least, so thought the man who entered the store just as she was leaving it—a tall, well-set-up, middle-aged man, with a heavy brown mustache and warm brown eyes. He cast her an admiring glance, whereat Miss Beulah blushed rosier than ever, jumped into her rickety democrat and, clucking to Mandy, the white mare, drove away homewards at a brisk trot.

Meanwhile, a slim, bright-eyed slip of a girl, in a jaunty blue jacket and red Tam o' Shanter, tripped eagerly into the store and demurely inquired of the new clerk whether there was any mail for Miss Berta Hoffman? The college student, after another hasty survey of the little pile of missives on his desk, shook his head, but smiled engagingly as he did so, for she was an uncommonly pretty girl. But she took no notice of his evident admiration and friendliness, and frowned and pouted, and flounced out of the store as an angry child might have done.

"How can I help it, if nobody sends her a valentine?" complained Silas' nephew to the crowd of loungers about the stove.

"By sendin' her one yourself," answered one of the latter, much amused at his own wit. "That's Squire Hoffman's only girl, spoiled like all possessed, and with a temper of her own, I've hearn tell. And she's been goin' with Nate Hines fer the last six months. He's got plenty o' money, and he's free enough with it, when he's out with the boys. Funny he didn't send her no valentine."

"Looked like a squall comin' fer him, the way she stomped out," chuckled Uncle Ben Biddle, as he spat with the precision of twenty years' steady practice at the saw-dust box in the corner.

"D'you see what Miss Beulah got?" said the first speaker, leaning over to sever a generous slice from the end of Uncle Ben's plug. "Looked to me oncommon like a valentine."

"A valentine!" echoed Uncle Ben, bending forward to empty his pipe in the stove. "Who'd send her one? She's thirty-four, if she's a day."

"Fifteen years ago, Miss Beulah was the prettiest girl in Henryville—and she's kept her looks well!"

The speaker of these quiet but emphatic words was Ned Harland, the middle-aged, well-set-up man of the warm brown eyes, whose chance glance had deepened Miss Beulah's blush as she left the store with her letter. As he finished, not waiting for answer or comment, he turned quietly to the counter, took up his mail, and departed.

Uncle Ben pursed his withered lips and emitted a low, significant whistle.

"Ill—be—dummed!" he ejaculated. "After fifteen years, too. And they ain't passed a dozen words in private since, to my knowledge. Yes, it must 'a been him as sent it to her, tryin' to make up. But Miss Beulah's dreadfully sot in her ways, like all unmarried people. Now I wonder—" he paused reflectively, and the clerk leaned across the counter, scenting a romance.

"Did they have a quarrel once?" he asked, hoping to start the old man's flood of eloquence that usually was on tap when it came to village occurrences of long ago. Uncle Ben really was a walking chronicle of the village's past, and woe be to him or her who fancied any crime so thoroughly lived down that its ghost could not arise and walk again while his tongue still wagged.

"Quarrel? Not edzackly. They weren't the kind to quarrel. Something happened— nobody ever knew rightly what but them two—and they simply stepped apart, and have staid apart ever since—each too proud, I guess, to utter the first word that might lead to'rd makin' up. The weddin' was called off at the eleventh hour, and that was the end of it. He didn't threaten suicide and she didn't pine away, neither did he set sail fer foreign parts as the heroes of romances do; ner did she marry another fer spite. He went on livin' on his farm—and a fine big place it is, too—raisin' cabbages and calves and totin' 'em to market, and she stayed with her folks till they all died, and then settled down by herself, on what was left her—mighty dum little it was, too, if one can jedge by the way she lives. Never was Beulah Hoffman stingy, and it makes me groan innerdly to see the red come into her cheek and the defiant look in her eye as she drops her lone penny into the contribution box on a Sunday. She needs a husband, and he needs a wife—two poor, lone critters that they be—and neither of 'em got sense enough to see it."

"Maybe she has, but is too proud or too modest to let him see it. She could scarcely speak first, you know," reminded the college student.

"Thet's true enough, and women are queer cattle," assented Uncle Ben. "I ought to know, havin' married and buried four as fine wives as a man ever had, and trottin' peacefully along by the side of a fifth. Women is queer cattle, as I have said, and you can't make nothin' out of 'em. The only way to get along with 'em is to let 'em alone."

"If he's really sent her a valentine, as you seem to think," went on the storekeeper's nephew, unobtrusively removing the box of prunes that was in dangerous proximity to the storyteller's straying right hand and placing it on the other side of the stove, "won't that be the opening wedge, and probably mean their complete reconciliation?"

"Might be," announced the old man. "Like the Almighty, Cupid moves in a mysterious way. . . . Lem Hudd, pass me some o' them prunes, will you?"

Miss Beulah was hardly out of sight of the village houses, behind the hedge, when she dropped the reins and, taking the precious missive from its hiding place in her grocery basket, tore it open carefully, with fingers that trembled as with the ague.

A valentine! A thing of beauty, of velvet roses and gilt lace and celluloid cupids, that breathed romance and lost youth and future hopes, as rosy as the little god himself, who was in the act of impaling a bleeding heart! The heart could be raised, if you possessed the curiosity that Miss Beulah did, and underneath it, in gilt letters, were two lines:

To err is human
To forgive divine.

What could it mean? Who could have been the sender? If she had had any doubts from the beginning, they were instantly and forever removed when she saw in a corner three magic letters—the initials of the only man she had ever loved! N. L. H.

Miss Beulah, with loving care, placed the valentine in her bosom, as near her heart as possible, for hearts know nothing about getting old and such nonsense, but throb on just the same when there are wrinkles at the corners of the mouth and threads of gray in the hair as when dimples and curls charmed the beholder. The college student was right—she had long ago realized that there was a better life than the cold, distant one they were leading; a life that lead down the smooth shining path of love together, with a setting sun at the end, that they might watch hand in hand, like little children.

Now, she found that he had at last realized it, too, and there was nothing wanting to her happiness.

The question that agitated her as she drove old Mandy homeward was the one as to the propriety of writing him that his token was received, and appreciated. How else could she let him know that he was forgiven—that her heart yearned toward him as his heart did toward her? She had just decided on sending him a simple valentine with a suitable inscription, if she could find one within her means, when she reached her own dooryard and discovered a buggy before her gate.

She knew the old roan horse well enough. It was his—Ned Harland's! He had even preceded his plea for forgiveness! Her heart throbbed painfully, her hands trembled, but her voice was firm, even cool, as she answered his greeting.

But when he came near enough to hold out his hand, her heart melted. The thought of the cruel years of separation, all endured for pride's sake, was too much. Her lip trembled and a tear glistened on her eyelashes.

What man who loves, and especially who has loved a certain woman for fifteen years, can be expected to withstand her tears? It is little wonder that the rest of that greeting was spoken from closer quarters—to be exact, very near the brown mustache —and that the long-delayed wedding became a certainty within the near future.

"I was going to answer your valentine right away," she said shyly as they sat beside the fire later, his adoring glance on her downcast face.

"My—valentine?" The question was accompanied by an involuntary start on his part, but she did not see it because she found it hard, as yet, in the newness of their tender relation, to meet his eyes.

"Yes—and it is such a lovely one! The very first I ever had, Ned. What ever put it into your head to—ask me—that way?"

Ned Harland considered a moment. Suppose she were to find out that he had never sent the valentine, but that the sight of it, coming, as he supposed, from some unsuspected rival, had driven him to seek her again at the earliest moment, lest he lose her forever? She would only be hurt and humiliated, and fancy that she had been forward and unwomanly. So he only answered, compromising with his conscience on a half-truth:

"I suppose Cupid must have done it."

So happy Beulah never suspected the truth, but treasured the valentine—whose envelope had been destroyed long since—as if it had been gold.

After all, Ned Harland was probably right, for Cupid himself must have been on the job!

4
CHAPTER

STORIES ABOUT THE HUMAN CONDITION

"NOT all the blossoms of the earth gathered into one mass would equal the beauty that radiates from the brow of twenty years, and if all the tender light of the stars could be focused together, all the blue of the sky and the sea and of the mysterious depths of the forests, it would not make anything comparable, O youth, to the light in your radiant eyes when hope dwells there, and love. And yet there is something more precious, more moving, whose radiance is rarer than your freshness; it is old age, come through the crucible of human griefs, refined like pure gold."

—Pacific Rural Press, March 1905

Readers who whiled away their spring and summer afternoons on shaded porches, magazines in hand, or devoured their favorite periodicals by the dim glow of oil lamps on bitter winter evenings may have found escape in exotic tales of adventure or romance and emotional catharsis in stories of tragedy. But on the whole they wanted stories about people who rang true, who in some way seemed like people they knew. They wanted characters in whom they could recognize some human condition.

Stories on the human condition appeared often in the American farm and rural interest magazines popular during the early decades of the twentieth century. Re-reading these same stories today, one understands why.

Literature has lasting value only to the extent that it has meaning for the reader. Characters are lifeless if readers cannot identify with them, do not recognize their emotions or feel empathy for their circumstances, find in them no real human values. But when the characters ring true, plot, setting, narration—all the other things that may go into a story—may become less important. The human condition is universal.

Each of the stories that follows has a rural or partially rural setting. Still, each setting is different. The characters are both men and women. They are old and they are young. Their respective positions in life are diverse. Themes of the stories range from the optimistic to the nearly hopeless. Plots are both simple and somewhat complex. The individual styles of the writers vary immensely. Yet each of these stories has a common element; each is a story of human condition, a story that readers today may find just as appealing as did the readers of those magazines in which they first appeared generations ago.

The finely-drawn characters of a spirited young country woman and her boy friend in the city, separated by more than distance, do not seem strange to us; we feel rewarded when they are brought together again. Is it more difficult today to understand the grief of an old man who has lost his lifelong mate, or the loneliness of middle-age without companionship? Probably not. And we know that in our time, just as was the

159

case decades ago, giving up the familiar habits of a lifetime on the land can be unbearably painful.

All the stories included here could have been used in other sections of this collection. But they fit here better, given the extent to which they are character-driven.

The editors who chose the stories that follow for publication in their magazines may have professed little or no concern about how well the literature they presented would stand the test of time. They might be amazed at how we, in our time, find them virtually timeless. But they should not be surprised; the human condition hardly changes.

The Real Gal

Richard Washburn Child
The Country Gentleman, May/June 1915

THIS is a wonderful country. It is full of drama. Fortunes fly into the laps of us as we sit. Immigrants soon ride in limousines. You can find traveling salesmen making small towns with a line of collars, and reading Homer in the original on layover Sundays. A woman is a manicure yesterday, a mayor tomorrow. No bare spot in the middle of the Western prairies can give assurance that it will not be the site of city subways.

I love it, not because of its drama alone, but also because good old human nature goes right on in it. In spite of all the money miracles, human nature is with us. To all the heavy-thinking intellectuals—the unskilled divinities who want to dissect our national life and put it together again on some free-thinking plan, or play in some other way amateur papas and mammas to mankind—human nature pays no attention and fairly shrieks with joy when it is turned loose to play. America is a wonderful country; it is human nature's own year-round resort. That is the chief reason for my patriotism; I am for human nature.

I was coming up from Dallas, Texas, in the spring. Not that I amount to anything in this story, but it was when I was coming up from Dallas, Texas, in the spring that I saw the Creels.

Fate had prepared me for the Creels, because, just before we came to the river flats, and the ferry, and the sight of Vicksburg, perched on the bluff across the Mississippi with the bronze of a sunset on the clinging city, a loathsome man came and sat across the aisle. He was not a rough man; he was a coarse man. He was too coarse and too natty in his dress; he was too sleek and too fat. He had a cropped mustache. He was the fellow called "a business man." One sees plenty of him, especially at annual conventions.

He had a letter, the envelope of which was pale blue; it looked scented. He read the letter over and over, for it was some appeal to his vanity. He leered at it.

After a little I looked sidelong at the letter, and then I saw that it was all a scrawl of an unsteady, untutored hand, and that it began "Dear Daddy." I was filled with shame, and this mortification prepared me for the Creels.

There were two of them. They got on at Vicksburg. The first one came to stand in front of me, looking up at me in a friendly way out of two beautiful blue eyes, set in the most horrible distortion of a face I ever saw. It was a child's face all torn into shreds, drawn and pulled into white and lurid pink patches and streaks by sinews, nerves, and veins that had healed all askew. The lower lip had been drawn down and adhered to the chin. It was a nightmare face.

Don't move! Don't go away! I did not move and I am glad.

"You are lookin' at my face," the little boy said accusingly. He was about four, but he looked squarely into my eyes, asserting silently that he must not be held responsible for his exterior.

I did not deny that I was looking at his face. I did not tell him that he was all right. I did not talk down to him. I did the right thing for once—I talked to this Creel Number One as if he were my own age; I spoke to him on the level.

"Yes," I said. "You have been burned badly. No doubt of that. What is your name?"

"It's Pipe Creel," he said, putting both his hands on my knee. Pain had matured him. It had deposited grownup character in the depth of his blue eyes.

"My real name ain't Pipe," he went on. "They call me Pipe. It's for Peter."

"Where you going now, Pipe?" I asked.

"Way off to—to—some place," he said, leaning on my thigh and evidently trying to remember. "I'm goin' to see a doctor. I'm goin' to get my face all fixed."

This idea illuminated his eyes. He drew a deep breath into his sturdy little frame, exhaling it with a sigh that told of the great relief being "all fixed" would bring at the end of weary suffering followed by the consciousness that, to the world of strangers, he had been made into a sight to cause shudders. Now he looked into the strip of mirror between the Pullman windows at his own hideous countenance and repeated, as he looked away: "All fixed."

"Don't go, son," I begged him. "Sit down here with me. Tell me where you live."

He climbed up beside me, and though he took much interest in the ribbon of country unrolling in the dusk outside the train window, and though he played with the ratchet device that served for a window catch, and though he pointed out each isolated house where lights had been lit in kitchen windows, he succeeded in making very real the picture and the story of his home.

The art of this is personal; it is not a matter of education, class, or age. The banker may travel in a strange and distant country and bring that country back, dead; the cabman may go over to the north side of town and on his return make the north side live again. And so Pipe, instead of painting for me detailed descriptions, rather made me see and feel his circle of life.

His father's was a clear portrait—that of a Texan from the Black Waxy Belt, a man of sandy hair that a hundred brushes would never keep in order. He had been a planter.

The boll weevil, mortgages, a houseful of children, visits of scarlet fever, trading with cotton buyers, laughing with neighbors, squinting under the Southland sunlight, driving across the prairie into the teeth of biting northers had lined his face, marked out the character of justice which we see in the thin lips and firm horizontal mouths in portraits of great judges, but it had put crow's-feet of geniality at the corners of his eyes. Such a man could never keep his trousers creased.

I saw him now, a widower, three of his daughters evolved from awkward, stem-legged schoolgirls into young ladies, two of his sons almost old enough to help, and the new house with the carpenter's shavings still blowing about the homestead lot.

He had gone out of the planting business into ginning and baling. Three gins were his. Prosperity had not overtaken him; he had overtaken prosperity. Pipe told me of a new six-cylinder car. The father had tried hard and toward evening he had won. The girls went to seminaries; the boys could choose their own higher educations. The family still stood, proud of each of its members—a decent group, founded on old virtues, powerful in defense of them.

Unconsciously Pipe pieced out the panorama of his people. Finally he allowed me to put my arm about his little shoulders while he watched the black, black Alabama Negro "making down" the berths, and he yawned comfortably.

"And who is going to the North with you," I asked.

"Alice."

Alice was one of his sisters, I supposed. I knew an Alice once. The name brought a kindly thought.

"I've thought of the place now," he volunteered. "It's New 'Ork."

Accordingly I thought of the metropolis, with which I was so familiar. I thought of its lights, its traffic rectangles, its battlements. I thought, too, of Pipe, of hospitals, of surgeons I knew, of nurses in white caps, of the smell of anaesthetics, of Pipe's distorted face and of his hope that they could straighten out the muscles, the sinews, and relax the tautened skin and "fix" it.

I was interrupted. The second Creel had come to my seat in the swaying train.

"You mustn't bother the gentleman, Pipe," said the voice. I listened for it again without looking up, for it was a pleasant young voice—this voice of Alice Creel.

"Oh, Pipe and I are having a fine time," I said.

"He must go to sleep," said she, sitting on the other Pullman seat. Reaching over, she pulled down his absurd little pique kilts which had ridden up until they exposed above his stockings two round segments of healthy bare legs. "You will catch your death o' cold," she cautioned. "Father said you could have trousers when you came back, and I will be thankful. You won't come apart so much."

Pipe laughed with me; then I looked up, because I wanted to see Alice Creel. I wanted to see her, though of course I did not know then how large a part I was to play in her affairs. I wanted to see the owner of her voice.

No one could say she was beautiful. She was plain. Like Pipe, she had fine eyes— blue, deep, observant, clear aquamarines. The rest of her features were not perfect. The best you could say was that the light of life, quick sympathy, active intelligence, and common sense shone from a setting little less than ugly. Her hair, naturally a very light brown, had been touched and engoldened by the outdoors and the sunlight.

Nevertheless, as to her ugliness I was forced to remember that Nature loves compensation. It is astonishing how few human creatures are not endowed with at least one beautiful attribute. "The ugliest woman I ever saw," says Haviland Beers, my artist friend, "was the wife of an attache of the German embassy, and she had the most perfect ears that ever grew on a human head!"

So Alice Creel, plain though she might be—ugly, if it pleases you to call her so— had her eyes and the light of her countenance, and more than these her body, which would delight sculptors, and her wonderful skin. This skin was not browned by the sun; like her hair, it had been made golden, and with health it bloomed upon her cheeks and upon her strong young arms from which she had pulled back the linen sleeves of a waist that spoke of homemade designs and of a country dressmaker with a mouthful of pins and a handful of bastings.

"Pipe, you must let me put you to bed," said she. "You must be in the best of health when you get to New York."

"He's been telling you?" she asked, turning to me. "His father wanted to come, but one of his buildings is being finished. I had to come with Pipe anyway. So I just persuaded Dad to let us take the trip alone. I haven't ever done much traveling."

She took Pipe's left hand while he gave me his right—a warm little fist. As I let go of it and they left me, I leaned forward to clear my bag and scattered magazines from the other seat. I wanted her to come back when the little Creel had been tucked away. And she did.

The porter had been trying to drive everyone to his berth by rattling the mechanism of those that let down from the top, ostentatiously shaking pillows into slips, turning down lights in the middle of the car. I ignored him. I wanted to listen to Alice Creel. And she, on her part, had something on her mind, I thought, that made it a relief for her to talk, even to a stranger.

"I reckon we're a funny family," she said, looking at me to see how broad my understanding would be. "We all stand together—especially in time of trouble. But no doubt all families do that. It is just so now; I can't talk about much but Pipe. He has so much courage! The doctor says that repairing all these burn scars will be painful. Pipe knows it. Yet he is the one of all of us who wants to try the experiment."

I took the folded letter she offered me. It was on the stationery of a man who, because of his research as well as his skill, has leaped into fame in the last decade. It was merely a typewritten note of a few paragraphs, and evidently had been preceded by other correspondence.

Alice went on to tell me that Pipe had been burned because he had tried to smoke a "coffee cigarette" and had set fire to a calico waist.

"That was like him," she explained with a laugh.

I laughed too. "He could not be mistaken for a girl," I said.

"No," she answered, studying me.

"Do you know any folks in Texas or Vicksburg?" she asked, hoping no doubt that I could establish myself.

I spoke of an attorney in Fort Worth with whom I had been engaged in a legal matter. Fortune was with me—he had been her father's attorney.

"Hasn't that man the most wonderful sense of humor!" she exclaimed. "And what a flexible mouth! He was the one who got Dad to send me to normal school when I was eighteen. I'm the oldest and that was four years ago, just after mother died. I didn't want to go on that account, and then besides, I knew I never *would* teach school anyway. And then besides—"

"What is the second besides?" I asked.

She blushed. "I reckon there isn't any real second besides," she said with a wistful smile. She became silent.

I wondered what she would do in New York, where she would find rooms, whether there was any danger in her going there alone, and I concluded there was no danger. She carried an aura of her wholesome life and home out into the world with her. Sense and instincts of decency were adequate defenses for her, I believed.

"No, Alice Creel," said I to myself as I gazed out into the night; "you need not fear New York—little as you know about it, unsophisticated as you are. The spirit of that metropolis will bow down before you, for it recognizes that without what you and your kind can bring to it from the East, the West, and the South, it can never reproduce even its own yesterdays."

She might have read a bit of my questioning.

"I'm going to a lodging house where the Jacksons stop in the summer when they go North," she explained, showing me a card. "Of course I had to have a good place to stay while Pipe was in the hospital. Dad wouldn't have me in any hotel. He doesn't know anybody in New York except a cotton man, who is in Europe, and a machinery salesman he doesn't like. And I don't know anybody—that is—"

She stopped suddenly. Galloping along in her conversation she had come to a hazard too wide to attempt. I thought of the "second besides." I had a part of her story already, I believed. He was in New York—whoever he might be.

She went on to talk of New York. Somebody had sent her inside information about the city; she never could have gained so clear a perspective through the periodicals. I thought she might have received her picture from letters.

"I have no grudge against New York," she said at last with a sad little smile; "only I think perhaps their ideas and mine aren't just alike. And then, besides, I had a friend—"

She stopped once more, and stopping, she looked at me steadily, perhaps to see if she were wise to go on.

"It was a long time ago—four years ago," she continued with a movement of her hands expressing very clearly that perhaps after all the matter would not seem important to me.

"He went North?" said I, helping her.

"Yes, he went North. We were both young. 'Deed he's a year younger than I am now—and of course he was then too. Maybe I was romantic. I'm older now. But he had so much ambition and enough get-up-and-get in him to leave our town. Everybody said he was bound to be a fine, able man. I didn't pay any attention to what most people said, but Judge Caxton said so, too, and I—I was proud. I encouraged Zed to go. I felt I might have a part in his—his growth."

Thus she told me without direct words that she had been engaged to Zed. She had looked forward to life with Zed, whoever he was. She had told me about it, not because she was lacking in delicacy, but because her weighing of life's values was much more accurate than that of the women of my own family, who would doubtless have criticized her. She had told me because her perceptions were clear. She had dignity; she could afford to tell about herself. I thought so, as I looked at her lovely hands, clasped about one of her knees.

She had been engaged to him, or at least there had been a tacit understanding that they would fulfill their comradeship in man's and woman's way, going on together into long stretches of time and growth, toward combined, completed life. It is the rare, worshipful woman who, when the time comes, turns her back upon coquetry and contest and makes half of a comradeship like this. She was one. She was meant for marriage.

None but a fool could be so blind as not to see that to deprive her of marriage would be to block the purposes for which she had been created. I began to wonder what had been the matter with Zed—what had happened to him in New York in the passing of these four years.

"Of course he still writes," I said, feeling my way roughly. The story was none of my business and I knew it; of course I am not my brother's keeper.

She smiled. "I had a postal card at Easter," said she. "Zed has just faded away into New York, I reckon. It's not strange. And I am not at all a heartbroken young lady. Life is too big for that, isn't it?"

Her appeal to my judgment pleased my vanity; it was an appeal to one older and wiser, more experienced. I leaned forward, ready to justify her good sense in asking for my comment.

"Yes, life is too large," said I. "And the interest that I know you have is not in yourself; it is in him—in this man you call Zed, isn't it?"

"Yes," she replied. "I've wondered about that. A girl still thinks. But that's natural. I had looked forward a good deal. I reckon, though, the real reason I hate to think of the day Zed started for New York, is something to do with *him*."

"I suppose he has made a failure," I said after a moment. "Or perhaps—"

"Depends on what you mean by a failure," she interrupted. "It seems to me a man hasn't done very much like a man should do when he hasn't dared to write me that he doesn't love me any more. It seems so, too, when he has gone into things that back among my folks no one can see as a man's job—a real man's job, no matter how honest or respectable."

"We at least expect a man to be a good provider," I said in an attempt to give the conversation a touch of humor.

She laughed outright.

"Provider!" she answered. "A provider? Goodness, he would make the most wonderful provider! Last year he cleared over thirty thousand dollars and now it will be more."

"Zed?" I asked.

"His name is Victor Rees."

"Victor Rees! You mean—"

"Yes, sir, I mean that one—that is Zed. Rees who owns the Jardin des Fleurs. Young Rees who is paid three hundred dollars to exhibit his dances and ten and twenty dollars for a lesson. I don't wonder you stare. Nevertheless, that is Zed."

Not a sign of pride was on her face. Now at last when she had told me she had no pride on her face. She blushed as if she were ashamed.

This is a wonderful country; it is full of drama. Fortunes fly to us as we sit—or dance. Zed, the son of a Southland planter, goes to New York to begin his way toward a fortune and fame. At the end of four years he is Victor Rees in rubbersoled pumps and evening clothes. Ladies bring him roses. Reporters bring him queries. Photographers bring him proofs. Limousines bring him rides. The mail brings him new contracts from uptown and new bank balances from downtown. The makers of tobacco ask him to smoke their brand and acknowledge it in the street cars. The makers of bizarre society ask him to eat their dinners and confess his presence there. Who would believe that Victor had once run barefoot along a Mississippi River levee to pot bullfrogs with a sling shot?

"Yet it is evident that you still care for Victor Rees," I said with a rising inflection of inquiry.

She raised her eyes to mine.

"For Zed—the old Zed," she corrected.

"And you will let him know that you are in New York?"

She shook her head. "Good night," said she.

I stood watching her as she went down the dim-lit Pullman path between the green curtains.

"But I'd bet my last dollar—" I said to myself.

And following that thought I wrote in my notebook the New York address of Alice Creel.

There was a time when life appeared to me as the Greatest Show on Earth. I did not like to play the part of an actor in the sweat and dust of this immense arena. I was content to sit in the bleachers in the superior position of a fascinated spectator. To strive is only human; to look is more divine.

But sooner or later we all become involved in the controversy, and now it is not often that I can close the desk, turn the face of the clock to the wall, suspend the rules, and fare forth as an impersonal ghost to sit in the reviewing stand.

Alice Creel, however, had given me an excuse.

Having gone to the Jardin des Fleurs on Broadway at after-theater time, and having seated myself alone at one of the little white-enamel tables, I made my relations with the waiter firm by the obvious metropolitan method, and then, with half-closed eyes, watched the masculine evening clothes and the gorgeous-colored vanity of gowns at play. I knew that by and by Victor Rees would come out to dance under the vine-hung, bacchanalian ceiling, and that he and his diaphanous partner, followed through the mists of swaying cigarette smoke by the moonbeam lights of concealed calciums, would be fleeing here and there as if from the pursuit of the chatter and the laughter. I waited contented and amused in my solitude.

The women, who dragged their wisps of perfume about after the gleam of their arms and of their pink, excited faces, were no more personal than garden tulips blown by the wind. The men, whose evening clothes were dotted with the red glow from lighted ends of cigarettes, came and went without distinction greater than that of being figures in black and white. I was alone, wondering how much of this was joy and how much of it was fever.

Before me on a table the waiter had laid a magazine devoted to the dance. It assured me that here I could find the wholesome expression of youth, and happiness in the movement of health-giving exercises. But the odor of degeneracy, I thought, was in the air, faintly.

This was not America. I recalled the personality of my aunts. Beautiful they had been in their day and spirited, but I felt that they would have sneered at this Jardin des Fleurs with its leers and overfed, perspiring persons. Alice Creel, too, had been right about Zed. It was a matter not for philosophy or analysis. It could be decided by instincts. She had condemned it all by an authoritative word from one who feels, if not defines, the rightness of life.

"But at the bottom Zed too"—I began, and then I repeated that which I had said as I had watched Alice Creel going down the dim-lit Pullman path between the green curtains: "I'd bet my last dollar." I looked about then to see whom I knew among the dancers and the onlookers at the Jardin des Fleurs, for I sought an introduction to the famous Victor Rees.

Fortunately for the variety of my acquaintance among people and observation among things, I have been unable to stop scribbling even at those times when my profession showed jealousy. This leads to acquaintance with actors and artists, newspaper men and illustrators, cartoonists and moving-picture producers, musicians and promoters, songbirds and playwrights, vaudevillians and wallpaper designers, interior decorators and bill posters, editors and office boys. These are the camp followers of art; a brotherhood is among them. So I looked about me in the Jardin des Fleurs, and there I spied George Hallingham sitting at a table with Mrs. Verner Bostwick and Mathilde Cruiks.

George comes from the idle rich, but is not of them. Years ago he rejected the idle rich and took up with the camp followers of art. He is fifty, but persistently he has lived enough of each year outdoors to retain the appearance of thirty-five. He is a weak man in a large muscular frame, hiding behind the face of a great statesman and the dignified, calm, and deliberate mannerisms of a great diplomat. He is an amateur actor, an amateur author, an amateur gentleman. The only thing in which he is not an amateur is philandering. Stockbrokers always like to find him when they go out to play because Hallingham knows the vanities.

Mrs. Verner Bostwick, who sat with him, is called "Vernie" by her intimate friends. By day she is said to be an invalid, haunting the offices of doctors; by night she is youth and unimpeachable respectability with a craze to see that which is not respectable. She has a perfect nose. For the moment she is friendly with Mathilde Cruiks, who is a pretty little thing possessed of baby-blue eyes and a heart of darkness.

"How is every little thing?" said Mrs. Bostwick to me, after George had beckoned me with his finger. "We never see you except in the magazines." Mathilde, without waiting for an introduction, gave me her warm and perfumed little deceptive hand, which said, as if it had a mouth: "I am sure after all that you and I are to mean so much to each other!"

Knowing Broadway, I smiled at her patronizingly, as one would smile at some child of inexperience. The device was a good one; Miss Cruiks powdered her nose somewhat nervously.

"Know this man Rees?" I asked, twirling my inquiry about in front of each of the three upturned faces.

"Spent a week on Cotton's 60-footer with him last summer," replied Hallingham. "Rather an ordinary chap, I thought—devilishly bored all the time. Wanted to fish. Struck me he would fish in a bathtub if he took the notion. Said fishing reminded him of something or other—maybe it was home. Ask Mathilde."

"Despair!" exclaimed that golden creature. "Women are mad over Victor. He has those soft brown eyes. I confess I have been a victim. When he looks at you it feels the way Chopin sounds. You never saw such a charmer, my dear. Evelyn Gormand, from Salt Lake City, with a million of her own sewed up in the old mattress, almost made up her mind to take arsenic in her tea instead of lemon because he advised her not to divorce her husband."

"Mathilde!" cautioned Mrs. Bostwick.

"Let's have a party," Hallingham drawled. "I want to have a party. Rees will come along. He's 'bored to death,' he says. Mathilde can look into them eyes. You can meet him, Jim, and Mrs. Vernie can have another evening with celebrities."

The celebrity word vitalized Mrs. Bostwick.

"Here is his last dance now!" she exclaimed. "Then we can go over to the place that the police never close and drink it out of those long-stemmed green glasses."

"He is doing the maxixe with Miss Lily Wycoska," said Mathilde, as the lights were lowered and the imitation stars came out in the imitation sky.

"Her real name is O'Brien," Vernie added in her felinity. "The nearest she ever came to the kingdom of the Czar was when she carried a Russia leather handbag. Why don't you all watch this? They *can* dance!"

They could dance. They could dance well enough for me to twist my neck, which I find is not so flexible as it was once, so that I could watch them weave their graceful way as lightly as if they were stepping on the rays of the calcium.

The smell of chemical heliotrope, of the Turkish weed, and of wet glasses was in the air; the sound of yearning violins was beyond the dark and haze; and Rees and his partner swayed like flowers on slender stems, looking into each other's eyes with a kind of desperation that said: "I'll be your affinity or die in the attempt. If I don't properly ape the affections cut my salary and send me back to the table-d'hote cabarets." I was glad that Alice Creel was not there to see.

Hallingham had gone to bring Rees back to our table; as the dance came to an end both the women watched the perspective of aisle through which the thirty-thousand-dollar dancer would come. Indeed, when he approached, several minutes later, I could see that coming reflected in their faces. Mrs. Bostwick cast a look about her that said to the other white devotees of black men's dances: "He is to be *our* guest"; Mathilde touched the lace fringe at her throat with the pink tips of her fingers. A woman at the next table looked up as he passed, and said aloud and in a coarse voice: "Hello, Vic. I've been in Europe ever since. How do you like the color of my hair?" I was glad that

171

Alice Creel was not there to hear.

The first remark Rees made to me, in a voice that still retained a trace of the South, was: "You are not a New Yorker?" He had a face that seemed to have grown a film of mask over its surface, but through this film a trace of anxiety now showed.

"No," said I. "Not at all, in that sense."

The others, understanding me, all laughed.

"What do you want to drink?" Hallingham asked in one breath, as if rolling out an oft-repeated formula.

"Oh, yes—to drink," said Zed with resignation. "All right. One of those."

"To drink is an obligation one owes to society," suggested Mrs. Vernie B. "It is so awkward not to drink. That's all there is to do to have an excuse to sit down here, isn't it?"

"It makes a delicious mental world of half lights," added Mathilde, twirling her glass.

"Do you know—" Zed exclaimed, suddenly turning his youthful torso so that he could meet my eyes of inspection.

"Do I know what?"

"Do you know that living in all this swirl of food and bottles and glasses a man has to watch out for himself? Nobody does it for him. He gets to be selfish, because he has to be his own keeper, and it takes all the time he has to do that well. Tonight I'm taking my last drinks until October first. And the only man in the length and breadth of Broadway who will say that to me is—me!"

"Signs of youth!" said Hallingham.

"Signs of a stormy night," said Mathilde with her infernal wisdom.

"Signs of fear," ended Vernie, wiser than all. "And shall I say broken resolutions?"

I thought I could see in Zed's eyes almost an admission of the truth of her cynical thrust. He was tired. A moment later, however, he turned on me with a look of self-confidence on a face that showed a good deal of square-jawed strength, and he motioned toward me with a hand that also had the suggestion of power.

"What do *you* say?" he asked abruptly.

"The city will take exactly what you give it," I replied. "It is the characteristic good nature of cities, and this City of Cities, I guess, is the best-natured city of them all. It will give any of us a monument—or the morgue. And it doesn't even shrug its shoulders over one's choice."

"Let's go!" Hallingham exhorted us with his eternal restlessness. "We'll crowd into a taxi. Let's go!"

"And when these girls start home, what are you going to do?" Zed asked me, as we faced the buzz and late night laughter of the cafe that the police never close.

"You?" I inquired.

"Anywhere you say—except to bed. Do you understand my wish?"

I understood it perfectly. Zed wanted the half-lights of that forgetful night world of unrealities. Zed wanted to abolish time. He wanted to hear the rattle of late vehicles. He wanted to exchange stories with strangers and find old acquaintances in men and women he had never seen before. He wanted to slide out of the skin of Victor Rees and be only a human being, whom a word from a lady could transform into a gallant knight, an oath into a brutal fighter, a thought from a bartender into a philosopher. If this world of adventure is a stranger to you, think of it with pity, not hate. It is kind, tolerant, and loving. With its falsehoods are mingled great truths. With its fleeting moments, eternity is concerned. Let those who know it not cease their prattle. For purposes of my own I wished to enter this magician's land with Zed. I was thinking of Alice Creel. And said I to myself: "Now that I have seen him, I will still bet my last dollar."

"Oh, surely," I replied to his question. "I understand you perfectly. Nothing more agreeable."

It was evident that he had made a test of the question he had asked me, and that my answer satisfied him.

"Listen to me," he whispered later, when we were in the process of saying good night to the party that the gallant George Hallingham was taking to their respective gilt-and-bronze and bay-tree and brass-buttoned apartment houses.

"Yes," said I. "Good night, Hal. Good night, Vernie. Good night, Miss Cruiks. God speed you!"

"I have so much money it is a nuisance," Zed went on. "Let's understand each other. If I have a whim, from now on let me pay for it without reasoning with me, will you?"

"For whims—yes," said I.

"Good fellow!" said he. "What's your name?"

"What's yours?"

"Zed," he replied. I wished that Alice Creel had been there to hear. He had chosen to call himself "Zed" for me. He liked me. I liked him. Zed was the name he had used.

First we went to the Van Amberger—a hotel with great plate glass doors, a chateau entrance, a fake magnificence, a cafe where Negroes serve glasses behind heavy green portieres to famous novelists, infamous stage managers, gunmen, police captains, rear admirals, adventuresses, ex-prize fighters, singers of Irish ballads, congressmen, lady circus riders, and the somebodies and nobodies who are out after two.

There, where Zed created a stir, where he attracted the eyes of grim, old, gray-haired men and weak-mouthed young ladies, he took pains to tell me about his success, about his golden success; about the fuss New York had made over him; how he came to New York a raw Mississippi youth, green and tender; about the attentions which by and by were showered upon him; about the glamour and the glory and the gloating.

The perspiration came out on his forehead. He was stating his case. He was trying to establish himself. He was seeking desperately for dignity. He was asserting his record. He was reiterating his pride in his achievements. He was insistent.

But doubt was in his eyes—I wished that Alice Creel had been there to see it. Zed was not sure of himself, I thought, and I played him like a fish on rod and reel.

From the Van Amberger we went to Mannihan's. It is on a corner. Sawdust is on the floor in the back room and a case of apoplexy takes the orders. A man and a woman—riffraff in a corner—whispered confidences to each other, leaning nearer and nearer until one knocked a glass over and the liquid fell with a splash, covering the round table with a wet film that for many minutes supplied slow drops which tapped monotonously on the floor. The woman ceased her whispering at this terrible tragedy of the night, and examined the frayed edges of her sleeves about her thin wrists; the man only stared ahead, amazed, as at this moment he had finished living and was on the brink of nothingness and eternal space.

Only when three young men, who might have been clerks in a haberdashery, came in, did Zed and the others become gay again. Stimulant now raised his spirit. He required song and listened in attentive delight to the performance of one of these youths who could play Yankee Doodle by beating with his knuckles on his young, white, even teeth.

"What is the matter with you?" he asked me, in a whisper that could be heard everywhere. "You don't join in this party. I know. It is because you are growing old."

His reddened, feverish face was bent forward near mine. He licked his dry lips with the tip of his tongue.

"Old! Do you hear that?" he muttered softly. "So am I—thousands of years old. It is terrible to lose youth. Look at me! When I think of that I turn pale."

He did not turn pale. He was as red as ever.

"But there's nothing like a *full* life, is there?" he went on. "And success! And you hear people run down money. But money counts. Gimme a light, old man. These fifty-cent cigars—I'll have the same—yes, ask the others. Why do you stare at me?"

"I was wondering," said I.

He uttered a silly laugh.

"Come on!" said he. "Let's go!"

Let's go! It was the slogan of the city. It was also the restlessness of Zed's soul. Let's go!

So we went. Zed knew of an apartment where a hopeless invalid held after-midnight salons. He was a creature knotted with rheumatic deposits in the joints, motionless, and ever burnishing up his memories of days when he had hobnobbed with the crowd of old Broadway—Jim Fisk, Evelyn Adams, Corcoran, the actor, and so on through a list of names to conjure with once, now faded like withered old flowers. Whoever would might come before the daybreak to his studio, where there would be hot tea and the smell of burning sandalwood.

He lay upon his eternal horizontal plane with great eyes staring into the faces of the furrow-browed men and tired women, knowing, perhaps, that they would comfort themselves by the inevitable comparison of their lots with his.

A frightened woman of fifty, whose hard face was lighted by the red glow of a brazier lamp, said to me in a terrible whisper in the midst of the light chatter: "What does he think of when he is alone?" I could not answer. I could not begin to answer; besides, I was watching a young thing who continually laid her hand upon Zed's.

"Don't do that!" he said to this girl at last. He examined his fingers to be sure no change had taken place in them because of her touch. "Don't do that. I don't like it."

As we went, her companion said to her: "Great heavens, Flo! Don't you know who that was? It was Vic Rees, the dancer."

And Zed looked at me under the light in the tiled corridor with a twist of distaste on his face.

"That's me," he admitted.

He said it again, but only to himself, as we stepped out into the city, where, as on the sea at dawn, one can count on a fresh breeze from the cool, moist lips of the new day.

Everything was gray: The luminous gray of the sky in which the stars are paling; the gray of the half mists which sway at this hour between the sleeping, shut-eyed fronts of buildings, great and small; the gray of early pigeons strutting on the gray, bedewed asphalt; the gray of lone figures of men who walk like gray and frightened ghosts; the gray which here and there is shocked by the yellow glare spilled out like liquid on the pavement in front of some nickel and porcelain all-night lunchroom. I wondered if Alice Creel was still asleep.

"You're not tired?" said I.

"No, no! It has all risen to my head now," he replied with a burst of gaiety. "I've been depressed. But now—"

"Good!" I said. "What now?"

"The sunrise!" he said wildly.

"One never sees it in the city," I said. "In the city the sky is nothing. In the city there is no sunrise."

"By jings, I can have a sunrise," he said, as we turned into Broadway. "You can buy anything here in New York. I'm going to buy a sunrise. Do you hear me, you weird old thinker? I'm going to show you the power of money. I'm going to purchase a dawn!"

"Wait a minute."

But he would not listen to me. He dashed across the aching emptiness of Broadway, across the broad expanse of street as shiny and cold as a serpent's back. To my shout of inquiry he answered over his shoulder and pointed upward at a great new hotel. He unbuttoned his light overcoat and showed me the gleam of his white evening shirt which in the half daylight was so incongruous. He pointed upward with his gold-mounted malacca cane. He shook a roll of bills.

"Come on!" he called. "Come on! Breakfast in the roof garden! In evening clothes. I'll order sunrise and grapefruit and coffee!"

It was a mad idea, I thought; the roof garden had been closed for hours. The elevator man shared my notion. But two ten-dollar bills pressed into his hand tingled his nerves upward toward his brain. He nodded.

"Now don't be a fool and tell the management," cautioned Zed. "Let us out on the roof and then send us coffee and rolls for two by a bell-boy, or waiter, or anybody you can buy. There'll be the same in it for him." He smiled at himself in the elevator mirror. "Oh yes—order grapefruit and *sunrise*!"

Rees knew his ground. The elevator man was newly shaven; I thought the varnish-glossed surface of his face would crack with a grim, dry smile of cynicism—and token of willingness. Twenty minutes later we were sitting in a desert of green tables the color of weathered copper. The wind had dropped, but it had left the smell of the salt and open sea behind, and this fresh smell contested the aromatic vapors arising from our coffee. We leaned for a moment on the parapet with our elbows, gazing out over the cubic waste of endless buildings below us; over their tops to the silver thread of the East River and the brown bridges on which cars were crawling; at the somber city beyond, with the flashes from its blast furnace, and then at the pink of a morning sky which suddenly burst into red and gold!

"The sun!" cried Zed. "See! The sun!"

But when I turned toward him he had leaned forward with his face in the cup of his hands. All his bravado, all his gaiety, all his vivacity had gone. When he raised his eyes I thought they were moist with tears that would not flow.

I said nothing. Presently, with the sun staring full into his face, he shook his clenched fist at the city below.

"Damn you!" he cried out to it; "I'm sick of you. I've loved you too much, you false thing!"

He was shaky.

"Rather extreme," I suggested in a cold voice.

He looked at me a moment; then, reaching over, he grasped both my hands with his own, searching for comfort. Back of it somewhere, no doubt, was the old yearning for the long-ago sympathy of some lost personality. But I would do. So he expressed it to me, squeezing my fingers till they hurt, speaking in a low and trembling voice.

"I like you," he said. "You understand. I want the things I haven't got. I want the cheap little things—the common life of common people. I want a home. I'm afraid of all this stuff I feed on here. It's poison. These beautiful creatures. They are terrible! And I—I'm only a high-priced clown!"

He coughed. He clung to my hands. He changed without thought to his Southern drawl.

"I want to see a woman once more! Do you hear? I want to live up to her—day after day. I want to see a real gal again!"

"Yes, yes, I understand," said I truthfully. "No doubt there will be those who do not. I know what you want, Zed. Will you take a chance on coming on a little ride with me, right now—this minute."

He laughed without mirth. He believed I had misunderstood, that I only sought new diversion. To be agreeable he nodded, and rising, without touching his breakfast, he followed me down to the street. There I tore a page from my notebook and handed it to the driver of a taxi.

The house where we stopped was without distinction. It was an old-fashioned brownstone front in a side street. Ancient pretensions which it had made had been outdone by the march of metropolitan elegance. Zed followed me up the steps, whispering inquiries about it that I would not answer. He shrugged his shoulders as we waited for someone to come to the door.

I held a whispered conversation with a dame in curl papers and middle-age; the door was closed and we waited a moment more. When it was opened again we were beckoned in.

"She says to come in there," the dame informed me.

I took Zed by the elbow. I turned the glass knob on the black walnut panels of the "front parlor." I pushed him in and pulled the door shut so hard that it rattled the shades on the gas chandelier above me in the dim hallway.

Waiting was not pleasant. The hall had a stuffy odor. I sat on the bottom step of the stairs, wondering what feet had worn the rose-patterned, brass-bound stair carpet. I counted the *fleur-de-lis* figures in the wall paper; there were twenty in a line from the baseboard to the plaster-of-Paris molding. A paper boy threw a morning edition into the vestibule beyond the ground-glass panes at the entrance. Far upstairs someone was drawing a bath.

After a time people came downstairs and went out—men and women—nice, commonplace, respectable bachelors and ineligible ladies, I suppose. I did not count them. I did not count the time. I was too tired. I waited.

And at last the door of the front parlor was opened, and it was Alice Creel who came out.

I saw her in the gloomy light. She was plain, but she was golden. Her hair had been touched golden by the sun, and her skin was golden. She was healthy, wholesome, and meant for marriage. None but a fool could be so blind as not to see that to deprive her of marriage would be to block the purposes for which she had been created.

"Thank you," said she to me.

That was all. As she said it, it was enough. It explained that everything had been well behind those black walnut doors. It was gratitude in truth. It was like Alice Creel. It was like her almost infinite ability to understand and to make understanding.

"He will wait for me here, and of course when they telephone him later he will come to me," she said.

I shook my head from side to side.

"I did not tell him," she went on. "I was afraid he would not let me go."

I shook my head again.

"It is this morning," she said with a laugh. "They are to fix Pipe's face this morning. And they are going to use my skin. You knew that?"

This had never occurred to me, and now I suppose I tried to express some admiration for the bravery.

She only laughed.

"Why, it happens every day! I've read of it in the papers over and over. You mustn't make anything of it. The doctor says it is nothing. I'm the happiest girl you ever saw. He's going back home with me. Don't be silly. Tell Zed if you want—but only after nine o'clock."

"Did he know I was waiting?" I asked.

She laughed mischievously. "I don't believe he cared," she said as she left me.

I went into the front parlor then. Zed was looking out the window between the stiff lace curtains.

He turned and smiled at me without a word. And I said to him, as I said a little while ago:

"This is a wonderful country. It's the year-round resort of human nature. And human nature is our best bet."

"Ain't it dependable!" said he.

THE LOST PASTURE LOT

Birdsall Jackson
Successful Farming, March 1909

FULL of sunshine was the June morning when Uncle 'Bijah Thompson drove slowly homeward in his rickety old calash-top wagon. Charley, the iron-gray, shambled on in front, drawing the vehicle just fast enough to keep ahead of the cloud of dust they were raising. He had long since learned that this was the only condition set upon his progress, and rolled along in his usual overfed complacency.

Wild roses besprinkled the hedges, filling the air with fragrance, and the trees looming over them cast patches of shadow across the roadway. Content rested upon the fields of rank-growing grain, content hung in the pellucid air above them, and content reigned in the heart of Uncle 'Bijah.

On they went, rattling down over the little bridge at the foot of the hill, then up again on the other side, the sage Charley cocking one ear forward in reconnaissance and inclining the other backward to assure himself that the whip stayed in the socket where it properly belonged and old Uncle 'Bijah sitting back comfortably and stroking his patriarchal beard with satisfaction.

The long rows of corn on the hillside enfiladed past them, first diagonally ahead, then straightway at the side, then diagonally again behind. Then the quince-tree hedge near the homestead swung into line, and beyond this came the whitewashed palings between which Aunt Mary's peonies thrust their beauty upon the grateful world.

When they drew up at the barn, the plethoric Charley heaved a deep sigh of relief and rattled the harness with a vigorous shake, expressive, doubtless, of his hope that some day it might come to pieces and fall from him utterly; and Uncle 'Bijah rose slowly, lowered his lanky frame to the ground, straightened it, and began to unharness, whistling and chuckling softly to himself.

"Goodness gracious! 'Bijah—why couldn't you have stopped at the house first and told me about it and unhitched afterwards? You are the provokingest man I ever lived with."

Aunt Mary, with blue and white checked apron thrown over her head, was coming toward him with eager steps.

"Didn't know you had lived with any other man," said he, turning away from her to lead the horse into his stall.

She stood looking after him patiently, almost pathetically. Forty years of household care had stamped the crowfeet at the corners of her eyes and set the dark circles beneath them; forty years of hard labor had given her shoulders the heavy droop typical of the farmer's wife. Her voice trembled with anxiety when she spoke again, as he came out.

"Tell me, 'Bijah, quick. I can't wait any more. I've waited so many years. How did you make out?"

"All right."

"Then it's sold?"

"Yes, contract signed and money enough paid down to make it good."

"And the price, 'Bijah, the price?"

"What we agreed on before I went."

"Forty thousand dollars"—she spoke in a half whisper, as though scarce comprehending, now that the fact was accomplished, "forty thousand dollars! What will we ever do with all that money?"

"Now ain't that just like a woman? Wishes for something, and works for it, and prays for it thirty-odd years, and when it does come, 'What'll we ever do with it?' says she. Mary, I'm 'most ashamed of you. We'll do what the rest are doin' with it, the ones we've envied all these years."

"But how did you ever get him to pay that much?"

"Well, I've always been pretty good at a business transaction. You know that. If I hadn't been, that five-thousand-dollar mortgage would be right here on this place, as it was when we started."

She looked up at him with silent assent.

"After talkin' with him a few minutes I could see he wanted it bad, so I asked my price and stuck to it. 'You're asking too much,' says he. 'You don't have to pay it,' says I. 'It's only worth about half that to you,' says he. 'But you're the one that's buyin,' Mr. Hilton,' says I. So he went up five thousand at a time till he got there."

"Well, I'm glad it's settled," said Aunt Mary. "But it'll be hard to leave the old home after all, some ways, won't it, 'Bijah? It'll be 'most like losin' one of the family. Think of what we've enjoyed here. I shall always love the place for that, no matter where we go."

"Why don't you look at it the other way?" he remarked quickly. "Why don't you think of what we've suffered here?"

"Well, 'Bijah, if I do, I'm not sure but what I love it just as much for that, too."

"I guess the forty thousand will make us whole for all we leave behind," said he.

They were now walking together toward the kitchen door. A flock of chickens trooped after them expectantly. A robin which had been hopping along on the white palings in front took wing and, alighting in the top of the big cherry tree by the gate, swayed up and down with blithe carol. Near the outer end of the grape trellis at the rear porch they stopped and looked about them—at the fields of flourishing grain below and the corn on the hillside; at the long line of five-rail fence Uncle 'Bijah had set upon his boundaries in the beginning; at the orchard he had planted soon after, pruned for a score of years, and gathered fruit from almost as much longer; at the piece of woodland he bought later to make his possessions complete. After a long pause, she turned to him again:

"Well, 'Bijah," said she, "I'm only sorry David couldn't have known of this. He was always talkin' about fixin' it so's you wouldn't have to work so hard. If this had only happened before David—before David—went."

There was a lowering of her voice toward the end, and a tremor upon the last word, the word she invariably substituted for that which she could never bring herself to utter.

He turned to her and spoke gently, even soothingly.

"He was just as anxious about you. And whatever else comes out of this for us, you shall never work so hard again as you have here, Mary, never again. I'll start in a day or so to look up a place for us to move to and we'll go right away."

And with hearts filled with joy, the old couple passed through the low doorway into the kitchen and thence into the sitting room beyond. The slowly moving squares of brightness on the floor by the eastern windows of the little room had not seemed so bright before in thirty years, and the clock upon the mantel shelf, the one with the pastoral scene on the front of the case and Gothic pinnacles on its corners, had never ticked so cheerily.

Many were their plans for the future; the purchase of some small homestead nearby with sufficient acreage to keep the old man busy, yet not enough to be a care to him; a house more comfortable and convenient than she had been used to; and, mayhap, some of the trips about the country which they had heard spoken of by others but had always considered wholly beyond their means. It was indeed an eventful day and a happy one for Aunt Mary and Uncle 'Bijah.

"'Bijah," said Aunt Mary as he came in one afternoon several weeks later, "I thought you were goin' to look up a place. We'll have to go right off, now that the deed has been passed."

"I know it Mary, but Mr. Hilton said we needn't hurry and I wanted to get our stock sold first. It's mighty exhaustin' work to sell livestock if you care somethin' about 'em and want to make sure they'll all have good homes. When they come after old Whitenose this mornin' and led her away, and Charley stuck his head out of his stall and looked around at all the other empty ones and then at me, as much as to say, 'This is a nice fix you're leavin' me in, here alone,' I don't think I ever felt so tired in my whole life."

"You do look played out, 'Bijah, and it's been hard on you, I know. But we're sure it's all for the best, and the thought of it will soon wear off after we leave. I think we'd better move as soon as we can find a place."

"Yes," said he, "so do I. I'll start right out tomorrow."

Every clear day for several weeks thereafter, the old calash-top propelled the sage Charley down the hill until its wheels rattled on the little bridge at the foot, whereat the somnambulist awoke and a cloud of dust arose in the midsummer air while the countryside for miles about was filled with the noise of their journeyings. From these pilgrimages, Uncle 'Bijah invariably returned despondent, but still hopeful.

Through some unknown agency, possibly that of the Gipsom girls, who had now been girls about thirty-five years and who conducted privately a very reliable information bureau, it became known that Uncle 'Bijah and Aunt Mary would buy a place if one could be found to suit them. After that, it was not through lack of neighborly advice that the purchase was not made forthwith.

On several occasions, upon receiving reports of an especially encouraging tenor, they set out together, eager in their quest and flushed with hope. But they were continually disappointed, and the summer waned away without any decisive action.

Others came to gather the crops Uncle 'Bijah had planted, whereat the patriarch, his round of accustomed duty steadily contracting, and for want of something better to do, went out to watch them at work. Nor could he forbear telling them how the harvest should be managed to best advantage. And when they answered him lightly, or not at all, and gave no heed to his counsel, the old man passed slowly homeward along the fence, steadying himself with his hand at the top rail, and betook himself querulously to his rocking chair for solace and rest.

"Who'd ever thought," said he, "who'd ever thought, Mary, that we'd live to see our place run over like this by a pack of numskulls who don't know a wheelbarrow from a mowin' machine? It makes me sweat all over to look at 'em. It tires me more than the work used to."

"Well, then, 'Bijah, stay away from 'em till we go. We'll be sure to find something to suit before long. You know I've been ready and anxious to leave these three months past."

"Not a bit more so than I have," the old man blazed. "You just show me a place that's laid out half-way sensibly for comfort and convenience, like this one, and a house where I won't feel like a cat in a strange garret, and a well of water that comes anywheres near the taste of ours and see how long I'll stay here."

Then followed several more days of fruitless search, and finally one at the close of which Uncle 'Bijah drove in wearing such an expression of satisfaction that Aunt Mary hurried out the kitchen door to intercept him.

"No, Mary," said he, "I haven't found what we want, but I've done the next best thing. I've got Mr. Hilton's word that we can stay here all winter if we want to. It seems he is going to turn the farm into a place where they play this new game—knock a little ball as far as they can with a club, then walk after it, so's to knock again, so's to walk again. On the way home," he added, "I stopped at the doctor's."

"Well, what did he say?"

"Said I was as sound as a dollar and good for ten years at least. Only one sign of danger, 'And what's that, doctor?' I asked. 'I don't hardly know how to tell you,' says he. 'You probably know already better than I do. It's your feeling that you ought to come here, or rather it's whatever is back of that feeling, what I might call the germ of the idea that you needed me.' 'Well, doctor,' I says, goin' for my hat, 'if that's all you can find wrong, I've got the germ of an idea that I don't need you at all.'"

"For my part, 'Bijah, I never did think it amounted to anything anyway," was Aunt Mary's comment.

With the coming of early autumn, the long rows of corn on the hillsides went into bivouac and the grain stacks in the adjoining fields, although lacking the military exactness Uncle 'Bijah exacted, stood guard above them.

For the most part, the old man kept closely to the house and his chair in the sitting room and, apparently, gave small heed to the changes, whether because he had no wish to note them or possibly could not bear to do so.

But late one gray afternoon in November, he went out and walked slowly though the fields, as had been his wont after the crops were gathered and all made snug for the winter. He came back at a shambling half-run with one hand at his breast. Aunt Mary saw him, ran out, and helped him in to his chair.

"Why, 'Bijah! What in the world is the matter?" she cried.

"The pasture lot!" he panted. "The pasture lot! It's gone! And the brook! The brook went too!"

He sank back wearily into the chair with closed eyes.

"You know the place, Mary, where I run the fence across the bend of the brook, so's they could go down and drink whenever they wanted to. Old Whitenose was there, just like she used to be. And when I went towards her with my hand out, in a flash, she was gone; and I was walkin' across on dry land. And the fence is gone, and nothin' left but one broad, open field."

She stood looking down at him in amazement and solicitude.

"There, there, 'Bijah! Don't go on so! You've run and got yourself overheated, and it's made you light-headed. They've taken down the fence and filled in the bend, I s'pose, in their improvements."

The old man sat for several minutes in silence. Then his faculties drew together and his mind slowly readjusted itself; the smoldering fire within him blazed up.

"Improvements!" he sneered. "Improvements! The fools! They've ruined the best pasture lot in the four townships! I'm goin' right off to see Mr. Hilton about it."

"Oh, don't, 'Bijah. Please don't do that. You can't change it any now. You'll only tire yourself all out again for nothing!"

But despite Aunt Mary's tearful protests, he rose, dragged himself to the barn, harnessed the old horse, and drove out.

It was nearly dark when he drew rein at the door of the Hilton countryseat and asked for the proprietor. But when the latter, who was just home from his afternoon on the links, came out and greeted him pleasantly, Uncle 'Bijah sat bent over in the dusk, fumbling at his whip and at a loss how to explain his errand.

"I thought you ought to know," he began, finally, "that somebody as taken down the fences and filled in the brook and ruined the pasture lot."

"I do know it—in fact, I ordered it done." Mr. Hilton's voice suggested good-natured raillery.

"Mebbe you didn't know it was the best pasture lot to be found in a day's drive," suggested the patriarch.

"Hadn't a doubt of it," said the other. "And now its going to be a part of the best golf links to be found in a day's drive, which, to my way of thinking, is a good deal better."

The impatient Charley lurched forward a little just then, and the light streaming from one of the front windows struck full upon Uncle 'Bijah's face.

"Great God! Man, don't look like that!" Mr. Hilton's tone and manner changed completely. "I wouldn't knowingly bring that look into a man's face for anything in this world. And I won't have my pleasure paid for so dearly as that by anybody. I'd rather lose ten times the few thousands I've spent on your farm than to have you feel so badly about what I'm doing with it. I insist on transferring it back to you immediately."

The old man's lank form straightened up in the seat as though a bullet had struck him.

"Not if you offered me twice what you paid for it to take it again. You don't know 'Bijah Thompson. I asked my price didn't I? And you paid every cent I asked. I never took water on a business deal in my life, nor went into one without lookin' on all sides of it. I know I've had spells of feeling tired lately, but there ain't anything the matter with me. And if there was, could ownin' a few acres of land more or less make me worse or better? No, Mary and I have acted for the best in this. It's just what we planned and agreed on. Why, Mr. Hilton, Mary and I have prayed for this over thirty years. And now we've got the chance, do you think I could ever look her in the face again and tell her I hadn't been man enough to stand by her in it? All the same," he concluded, "it's good of you to offer it, and I'm glad to know that dealin' in stocks don't keep a man from bein' a gentleman."

"Nor does farming," reciprocated Mr. Hilton smilingly.

Whereupon they shook hands, and Uncle 'Bijah drove homeward. Aunt Mary awaited him at the barn, helped him from the wagon, half carried him to the house, and, with much difficulty, succeeded in getting him upstairs to bed.

There the old man fretted for several days like a petulant child, now sitting up in bed to see from the window what was going on about the place, now sinking back again in wearisome complaint, assenting to his wife's plea that his interest was a passing one but invariably reverting to the same monotonous theme.

But finally, one bright, keen December morning, as Aunt Mary sat at her little sewing table in the sitting room, she was astonished to hear steps in the stair-hall adjoining and, before she could rise, the door opened and Uncle 'Bijah stood before her, fully dressed and as erect as in his prime. She was still more astonished when he walked with strong, firm step to his chair by the window.

"Why, 'Bijah! I never was so taken back in my life. I'm afraid this will be too much for you. I wouldn't have believed you had strength enough to get half way here."

"Well, Mary, I didn't feel as if I could at first, but you see I had to come. Why, I couldn't see down towards the orchard at all from the bedroom window. But I'm better, now I've got here. And stronger, yes, a good deal stronger. Only this pain gnaws me some here in the side. But I'm gettin' used to that, now. That'll never kill me. Oh, I'm good for ten years yet. Don't you worry about me. And I had to get up, so's to see if everything was all right at the orchard. I wish you'd come over, Mary, and run up that shade. Mebbe I've been dreamin' up there, but for several days I've been hearin' a sound, kinder dull and heavy, like clods fallin' onto something down in the ground. And this mornin' it was stranger and worse, more like something or mebbe somebody bein' struck by an axe."

Aunt Mary laid the white kerchief she was hemming upon the sewing table, crossed the room to the window, and raised the shade. At the first glance, the old man's hand went to his breast, and his whole body seemed to droop and shrivel before her.

"Oh, Mary! They're gone! The ones we set out first! All we planted before Davy was born! Don't you remember how he used to laugh and hold up his fat little arms to the blossoms? And how he cried one day, and ran and struck one of the trees with his fist, 'Tause you fwoded 'at apple down onto my papa's nose,' says he? That was Davy every time, lookin' out for his daddy."

"Oh, don't 'Bijah! Please don't! I cannot stand it!"

But he heard not, or heeded not. "And now they're cuttin' the ones he and I set out together. 'For your use, father, in your old age,' says he. 'No, for yours, when you marry and start out,' says I, and argued with him, not knowing he was right."

"'Bijah! Stop! Look here! Look at me!"

But the old man could see naught else but one thing. He had half risen from his chair, with one hand on the arm, and with the other plucking alternately at his beard and breast.

"But the old tree between! They've left that! That's the one his little swing used to hang from. Put it there myself, so's I could watch him from the cornlot. Back and forth, back and forth, he used to go, in the shade and out again like a shuttle. See! They're goin' right past it. They won't touch that one! They wouldn't dare!"

His voice fell to a whisper, a tense, incisive whisper, that pierced the stillness of the room like a dagger.

"Why, if they tried to cut that one, Davy'd come back and stop 'em. Oh, Mary! Look!" He pointed with one trembling hand. "Look! They've turned towards it again! And he is there now! And they're swingin' for him with their axes! Oh my God!"

The old man sank heavily into his chair, threw back his head, and sighed deeply. Aunt Mary bent over him for a moment in silence, then tottered in bewilderment to her chair.

On the third day thereafter, the astute Charley, neighing his protest against hunger and neglect, drew to his aid one of Mr. Hilton's workmen, whose curiosity led him thence to the farmhouse. He went in at the kitchen entrance, crossed the room softly, and swung wide the inner door. At one side of the sitting room, an old woman with bright eyes and shrunken features was swaying to and fro in her chair, droning weirdly as though to a child held in her arms, while at the other side the motionless figure of the patriarch sat by the window and stared out with stony eyes.

His Traveling Mate

Robert Carlton Brown
Farm Life, January 1916

THE tickling of a wisp of hay in the colonel's open mouth awakened him. He spluttered, and catching for breath, sucked the straw farther down his throat. Choking, coughing, and scratching away the hay, he made an opening through which he forced his apoplectic face. With his gaze fixed on the top of the stack, he dragged out one arm and rubbed the water from his weak eyes on the ragged coat sleeve.

"Mornin', and the rain's stopped," he commented blankly, squinting up at the rising sun. "Hum! Can't lay in the hay while the sun shines. Guess I'd better move along."

His wasted cheeks twitched sharply with pain as he hauled one stiff limb after the other. With a plucky smile, he crawled to his feet, rubbed a rheumatic thigh, and brushed, pulled, and straightened his clothes into a semblance of order. Then, reaching back into the warm cubbyhole that he had just vacated, he drew forth a quaint stick with a worn bone head and hobbled through the stubble toward the road.

A mile farther on he stopped, seated himself on a stone, and produced from the threadbare lining of his coat a frayed wallet. Unclasping the stout rubber band, he shook the contents of one compartment into his hand.

"Ten cents—ten cents!" he ruminated wistfully; not without an effort at brightening, however. "Just the price of a—hum, guess I need breakfast more'n that!"

The coin slipped back, to roll about lonesomely. Mechanically the colonel pulled up a leather flap, softly inserted a hardened, twisted finger, and drew out a ragged photograph. Listlessly he held it, not looking directly at it, and yet conscious of a strange sense of companionship, a warmth of friendship. With a caressing movement, he rubbed his harsh palm over it. Then, holding it close to his watery eyes for a moment, he pressed it to his lips, sighed, and quickly replaced it in the wallet.

"Mary, Mary!" he mumbled. "If she knew what I've come to since she went, an'—an' what this picture's kept me from!"

Then he arose stiffly and stumbled on his way, looking far ahead, but seeing nothing.

In time the colonel came to a town, wandered about till he found the local weekly newspaper, asked for the proprietor, and being shown to him, explained anxiously, eagerly:

"I can do anything in the shop. I was a quick type-setter afore—well, some time back—"

"All right. I can use you, I guess. There's a little copy here that you might work on this mornin'," the editor said.

Feverishly the bent old man clattered his cane on the table, drew off his battered coat and placed it beside his battered hat. Then, with a will, he went to work.

No compositor could work faster than he, though his eyes were dim and his fingers hard and tremulous. He smiled indulgently at his fellow worker, a far younger man, who watched the colonel's astonishing speed.

At noon the tramp printer shuffled into his coat and limped out into the street.

"Ten cents!" he repeated again, taking the worn dime from his old wallet. "Just the price of a—"

He paused a moment before the town saloon, clutched the coin in his hand, and started to close the wallet. Then a queer light came into his eyes; he opened the second compartment and saw the ragged edge of the photograph.

"She always said, 'Feed a man well, an' be a mate to him, an' he'll stay to home of nights'," he ruminated.

With another glance at the saloon, he zigzagged past it and ducked into a little lunch room.

"Coffee and a ham sandwich," he ordered. "Breakfast and dinner," he commented to himself.

Half an hour before his time he was back at the case. The editor looked at the rapidly filling galleys in astonishment, and went back to his work with admiration in his eyes for the capable old printer and a wonder in his mind as to how long he would stay.

It wasn't a great while before the question was answered. At five o'clock the colonel shambled into the office and interrupted the busy editor, perspiring over his literary efforts even in his shirt sleeves.

"Work's all finished up—guess I'd better move along," the tramp printer informed him.

"All right, all right, if you can't stay over," cried the editor, with a frown, not looking up from his work.

"If I've earned anything, I'd—I'd like to have it," ventured the colonel.

"Oh, yes, sure enough! Here's a dollar. That all right?" snapped the nervous little man.

"Yes, sir; thank ye, sir!" mumbled the old fellow in appreciation.

He hurriedly slipped the dollar into his trousers pocket, rustled into coat and hat, grabbed his bone-headed stick from the table, bid the editor a hurried good day and shuffled out.

Ten minutes later the rural litterateur signed a sample of best sarcasm "Vox Populi," and threw down his pen. Removing the stump of a stogie from his tobacco-browned lips, he looked at his watch, slammed down the desk cover, and stretched.

"Supper-time!" he reflected. "Well, I've earned my meal, I guess."

Springing from his chair, he caught up his coat from the table and plunged into a sleeve. The hand refused to enter the armhole. For a minute he tussled and fretted with the thing behind his back; then he pulled it away with a jerk, held it at arm's length and glared at it.

"Not my coat!" he cried. "Let's see—let's see," he mused dumbly. "There was that collection from Perkin's dry goods ad, and the money that Cummins paid me—whew, seventy dollars or more in it! Who's got it? Who stole it?" he shouted, tearing around the room and looking in the most impossible places for the missing garment.

Coming back to the substituted coat, he looked at it.

"Oh, the colonel—to be sure! Who else?" he cried suddenly. "And he's left me this thing of his. What drunken scoundrels all these tramp printers are! No wonder the old thief said a dollar was enough! Well, I'll never see him again!"

A creak of the stairs caused the energetic editor to spin around and face the open door. There was the colonel, mounting the last step. He advanced nervously, a hunted fear in his eyes. At the office door he hauled at his coat, removed it, stepped into the sanctum, and handed it tremblingly to its owner.

"Guess this is yours," he said in an excited tremolo. "I took it by mistake, an' didn't know it till—till I found your wallet with more money in it than I've had since—well, for many a day."

"Yes, you bet it's mine!" snapped the editor, snatching the coat and counting the money greedily.

"Guess I'd better move along," said the colonel, putting on his own coat with a wonderful sense of satisfaction.

Clumping down the stairs, he paused at the bottom and reached into the shabby coat lining. There was an anxious gleam in his eyes. His hard fingers clicked against the wallet; his eyes lighted. Holding one hand on the frayed leather, he threw back his head, squared his shoulders and started up the street. The lights of the corner saloon lured him.

Then mechanically he pulled out his wallet, unclasped the band, reached into his trousers pocket and placed the earned dollar in one compartment of the pocketbook. Lifting the leather flap, he inserted a hardened finger cautiously, and drew out a ragged bit of photograph.

"Mary, Mary!" he repeated softly, a bright smile lighting up his old face. "I missed you first when I couldn't get past that corner there. I was crazy when I thought I'd lost you!" He closed his fingers tightly over the battered picture. "But now I've got my mate again, an' in your company I couldn't very well stop at that place."

Clutching the old picture between a blackened thumb and forefinger, as if it were a sacred talisman, he walked squarely past the gilded palace and dropped on a little stool in the fly-infested lunch room.

"Baked beans an' coffee," he ordered, "an' make the coffee good an' strong."

191

AS A DREAM WHEN ONE AWAKETH

Jessie M. Heiner

The Ohio Farmer, July 1910

L'cindy walked slowly about her garden. Since the heavy frosts, its drooping border plants and ragged chrysanthemums presented a desolate appearance. As mothers are tenderest toward the weak or crippled one of their little band, so L'cindy viewed with a loving pity the stricken flowers, that so short a time past had flaunted their saucy faces in seeming defiance of wind or shower. Crushed was their pretty bravery—broken their gay spirit—ended their little playtime in the sunshine.

"You mus' res' a bit," she murmured, stooping and carefully covering with bits of rag carpet the dahlia roots. "Them thet allus are noddin' an' beckin' grow faded an' ugly. Them thet res' in quiet places gain a heap t'others never hev. You mus'n min', dearies—you mus'n min'."

Her voice sank to a soothing croon.

This annual farewell to her garden held much the same mournful pleasure that walking in the cemetery Sunday afternoon held—walking slowly—pensively chewing dried mint leaves, and reverently mumbling over the epitaphs of those who, boasting the last doubtful luxury of a marble headstone, slept dreamlessly.

The last root being covered, L'cindy passed up and down the walks in silent leave-taking. The pale afternoon sunshine had faded, and the air grown suddenly chill. A breeze blowing straight from the river fluttered her scant calico skirts and caught at the black sunbonnet hanging limply about her face. The western light touched unsympathetically the lines about her mouth and eyes. The latter were hopeful. Youth and its unfulfilled longings lingered in their wistful depth, revealing the heart of the owner. Dreamily she noted the fading light, the rugged lines of West Virginia hills showing darkly somber against the sky—the Ohio sluggishly crawling through its valley bed, the trees upholding boughs guiltless of screening leaf, to face the coming wrath of winter.

High revel of the autumn!

Bittersweet red on every hill; cornfields showing ragged shocks of fodder, ready for the winter's feeding and bedding; here and there in field or meadow, shining pumpkins—the unclaimed trophies of the harvest battlefield.

How many autumns she had seen slip away, gray and rain-drenched, L'cindy scarcely remembered—or cared. One was like unto another. A summer of her life counted with the yesterdays—the ingathering of herbs and vegetables from the garden, the tying up of sage and dried beans in paper bags, the filling of the woodbox. A little later the excitement of stuffing every crevice of the house with strips of cloth—strips guarded most sacredly through the summer from moths, awaiting this very autumnal service.

Then the winter, white and solemn; every day bringing its round of duties, its unconscious endurance of monotony; the impatient patience with her father, crippled and querulous, whose oft-told stories and asthmatic coughs were as the continual dropping on a rainy day; the quiet acceptance of her niece Maria, who lived with her, and whose exuberant vitality impartially expended itself on protracted meetings and barn dances down at Porter's Settlement.

Back of all, as a streak of light gleams whitely between clouds, was Jacob. This afternoon, when her musings had reached this timeworn and oft-lingered-at crossroad, her face brightened, and with one last backward look she briskly crossed the garden path to the chip yard.

Quickly she heaped a great basket with chips and, bending under the weight, carried them to the sitting room grate. A coal from the kitchen stove transformed them to things of beauty. How they roared and crackled, those mimic forest kings, shouting as if in glee at their own warm splendor! L'cindy knelt and watched them, her eyes reflecting the flame light. That blue curling smoke, that smell of hickory. How they cried of the woods and hills! The yellow light showed the whitewashed stone mantel with its blue jug ornaments; the wooden rockers; the canton flannel cat with green bead eyes, keeping guard at one side of the hearth.

The door opened noisily and Maria, tall and healthfully beautiful, crossed the room. She swung her bonnet to and fro, the little frown between her eyes unbending at sight of the fire. "Ef you hav'n lit the fire, Aun' L'cindy! Well, it's about time! I was a-wonderin' ef ever you was agoin' to, or ef we was to keep on chillin' to save a little wood. Aun' Tab's hed a fire nigh on to two weeks o' evenin's. Aun' Tab tol' me this afternoon as how everybody in Porter's Settlement has lit fires."

The voice, shrill and unmodulated, succeeded in expressing considerable injury.

L'cindy, with as much dignity as her stiff knees would allow her to exhibit, rose from the rug. For a minute she looked steadily at Maria; then, crossing the room to the corner cupboard, she produced from its depths a battered looking turkeywing. Spreading it fanlike, she carefully brushed the hearth and, seating herself, said quietly, "Yer Aun' Tab's a great woman fer burnin' an' wastin' an' not keepin' an' eye to the main chance. I've knowed her, in times past, to keep girls in the kitchen who, bein' fon' o' vegetables, would shif'lessly eat up the seed onions laid away on the lof'. When plantin' time'd come, yer Aun' Tab'd hev to turn out an' borry sets o' young onions. Uncle Nat Enderby used to be a well doin' man, but thet was afore Aun' Tab got to runnin' things with such a high han'."

She balanced the turkeywing on her finger as she spoke, a primitive scale of justice. When it fell floorwards, she considered the point satisfactorily settled, for with added dignity she carefully replaced the wing in that darkened mystery—the cupboard. Maria's face went darkly sullen at the references to her absent relative's extravagance. She kicked the fender with no gentle foot.

"You allus talkin' o' wastin', Aun' L'cindy, til I'm sick o' hearin' the very name o' waste an' save. Aun' Tab says as how if things is allus dinged in a body's y'ears, you git clean disgusted with everything. An' Aun' Tab says I'm gittin' to look as ol' an' fogeyish as you all, though I'm s'much younger."

Her red cheeks grew redder as her injuries, with discussion, piled mountain high. L'cindy, with half-bent body, moved dangerously near the edge of her chair. She kept creasing her apron and staring with startled eyes at Maria. The foot opposite continued its vigorous kicking to emphasize its owner's utterances, as the piercing voice broke forth again.

"Anyway, I jes' allus hate bein' without a decent thing to wear, an' hearin' folks' remarks every time I go down to the Settlemen'."

"Do folks—at the Settlemen'—say—things?"

L'cindy's voice quavered childishly.

"Ef you could hear 'em," burst forth Maria, "they say you all won't le' me hev my li'l' day fer savin' every cent to help Jake Sykes lif' the mor'gage off'n his ol' farm— jes' cause you all expect to merry him some day. Aun' Tab says as how some folks are bigger dunces than Thompson's colt, that swum the river to git out'n the rain. Jake Sykes don' mount to nothin', people down at the Settlemn' say. He never will be nothin' now or he'd a-cleaned off'n the mor'gage 'thout a woman's help. He has no idees of his own. He'd soon say 'twas night when the sun was shinin', if his ol' witch of a mother tol' him. Leastwise thet's how people down at the Settlemen' talk."

L'cindy's cheeks were a dull white. She looked helplessly at Maria—then furtively about, for some tangible object by which to weigh this revelation that was depriving her of speech, killing her courage—stealing the very life blood from her heart. She moved forward—and sank down on the gaily woven rug, at Maria's feet.

"Do folks at the Settlemen' say them things of Jake—an' me?"

"Yes, an' more," cried Maria, with the fine tact and feeling that such natures show when witnessing the first shivering dismay of the unsuspecting attacked.

"Don'—" L'cindy raised her poor shaking hand. "No matter w'at they say—don' tell me, Maria—don' tell me!"

To and fro rocked the thin body as though in pain.

"Hev I scrimped you, Maria? 'Deed I never meant to. You hev allus been my first tho't, fer sister Nell's sake. W'en your shif'less father deserted Nell an' you, 'twant his people thet opened their hearts to you. In them days yer Aun' Tab never come a-nigh us, even w'en Nell was dyin'." Her face worked painfully. "Ef you have'n as many things as some girls down at the Settlemen', it don't seem nateral to hol' feelin's agin a person who's fed an' clothed you, an' loved you better'n any one else."

Maria preserved a cold silence. She had fired her long treasured shots.

"I've allus hed sich a little in my lot, M'ria," pleaded the quavering voice, "nothin' but scrimpin' an' hopin' fer things that never come my way; mebbe I've got mean an' selfish. Do you think so, M'ria? I wa'nt blamin' you in anything min', but do you honestly think so?"

Maria shrewdly took her bearings.

"Mebby you are, Aun' L'cindy," she said slowly, "mebbe not s-much as folks say. Folks allus is sayin' somethin' or other 'bout somebody or 'nother. This afternoon down at Aun' Tab's quiltin' w'en they all was a-givin' you fits, I tol' 'em you wa'nt' as close as they all was a-makin' out; thet jes' as sure as my name was M'ria, you would gi' me a new white dress an' blue sash to wear to the dance down at Porter's Settlemen'.''

"Folks at the Settlemen'—talkin' thet way—an' me a-thinkin' them good friends!"

Maria nodded her head sagely.

"Aun' Tab spoke up an' said as how Cousin Betty'll hev a pink poplin, ef the money can be squeezed out'n Uncle Nat. It's my notion Uncle Nat's been squeezed too often to give in very quick like."

L'cindy's mind did not work quickly, under mental distress. She did not notice the adroit whisking in of the dress subject under the guise of her own defense, as held up by Maria. Everything seemed hopelessly snarled, and she was too tired to attempt getting at the straight of things. Many a time in the years gone by, Maria's baby cry at midnight had struck pitifully upon her ear, and jumping up, warm and drowsy, she had been sharply awakened by the contact of her bare feet with the cold floor. Some such shock in the last minutes had come to her. The drowsiness had passed away from her soul—the sharp awakening had come, and the chill of winter accompanied it. She peered at the fire. It was dying; and reaching for the basket, she piled on the few remaining chips, and unsteadily rose to her feet.

"I can go, Aun' L'cindy, an' hev my dress?"

A note of anxiety pierced the shrillness.

"Certainly, ef you care so much!"

"Care? You all don' realize how much I care. W'y Cooney Bean tol' Betty at singin' thet it'd be the biggest dance till Chris'mas. The boys are goin' to trim Milligan's barn with wintergreens. Three fiddlers are comin'. The regler one from the Settlemen', an' two from beyon' Pine Center.

"Cooney Bean says as how all the hitchin' racks down at Porter's Settlemen' won' hol' the horses an' mules thet'll come cross country the night o' Milligan's dance."

For answer, L'cindy took from the cupboard a small tin box. Fumbling in her pocket for the key, she slowly unlocked the box and took from it one of its rare gold pieces.

Before Maria slept, she had, in fancy, fashioned the white dress a dozen ways and whirled through as many dances with the goodly company that were to cross the hills on mules and horses, till of hitching space in Porter's Settlemen' there should be none.

Two evenings later, it would have been hard to find a more complacent soul as she carefully folded and packed the coveted dress, the blue sash, and a pair of cheap dancing shoes.

"We'll hev a great time dressin' tonight"—she laughed gleefully. "Cousin Betty allus gits in a rage w'en she dresses, 'cause she's so fat an' dumpy, an' her eyes and lashes so light—mos' the color o' buttermilk."

Maria complacently tied a crimson hood over her masses of black hair.

"Goo'bye, Aun' L'cindy. Don' look fer me till I come. Betty allus coaxes me to stop, an' Aun' Tab says she knows it's mighty lonesome fer me way up here, with jes' you all an' no one ever droppin' in, but thet simple Jake Sykes. Goo'bye, tell gran'fer thet he mus'n get any more wheeze. No, don' watch me out of sight."

L'cindy turned from the door with an odd sense of relief.

She replenished the fires, carried a basket of golden grain to the chickens, and housed them for the night. When she returned to the house, her father had hobbled to the kitchen window and stood watching the evening sky.

"Might be snow in them clouds, ef the win' don' raise, L'cindy."

"I hope not, father," anxiously. "I wonder ef Jacob'll clim' the hills tonight? He has'n been nigh fer a week."

"Tain' no long stretch ef he ain', L'cindy. Shucks! When I was co'tin' yer mother, I see'd her onct in six months. O'ny see'd her twice though, till I asked her dad fer her. I loved her jes' as well, an' better mebbe, than them thet see their pardners every week."

L'cindy creased her apron.

"I reckon he'll come tomorry—ef he don' come tonight. His mother ain' well. His cousin Milly's goin' to stay all winter. The ol' lady has tuk a fancy to her. Somethin' strange fer her to like anybody 'cept Jacob."

There was a perceptible bitterness in the drab-colored voice.

"Well, there's no dependin' on wimmen. Now w'en I was a young buck down at Salt Fork—"

L'cindy knew well the story that was coming, and through its present recital walked uneasily about, turning the geraniums from the window and watching the darkness settle over the hills. Down the roadside she could see the light streaming from the little chapel of St. Anthony. Often she sat and watched it, and as the night deepened, she fancied, yes, could almost see the gentle black-robed sisters pass in and out to prayers.

The wind was rising. It howled down the chimney, puffing the smoke into the face of the old man.

"No snow in thet win'," he said fretfully.

"Jacob mus' a give up comin'," answered L'cindy dreamily.

A day later, when she had grown quite haggard from watching, Jacob surprised her by suddenly opening the kitchen door and settling himself by the stove.

"Wy'y Jacob," letting fall the tin she was polishing. "We all thought you all was sick or dead, you hevn't been up the hills fer so long!"

"Sho, now, L'cindy—not dead!"

He carefully unwound an awful length of green and red yarn comforter about his neck, and with some dignity removed his coonskin cap. Awkwardly he stretched out his long legs, thought better of it and stretched them either side of the chair. L'cindy, beaming cheerfully, subsided at the other side of the stove.

"How's your mother, Jacob?"

"Quite porely."

"How's Milly?"

"Fair to middlin'."

His vacant eyes moved uneasily about the room.

"How's the stock?"

"Star's got the distemper, an' White Foot seems doncy."

"Maria's down at the Settlemen'."

"Sho now!"

"Some folks fin' pleasure a-runnin' to an' fro. Some jes' stan' an' wait, hopin' thing'll come their way, by an' by."

"Sho!"

"How's money matters?"

Jacob fumbled in his pocket for a minute, drew forth a small package and laid it on the table.

"That's the money, L'cindy!"

"W'at money, Jacob?"

"The money you lent me on the mor'gage. I can't keep it, seein' as how things air turnin' out."

"Turnin' out? W'at you mean Jacob? You'r welcome to't."

For the most fleeting instant, his eyes met her honest faithful ones, and then continued their vacant roving.

"'Tain' no use L'cindy," he said doggedly, "a-takin' on. I argeyed an' argeyed fer w'at seemed square dealin', but Ma'am she's thet sot on Milly—an' so I brought you back your lendin's."

"Sot on Milly?"

"Yep, on Milly an' me merryin'." He waved his hand airily to make plain his meaning.

"You an' Milly marryin'? W'y Jacob!"

"Thet's w'at I said, L'cindy. 'Tain't no use takin' on. 'Twar a long time ago w'en me an' you first talked o' these things, an' Ma'am's kind o' got scunnered out'n with the hull thing—an' changed her min'. But I argeyed fer you to the las'." He grasped his cap as if to show how firmly he had tried to hold ground, then with an air of finality settled it upon his head, slowly pulling it down over his fan-like ears. He glanced uneasily at the woman opposite. If she would say something or "take on" as his mother, laughing shrilly between puffs from her cob pipe, had predicted. But that white face— that breathless silence—those unseeing, unblinking eyes!

He tiptoed across the kitchen and softly lifted the latch. A gush of outside air revived his fainting courage. Starting away, he put his head inside the door, and called gruffly: "L'cindy, I argeyed fer you to the las'."

The morning passed—but L'cindy sat on and on by the stove, her elbows on her knees, her head in her trembling hands, vainly trying to grasp the new phase of affairs, to see in all its details the broken dream, that through so many years she had clothed with all the beauties of her loving and faithful imagination. The afternoon found her starting down the hill path, and a half hour's walk brought her to a shabby house at the very edge of Porter's Settlement. The grave old man who answered her knock grasped her hand warmly.

"I did'n' come to stay, Mr. Davis," she quavered. "I—we—noe o' us had paid our stipen's to the church lately, an' so I brought you some money. There's some over an' above, but you can use it as you see fit, to help somebody, or somethin' like thet."

The old man gasped at the roll of bills. "Why—why—Miss L'cindy!"

"Yes, keep it," she cried breathlessly. "It's some money I saved along to help, but it wa'n't needed for w'at I saved it." In an instant she had gone.

All evening the old man would have vowed that he had dreamed dreams or seen visions, if there in the drawer of the writing table had not reposed the two hundred dollars.

L'cindy went on into Porter's Settlement, stopping a minute at Aun' Tab's. Maria was boisterously voluble over the dance, and the fact that Cooney Bean and Betty were to be married at Christmas.

"Aun' Tab wants me to stay an' help get things ready," she whispered in parting with L'cindy. "Betty's no earthly account about mos' things, 'cept dressin' up."

"Yes, stay," answered L'cindy, dimly seeing in this temporary absence the days to be.

The early twilight had settled over the hills, as she climbed the path homeward. Suddenly something grazed her cheek—again and again. The winter had come! It was the first fall of snow! L'cindy stopped for a minute, her breath coming in little gasps. Her mind ran slowly backward through the years, to her little girl days—so long ago. She had stood at the window, her small hand clasped in her mother's, that dear mother, with the strong warm hands, and blessed mother eyes! L'cindy felt a rush of longing for the past joy. If she could but hurry homeward, and creeping softly in, lay her tired, bruised life down at that mother's feet! The ache was in throat and heart, as she passed through the garden and entered the kitchen.

The teakettle steamed merrily on the range. Through the half-open door, she could see her father sitting before the fire. He was shelling corn for the chickens' morning feast. In the basket he had found a blood-red ear. He held it tenderly in his old trembling hands, his face working with memories. Years agone, the husking, the bright-eyed girl at his side. She had found the blood-red ear! Later their great happiness—a few years—and the greater sorrow! So long ago he had lost her. "Into the shadow land," her feet had so early wandered. Almost traveled was the road for him, nearly lived the long day without her. Would he find her at the end of his journey, waiting? Who can tell?

There were tears on his cheeks as L'cindy crept quietly into the room. She saw them and the sight hurt her. Never before had she comprehended *his* loneliness or suffering. A great regret came to her, as for the first time she realized how little they had really been to each other. In the days to come, she would remember. She crossed the room and knelt down beside him, so that his hand rested upon her bowed head.

"You're lonesome, ain't you, father, w'enever I leave you? Well we're goin' to stay right by each other. M'ria don' need me, an'—Jacob—won't hev me, so we'll stay close together."

For answer the old man bent and awkwardly kissed her forehead; and in that mute caress, the bitterness of the one and the sorrow of the other were counted with the hurts of yesterday.

5
CHAPTER

STORIES OF COURAGEOUS WOMEN

"MEN have trained themselves to believe, and trained others along with them, that they are so constituted by right of sex as to be the 'sturdy oak' of the clinging feminine vine. This, alas, is mostly tradition. What truth there is in it comes from the fact that men, having taken the initiative and become aggressive, are better trained and more competent in a business way. If women had had the same training, the sexes would be neck and neck, universally speaking. The sad fact confronts us that men insist on keeping up the clinging vine tradition. The little woman who milks eight cows, feeds half a dozen pigs, cooks for a round dozen, cleans, scrubs, chops her own stovewood, makes her own clothes and her children's, trims her own hats and plants her own garden, and then maybe weaves rag rugs for her neighbors for recreation is, in her husband's sight, only a member of the weaker sex, a clinging vine, a zephyr, too frail to stand at the polls and vote, and certainly not capable of having ten dollars for her own individual disposal."
—The Orange Judd Farmer, November 1913

Those who tend to think of the modern drive for women's rights as a movement that took shape in the 1970s simply have forgotten important episodes of American history. The suffrage movement that ultimately led to passage of the Nineteenth Amendment to the United States Constitution, giving women full voting rights nationwide in 1920, actually was carried out state by state over preceding decades. These campaigns had succeeded in gaining women full voting rights in four Western states before the turn of the century, and at least limited suffrage in two dozen more, from Maine to California, before the Constitutional amendment. The names of suffrage leaders such as Julia Ward Howe and Frances E. Willard were well known to the American public. This meant that the suffrage movement was highly visible to most Americans during the first two decades of the century, and a common topic of discussion in the nation's newspapers and magazines.

The farm and rural interest magazines dealt with women's suffrage in predictable fashion. They carried editorials on the topic from time to time, generally approving the idea, and they offered their pages as a channel for the expression of opinion.

But viewed as a whole, the discussion we see in the rural magazines went well beyond the question of women's right to vote. It was more fundamental. It related to the full participation of women in the economic and social arena, as equal partners with men. The farm provided a perfect backdrop for the intense debate encouraged by the magazines; on the farm, the work load virtually demanded that women contribute a significant share of the labor. The question essentially was whether the woman's labor

201

was of equal value, and whether she shared equally in the rewards.

Short-story fiction in the rural magazines often used the woman's role as a theme. One common formula made a heroine of the long-suffering farm wife who asked for little more than a few household conveniences and a bit more appreciation from her hard-working husband. Gratification came easily, in the form of a pump in the kitchen so that she no longer had to carry water from the well or an agreement that she should have full control over the butter and egg money and thus be able to buy an occasional new dress or something for the home. But her fortune still rested in the hands of her mate, and the necessary step toward her fulfillment was *his* enlightenment and ultimate willingness to do the right thing.

Less frequent were stories in which the women truly were forceful individuals, competing in situations normally reserved for men. But when such stories did appear, they gave readers heroic and memorable women.

In the first of the following stories, the conflict faced by a courageous woman farmer stems not from the prejudices of men but rather from the caprices of nature. We find her most enduring because of her willingness to share. Two of the stories depict strong farm wives who struggle with problems created by less than perfect husbands. One is about a young country woman who responds heroically in difficult circumstances over which she has little control, while another tells of an old woman of remarkable spirit.

The stories included in this section were selected initially because they are interesting and convincing characterizations of strong women. They were kept, in the final analysis, both for that reason and because they represent an exceptional cross-section of the varied settings in which such earnest female characters appeared in the pages of early American rural magazines.

AN EARLY SPRING

Elsie Singmaster
The Farmer's Wife, March 1923

ARLY in the morning of March 30, Mrs. Taggart started nervously and opened her eyes. She had been awake until after three o'clock and it was not yet daybreak, so she could not have slept long. She felt stifled as she pushed back the covers. Usually one needed blankets in March but in this unseasonal weather a sheet was sufficient. There had been no real winter and it seemed now as though summer were coming without an intervening spring. For weeks, killdeers had been crying high on the soft wind, blackbirds and robins screamed and chirped on the ground, and doves sought nesting places in the bare trees.

Presently Mrs. Taggart turned to look out the west window. She watched the full moon setting languidly and she could tell that dawn had paled its brightness. At once she sprang up and, without stopping to put on slippers or bathrobe, entered her living room. Her house was a bungalow and the living room, thirty-five by twenty feet, occupied the southern front, a doorway with a hooded entrance in the middle. On one side were two windows, on the other the deep bay. Opposite the door was a fireplace, built, like the house, of native stone.

Mrs. Taggart knelt with one knee on the window seat of the bay and looked out. The seat was uncushioned but she did not notice its hardness any more than she felt the cool air of the large room. The room was unfinished, the built-in book shelves were almost empty, the curtains were of rough burlap and the furniture was scant and plain. Either the owner had planned to build only a substantial shell or his money had given out before he finished.

Mrs. Taggart looked on a gray world. To her right and left, on the summit of the highland, the masses of forest were pale gray. Below her was a dim gray abyss. She pushed open the window and, as though by her volition, the gray brightened and the outlines of the whole landscape became faintly clear. From her door to the plain far beneath and as far as her eye could reach on the gradual slope on either side extended even ranks of vegetation, too tall and dark to be grain, too short and uniform in height to be forest trees. On the miles of open plain the eye could dimly discern houses and barns, several villages and one settlement large enough to be called a town.

It was at the vague, even ranks beneath her and to the right and left that Mrs. Taggart looked. These were apple trees. These nearest her were her own, a hundred acres of York Imperials, a late-ripening variety with fine keeping qualities. This was the first year of their full bearing.

Upon this crop depended all Mrs. Taggart's hopes. Into this rugged land, secured at a bargain, she had put all she had in the world and all she could borrow. She had cultivated it with her own hands and watered it with her own tears. In her youth she had asked for fame as a singer and her voice had failed; she had then asked for love and had been cruelly deceived; now she asked only for peace and a livelihood from this land. If her trees bore merely a fair crop, she could this year pay her indebtedness, add comforts to the meager furnishings of her house, order books for her shelves and magazines for her table and lay her head upon her pillow in peace. Next year she could have a car. A half-mile away a state road crossed the shoulder of the hill and an hour upon it would bring her to Harrisburg where there was a library and where there were occasional concerts and plays.

She did not often allow herself the luxury of this dream, but when she did, her throat tightened and her eyes burned. She *must* not be cheated again! She was almost fifty and she could not make another beginning.

As she knelt, straining her eyes to look down upon her orchards, sudden tears rolled down her cheeks. That which she had dreaded as the last stroke of a cruel fortune was upon her. Her trees were not coming into bud! In the other orchards, twigs were green, and little leaves were showing. The owners were jubilant. They had feared frost but now that danger was past. Yesterday Mrs. Taggart had met Thomas Hoar in the road, he, standing beside his long car while his chauffeur changed a tire, she, sitting in her ancient buggy behind her ancient white Jenny. Thomas Hoar's orchards were like a rich mine or a gushing well. The storage plant in the town and a dozen farms were his. Even if he neglected to spray and prune and cultivate his trees, riches would still flow in upon him. But he neglected nothing to increase his crops and improve their quality.

He lifted his hat and smiled at Mrs. Taggart.

"Every prospect pleases. I hope your hopes will come true."

Mrs. Taggart uttered a grave "Thank you" and drove on. She would have liked to stop. She was impelled for one wild instant to ask Mr. Hoar to come and look at her trees which seemed less than alive. But she drove on. Her misfortunes had made her shy and she was now too sick at heart. A week ago she had secretly inspected Mr. Hoar's York Imperials on the lower slope of the hill two miles away. The twigs were green, the buds swollen thickly. By now there would be little leaves. The twigs on her own trees had a gray, unnatural appearance; there was sap in them but it was not the abundant, pushing sap of spring. She had had to buy her own stock as she bought her land, at a bargain. She feared she had erred fatally.

The tips of the forest trees above her were touched with yellow light and the gleam stole downward, gilding her sturdy, well-planted little house, her yearning face, her trees, the vast orchards on either hand and the great plain itself. A point on the eastern horizon brightened to orange, the rim of the sun showed, then a glittering segment, then the whole disc rose magnificently into a clear sky. Mrs. Taggart turned away and went into her bedroom and began to dress. The sunrise mocked her.

When she had re-entered her living room, the morning light showed its good proportions and designs and all the grandeur of the view from its windows. Here, with heat and food and books and an occupation and peace of mind, a soul contented with itself might establish paradise.

From the east end of the living room she entered her kitchen and made a fire. She hoped that this year she might afford coal for her stove. The constant tending of a wood fire was a burden and she wished to save the old trees in her woodland for her fireplace. But she could indulge this hope no more. If the bank which held her mortgage allowed her to stay, it would be only as a charity lodger in a useless house.

When she had finished her breakfast, she yielded to a temptation. She would postpone her dishwashing, feed her old horse and her chickens and then go down the hillside to look again at Mr. Hoar's York Imperials, two miles away. She would take a few twigs of her own and compare them.

She hurried across the yard to the little stable. She had expected to give poor old Jenny the reward of her long years of hard work by putting her out to grass, but now Jenny might have to serve her still farther in whatever price an old horse would bring.

Hurrying back to her house, she put on her old coat over her old woolen dress. She had no decent clothes. That was one of the reasons why she had not made friends with her prosperous neighbors, who wore furs in their elegant cars and lovely gowns at their evening parties.

When she had locked the door she stood still, amazed. It was not quite seven o'clock and she could not bear a wrap of any sort. She opened the door and, taking off her coat, went to look at the calendar. It was March 30—she had made no mistake. Such weather!

Locking her door again, she crossed her property on a downward and diagonal course. Here and there she broke off twigs and studied them. To her anxious eyes, they did not seem to have changed. They were not dead, but she was sure that they were dying.

Having passed through her orchard, she came to a stretch of woods which extended downward into the cultivated land. The moss was green, anemones and hepaticas were in their last bloom; the red maple shed a shower of blossoms on her head. She smelled the early bloom of some sort of wild fruit and she saw tiny white violets on a wet bank by the stream, blossoming a month before their time. The water weeds were a brilliant green and the cress had passed its tender deliciousness. Even the dogtooth violets were pushing their tender spears through the dead leaves. Frogs croaked in the marshy places.

She was not disturbed by the thought that Thomas Hoar might think it strange to find her on his land. There was little chance of his coming. Until the young apples formed there was no more spraying to be done and there was no reason why he should visit this orchard for days to come. She climbed the last fence, still clutching the twigs in her hand, and stood earnestly regarding the tree nearest her. Then she let the twigs drop. Here were little leaves. The difference between these trees and hers was not to be accounted for by difference in location. *Her trees were dying.* Her hopes were dead!

She stood for a long time by the fence, then she climbed over and took her slow way homeward. She reviewed her life as she went, preparing for another change. It divided itself into four periods. When she was fourteen her father had died; when she was sixteen, her mother. That was the end of childhood, of girlhood, of unthinking happiness.

"But I had ambition," she said aloud.

She saw herself still ardent, dulling her grief by hard work, spending her little patrimony in foreign study. She heard the praise of her teacher, the applause of connoisseurs, then she felt again the fierce anguish of that stricture in her throat. Her master had been too ambitious for her, had driven her too fast and too hard—ruined her voice.

"Then I thought I had love!" she said aloud again.

She was walking in the woodland, stumbling over roots and rocks. Love proved to be an apple of Sodom, bright and blooming without, ashes within.

"Then I had this place and my little house and my hope of earning a competence. Now I have only the dreadful necessity of living."

When she reached home, it was ten o'clock. Mechanically she finished her work in the kitchen, made her bed, put her house in order, and sat down on the uncushioned seat in her bay window. She had hoped to have plants here on the wide sill and she had a memorandum of measurements for a galvanized pan in which all the pots could stand. This was one of the simple luxuries she had promised herself.

Presently the direct heat of the sun proved overpowering even in the unheated room. She stood, withdrawn a little from the window, and looked down at her ruined hopes. No lord in his castle had had happier dreams than she in her little house until now.

When she had eaten her simple dinner she decided that she could go to town. She had a matter to attend to at the bank and she must buy coffee. Her supply would last only a few days. She could do without heat and she did not need a large quantity or a great variety of food but the stimulus of coffee she must have, especially if she was soon to meet ruin.

She hitched Jenny into the buggy and started down the hill.

Beyond her own property she came first of all to Mr. Hoar's orchard of Grimes' Golden apples. They were the first to bloom and already a green haze touched all the branches. She visioned not only this delicate spring foliage but the dark rich leaves of early autumn, a sumptuous tapestry dotted with golden globes. That was the way she had expected her own to look, only richer and more beautiful with darker foliage and red fruit.

Her business at the bank was the borrowing of money. She must have money and she expected no difficulty in getting it as long as it was not known that her trees would not bear. She had never been dishonest in the least particular in all her life, but now she must have money at any cost—at least enough to get away when the crash came. That it would come soon she did not doubt. A passer-by would see, perhaps had already seen, that her trees had a strange appearance. In another week they would show dark, blighted, conspicuous as a dead rock in a sea of living green. No chance of borrowing money then!

On the lowland, the unnatural forwardness of the season was more obvious. The grass in dooryards needed cutting, the willows had exchanged their yellow for green. Forsythias had already shed their yellow blossoms and so had peach and cherry trees their pink and white. Daffodils and hyacinths and tulips and masses of white spirea were in bloom and there were a few imported and prized magnolias in blossom a month too early.

Mrs. Taggart moved on slowly, chirruping constantly to old Jenny, who seemed scarcely able to set one foot before the other. The air grew heavier. Behind Mrs. Taggart, to the west and above the hills, the rosy edges of a few clouds were showing, but she saw only the clear brilliant sky before and above her.

In the streets of the town few persons were abroad and these were dressed in summer clothes. A gay parasol bobbed down the street and a few barefooted children played on the sidewalk. The clerk in the grocery store moved languidly.

"This is an awful day!"

Mrs. Taggart considered discussion of the weather bad form but this day was not to be passed unnoticed.

"Dreadful!" she answered, briefly.

"I say it's because we aren't accustomed to summer heat that it's so hard to bear."

"I'm sure you're right," said Mrs. Taggart, faintly amused.

She took her coffee under her arm and went out. Jenny's head had dropped over the pavement as though she were ashamed of the homely rig behind her. Mrs. Taggart patted her nose and said, "Cheer up, Jenny!" A hot wind had begun to blow; it lifted the dust and hurled it into Mrs. Taggart's face. She crossed the street, going toward the bank; then, with her foot on the step, she paused and turned away, her face crimson. She could not thus suddenly abandon the principles of her whole life! What had she been dreaming? She would go home and await destruction honestly, squarely. She crossed back to the other side, a tall, erect figure that would not be beaten, untied old Jenny and got into the buggy. As she did so, the curtains suddenly began to snap like sails. Jenny uttered a low whinny and Mrs. Taggart looked up at the sky. It was cloudless.

It was not until she got outside the town that she saw the clouds, massed high above the hill on which she lived. The air was perfectly quiet again; the landscape looked exactly as it had when she drove through it a half-hour ago. Yet there was a change. She tried to hurry Jenny, not because she anticipated a storm but because she wanted to get home. She thought of her home with yearning. She might not be in it long.

She had traveled almost an hour, making three difficult miles of the seven, when suddenly a shadow fell upon her and the buggy and the wide fields. She looked up sharply. The clouds had risen to meet the sun, which was about thirty degrees above the horizon. Moving swiftly, they covered it entirely in an instant.

Without urging, old Jenny started to run, but she could not run far. Before her mistress had finished her contemplation of the sky, she had dropped back into her stiff and broken stride. The wind lifted her mane and blew her tail to one side—she seemed to be holding back rather than advancing.

If Mrs. Taggart had been wise, she would have asked for shelter for Jenny and herself at the next farmhouse, which was the last between her and home; but she felt only a desire to get on. The sky was darkened as though the cloud had destroyed the sun but there was as yet no rain, only a hollow, roaring wind which wrapped the buggy in a cloud of dust. She looked forward hopefully to the shelter of the hill.

As the buggy tilted a little on the first upward slope, Jenny stopped short.

"Go 'long, Jenny," said Mrs. Taggart. "Only two miles more. Come, Jenny!"

Jenny took a dozen steps in answer to the friendly encouragement and stopped. Mrs. Taggart touched her lightly with her whip.

"Come, Jenny," she said coaxingly. "You'll soon have a good supper."

But Jenny did not stir. Mrs. Taggart got down and went to her head, holding to the shaft as she walked. Suddenly a chill wind struck her to the bone. She looked up, expecting snow or hail. But there was not even rain. She seized Jenny by the bridle and pulled it sharply. She was now a little frightened. Perhaps it seemed as though something was going to happen contrary to nature. The unseemly heat had been out of all order. It would not be strange if the restoration of balance were also unnatural. The strange green twilight was ominous.

"Come, Jenny, we must get home!" she said as though she were speaking to a stubborn child.

Jenny took a few steps; then, dragged by Mrs. Taggart, she took a few more. As she did do she uttered strange sounds.

Half way up the slope Mrs. Taggart was aware of an impending change in the aged horse. Suddenly the bridle was wrenched from her hand and Jenny staggered to the side of the road as though in death as in life she meant to be as accommodating as possible. There, the buggy crashing over behind her, she lay down.

Mrs. Taggart stood for an instant with her hands hanging at her side. There was no question that Jenny was dead; not a heart throb stirred her poor side. Mrs. Taggart shed a few quiet tears, then blindly she started on. There was nothing she could do until morning. She had taken a few steps when she remembered the coffee! Spilled! Its heartening odor reached her and she realized that she could smell it but that she could never gather it together. She stood for a long moment staring at the road. What, she wondered, would happen next? She had enough coffee—and other things—for several days and now a queer conviction that beyond tonight it was not necessary to provide.

The greenish light was darkening each moment. She surmised it was about five o'clock. At this moment the first heavy drop struck her cheek. On her cold skin it felt warm.

At half past five, wet and utterly weary, she reached her house. Dripping as she was, she fed her chickens, then made fires in kitchen and living room, changed her clothes and drew her curtains. Before the fireplace in her living room she sat down. On a table beside her were bread and butter, coffee, and a little can of delicate tongue. A friend, one of the few she had, had sent her a box of canned meats and fruit and of them this was the last.

Before she began to eat, she went to her little store of books and selected one at random. She took now a sip of coffee, now a bite of her sandwich and as she ate she read *Moby Dick*. There was sharp lightning, a few heavy claps of thunder, and the rain continued to pour for an hour, then abruptly ceased; but she was oblivious to all. Nature had restored her balance with less commotion than might have been expected. But Mrs. Taggart's heart was numb within her.

At about ten o'clock she went to bed. If she had looked out of her south windows she might have seen a strange sight. The whole hillside appeared to be inhabited. Instead of the two or three scattered lights which usually were visible from her window, there were a hundred. Some were stationary and some moved about. When the full moon rose in a clear, deep blue sky, it shone upon masses of white smoke drifting low among the branches of the pollarded trees. The moving lights twinkled far to the left, far to the right, and far down to the distant plain.

Mrs. Taggart opened the window which looked out into the woods and returned to sleep. She was conscious only of the weariness of her body and of the blessed softness of her pillow. Trouble can be so heavy we do not feel it.

When she woke, she saw with a start that it was eight o'clock. As she sprang up, the recollection of yesterday rushed back upon her. She would have no apples, she would pay no debts, she would lose her property. Thomas Hoar might buy the place, as he seemed anxious to extend his possessions until they included the whole country. Eventually he would root up her trees and plant good stock. He might put a tenant into her house or a summer dweller who would exclaim over the view.

When she heard a knock at the door, she thought of poor Jenny—possibly this was a health officer coming to tell her to dispose of the carcass. The buggy would have to be disposed of too; it was, she was certain, a hopeless wreck.

As she went toward the door she heard voices—there was more than one official! But even the sight of five men outside her lonely door did not startle her as much as the rush of icy cold air. The night had been quiet and her snug house had remained warm. Outside it was wintry. The men wore heavy coats—Thomas Hoar's was of fur. Besides Hoar there were three orchard owners and Harry Miller who had ploughed and sprayed for Mrs. Taggart.

Her first impulse was to offer them shelter from the bitter cold.

"Won't you come in?"

Thomas Hoar thanked her. She saw that he was pale and heavy-eyed and that all the company looked wretched, but her tired mind advanced no farther.

"No, thank you. We've been going the rounds and we stopped to congratulate you on your good luck."

Mrs. Taggart stared. What "rounds" had they been going on, and what had *she* to do with "good luck"?

"I don't know what you mean." She spoke stiffly.

"The crop is dished for this year."

"I know that," said Mrs. Taggart, her face flaming. What sort of men were these who had come to insult her? "I could tell that two weeks ago."

"You were smarter than we," said one.

211

"I had some fears till after the middle of the month," said Thomas Hoar. "But I didn't expect any such April Fool as this."

Mrs. Taggart wished she could close the door. But one must act with dignity. She realized that her callers were distressed—it was good of them to be distressed for her. A vague thought startled her.

"What crop do you mean?" she asked.

"Ours," answered Thomas Hoar. "Everybody's—except yours. Frozen. The buds are black. It's hopeless."

"But mine were gone already," said Mrs. Taggart. "The leaves were out on your York Imperials. I went to see. But my buds haven't swollen."

"You may thank heaven for that," said Hoar.

"You mean . . . What do you mean?"

"You'll have the only crop in the county, probably a magnificent crop, to sell at your own price." Hoar saw suddenly the dreadful whiteness of Mrs. Taggart's face. "Don't take it so hard," he said jocosely. "You have the latest variety and the coldest spot and stock which wasn't forced and land which, while it is good enough, isn't too good. It can all be explained. You are the envy of us all."

"Oh, don't envy me!" cried Mrs. Taggart, as the truth rushed home. "Don't envy me! If this is luck, it has just come in time. You have other resources and friends and you are all younger than I. I have only *this*!" She flung the door wide. "It's very warm and comfortable here. If you will rest, I'll make you some coffee. I can make it quickly."

"No, thank you," said Hoar. "We've had about a dozen cups since yesterday. We were up all night, doing what we could. We might as well have slept. If I can do anything for you, let me know. I can be of help about markets."

"I speak for your work," said Miller.

Mrs. Taggart watched them go down the hill, then she closed the door and walked to her bay window. There was no longer a shimmer of green leaves anywhere. The landscape looked as it looked in January; all the other trees were like her trees, but their buds were dead and in hers remained life. She thought only of herself. She began at once to plan what she should do. She must eat. She must see that poor Jenny was disposed of. She must give orders for the next spraying. She would go to the bank and arrange for a loan upon an honest expectation. A second-hand car seemed suddenly possible. She would see the dealer who had offered her one. She remembered a little interest which was due upon a tiny investment, an item which would not have mitigated her ruin but which was now an aid.

She looked down once more upon the sunny plain and as she did so other thoughts flowed in. She began to think of her neighbors. These men who last year had had ten, twenty, thirty, even a hundred thousand dollars for their vast crops could meet cheerfully one year's loss, but along the edge of the valley were little owners to whom the blow would be severe. There would be difficulty in providing shoes and clothes for little children; perhaps there would be actual suffering.

"I can help!" she whispered, as her soul aroused itself. "At last—once more—I can help."

ENOS B COMSTOCK

THE RATTLETRAP GUN

Samuel A. Derieux

Farm and Fireside, January 1921

TESS hardly saw the dishes she was washing, or the hot shabby kitchen, reddened by the setting sun, or her aunt Martha's sallow face. The girl's breath was coming fast, her heart was pounding, her pretty, sunbrowned face flushed with more than heat.

She started when she heard her father out on the front porch knock the ashes out of his pipe. He had driven to town that morning and he had said he would not be back until tomorrow; he had sent for Martha to stay with Tess. All unexpectedly, an hour before, he had driven into the yard. His face at supper had been swollen and red, his eyes hard and suspicious. Sometimes when he was this way he went to bed early, sometimes late. Tonight, she hoped as she had never hoped for anything before, that it would be early.

She waited, breathless, after the knocking of the pipe out on the porch, the water from the dishcloth dripping idly into the pan. Her heart sank when she heard him strike another match. She went on washing dishes and handing them silently to Martha. She dropped one, and as it shattered on the floor she almost screamed.

There was no occasion for Martha to stay now. She would be going home before dark. Tess started impulsively to beg her to remain, to confide in her, to ask her help. But Martha had been watchful that day, she thought. Tess had seen her talking secretly to her father before supper. And Martha's days were spent in ceaseless rounds of drudgery; her mind was as colorless as her face, her spirit as shrunken as her flat chest.

Tess smothered the impulse quickly, as if it had frightened her. She was afraid even to look at the older woman. She followed her out on the back porch. Martha lived a mile away through the woods.

"Come again, Aunt," she said mechanically, and leaned against the support of the porch.

Tess was a slender girl of eighteen, her bared arms shapely, her soaked hands strong with toil, her hair crisp and dusky, her eyes gray and brooding.

With a sinking sensation of loneliness and dread she saw this fellow woman shuffle off by a path that led through the flat cotton field to the blue horizon of pine woods. She saw the dusk rise out of the ground and swallow up the drab figure. She looked up at the pale green sky, out of which came the twitter of a few belated bullbats. She was alone in this house with her father—and Ben was coming out tonight.

She turned quickly, hurried down the hall to the front porch and stopped in the doorway, breathless. Her father still sat on the edge of the porch where he could see, across the cotton fields, the whole line of the woods—the woods in whose border Ben had said he would strike a match.

He was tilted back against the wall of the house; his bulk seemed to crush the chair. His clumsy shoes sat on the floor beside him, and his head was bowed slightly forward on his chest; but she knew he was wide awake—wide awake and silently watchful.

She tried to make her voice casual and weary, as if with the strain of the torrid August day.

"I reckon you're tired, Pa."

He did not reply.

"Ain't you goin' to bed?"

"No," he growled. "Too hot."

She collected herself quickly.

"There's a nice breeze in your room."

Again silence. She had gone too far to stop. She went to the other end of the porch and sat down on a bench against the wall.

"Seems like," she ventured, "seems like its cooler over here."

He looked toward her. In the weird mingling of the moonlight and the sun's afterglow she saw the blunt heaviness of his face, the yellow underlook of suspicion in his eyes.

"What's the matter with you, gal?" he demanded. "There ain't a leaf stirrin' nowhar!"

She leaned forward, her elbows on her knees, but the tune she tried to hum died in her throat. She still felt on her face the shrewdness of his eyes. She straightened up and looked languidly off toward the road with an air of tired indifference, her little foot swinging aimlessly. Still she felt those eyes on her. Her breath, panting to be free, choked her. She could not sit out here.

She got up and, eyes straight ahead, walked toward the door.

"Guess I'll turn in," she yawned.

"Tess?"

She turned in the door. "What is it?"

She knew he was trying to think of something ordinary to say—something to make her think he hadn't noticed anything.

"What is it, Pa?" she repeated.

"Whatever become o' that ol' rattletrap shotgun used to be about here?"

"It's in the plunder room. Why?"

"Sold it to a nigger today. He's comin' after it tomorrow."

"It ain't any good, is it?"

"Well, I'll have to file down the lock. It'll go off if you look at it."

She went eagerly into the house and into the plunder room. If she could only start him working on the gun! He was a child when he was this way, and loved to tamper with things. She found the gun, a heavy old hammer-and-lock affair. She picked it up gingerly—it might be loaded. She was as afraid of it as of a kicking mule. She carried it into his bedroom, and laid it fearfully on a table near the door, the muzzle pointed at the wall; then she went back to the porch.

216

"I put the gun in your room, Pa."

"What?" He turned on her almost savagely. "That ol' rattletrap?"

"You said you wanted it!"

"I never said no such damn thing! Great God, gal—you reachin' over them chairs for that ol' gun! Maybe loaded for all I know! Liable to go off if you crook yo' finger at it! Don't you never touch it again—hear?"

His hand shook as he lit his pipe.

"The file's in your room, Pa," she ventured, "if you want to work at it."

He had resumed his tilted position against the wall, his attitude of watchfulness. Now she thought he glanced quickly at her out of the corner of his eye. But she must not give up now.

"There's matches on the mantel, Pa."

He did not seem to hear, and she went back into the hall and leaned against the unfinished banisters of the staircase. She ought not to have let her aunt Martha go. She ought never to have gone out on the porch. Her father had been suspicious of her ever since he had the quarrel with Ben, and he was always doubly suspicious when he was like this, and doubly stubborn. She had done so much worse than fail!

"Oh!" She let out her pent-up breath. "Oh!"

She ran upstairs to her room under the hot roof, sat down in her only window and fanned her face with her apron. She saw the dim, hot red above the horizon of pines fade, the moon begin to cast shadows across the fields. Its light fell softly across her slender hip; it made an aura of her cloudy hair and dimly revealed her room, neatly furnished in contrast to the rest of the house.

Her father had papered it clumsily with his own hands—hands that trembled, for he had just got over a spell. Then he had driven to town and bought her a shiny new suite of furniture, hauling it home in his wagon and proudly calling her out to look at it. He loved and cherished her when he was right.

The roar of a train on the railroad three miles away brought her back to her situation. Sometimes after this train, Ben closed the station; sometimes he had to wait until the ten o'clock passenger; sometimes he had to work over his yellow express book until midnight. Her hand slipped into her bosom and closed over the note that an old Negro had brought her secretly that morning. Somebody had told Ben her father had gone to town, and he was coming out after supper. He wanted to talk to her, he wrote, about the cottage he had bought near the station. She could see it now, with the small barn behind, the trim garden palings, the cool water oak in the front yard. Ben was going to paint the house and barn white—if she liked white.

There was another note, too, hidden in her dress—the note she had written in answer begging him not to come, telling him that it would only make things harder, that her father would never give in, that he must never come any more. All day she had watched the road, sure there would be someone who could take it in to Ben. But nobody had passed and the day had worn away, and then her father had driven into the yard.

He had been worse than he had ever been, since he had the quarrel with Ben at the station about some express. She had not heard it, but neighbors had told her. It was terrible, they said. Ben had lost his temper at last.

"Get out of this station, you soak!" he had cried.

Men had rushed between them and dragged her father away. But at the door he stopped.

"If you ever step foot on my place, young man," he said, "I'll kill you!"

She would never forget his face when he came home that day.

"Don't you never let him come on the place again, Tess," he said. "Never again!"

The distant puffing of the train as it pulled out from the station startled her. If Ben left now he might be here in half an hour. Sometimes he came on horseback, sometimes he walked. If she knew when he was coming she would run out and warn him. But he might be detained at the station; her father might come up here while she was gone, looking for her.

She could not stay here. She jumped to her feet. A sudden dryness in her throat gave her an idea. Her father was thirsty when he was this way. She tiptoed down the narrow stairs, into his room. She picked up the pitcher from the washstand, and hurried out by the back porch, across the yard, to the well.

The screaking of the chain as her white arms pulled hand over hand in the moonlight filled the air with an alarmed scream, made the night alive. Maybe Ben, if he had reached the woods, would hear this, would come to the edge; then she would run to him quickly, warn him, run back.

She waited in the stillness that followed the screaking of the chain. No sound. She filled the pitcher and hurried up the back porch. For a moment she stood panting, looking toward the woods; then she went in, the water splashing on the floor of the hall. She hurried into her father's room, set the pitcher in the basin, and turned.

The moonlight, falling at a sharper angle through the window than it had done formerly, shone on her father's new double-barrel shotgun. It leaned against the wall, near the bed. Her father would come after this if he saw Ben. It glowed dull, satiny, sinister, there against the wall. She ran out as if she had seen a snake.

Her father still sat glowering on the edge of the porch. He looked up at her underneath his eyebrows, and she tried to smile. It was too hot to sleep, she said, and leaned against the wall.

"I fetched some nice cold water in yo' room, Pa."

He filled his pipe and lit it.

"Bring me a drink."

He gulped down the water she brought him, then handed her the gourd.

"More," he said.

He was holding the dipper out to her, his big, blunt face raised to hers. She could touch his bristly hair, thin at the top; he must hear her heart pounding above his ear. She brought him another drink, then she walked over to the steps and sat down, her head against the post, her hands clasped about her knees. Breast rising and falling, she studied his face furtively. She would tell him boldly Ben was coming, she would plead with him, if only he were not as he was tonight. He had liked Ben, at first, had bragged of him to her.

"He's a fine, sober young feller, Tess," he had said, "without no bad habits."

She knew, everybody knew, that her father was a kind enough man when he was right, too generous for his own good, impulsive, hospitable.

But, better than anybody else, she knew how far to go with him when he was like this. She knew how the animosities of one drunken spell remained stubbornly over until the next, how more and more, since her mother died, his worst moments guided his life. She had tried every way she knew to help him. Just once he looked at her with strange eyes. "I get lonely, gal," he said.

Everybody was afraid of him when he looked as he looked now, sullen, heavy, flushed. She was seized with a sudden loathing of him as he sat there, his sock feet up on the rungs of his chair.

A match was struck in the edge of the woods opposite them. It flared up quickly and was jerked out quickly, but it seemed to light the whole side of the house and her own face like the flaring-up of a rocket.

She looked at her father. He had not stirred. Perhaps, if he had seen, he thought it was a smoker passing along the road on the other side of the pines. They were thin here. But around them the road turned at right angles and passed in front of the house. Her father would watch for the appearance of the smoker.

She sprang up—sprang up too quickly, and remained standing. She must not seem to hurry; she must not make any more mistakes; but Ben must not strike another match. She must warn him—now. She crossed the porch, her eyes straight ahead. When she spoke her voice was unnaturally calm.

"Guess I'll turn in. Good night, Pa."

She ran up the stairs, pressing heavily on them so they would creak. At the top she paused, sick with fear. Then she tiptoed back down and stopped, out of breath, in the hall.

Through the window of the front room she could see his broad heavy back into which the head was sunk without a neck. The back was moving. Deliberately he was easing himself to the floor. He held his pipe in his hand as if he had just taken it guardedly out of his mouth. He was leaning forward, like a man about to spring.

She went swiftly down the hall and stopped at the bedroom door. Her father would come after that new gun, glistening there against the wall. She darted into the room and grabbed up the new gun. She left the old one, the rattletrap, on the table where she had placed it. After she had run out of the room she wished she had hidden that other gun. But it was too late now; he might be coming; she had thought she heard him rise.

She darted out on the back porch, across the sandy yard, white as if snow had fallen, along the hot fence, into the shadow of the barn. She looked across the fields between her and the woods, white with a weird secret brilliance.

Once she was out of the shadow of the barn, the moon shone on her with bald brightness, revealing her flight. The cotton was up to her waist and the open bolls scraped her free hand like fuzzy worms. She hugged the gun to her body; it stood no more ready to her father's hand. As for the rattletrap gun, probably he wouldn't see that. It lay in the shade, and her father didn't see very plain when he was as he was tonight.

She ran into the shadow cast by the pines, then stopped and looked back toward the house. She could see the end of the front porch. Along the straight edge where it joined the house she made out a protuberance. Her father had risen and was standing there against the wall.

She started to scream, but that would bring Ben running. She could only wait, panting, here. A stick cracked in the woods and her father jumped off the porch. She could see his burly body above the hip-high cotton, his white shirt, his hair in the moonlight, white like an old man's hair. He broke into a crouching run toward the match that had struck and the stick that had cracked. He looked like a white ape, bent forward, running.

It would not stop him to scream. He would understand, he would rush on at Ben. She pointed the gun at the moon, shut her eyes, and pulled convulsively. Both barrels went off. In her excitement she had pulled both triggers. The kick staggered her; the echoes rolled from the amphitheatre of woods like an army firing. When she opened her eyes her father had stopped. He could not see her here in the shadow of the woods. He turned and ran toward the house. She heard him stump up on the porch, down the hall, into his room; she heard his muffled, maddened voice calling her upstairs. She looked at the gun in her hand and smiled.

Somebody was running along the edge of the woods toward her. She could see him brushing through the cotton, see his white shirt, then his white face, then hear him panting. He caught her hard by both shoulders, his eyes burning down into hers.

"Ben?" she whispered.

"Are you all right, Tess?"

She nodded and smiled.

He straightened up with a profound breath, brushed his hat off his head, ran his hand over his hair.

"I thought you had shot yourself!"

"I stole the gun," she said.

He was looking toward the house, his head and shoulders rising above the shadow into the moonlight. He seemed to swallow something hard down his throat.

"Here," he said quickly. "Give me the gun." He unbreeched it. "It's dead," he gasped, and drew out the empty shells. "Stand aside, Tess—there, toward the woods."

She backed away, her eyes on his face.

"Here, Ben?"

"Yes."

He stepped boldly out into the moonlight. He was looking toward the barn, as if he were trying hard to see something.

"It'll be all right, Tess," he said. "Sure it'll be all right. Just don't move."

His gun flashed an arc through the air as he waved it toward the barn.

"Stop, Bill Simpson! Stop, man!"

Out of the shadow of the barn her father had burst and was hurrying toward them,

as she had seen him hurry toward the cotton pickers when they were loafing. There was something in his hands, thrust forward at the hip. The moonlight flashed on it—the rattletrap gun she had put in his room.

She smothered the cry that came to her lips; she fought down the momentary dizziness in which the silvery field of cotton swam round and blurred. Just a wistful glance at Ben standing there bareheaded, terribly tense, terribly watchful; just a longing in her soul that he might go back to his yellow express papers, to his cottage that he wanted to paint white—and the girl had darted out of the shadow ahead of him and was running toward her father.

"Git out o' the way!" he yelled. "You fool!"

He went on filling the night with his yells. He raised the gun—she was in front of it, and he lowered it with a choking oath. For all his bulk, he jumped aside like an athlete and raised it again.

She sprang suddenly forward and caught the barrel with both hands. Clinging to it, she was jerked powerfully back through the cotton. He was twisting and turning the barrel viciously through her hands, his face horrible with its effort. The muzzle was pressed against her body below her breast.

"I ain't going to turn loose!" she panted. "Never—never!"

She closed her eyes—she heard steps running up behind her. Again she was jerked back; again the barrel twisted this way and that. Then he had stopped still and she opened her eyes. He stood panting above her, his protruding eyes on her hands clenching the barrel, on the muzzle pressed into her breast.

"Hit's the rattletrap!" he gasped.

He choked and swallowed.

"Hit'll go off!" he roared. "Hit'll shoot you!"

"I don't care, Pa."

He was shaking all over; his soaked shirt was clinging to his arms and shoulders.

"Look, gal—into yo' pa's face! You remember—the ol' gun! Won't you turn loose? Turn loose for your pa, like a good gal?"

He was looking above her now, helplessly.

"Hit's a old gun, Ben," he was panting. "Hit's cocked. I'm all shakin'—I'm afeerd to let the hammers down. They're wore out. Ben, you want to see her blowed all to hell? Don't touch her, man!" he screamed. "She might jerk! Here gal—see? I turn loose. Easy, gal, easy! Throw it away from you. Thataway! God A'mighty!"

The stock had come heavily to the ground. With a convulsive shudder she threw the muzzle away from her. For a moment it pointed uncertainly at the sky, and Ben sprang forward. Just in front of his grasping hand it tottered and fell; a flame shot along the cotton rows, the mowed-down cotton tumbling in after its passage. The roar shook the ground under them.

Off there her father stood, chest heaving, face flabby, with sobered horror.

"Ben," he choked, "I might-a killed my little gal. Ben—I ain't a soak no more."

He turned and stumbled through the cotton toward the house, wiping his face on his shirt sleeve.

"Pa!" cried the girl, and started to run after him.

But Ben caught her by the shoulders and turned her round, his face stern, his eyes blazing.

"Not yet," he said. "Let him study about it. It won't do him any harm!"

They stood side by side, looking in the direction of the house. When at last Ben spoke, the anger had gone out of his voice, the terrible look out of his eyes.

"We'll go now, Tess."

They did not find him on the porch; there was his empty chair, and beside it on the floor his pipe and his shoes. Alone the girl went softly down the hall to his room door, and looked in. When she came back to the porch where Ben waited, her eyes were swimming.

"Ben," she whispered, "he's sittin' by the window in the moonlight—an' Ben—he's cryin!"

Then she too began to cry softly. But out in the border of the woods, where a match had been struck, a mockingbird, perched lightly on the top most twig of the loftiest pine, was filling the brilliant night with song.

OH GRANDMOTHER

Anna Phillips See
The Farmer's Wife, July/August 1921

P OLISH Katie vigorously kneaded the bread dough, but swift as were her capable fingers they could not keep pace with the glad thoughts that raced through her brain. As soon as she had patted the bread into tins she took a letter from behind the kitchen clock and read it, smiling, though she knew its every word:

Poland,
June, 1919

Dearest Sister:
   Praised be Jesus Christ and I hope you will answer me "in centuries and centuries, Amen."
And now I write these glad words that you will see me soon after my letter, for the ship-ticket is already bought.
Matters are so at the farm that I cannot longer endure it. We sit as in a bees' nest. No one but grandmother could withstand this Mikal. Great sorrow has my betrothed, Piotr Fronczak, that I leave Poland for he cannot arrive in that golden America for one year. Soon shall I embrace you, my Katie. Remain with God.

I, your loving sister,
Julka

At the sound of footsteps Katie looked up to see her young mistress, white-clad and pink-sunbonneted, tripping in from the summer morning. She dropped into a chair by the window and renewed a discussion of what the girl had considered settled.

"Katie, will you stay with us if we hire your sister Julka too? It *is* lonely here for you on the farm. I thought I should die myself when we first came out from the city, though of course I endured it for the sake of Mr. Pierce's health. I had no friends! You have the Krupas for company—"

"The Krupas! What company are they? John and Ewa working night and day in the onions and tobacco, and old man Krupa always quarreling with Ewa. My sister Julka she also has enough of farms; we both wish the city where it is lively. I guess I told you, Mrs. Pierce, how we all live on great large place in the country—my big sister Mania, my little sister Julka and me, with our grandmother managing everything after our parents die?"

Mrs. Pierce, wearing a worried frown, nodded absently.

"Well, we were happy with plenty of comfort for we have much land, till Mania married with Mikal who comes to live at the farm and tries to run it against grandmother. This was a madness of the reason for Grandmother Franciszka all her life has

225

her own way. You never saw such a woman as she is! There is so much unhappiness that I travel to America and work for wages—something I would never do in the old country—and now Julka comes too. When she arrives," continued Katie with an independent toss of her blonde head, "I leave you pretty soon. Nothing can keep me here."

A rumble of wheels on the driveway and loud "Whoas!" interrupted the talk. Katie opened the door and beheld old Walenty Krupa's farm wagon laden with boxes and bundles; then with a shriek compounded of consternation, surprise, and joy she recognized the small person perched on the high seat.

"Grandmother Franciszka!" she cried, running with outstretched arms.

There was a babel of Polish ejaculations; hissing consonants varied by an occasional unobtrusive vowel shattered the morning air.

"Here am I, Franciszka Pedewski, at last in this massive America! Many sorrows of the stomach did I suffer on that ship and many bewilderments of the head in that New York but now all is as a turning of the head because I see you again, my little dove!"

"But Grandmother," demanded the breathless Katie, "where is Julka?"

"Julka sits yet in the old country in the house of Piotr Fronczak her husband! At the last when the boxes were already filled with the bed, the cheeses, and the gifts for you, this Piotr pulled the hair with grief at her going and she — she covered herself with the veil instead of traveling to this America. And who should now use the ship-ticket but her who had paid for it, Franciszka Pedewski? To be sure I am in my old years and not expected to travel, but you know, my Katie, that at home I sit with that Mikal who was surely educated among cattle. If you love me, you will surely abuse him!"

Breaking in on this animated recital, Walenty Krupa began to explain how he had happened to be at the railroad station awaiting a load of fertilizer and had received instead "this old woman" tagged to the Pierce farm at Underfield.

"Old!" burst from the grandmother, who fixed him with keen blue eyes that twinkled wickedly. "Old goat yourself!"

At such brilliant repartee Krupa chuckled delightedly. Never before had Katie heard him do more than grunt his appreciation of a pleasantry. Old Krupa laughing was a different being from the man who constantly warred with his daughter-in-law Ewa. He was still grinning and chuckling as he mounted his wagon to drive away.

In the kitchen, when Katie had removed her grandmother's head-handkerchief and placed her in a rocking chair (a novelty that greatly delighted the old lady), the resemblance between the two was noticeable. Just such a fresh-looking, blue-eyed girl with a weight of fair hair must Franciszka Pedewski have been in her youth; now she was like a well-wintered russet apple, brown and slightly withered but with no sign of decay and with a pungent flavor all her own. This pungency spiced the words with which she concluded her relation of affairs at the home farm in Poland:

"And then one day, my Katie, after such a large quarrel as my head would not hold out to think of, this Mikal tells me that I am now old enough to go home to God and leave the place to him and Mania. At that I went from my reason and seized the ox goad, but happily the carcass fled away! Then for many days I turned over in my thoughts how these two, Mania and Mikal, should not get so much when I die, and secretly I sold everything except the naked farm and put the money in the bank in the name of myself, Franciszka Pedewski, that you and Julka may sometime have it. When this thing comes to the daylight it makes so much trouble with that Mikal, that gladly did I use the ship-ticket to step away from his beast's eyes!"

At set of sun, old Franciszka retired to the larger half of her granddaughter's bed, leaving the girl free at last to draw her breath. Still dazed with surprise, Katie sought the Pierces in regard to the responsibility so suddenly dropped upon her shoulders. Gone was all her pert independence. It was she who now wore the anxious frown.

"*What* shall I do? She is my grandmother and I must be good to her but *why* did she come to America? This is no place for old Polish people. I cannot take her to the city, so I ask now that you keep me here, yet you do not want her. She would boss the place in a week."

"Not if I know it," declared Mr. Pierce, whose firm jaw and decisive manner supported the statement.

"How could she 'boss' you, Henry dear, or me?" piped Mrs. Pierce. "Such an old lady and not knowing American ways."

Ignoring these words and with a pitying look that at the time was incomprehensible to her employers, Katie went on:

"This afternoon Grandmother would walk through all the orchards. Of course she does not know American fruit farms like this but she has much wisdom. All your trees she has blessed and you will have a fine crop, Mr. Pierce. When we came to the little empty house she sat down on the steps and declared that there she would live."

"A good idea, Henry!" cried the mistress, who no longer feared Katie going but her *staying* if this relative was to be a fixture in the farmhouse. "With a few repairs the cottage would be quite comfortable."

Mr. Pierce turned to Katie, saying that there was only a fireplace.

"Could your grandmother get along without a cookstove?"

"She never used a stove in her life. The little house will please her if you let her build a pigsty. She said she would be happy if she had a pig for company. And she will work for the rent money, Mr. Pierce; she can farm as well as a man. She wants to work because she likes it, not because she is poor. It scares me to think how she brought all her money from the old country sewed into her clothes. Suppose she had been drowned dead in that ocean with the money that should come to Julka and me! When I told her that, she snapped her fingers and said, 'But you see I did *not* drown!' You can't reason with Grandmother."

In a few days the old cottage, once the home of a hired man, received its foreign tenant. Franciszka herself had whitewashed the walls and ceilings, scrubbed the floors and carted the furniture gleaned by Mrs. Pierce from the farmhouse attic. In the bedroom, the enormous feather bed that had traveled all the way from Poland rose imposingly under a crocheted counterpane of her own making; in the kitchen fireplace hung iron pots and kettles that had served generations of farm folk before ever the city-bred Pierces had purchased this ancient homestead.

The gem of all her belongings, in Franciszka's eyes, was the promising young porker, grunting in his pen behind the house. He was a Polish pig bought from the Krupas with her own Polish money and, being mentally endowed, he already knew that his name was Pawel.

As our dearest possessions are often the cause of our greatest anxiety, this pig had it in his power to wring the heart of his owner. One day Pawel refused to eat; later he displayed signs of serious illness. When Polish nostrums failed to relieve him, Franciszka went to a field where grew a certain herb, and after weighting it down with stones, she said: "As soon as Pawel is well I will release you."

The next morning was Sunday. The old woman poured out the plaint of Pawel's critical condition to the Krupas, who had stopped their wheezing Ford at her door with an invitation to ride to church. Whereupon old Walenty, though garbed in his best, deserted religion to assist a neighbor (and pig) in distress. At noon, Katie, coming to the cottage with inquiries, found her grandmother and old Krupa finishing a sociable lunch of black bread, Polish cheese and cabbage. As the pig was better, due to Krupa's treatment, this was in the nature of a thanksgiving feast. With a look of intense satisfaction, the old man lit his pipe and seated himself on the doorstep of the cottage.

"Now this Ewa," he said, evidently continuing a previous conversation, "this daughter-in-law, she would give me no such good food. Always she lays on the table the insides of cans and the white bread from the baker. What work is that for the teeth? And the things she would put over our skins! What think you, Franciszka, she has tried to lay on me already? *Pajamas*!"

With a frightened look the old woman crossed herself.

"Tell me, Walenty! Is that an American *curse*?"

At this Krupa and Katie burst out laughing.

"A curse it is, Franciszka, but only if one puts on these clothing for sleep. If one throws them to the corner, as I did, they harm not. When this Ewa saw them there, the devils took her. Such words she said to me that I had a hot wish to go back to Poland."

"I know our old years are tormented with these daughters-in-law and these grandsons-in-law that wish us away for eternal times," cried Grandmother Pedewski with sparkling eyes. "But we do not go hence for *them* but as God wills. And we are healthy, very healthy! Besides we hold yet the purse. Eh, Walenty?"

This humorous light on the shadows of old age amused Krupa. He slapped his knee laughing: "Yes, yes, we are healthy, *very* healthy, and we have yet the money! But come, let us look at the pig. May he also be healthy."

Alas for pool Pawel! When his three friends bent over the pen they saw him lying with pitiful outstretched legs. Pawel had "gone hence." Franciszka gazed sorrowfully at the deceased, then cried aloud as for a dead child.

"God gave it, God took it away, may He have honor and glory. He afflicted us but He will also comfort us."

The comfort was almost immediate, for next day Krupa appeared with a gift, the replica of Pawel. As this animal inherited not only the home but the name of the departed, he kept warm the affections of Franciszka Pedewski.

EARLY STORIES FROM THE LAND

The days of early fall found the old woman busy at her cottage. Within the cellar she stored much food; without, she banked the foundations with leaves and sawed much wood in preparation for winter. This work, however, counted in her mind for naught but chores; her real responsibility was the farm itself, and on it she exercised all her energies. With dismay the Pierces came to realize that they and all their belongings had been commandeered.

It was at the time of the County Fair, when Henry Pierce (with Franciszka as adviser!) was selecting his fruit for display, that the Oregon letter came. Katie heard discussion of it as she waited on the table. She was not unprepared when Mrs. Pierce, all in a twitter, announced one morning that they (the Pierces) were going to move to Oregon as her husband had inherited an apple farm there. She ended up by saying that they were sorry to turn Grandmother Pedewski out of the cottage but they hoped to sell the homestead immediately.

The words were still on the lady's lips when old Franciszka herself, wearing overalls and cowhide boots, clumped into the kitchen. Katie mournfully interpreted the words of doom but Franciszka remained calm.

"You go to the city, Katie, for you must earn the money, but I shall stay here. My house is fixed for winter already and I have Pawel for company. If anything happens, are not the Krupas beside me?"

From this stand no argument of mistress or maid could move her. The man of the house, who now joined the circle, took his turn with cajolery, bluster, commands. Nothing affected the resolve of his tenant.

"Good heavens, Katie!" exclaimed Mr. Pierce to the unhappy interpreter. "Can't you make your grandmother understand that it is impossible for her to stay on my property if I tell her to get out? I could have her arrested for—for—well, I don't know for *what* because she pays the rent, but for *something*! The place is on the market. No purchaser will allow her to stay."

Here Franciszka interrupted with an energetic sentence and the girl translated: "She says *she* will buy the little house with a bit of land around it."

"Impossible! Cutting up the place would spoil any sale. Besides, if I could dispose of it that way, as a neighbor she would be—oh, tell her she can't buy it, Katie, and that she *must* prepare to move out!"

Franciszka did not prepare to move. On the contrary, she spent two whole days sawing more wood. On the morning of the third she dressed herself in all her petticoats and a large purple hat—the first hat she had ever owned in her seventy years—for was she not going in the car with Katie and the Krupas to the County Fair?

After an exhilarating drive, the viewing of the exhibits and the eating of the noonday lunch, there occurred the most thrilling experience of Franciszka Pedewski's life— a life that had been not wholly without excitement. In a field near the fairgrounds the Eagle, a small airplane, was carrying passengers skyward at the rate of ten dollars for ten minutes. Many men produced the price and took their turn in the air, among them John Krupa. Old Walenty, when urged by his daughter-in-law to fly, declined with a dark look that said: "I take no chances on going hence."

230

With rapt interest Franciszka watched the Eagle whirring into the heavens or slanting down to earth. At last she could restrain herself no longer and, shamefaced, whispered a request to her granddaughter. Katie shook her head, displaying an empty purse.

"But I cannot live if I have not a fly in the boat with wings! To rise like a bird among the clouds! I must! I must!" muttered the old woman, and undeterred she importuned Walenty Krupa to lend her ten dollars. Something in Franciszka Pedewski always exhilarated him; now the thought of her going up in the airplane so tickled his imagination that he produced a soiled bill and accompanied her to the machine. As she rose "on eagle's wings," he cried to Katie:

"Look at the woman! Wearing the double eyes and the coat of leather and daring to fly above this earth of God! There is no one like her!"

Poor Katie, guarding the purple hat and filled with apprehension, could not understand his enthusiasm.

On the ride home Walenty encouraged his contemporary to relate her sensations while in the air. This was with a twofold purpose: to irritate Ewa, who had not been offered a "fly" by either husband or father-in-law, and to give himself the pleasure always afforded by Franciszka's talk. She needed no urging; speech bubbled from her excited lips.

"I was not like an eagle, Walenty, but a swallow dipping and skimming. My head did not leave me nor my breath, neither did I feel fear but I was as one behind the stove in God's house. Never shall I forget, Walenty, that you loaned me the money for this air pleasure."

During the hurried days before the departure for Oregon, Mr. Pierce tried by every method except forcible eviction to separate the tenant from his cottage, but always with a noticeable lack of success. When the family had at last arranged everything, even to the final meal, and Katie had tearfully packed her trunk, Mrs. Pierce unwisely questioned her Henry as to his disposition of Franciszka Pedewski. The exasperated man exploded: "Do with her! What can anyone do with *her*? Let the next owner of the place settle that question!"

On the evening of the same day came old man Krupa, shaven and adorned with a clean collar. His errand he announced without preliminaries.

"I buy your farm at your price."

Astonishment laid hold on Henry Pierce, for he knew that these neighbors already owned more land than they could cultivate.

"Why Mr. Krupa, I thought you were planning to go back to Poland."

"I know, I know. John say that too. But Franciszka Pedewski she want me to buy this place. Such a woman, that has the dare to fly above this world of God! For her I would do much. Sunday the first banns will be in the church and soon I go to live with her in the little house."

THE MAN FROM THE CITY

James Hay, Jr.

The Country Gentleman, May 1914

G EORGE Wayne had left the city because the time had come when he could not think.

"I can think, but not enough," he had characterized his illness.

"Bunk!" his cheerful physician had replied. "You think too much. Your brain's going round like a flywheel. It's overdoing things. Get out to the country—deep country—where a real thought is as rare as a pterodactyl."

Now, swaying from side to side in the hired carriage that was taking him over the nine miles between the railroad station and the Millwoods' house, he already was beginning to think—to think differently. Pictures that had hung forgotten in the galleries of his brain became new and fascinating. A stretch of the road, white as paper, straight before him in the moonlight and lost at last in the woods beyond, reminded him of a drive he had taken in his boyhood with a girl—a girl of whom he had not thought once in the last fifteen years.

Clouds, thin and fleecy as down, half veiled the moon in such a way that he had before him all at once a night when he had wandered from the ballroom with her to stroll aimlessly beneath the trees. Unconsciously as he thought of it and as he heard the crickets and all the chorus of the soft, murmurous night, he whistled a bar from an old waltz, a tune that had been magic long before the days of the tango and the trot. Then, involuntarily, he became keenly conscious, greedily desirous, of all the pleasure to be derived from the heavy perfumes of the fresh, dewy night. The hoot of an owl far away was, in some indefinite manner, full of music. And the velvety blacks, the very deep purples, the splashes of silver, the long, gray vistas—all the catalogue of mystic coloring written on earth and trees by the moon made him tingle with enjoyment. His delight was so keen that it was an excitement, a new sensation.

George Wayne, author, had won his fame by writing about the tragedies of great cities. More than any other man he had sensed and had expressed the misery of the tenement houses and alleys. His sentences had been sledge-hammer blows beating the public consciousness into reluctant admission that things were not as they should be. Possessing a rare imagination, he had developed the faculty of sympathizing with the individual, of getting his viewpoint, of eating with him his miserable dinner, of lying down beside him on his rag pallet, of going out with him in the morning to his heart-breaking work for wages that could not conquer even hunger. And, having done these things, he had written of the ideals destroyed under the countless wheels of trolleys, of the hopes beaten down by the hydra-headed disappointments born in great towns, of the high ambitions made drab and dirty by the dust of millions of feet tramping the pavements. His prose was hailed as the epic of the sorrows of the cities.

Once during the ride he thought of the heavy-eyed women, the white-lipped children and the sullen-faced men—all prisoners in the jail of poverty—whom he had left behind. His exquisite sympathy for them had helped them much, and it had blazoned him as the preacher of a new gospel—the apostle of the value of personal charity. But tonight his weary brain was unstirred by memory of them.

"Thank heaven," he said half-aloud as he got out of the carriage at the Millwoods' gate, "there'll be no tragedies here! Nothing but peace."

He paid the driver, swung open the gate and flashed up the walk, all his movements quick, flamelike. So swift was his approach that the woman who had been sitting on the porch had scarcely come to the top of the steps.

"This is Mrs. Millwood?" he asked, putting out his hand.

The moonlight falling upon her as she stepped forward from the shadows showed her tall and slender.

"Yes. And this is Mr. Wayne?"

Her voice was pleasant, with full, rich tones; and her smile was gracious, strikingly attractive. She was pretty, he decided, almost beautiful, and there was in her face some sort of strength, some picture of self-reliance, which stamped her as efficient. Later he analyzed that expression.

"Please sit down," she added, "while I tell the driver where to put your suitcase."

Then, as she went down the steps, he following, she explained over her shoulder:

"It's too bad that your trunk couldn't come over tonight. But the mail wagon will bring it in the morning. We had nothing to send for it."

She led him to his room and left him to plunge his face into a tremendous basin of cold water. The window shutters were thrown wide open, so that the slow breeze filled the room with the perfume of the honeysuckle, a fairy sweetness with which he filled his lungs as if it had been an anodyne.

"All this is life, real and best life!" he said joyously when he had taken his seat at the supper table.

She was serving the meal, disappearing now and then to reappear with more dishes— broiled chicken, real batter bread, fried apples, hot biscuits, honey and cold milk. And again the thing that impressed him was her calm efficiency, her doing the work with such satisfactory smoothness while she herself, impervious to the heat of the kitchen, remained freshly cool in her simple white dress.

"You couldn't get a meal like that in New York for the price of the tallest skyscraper," he said when he finished.

He went out to the porch to smoke a cigar—which was against the doctor's orders—and she joined him there, taking her place on the top step and leaning her chin in the cup of her left hand except when she looked up to him occasionally in sudden interest. He studied her intently for a moment and decided that there was in her eyes a suspicion of sadness. He had noticed it when they had been in the lamplight in the dining room, and he was more conscious of it when her lowered lashes lay for an instant like shadows against her cheeks.

Somehow she astonished him. In a vague way he had fallen into the habit of thinking that farmers' wives neglected to preserve their attractiveness. He thought they threw away their youthful freshness simply because they did not value it. But here she was, a denial of all his ideas, with a self-possession and poise that compelled his admiration. He was glad to see that she was what she was in a scene of such beauty.

"I envy you all this," he declared, waving his hand comprehensively.

"All of what?" she asked, and looked at him quickly.

"This loveliness. Why, this is the most wonderful night I ever saw!" He drew a deep breath. "It's the first time in my life that I ever realized that there must be forty million stars in the heavens. The sky is so big, so immense! The earth round us is just a little bit of a fairy garden full of perfume and flowers and silver—and all the rest is distance, marvelous distances with great, shining glory and bursts of light beyond them. Isn't it wonderful?"

"Of course it is," she agreed without looking toward him; "but we get used to it in a way."

"Yes; but you could never get used to this as I have gotten used to the city—the cafes, the orchestras, the theaters." He leaned forward swiftly and talked down to her rapidly. "You know, men are poor manufacturers of beauty. When they begin to imitate God in the making of loveliness they're utter failures."

"And yet," she suggested, looking far into the night, "the people there have good times, awfully good times, don't they?"

"Oh, in a way," he agreed, leaning back in his chair. "But they never have what you have—contented happiness. That's your treasure. In the city men and women are hunting so desperately for pleasure and what they call happiness that they are willing to kill each other in order to get it. By George, they do kill each other! Men and women are being sacrificed and killed there day by day and night by night to give other men and women the feverish thing they mistakenly call pleasure!"

"That's terrible," she said thoughtfully. "I never thought of that before."

"But here it's all so different," he went on in his imperious suddenness. "All you people know each other and like each other and help each other. Your life, your very work, is in the midst of flowers, surrounded by the everlasting freshness of nature itself. There can't be anything very bad in such a life. You work hard. I know that. But, after all, it's a blessing to work when so much enjoyment in the evenings, in the rest times, is within your reach—isn't it?"

"Oh, yes," she answered. "I think—"

The sound of a child's crying interrupted her. As the first note of it came from a room upstairs, she was on her feet, accomplishing the process of rising in one continuous, graceful motion.

"That's Richard," she said, already on her way into the hall. "He's not very well."

When the child's cries had died away she returned.

"Aren't you tired?" she asked. "Don't you want to go up to your room?"

"Not on such a night," he said gaily, and added: "This wonderful night! I'm gloating over it as I might do over a gorgeous painting. I'm watching it as misers watch precious stones. I'm drinking it in like wine."

"Then you'll like it here. You'll enjoy the country."

"How many children have you?" he asked abruptly. Somehow he had not regarded her as a mother.

"Two—two boys. Henry, the older, and Richard. I'm sorry Mr. Millwood is so late. He had to go to the store. It's only a mile and a half down the road. I thought he would be back by this time."

The purr of an automobile sounded down the road, and a touring car, its brass glittering in the moonlight, swept past.

"That's Tom Thornton in his car," she explained. "He lives a mile above here."

"Are all the people here well-to-do?" he inquired.

"Oh, no," she said, laughing lightly; "not so much that they can afford automobiles. But Tom Thornton's been awfully lucky."

He thought there was wistfulness in her last two words.

"What does he do?"

"He farms—but he makes money."

There fell a pause. Somewhere down the road the notes of a guitar rang gently, and a youth's voice, softened by the distance, went slowly through the opening bars of a love song. Against the deep blackness of a hill far away to the right a lighted window shone as dimly as a candle flame. And on the last notes of the young lover's song came the melancholy music of the owl's long call.

Mrs. Millwood lifted her head slightly and listened attentively.

"Harry's coming now," she said simply.

He opened the gate slowly and came leisurely up the walk, a peculiar, dragging heaviness in his movements. His great bulk loomed grotesquely big in the shadows. He wore overalls, and heavy field shoes that scraped loudly on the gravel.

"Harry," she introduced the two men, "Mr. Wayne has come."

They shook hands, Millwood exhibiting a cordiality that was surprising in view of his slowness and heaviness of demeanor. After they had talked in desultory fashion for a few minutes Wayne went to his room.

It was twenty minutes later when he leaned out of the window on the side of his room overlooking the roof of the porch. He wanted to look again at the most wonderful night he had ever seen. He could not explain its hold upon him. Perhaps, he concluded, it was because for the first time in many years he had it before him virginal, unprofaned by artificiality. He had seen it often enough from the verandas of country clubs or from the deck of a yacht. But here there were no driveways lit by electricity that vied wanly with the starlight—no pumpings of engines or trailing storms of smoke and cinders. And again he felt that he could not drink in enough of the scented, dewy air.

Voices came to him at first without meaning, so deep was his absorption in what he saw. It was several minutes before his ears took actual knowledge of what they heard.

"Harry," she was saying, "won't you let me have fifty cents until next week?"

"I haven't got it." The reply was distinctly surly.

"I don't know what I can do," she explained, a trifle desperately. "I did so want to

236

get a ham boiler tomorrow. Mr. Wayne said tonight he was especially fond of ham."

"Now, look here," the command was ugly; "don't bother me about him. I told you I didn't want you to have him in the first place. It's more trouble than it's worth anyway. If you can't—"

"But I'm only doing it to get the money for the boys' winter things, Harry," she interrupted him with singular dignity. "They must have overcoats, and you know we haven't the money to get them anything in the fall. You said I might have a boarder if I could—"

"Well, you've got him! That ought to satisfy you. Don't bother me about him!"

"Harry, can't you let me have just fifty cents! You know Mr. Carson won't let us have any more credit. And if Mr. Wayne doesn't stay his three weeks I—I don't know what will happen. You know Richard's not well anyway."

"Listen!"

As well as if he had seen it, Wayne knew that Millwood had taken his wife by the arm in a cruel grip. The thought sickened him.

"Listen!" the man's voice repeated. "I haven't got fifty cents, and I don't care a damn whether Wayne stays or goes. Now, I hope that's plain."

There was the noise of heavy footsteps on the porch and the banging shut of the door, followed by the man's progress up the stairs and down the short hall to a room.

Wayne looked once more into the distance. The silver slashings of the night were growing dim.

He awoke early enough to watch, through the open window, the coming dawn lift its pink fan against the sky above the greenish-black outlines of the hills. He marveled that he should have slept soundly, and on the heels of that thought came his consciousness of the stillness that yet was everywhere. When the birds began to punctuate it with calls and drowsy notes he sprang out of bed.

Mrs. Millwood had told him that he would find cold water in the bathroom.

"We have a wonderful tub," she had laughed, "but no water in the pipes."

In bathrobe and slippers he made his way to the bathroom, finding there three big buckets of icy water freshly brought from the pump. Idly curious, he drew back the white curtain of the window and looked out. In the yard beneath was the woodpile and, as his glance fell to it, Mrs. Millwood, ax in hand, drew forward a log and began to cut it up. There was nothing unskilled or hesitant in the way she worked, and he knew intuitively that this was one of her daily tasks. He noticed also that she wore a long, close-fitting apron over her dress.

"By George!" he muttered his bewilderment, as he stepped into the cold water and slid deeper into it.

"There's something great about this country, this deep country," he thought as he got back into his bathrobe. "A bath in the city never felt that good."

The sound of a rattling pump handle came up to him, and he looked out through the curtains again. Mrs. Millwood pumped one bucket full, and then another. He watched her carry them back toward the house, her walk even and graceful under their weight; and, as he looked, he remembered having read in a newspaper an estimate made by the Department of Agriculture to show the tons of water the average farmer's wife lifted in a year. He had laughed when he read it. Now he was indignant.

While he was dressing, the children rushed out of their room and downstairs, their laughter high and clear, and the echo of their tempestuous meeting with their mother mingled with the clatter of plates. Also, he heard a little later the rattle of the pump handle again. Evidently Mrs. Millwood, while her husband looked after matters at the barn, was doing many things—chopping wood, carrying water, cooking breakfast. She had done all that, and it was just a little past six o'clock!

A door down the hall opened, and the heavy field shoes scraped loudly on the stairs.

Wayne, who was preparing to brush his hair, put the brushes down with a bang, thrust his hands deep into his pockets and stood stock still, scowling. He was thinking that Millwood had been asleep while Mrs. Millwood had carried up the water for his bath! He was nervous, irritable. That had been his normal condition for weeks. But his sudden realization of Mrs. Millwood's work that morning brought from him an audible oath such as he had never used before.

He went down to the front porch and made the acquaintance of the two boys. Henry, the older, was a healthy, strong youngster of about ten, with light, bristly hair like his father's. Richard, a boy of seven, was delicate-looking, but he had the dark-brown hair and frank manner of his mother.

When Mrs. Millwood came to call them to breakfast, Wayne had arranged a picnic.

"We'll be gypsies," she heard him say as she stopped in the doorway, "and we'll get all those things and cook a regular gypsy stew up there in the hills."

"And I can shoot the birds for it, can't I?" Henry put in eagerly, dancing his delight.

"And me too?" young Richard urged anxiously.

"Of course, all three of us. I tell you, we'll be some hunters, all of us. And I'll be the cook."

"What you going to cook in?" inquired Richard.

"I hadn't thought of that," Wayne hesitated. "Let's see. I wonder if we can't get something at the store; a great big skillet or a pan of some sort—a great big pan."

"That's it! That's it!" yelled Henry. "Let's have something new."

"Breakfast is ready," she called, and as they turned into the house added: "Don't desert my cooking so soon, Mr. Wayne. You mustn't let them drag you into the woods."

"I have to thank them for going with me," he smiled. "The doctor's orders are to get as far into the deep country as I can. I shall have—"

"Oh, Mr. Wayne," yelled Henry from the porch, "I'll tell you what we want, a great big boiler. That's the thing to make a big stew in."

Mrs. Millwood looked back at the boy reprovingly, but she showed no embarrassment.

"You mustn't make such extravagant suggestions."

"The suggestion was mine," Wayne assured her.

As they entered the dining room, Millwood, who had been standing near a window, pitched a cigarette stump into the yard and came forward with a pleasant greeting.

Wayne recoiled inwardly. It was a hobby of his that anybody who smoked cigarettes in the morning was hopeless. Moreover he could not get out of his mind what had occurred on the porch the night before. Millwood, however, made himself agreeable, his smile always ready, his talk hinging on what he had read in the newspapers and magazines.

Mrs. Millwood, pouring the coffee, seeing to the needs of the boys and serving hot cakes in the intervals, was the perfect picture of a contented wife. Looking at her Wayne could hardly believe that he had heard correctly the things said beneath his window.

"Are you going to see about threshing wheat today, Harry?" she asked when the meal was almost over.

"If I see old man Jenkins down at the store I'll ask him about it," he said carelessly.

"I think it's most important," she persisted, looking at him steadily. "The wheat's been left too long anyway."

"Well, what of it?" he asked a little sharply. "What difference does a day or two more make?"

She turned to Wayne with a smile:

"That's what all of us have to fight against in the country—delay. We put off too much, even in the matter of crops." She looked at Millwood again: "Tom Thornton's had his threshed more than two weeks ago."

"That's all right," he dismissed the subject. "Thornton's no pattern for me."

Wayne and the boys overruled all objections and started out for the picnic, stopping at the store on their way and buying a huge cooking implement.

"It's what we call a ham boiler," explained the old storekeeper, whose long, thin whiskers contrasted strangely with the shrewdness in his eyes.

"That's exactly what we want, isn't it, fellows?" Wayne inquired, and made them carry it between them.

They struck out across the fields and were swallowed up in the woods. That was a wonderful day for the boys. When they returned late in the afternoon, the boiler full of ferns and wild honeysuckle, they had learned how to shoot "the boarder's rifle," had helped him cook the wonderful stew and had made up their minds that his stories about the James brothers were the best they had ever heard.

"Mamma," Richard confided at bedtime, "Mr. Wayne's the nicest man I ever saw. He's something like you, Mamma. His hands are so soft. And he's kind as you are. He ain't like the men we know."

In the meantime Mr. Wayne, with a fine disregard for his weary feet and aching muscles, had disappeared. In collecting material for his novels he had learned how to get at the real facts and, as a result of much thinking during his day in the woods, what he wanted now was information. He brought up finally on the Presbyterian minister's porch two miles from the Millwood home.

Mr. Naughton was cordial. In a short while he was communicative, a trait which also was shown by Mrs. Naughton. They were middle-aged people and their lifework had been in the country. This impulsive, nervous young man with his swift gestures and lightning-like smiles won their confidence; and his deference, unlike that of their parishioners, was always evident in his manner, a constant tribute to them. In the fullness of time, while the moon hung in a basket of filmy silver and the breeze came up with its inexhaustible burden from the honeysuckle, the conversation turned to the Millwoods.

"He's a fine young fellow. We so consider him," Mr. Naughton explained, rubbing his hands gently together. "He comes from a fine family. I think in the whole family, connections and all, there are thirty-three votes. And all of them, Harry's father particularly, contribute liberally to the churches. They are prominent in the community."

"But Harry's a little lazy," hazarded Mrs. Naughton.

"Tut, tut!" put in Mr. Naughton apologetically. "He does like all the rest of the young men. He hangs round the store in the evenings and that sort of thing. Occasionally he plays a little cards, I believe. Of course, that shouldn't be. But what can you expect, Mr. Wayne? None of us is perfect. And Harry's unusually well-read. He subscribes, I believe, for nearly all the magazines—at least six or seven of them."

"Yes, I've noticed that he's up on the news," Wayne agreed.

"They say"—Mrs. Naughton contributed this with a degree of timidity—"he knows more about national politics than anybody round here."

"And Mrs. Millwood?" Wayne put the casual question.

"We don't see much of her." Mrs. Naughton's tone was more assertive, almost hostile. "She doesn't visit much—in fact not at all. I think she's a little peculiar. I know she hasn't had a new hat in three years."

"And she dresses her children very poorly," Mr. Naughton commented. His tone indicated that this was excusable on the ground that, if women were not failures in one way, they would be in another.

"But perhaps she hasn't the necessary money," Wayne suggested. He was avid of facts.

"That can't be it," the minister objected. "Harry has enough to keep himself reasonably well dressed."

"Besides," his wife chimed in, "if she can't get enough from him for a new hat there must be something wrong somewhere. I agree with Daniel. She's careless about her children."

The impulsive young man remembered that the boys' clothing had been scrupulously clean but decidedly threadbare. Since he was sitting in shadow he permitted himself to grind his teeth.

He found her seated on the top step of the porch, her chin in the cup of her left hand. When she welcomed him she smiled brightly, but he knew that tears were in her eyes.

"Mr. Millwood hasn't come in?" he inquired, taking the chair he had had the night before.

"Not yet," she said easily. "He's down at the store. He likes to go down there at night and hear the news about people."

He remembered having seen him there that morning, but he refrained from mentioning it.

"Did you enjoy your day?" she asked after a pause.

"Oh, immensely," he answered enthusiastically. "It has been finer than I thought possible."

He leaned back in his chair and looked up to the stars. The charm of the night was gripping him again—the charm of the night and the majesty of the woman on the steps.

"Where a real thought is as rare as a pterodactyl," his doctor had told him.

And here, under myriad stars, at the foot of eternal hills, amid wandering airs laden with fragrance, near forests silver-spangled by the moon, he sat face to face with a woman whose every hour was heroism, whose every dawn was tragedy! And twenty-four hours ago he had babbled to her of contented happiness, calm delight. Why, as a matter of fact, her only peace was loneliness, solitude, stagnant minutes. Made in the form of beauty and schooled in her youth to believe that later years would bring her joy, she was a slave, an incessant server, a drawer of water, a hewer of wood! Her children were in rags, and she herself in three years had not had a new covering for her head. In order that the two boys might have overcoats in winter she slaved for him in summer while her husband gossiped at the store and left his wheat to rot in the fields. And, when she had asked for fifty cents, she had received only bruises upon her flesh!

He started to speak, but his voice caught in his throat.

She looked toward him expectantly. "I—I thought you were speaking—about to speak," she said, and laughed oddly.

"I was about to say," he explained, "I telephoned over to the station from the store today and got the agent to telegraph to town for a phonograph. I love music, and it's the only thing needed to make these nights perfect."

"Oh," she commented in a low tone, "that will be nice."

"Don't you like music?" he asked gently.

"Of course, I do!" she answered slowly, "but I haven't heard any for so long—so very long."

There followed a long pause, he looking up to the stars, she with her chin in the cup of her hand.

"I know," he said at last, "that you and I are going to be good friends—great friends. I think we know each other well—already."

She did not answer.

"Because," he elaborated, "we like the same things—and the same principles."

"It is very good of you to—to think so," she said simply.

Her head was turned entirely from him and her shoulders moved once, spasmodically. He watched her intently and saw that she was weeping.

He got to his feet with the lithe quickness of a tiger, and for a moment his figure inclined toward her. But he did not take a step in her direction. Instead he went into the house and up to his room. As he reached the stair landing, Richard, calling querulously for his mother, began to cry. And immediately he heard her coming, light-footed, across the porch and up the stairs.

In the two weeks that followed, Wayne naturally learned the routine of Mrs. Millwood's life, her daily program, the long list of her tasks indoors and out. One thing which he regarded as being in the nature of a miracle was that she had only one dress, and that she always appeared delightfully fresh and neat. Her resourcefulness was a constant wonder to him. And, as his admiration for her grew, his dislike for her husband was intensified many times over. While she went through with a ceaseless round of work he led what was in reality a life of leisure.

Wayne included the boys in all his expeditions. There were times when Richard, quiet and pale, preferred to stay behind, but as a rule both he and Henry accompanied the energetic, restless boarder. They could not help liking him. He had installed the phonograph on the front porch for the evening concerts. He had added to the hunting arsenal two air rifles to be used under his direction. And he had held two shooting matches at each of which two prizes were offered, the trophies being on both occasions what they wanted most in all the world.

One afternoon, when he had returned early from the hills, he found her mowing the front yard. She was hatless in the sun, and her heightened coloring made her look unusually brilliant. He came up behind her so that she did not see him until he put out his hands to remove hers from the handle of the machine. She started as she turned.

"Oh!" she exclaimed. "I didn't think you would be back so soon."

"There's a lot of shade on the porch," he said in a businesslike tone as he took possession of the mower; and, running the machine away from her, added over his shoulder: "You go up there and watch me. I'll lay this grass low in a jiffy."

"You're the most industrious person this country ever saw," she said laughingly, following his instructions.

"Except you," he corrected, and there was in his voice a resentment which he immediately regretted.

That evening at supper she was unusually gay. She had wanted to go to a store three miles away, she explained, and had hitched up their one old driving horse to the buggy.

"When I got to Rocky Creek," she related, "down dropped the shafts. Fortunately old Rollins hasn't spirit enough left to kick. But I had an awful time fixing those shafts with wire, and I didn't get to the store." She turned to her husband. "Harry, you ought to have fixed that bolt."

"What's the use?" he rejoined, laughing his enjoyment. "You fixed it with wire."

"I know," she replied, serious for the moment, "but I'm not supposed to be a carriage builder."

Wayne, thinking over such incidents as these, often asked himself why he stayed on, and always he knew it was because she must have enough money to buy the winter things for the boys. It became painful to him to watch her day by day. It seemed to him that she was possessed by a mania for self-sacrifice. This was the only explanation he could find for her enduring all the things put upon her—burdens unlightened by anybody's help or sympathy. Sometimes, he thought, while her body drove itself to the never-ending labors, her soul, wrapping itself in sackcloth, must be mourning its own crucifixion.

Then came Richard's illness. All day long he had been lying on his little bed, very quiet and very pale. After supper Mrs. Millwood found Wayne in his accustomed place on the porch. For the first time since he had known her she seemed embarrassed, painfully ill at ease.

"Richard is feeling very bad," she said, her voice tremulous, "so bad that I must impose on your kindness—if you will permit."

"Yes," he said eagerly, getting to his feet; "let me do something to help. Please do."

"Once before," she went on, not sure of herself, "when he felt this way the doctor said he ought to have a lot of sherry wine and eggs. He has so little vitality."

"Certainly, we can get that at once. I'll—"

"It will have to be ordered from town," she interrupted him hurriedly. "I know that because, when I spoke to Mr. Millwood about it then, he said he would ask the store here to order it. But somehow—somehow, it never came. And now the child needs it—oh, so badly—and—"

He was already halfway down the porch steps.

"I'll telephone to the station and have them telegraph for it," he said, and was gone.

In the road a hundred yards from the house he met a half-grown boy riding a work horse bareback and stopped him. In two minutes he had slipped a dollar into the boy's hand and had mounted.

"Come to Mr. Millwood's house in an hour and get the horse," he called back, and rode off toward the store.

Millwood was among the loafers, but Wayne did not take the time to talk to him. His feverish impatience stirred the old proprietor into something like haste, and in a few minutes the order had been telephoned to the station agent.

On his way out he snatched up a riding whip.

"Pay you for this tomorrow!" he said shortly and strode out to his dispirited steed.

Once more in the road, he turned back toward the Millwood house. When he reached it he had urged the horse to a gallop, and he did not stop. When he drew rein and slid to the ground he was in the Naughtons' yard.

"Mrs. Millwood's little Richard is sick," he said, without preamble, to Mrs. Naughton; "and he needs sherry wine. Have you any?"

"Well, of course, wine— That is, we don't encourage anybody to—"

"It's medicine—medicine, I tell you!" Wayne said sharply.

Mr. Naughton appeared on the porch.

"Certainly, my dear," he said smoothly, "if it is for medicinal purposes—"

"Then, sir, please give it to me—a bottle of it," Wayne commanded. "It may be a case of life and death. I tell you it's the doctor's orders."

He got the wine, and when his voice no longer kept the horse to a gallop he used the whip cruelly. The boy, who had been waiting for him at the Millwood gate, began to protest that the animal had been ridden to death.

"Shut up!" Wayne said fiercely, and threw him another dollar.

Going through the gate he forced himself to walk slowly to the house. He felt the need of showing no anxiety. He went quietly to his room, and, when he heard her go downstairs, followed her, the bottle of wine in his hand.

"I'm convinced that my mind's failing me with a vengeance," he said regretfully. "I forgot altogether that I had a bottle of wine in my trunk. Here it is. I have telegraphed for more."

"How fortunate!" she said with such relief that he was almost unmanned. "It's a miracle. Richard hasn't eaten anything today. I must fix this for him at once."

At ten o'clock Millwood came home and found Wayne on the porch.

"How's Richard?" he asked casually.

"I think he's still awake." Wayne was polite with difficulty. "I've heard Mrs. Millwood moving about several times."

"I guess he'll be all right as soon as he gets to sleep." The other dismissed the subject. "Aren't you going to bed now?"

"No; I believe not. Think I'll have another cigar. By the way, mightn't it be a good thing to send for a doctor?"

Millwood had entered the hall.

"Oh, no," he answered. "There's nothing to worry about. Women get scared about nothing."

An hour later she crept downstairs and came out to him. Her face was a dead-white blur in the darkness before him.

"How is he?" he asked softly.

"He's asleep now, I think," she said, "but he's very sick—very sick. Oh, I'm afraid—afraid!"

For a moment his wrath against her husband dominated his special, personal concern for her. He thought angrily that, if he had not been there, she would have had nobody to whom she could turn for help or counsel.

"What does Mr. Millwood say?"

"He—he's not uneasy at all. He's gone to bed."

She said that without realizing how it accused her husband.

"I think," she added wearily, "Richard was delirious for a little while tonight. But he—"

"Why on earth don't you have the doctor?" he burst forth. "You know the child is ill."

"Harry said he telephoned for him this morning from the store," she explained, turning half away from him; "but—he hasn't come."

"And he knows the child is ill?"

"Yes; oh, yes."

"Then, why doesn't he come?"

She did not answer.

"Mrs. Millwood, why doesn't he come?"

She put her finger to her lips and listened. The sound of the child's weak crying came down to them, and she turned toward the door.

He touched her lightly on the arm.

"I'll go up to him" he said imperiously, "while you wake your husband and tell him to go after the doctor." He was behind her on the stairs. "Richard likes me," he reassured her. "I can quiet him."

"Oh, yes; he likes you, of course," she said, a catch in her throat.

He went into the dimly lit room and took the boy in his arms. The little body was aflame with fever.

"How does it feel, old fellow?" he asked gently.

"It hurts—hurts awful," the boy answered weakly.

"Where does it hurt? Show me where."

He held him loosely so that he could put his hand where he wished.

"It's my side," Richard explained; "right there. Sometimes it hurts. Sometimes— it don't. It hurts—now—awful."

"Then we'll have to be brave Indians," Wayne comforted him. "The brave ones never whimpered."

"That's right," he said. "And I've tried not to cry. It scares Mamma so—so much."

Wayne, cautious-footed, paced up and down the room, holding him close and cheering him:

"We'll play it's an Indian, a bad Indian, after us. He's shooting at us, but he can't hit us. He just worries us. But that doesn't matter. If we keep running we can get to the shelter of the hills and build a fort, build such a high, strong fort that he can't get near us any more. And we can take our rifles and have lots of fun watching him dodge about and run and —"

He looked up and saw her standing in the doorway. He knew immediately that she was panic-stricken.

"What is it?" he asked, going close to her, the boy still in his arms.

"Harry says it's no use to go after Doctor Bronill," she answered, wringing her hands one against the other.

"Why?"

She looked at him a moment and let her hands drop limply at her sides, and stood helpless, hesitant, her eyes downcast.

"Oh," she said at last, making the exclamation a low wail, "we owe him money. Harry hasn't paid his bill since little Henry was born."

Wayne put the boy into her arms.

"How far away does Bronill live?" he asked. "About six miles, isn't it?"

"Yes," she said; "but—but it will take a long time to get him. And you can't telephone. The store's closed. And the horse is out in the far field."

"I'll have him here in less than an hour," he promised, starting to the front door; then, seeing her terror, turned back: "You know I'll have him here in less than an hour."

She nodded her belief, and he was gone.

Somewhere in the hall downstairs he dropped his coat and hat. He took the porch steps in one bound, but once on the ground settled immediately into a swift trot. He had decided what he must do, and, in order to cover the mile between the Millwood house and Tom Thornton's, he had to keep to a regular, unbroken pace. He ran as he had run at college, doggedly, getting as much speed out of his will as he did out of his feet. Before he had reached the Thorntons' gate his mouth had gone dry as a chip and he had wished for a handkerchief to crowd into it. At the end he leaned against the fence a moment, the blood pounding his temples, and reached down for a handful of the dewy grass. This he crushed into his mouth for moisture, so that he would be able to speak.

He stormed the door with fists and feet, calling out in the meanwhile in a voice that grew from shrillness back to its natural tones.

"Your machine!" he said furiously to the amazed Thornton who at last had come to the door. "I must have it! You've got to drive me to Doctor Bronill's. Mrs. Millwood's Richard is dying—dying, I tell you!"

"Say!" Thornton was inclined to be angry because of the other's fierce commands. "I've got a bum arm here. I can't drive—"

Wayne shook the uninjured arm. "What's the make of it? Quick!"

Thornton gave him the information mechanically.

"I can drive it myself!" Wayne pulled him out on the porch. "Lead me to it! Don't hang back, man! I tell you the boy's dying. Give me the machine!"

"My feet will—" Thornton began, hesitating.

But Wayne would take no denial. He dragged him, half-dressed, down the steps and toward the buildings on the right.

"I'm hiring it." He talked rapidly, as if that carried him nearer to the doctor. "I'm paying you anything you want for it. If I injure it I'll replace it. Come on, man!"

In four minutes he was rolling out of the shed.

"Better light the lamps," Thornton called after him.

"Darn the lights!" Wayne muttered to himself, and took the sharp turn into the public road at thirty miles an hour.

His driving was automatic. Almost involuntarily he handled the machine so that he got the greatest speed possible out of it. The thing that dominated his mind was the picture of the terrified woman, the child in her arms.

"Where a real thought is as rare as a pterodactyl!"

And here he was in a situation so big that he wanted to kill a man and save a child's life and comfort a woman. He felt the impulse to shriek forth the name of God in desperation. It was like being in a shipwreck, or among falling, crashing buildings, or at the mercy of a tornado. He was crushed by the sense of his own impotence. The wild ride, this night, was but an incident in the great horror he had learned—the plight of a woman who had to be the victim of one man that she might give to the world two other men; a woman who had to be always heroic in solitude, mighty in martyrdom, smiling in sorrow. Fate, fortune, something, had stripped from her even the cheap silks and baubles with which she might have been adorned; and chance, destiny, something, was burning her soul hour by hour at the stake of loneliness. Even her imagination had ceased to look for the gateways to happiness. Her one hope was for solace from her sons in the future years.

There was no escape, none. And yet she might—were there not limits to what a woman could—

He was out of the machine and pounding on the doctor's door.

His first question sounded like a maniac's: "How much does Harry Millwood owe you?"

The astounded physician answered automatically:

"A hundred and twenty-five dollars."

Wayne crushed some bills into the doctor's hands.

"Here's two hundred," he said. "Now come with me."

Doctor Bronill was indignant.

"I don't want your money," he said testily. He was a little, wiry man, with a long, lantern-jawed face. "Is Millwood ill?"

"No; but his child is; Richard is. It's appendicitis, an acute attack. Won't you come—come at once?"

"Of course I will," the physician said readily, and turned back into the house, carrying the money with him.

"Hurry!" Wayne called after him. "Never mind about your horse. I have a machine here."

They started off with a rush, the car swaying from side to side, stones flying from under the tires as if they had been thrown out of slings.

"Don't drive so fast!" the doctor said loudly, above the noise.

"I can't go fast enough," Wayne told him, and added, his gaze intent on the road: "Do what you can to help him through the night. Don't leave him. The expense is no matter. I'll guarantee that. There'll have to be an operation. If you don't mind, I'll have a friend of mine out here tomorrow for a consultation with you. Will that be agreeable?"

"Certainly," the doctor answered, somewhat calmed by the other's disregard of danger.

"Did Millwood telephone you this morning?" Wayne lifted his voice.

"No."

At that, Wayne lifted one hand and struck the steering wheel a blow that swerved the car far to one side.

Doctor Bronill clambered out of the machine at the Millwoods' gate, repeating his promise to stay with Richard until the arrival of Doctor Leibold from town.

Wayne turned the car round and headed for the railroad station nine miles away.

At one o'clock the next afternoon Doctor Leibold and a trained nurse, stepping from the train, were met by a tired-looking man who wore a new hat but no coat.

"There's not a minute to lose," he said feverishly, grasping the doctor's heavy valise. "Please hurry. The car's just round the station here."

"Now, see here," Doctor Leibold said when they had started; "I know you're a crack chauffeur and all that, Wayne. But be careful. Also you might tell me something about this case. How do you know it's appendicitis?"

"I knew it as soon as I saw him," he said. "Besides, I drove back there this morning. Doctor Bronill says it's appendicitis—and we haven't a minute to lose."

He took the short hill in front of him with such speed that the car seemed to leap the brow of it and land halfway down the decline on the other side.

"And you've got to operate, Doctor"—he made the statement a combination of pleading and command—"got to operate right there in that house."

"Very well—if it's necessary," Leibold agreed.

Millwood met them at the door, but he did not lift his gaze to Wayne's.

Mrs. Millwood came down the stairs.

"Take Doctor Leibold right up," Wayne directed her.

He turned away and, disregarding Millwood, went out to the car. When he stepped out of it in Tom Thornton's yard he was not an imposing-looking figure. His light flannel trousers were stained from the sweat of the horse he had ridden the night before. His face was layered with dust. His shirt, which once had been white, hung upon him like a gray rag. And he stumbled as he went to meet Thornton.

"I'm greatly obliged to you," he said politely. "I feel like a robber. How much do I owe you?"

"Great cats, man! Not a cent," Thornton said with enthusiasm. "We've all heard the whole story. If you've saved that kid's life we'll give you a medal."

"Instead of that," he laughed weakly, "give me a basin of water. I want to wash my face."

After that was done Thornton got more gasoline and drove him back to the Millwoods' place.

The operation was successful. Leibold told him so at six o'clock, adding:

"We—you—literally pulled him out of the grave. Half an hour later would have been too late."

Mrs. Millwood came out to him on the porch late that night. Her face was a white blur in the gloom, but this time he knew it was radiant.

Neither of them spoke for a long time.

There was no moon, and the sky was like unending folds of deep purple held together by the stars. A vagrant breeze brought to them now and then the breath of the honeysuckle. Far down the road a dog barked once, sharply. And against the soft blackness of a hill far away the same lighted window he had seen on the night of his arrival shone as dimly as a candle flame.

He stood beside her, leaning against the railing. Both of them looked out into the whispering distances, seeing nothing.

"Of course," she said at last, "there is no way for me to thank you."

"You shouldn't think of thanks," he said steadily. "If I did anything at all, I helped to save your boy for manhood."

"Ah," she sighed, as if he had lifted the weight of a world from her shoulders; "I scarcely dared hope you would realize that. It's the way I feel. Of what avail am I if I do not give the world my boys, my men?"

"It is that, exactly," he agreed.

She was silent again.

"But there is something more," he said, his voice exquisite in its gentleness.

"No," she objected; "there is nothing more."

"For me, I mean," he persisted. "You have taught me much about the—the possibilities of human nature, the nobilities of human nature. You understand, I know."

"My life, you mean," she answered with the simplicity of a child. "Yes, I know. But you mustn't overrate it. There are so many more like me. It isn't a new story—this poverty, the solitude of a woman in the country, the denial of a girl's dreams, the terrific manual labor, the failure of everybody to understand, the ridicule of the neighbors, the—I was about to say the solitude of the soul. Even if a man strikes—"

She stopped and caught her breath.

"I shouldn't have said that," she rebuked herself.

"Yes," he said, the tenderness of his voice caressing her; "I knew that too."

She was sobbing. She stood looking far into the night, her tears flowing unheeded.

He leaned toward her and put his hand upon hers as it lay on the railing. For a moment the stars came closer to the earth. "If—if," he said brokenly, "the time ever comes when you cannot stand—cannot endure—"

She withdrew her hand suddenly and brushed it across her eyes. It was as if she stepped forward, unafraid, to new torture.

"It will never come," she answered. "You forget the—the little men."

She turned slowly and left him. And for a long time afterward the memory that she went from him with dragging steps brought to his eyes the light of happy fancies.

THE RESURRECTION OF LEMUEL

Isabel Richmond Hidy
The Farmer's Wife, April 1925

The sharp tattoo of the mare's hoofs on the cement driveway brought Fanny Beeson hurriedly to the window. A little figure of anxiety she was as she stood there, her face puckered into a score of worried lines and her worn hands nervously clasping and unclasping before her.

As Lem Beeson grasped the swinging handle that released the iron gate, the mare shied instinctively, almost wrenching the lines from his hand. The lightning of retribution flashed swiftly above her and Fanny could hear the whine of a descending whip. Quivering, tense, ready for the plunge, the little mare hesitated for a second; then, recognizing the mastery of the grip on the lines, shook herself into submission and set off down the road with a steady, though nervous gait.

Fanny watched until the buggy disappeared round a turn in the road. A long sigh escaped her. "Oh, why'd Lem have to take that little half-broke horse *this* morning!" she murmured. "Just to work out his spite on, I reckon. If she devils him, he'll about kill her. Or she him!" she added fearfully.

She glanced at the clock—barely ten o'clock and Lem would not be back till noon at the earliest. Yet, there was a furtive haste about her movements as, after a last look down the deserted road, she climbed the steep stairs that led to the little attic. Here, picking her way among the odd pieces of discarded furniture and stooping under the eaves, she drew out a small trunk which, when opened, gave forth the delicate, musty fragrance of withered lavender.

A few pieces of linen lay carefully folded on top and some exquisitely embroidered undergarments, but these were not Fanny's objective. From the very bottom of the trunk she lifted out two bundles, handling them with reverent tenderness. These, when her trembling fingers had unpinned their wrappings, proved to be baby garments of finest flannel and linen, scarcely yellowed with age though it had been thirty years since Fanny Beeson had laid away her hopes and happiness in the two fragrant piles. Many times she had stolen up there alone to dream over them, but this morning she allowed herself no time for thought or hesitation. Carefully replacing the other contents and pushing the trunk back into its hiding place, she hurried downstairs and out of the back door, pausing only to catch up her sunbonnet, for the day already was oppressively warm.

The Beeson house and the big barn that completely overshadowed it stood on a little rise of ground with the rich farm and pasture land descending from it on all sides. Just visible in the hollow beyond and across the tiny creek was a small house set in twenty acres of bottom land. It was toward this cottage that Fanny directed her course, cutting across the fields and scrambling through barbed wire fences with the ease of long habit.

The house, at first glance, appeared deserted; but Fanny opened the kitchen door and stepped in, calling softly, "Ruthie, are you here?" A stir in the next room answered and a girl came slowly out, evidently reluctant to appear. Her dark hair was disordered and her eyes were swollen with weeping. She moved heavily, with an air of utter abandonment—the tragic picture of a woman bearing her destiny in sorrow rather than in joy.

Fanny gave a little cry, ran forward, and took the girl's hands in hers. "Ruthie, Ruthie!" she entreated. "Whatever is the matter, child! Sit down and tell Aunt Fanny! Where's Harley?"

The young woman shivered and withdrew her hands from the eager clasp, but obediently sat down in a low rocker, listening to the kind voice reassuring and beseeching in turn. Finally, she looked up and said slowly, "There's no use talking to me, Aunt Fanny. There's no use in anything when next week there won't be a roof over our heads and not a place on earth to go!"

Fanny stared at her incredulously. When she spoke, her voice was a whisper, as if she feared even to speak her apprehension aloud. "Ruthie! Lem ain't going to do anything like that! My God, he couldn't!"

"Oh yes, he could, too, Aunt Fanny!" said the girl, suddenly roused to defiance. "Harley's talked and talked to him! We could have paid this year if the cow hadn't got that hurt and the lightning struck the barn and all the hay lost. We've had such hard luck all round. We could pay yet if he'd only give us time! He's told Harley it's final and out we go. Harley's gone up to town now to see if there's anything he can do, but we know it's no use."

Lem Beeson's wife did not answer. She sat gazing straight ahead of her, her lips moving silently, her whole soul engrossed with this latest revelation of her husband's character.

Ruth experienced a swift contrition. "Oh, Aunt Fanny, I ought not to have told you! You can't help it and you've been so good! Try not to think of it, Aunt Fanny!" She saw for the first time the package Aunt Fanny had laid upon the table; her question of, "What's in your bundle?" recalled her visitor to her original errand. The joy was all forgotten and even Ruth's sobbing gratitude could not fully arouse her. Presently she rose.

"Well, I must go, Ruthie. I don't know *what* is to be done but I know there's something. God won't let him do this awful thing and don't you worry. You tell Harley it's going to be all right. It's going to be all right!"

All the way back across the fields she communed fearfully with herself. "If they meet in town, and Lem so black!" This was what had ailed him. "That mare'll kill him yet! Not yet, God, not yet, with these sins on his soul! Give him another chance, Lord! Give him another chance!"

One thing forced itself upon her; she must speak to him of this. Year after year she had been like this, shrinking before him, letting him drive on into deeper morasses of injustice and meanness, yielding what influence she once might have had with him in

252

her blind terror of these black moods. She had wandered in a maze, knowing of his reputation vaguely, trusting that hearsay was, at least in part, untrue. Now, this blow at the happiness and welfare of those she deeply loved had cleared her understanding and made the situation plain. She felt a large measure of blame pressing in upon her, the responsibility of the negative assent. Through her silence she had become a partner in his wrongdoing.

By the time her hurrying, stumbling feet had brought her to the kitchen door, she had determined on her course of action. The very fact of having something concrete in mind steadied and strengthened her; she went about her duties almost calmly. Once, pausing to look out, she recalled the scene of the morning. "I'm just like the bay mare," she said to herself, "it's in me to bolt, but he's got his hand over me!"

It was almost one o'clock when she saw Lem drive through the big gate. Foam-flecked and trembling, the little mare still obeyed the taut-drawn reins and entered the barn door quietly.

"I'll not speak to him till he's had his dinner," thought Fanny.

One look at Lem's face as he came in shattered the carefully reared structure of her courage. Accustomed as she was to his sour looks, she never before had seen him quite so forbidding. She wondered if he had met Harley Holt.

Silently she put the food on the table. Lem Beeson ate ravenously, almost savagely, in spite of the heat that now seemed well-nigh unbearable in the small, narrow kitchen. Fanny could not eat, but patiently waited upon him, answering his surly commands with quick, efficient service. Each furtive look at him confirmed her apprehensions. His face, always ruddy, was today a peculiar dark hue, almost purple in strange congested blotches. With a despairing heart, she watched him take up his hat and start out across the fields toward the Holt farm.

Terror possessed her. She ran frantically to the door and called his name. There was agony in her voice. He turned halfway and asked savagely, "What?"

Fanny never knew what spoke in her, what spirit uttered those strange words in that unfamiliar voice; certainly they did not come of her own consciousness or volition.

"Lem!" she cried, "Oh Lem, *I love you!*"

Her husband looked at her open-mouthed for a moment; evidently he believed her to be demented. Deep within him there must have stirred a response—he paused irresolutely, then strode angrily away.

Standing motionless in the doorway, Fanny saw him cross the upper field and enter the pasture. Suddenly he stumbled, staggered, and fell in a curious, crumpled heap. It seemed to Fanny as though she were witnessing something unreal, she herself unable to speak or move, only to gaze. She knew that Roger Dale, the neighbor across the pike, had come to the low fence and stood looking intently toward the field. She saw him vault over and heard him call to the occupant of a passing buggy, "Here, Thompson, lend a hand; Lem Beeson's fallen; guess he's sick or something!" She heard, too, the answer, "Let him lie! It's what he'd do to you or me!" And Dale's challenge, "Show yourself the better man, then, and come along!" A good man was Dale, an elder in the village church and therefore the object of Lem Beeson's open contempt.

Gradually the power to speak and move came back to Fanny; when the men at last brought in their heavy inert burden, she was ready. She accepted Thompson's offer to send the doctor but she did not need Dale's kindly warning, "I'm afraid it's too late, Aunt Fanny." She knew that Lem was gone.

It all seemed marvelously clear to her—the Lord had stopped him because she had not. Fortunately, this thought did not bring an overwhelming sense of self-reproach—it seemed to her dazed mind quite natural. Ruthie must be spared at any cost and since Fanny herself had failed to intervene, Heaven had saved her in the only way possible.

The next two days were lived through. Kindly neighbors came and went and Fanny accepted their ministrations gratefully, feeling a sense of kinship unknown for years. To them all she said, in effect, the same thing. "Lem appreciates this!" or, "Lem thinks it kind of you!" or "Lem's glad, I know, you're all so neighborly and good to me!" The presence of death sealed lips that might have made sharp rejoinder and the general impression prevailed that Fanny Beeson was "a mite touched" by the shock.

Young Gaylord, the Presbyterian minister whom Lem Beeson had so loudly and repeatedly flouted, said to his wife after his return from the funeral, "It's strange about these hearts of ours! Everyone that knew Lem thinks his wife ought to be thankful enough for her release from him, but I watched her today and there's grief there, far beyond the ordinary, for all she's so quiet."

Mrs. Allen remarked to her husband, the judge, "What do you suppose Fanny will do now, Adam? She's been crushed so long by that tyrant she won't even know what to do with her freedom!"

"What worries me," said the judge, "is what Fanny'll do with her money! Fanny's a rich woman and has no more idea than a two-year-old how to use it."

"Well," rejoined his wife, "it's a good thing that Lem had to leave her his money; he wouldn't have if he could have taken it along!"

The judge laughed. "That's just what I told him. Lem came in one day to have me fix up some papers in a land deal and I says to him, 'Lem you ought to make a will.' You could see he shied at the very idea; hated even to think of leaving his property behind him or of having anyone else get the benefit of it. 'What I need a will for?' he says. 'Well,' I says, 'we all have to hit the trail some day and most of us travel light on that journey. Do you aim to take your money along?' I says. He didn't answer, just sat there studying it over. 'Besides,' I added, 'I'd like to see Fanny provided for.' 'Oh!' he says, 'the law'll look out for her, I reckon!' 'Not so well as you can,' I told him; 'the law gives her the widow's exemption and up to five thousand dollars but only half of the rest.' I could see he was interested then. 'Who gets the other half?' he says. 'Oh, that boy of your sister's over at Ellensville,' I says, 'and you know just how long it'll take Bert to go through it!' I sure had him there; you know how he hated that sister, and the boy's no good on earth, they say. So that was how Lem made his will and I'm glad he did; but heaven only knows what Fanny'll do with the property—get cheated out of it, I suppose!"

They did not know Fanny Beeson.

That evening she refused all offers of company. "But you'll be so lonely, Aunt Fanny!" said gentle Anna Dale, the last to leave her.

"Oh no, I won't, Anna! You see Lem and I have so much to talk about," she said. "He was never any hand to talk—before!" she added dreamily.

Anna Dale looked at her anxiously, wondering if it were safe to leave her, but finally she decided to let her have her way and went reluctantly home.

All that night Fanny sat by her open door, living again the life that had been hers and making her plans for that which was to come. Often she had tried to force her mind to the deliberate recollection of her early married life, striving, perhaps, to regain the mental attitude of those days when something like happiness had been her portion. But, at certain remembrances, her mind had closed instinctively, shutting away the loveliness of the past from the ugly present. On this night of vigil, however, all barriers were down and that which memory had preserved, sweet and sacred, rose and overflowed her soul, purifying and enriching all recollection. She remembered her orphan girlhood, "living on friendship," as she so quaintly put it, yet happy enough since the home in which she was placed was a good one and the family kind and thoughtful toward her. They had given her schooling and at nineteen she was adept in all the housewifely arts.

She recalled the day she had first seen Lem, coming through the woodland with the master of the Kentucky estate. He had come down to buy a team of horses and, his fancy caught by the slender little figure with arms upraised to push the old swing, had taken back a wife to his Pennsylvania home. His wooing had been swift and tempestuous and Fanny realized afterward that she had always feared, even while she loved him.

Love had been uppermost; through that first happy year it was her joy to yield herself utterly to that compelling mastery. He was ten years her senior and it was a new experience for Fanny to belong to anyone. Her baby had not lived, and with this event and the realization forced upon them that there could never be another child, Lem's attitude had begun to change. Fanny knew absolutely that the desire for children was dominant in Lem. Since she failed to fulfill this ambition, she was the first upon whom his bitterness began to vent itself. Yet, she had loved him through it all and now she seemed to know, in some strange intuitive way, that her loyalty was justified. She no longer felt the pain of self-reproach; she was only thankful that her last words to him had been of love instead of upbraiding.

As the dawn brightened and reminded her that a new day was at hand, she rose and closed the door. Lem's old coat hung upon the back of it and pressing her cheek against its rough folds, she whispered softly, "Lem, you shall have your chance, dear—you shall have your chance!"

That afternoon when the judge returned from dinner, he found Fanny Beeson waiting in his office, on her lap a dispatch box filled with papers. "Why, Fanny," he said in surprise, "I was aiming to come out this evening to see you about those. I didn't think there was any hurry!" It seemed so unlike Fanny to be concerned with worldly affairs and he had supposed she was familiar with the will.

It was not, however, Lem's last testament that her anxious fingers sought as the pile of documents grew on the desk before her. Deeds, mortgages, mortgages, deeds— Lem Beeson had indeed been a man of property! At last she found it, the deed to Harley Holt's little farm, with the mortgage attached. She held it out.

"Adam," she said, trembling with eagerness, "I want you should fix this up right away to show it's paid."

"Paid!" exclaimed the judge. "*Paid*! Why, Fanny, Lem was foreclosing that mortgage the very last day he was here!"

"I know," said Fanny, "but it's paid now and Lem knows it. He wants it should be done!" she added earnestly.

"Well," replied Judge Allen, "I'm glad enough to hear it. Harley's a good hardworking boy and if I had seen any way on earth to raise the money, I'd have done it that day rather than see him lose his place."

Only after this matter had been settled to her satisfaction would Fanny listen to his explanations about the will, and even then she was obviously impatient to be gone. She concluded happily, "Lem thought for me, didn't he? Lem did well by me!"

The judge smiled grimly. "Yes," he answered, "you're a wealthy woman, Fanny, something like two hundred and fifty thousand it totals. I suppose you'll be buying you a great limousine and going to Europe!"

"In the limousine, I reckon!" flashed Fanny, laughingly.

The judge looked at her. "Fanny, you spoke that like your old self!" Fanny laughed again.

"I was a prankish girl, wasn't I?" she said wistfully. Then, with a sudden look of eagerness, "Adam, do you remember that about the 'years that the locust hath eaten?' I've been thinking about that! And you needn't worry about me, Adam, there's plenty to be done right here and Lem's laid it upon me!"

Ruth Holt had paused in her task of preparing supper to speak sharply to her young husband. "Harley, what you worrying for? Don't you know Aunt Fanny'll give us time on that mortgage? She'd never in this world turn us out!"

"I know that," assented Harley gloomily, "but the old devil may have tied it up so she can't help herself. I tell you, Ruth, there was too much meanness in Lem Beeson to be put under ground all at once; it'll show up somewhere. No, I ain't afraid to talk about him. I couldn't be more scared of him dead than I was when he was alive, could I? Besides—"

"Hush!" said Ruth, hastily, "here comes Aunt Fanny now! My, to think what's happened since she was here that morning!"

Aunt Fanny came in hurriedly, with the unselfconscious eagerness of a child, unaware of either Harley's sullen look or Ruth's troubled face. Her whole thought was centered in the papers which she thrust into Harley's unreceptive hands.

"There!" she exclaimed joyfully. "The place is yours, Harley, 'free and unencumbered' as Judge Allen said, and not a mite more worry for Ruthie, praise be!"

The young man stood gazing stupidly at the deed. "But—" he faltered.

"I know, I know!" said Aunt Fanny quickly. "But Lem's thought better of it now and he wants you should have it, Harley!" Again she spoke with the deep earnestness that had impressed the judge. "Nor you mustn't thank me," she went on, in answer to their stumbling words, "it's not from me, it's Lem. And Harley, I want your promise on one thing—" She paused.

"What's that, Aunt Fanny?" asked the boy gently. "Guess there's nothing I wouldn't promise you!"

"It's this," said Fanny Beeson slowly. "That you'll put away all hard feelings toward Lem. Not all at once," she added hastily, reading his unspoken thought, "but as you can and for always. Will you do this, Harley?"

"Yes, I will, Aunt Fanny," replied Harley soberly, "and I guess it'll be a blessing to me, too!"

When she had gone, he looked once more at the precious deed. "Lem Beeson!" he exclaimed incredulously. "It's a wonder he didn't rise in his grave to take it back."

"Harley!" cried his wife. A deep flush overspread the handsome young face. "There I go!" he said contritely. "But never again, Ruthie. You'll see!"

So Fanny Beeson began her work. The little village rocked with the news of her. "What will she do next?" became the absorbing question.

Carpenters came to the white house on the hill. In one end of the long sitting room appeared a conservatory filled with the plants and flowers that Fanny had always loved so passionately but with which Lem would never allow her to "clutter up the house." A deep fireplace brought back to her the cheer of her Kentucky home. She said tenderly to Anna Dale, "Lem never rightly understood before how much I wanted all this, but he knows now." Anna smiled and assented. She felt one should humor Aunt Fanny in her queer ideas, since they harmed no one.

Lem's good-for-nothing nephew came to live with Aunt Fanny. She told Reverend Gaylord about him. "Of course he's done wrong," she said, "but he's only twenty and no mother and no home—no folks at all! He'll be a good boy when he gets to know the home feeling!" She did not say this to the lad himself. "I'm a lonely old woman, Bert," she said to him. "I had to give up my boy and now Lem's gone and no one in the world to belong to me but you. Don't you think you could be contented to stay with Aunt Fanny when she needs you so much?"

Bert went with her to the little village church where she had resumed her old place and young Gaylord took him into a warm friendship. It was he who discovered the boy's secret ambition to become a civil engineer and Fanny rejoiced beyond words in the power to put him in the way to be a useful and happy man. One day the minister was surprised to have Bert say to him, "The way Aunt Fanny talks, you'd think Uncle Lem had it all fixed out for me and darned if I haven't almost come to believe it, listening to her!" In a flash Gaylord understood. Thenceforth, he was Aunt Fanny's strong aid in her purpose, speaking a quiet word here and there, expressing what was really in his heart, since he, too, believed in the present tense of the spirit.

When Ruth Holt's little son was born, it was Aunt Fanny who must see him first.

"You haven't asked me his name," said the young mother, smiling through her weakness. "It's Lemuel!" Above Aunt Fanny's head, bent over the baby, her eyes challenged her husband but he made no dissenting sign. Thus Fanny Beeson's life gathered sweetness.

One day she sought Judge Allen in his office. "Adam," she said in the direct way that had become habitual with her, "you're my friend, aren't you?"

"Sure I am, Fanny!" replied the astonished judge.

"And Lem's?"

The judge blinked rapidly, but he could not shut out those entreating eyes.

"And Lem's," he affirmed.

"Well, Adam, I want you should do something for me and Lem. You know folks everywhere and they talk freely to you. I'm sure you know many that feel hard to Lem for things in the past. Will you seek them out and send them to me?" Unwilling but helpless, the judge promised.

And so from time to time they came, gruff, suspicious men and puzzled, apologetic women—accepting the judge's advice to go, yet wondering what might be in store for them in the house that had been Lem Beeson's. Patiently Fanny labored, probing like a skillful surgeon, deep into the root of the bitterness and seeking, with a wisdom astonishing even to herself, to right the wrongs. Many times her soul shrank from the revelations. The harshness and injustice of which her husband had been capable was bitter to her. But her heart was undaunted, and to each of them she said what she had said to Harley Holt. "Don't thank me! It's Lem's money and I'm only carrying out his wishes. I want to feel that you'll put away hard thoughts of him, from this day, and remember only that he sees it differently now and wants to make amends."

Ruth Holt understood her purpose. Bending over her baby's cradle one day, she said to Aunt Fanny, "Now watch him! Lem-u-el!" The name was a caress; responding to the sweet mother tone, the baby smiled and cooed. "See," cried Ruth, "he loves his name already!"

"It's a good name," said Aunt Fanny proudly, beaming with delight.

Gradually the name of Lemuel Beeson was wrought into the fabric of the village life; and if the spirit behind it was solely that of Fanny, his wife, the community was increasingly unaware of it. The contributions of Lemuel Beeson enabled the orphanage at Ellensville to expand and develop in an unprecedented way; there was a Lemuel Beeson scholarship at the state university available to the boys of that county; Lemuel Beeson supported a missionary on the foreign field, and when a new brick church supplanted the old frame structure that Lem in his lifetime had scorned to enter, it was his name that appeared as the principal donor.

"Ruth," said Harley Holt one evening as they sat on their little front porch, watching small Lemuel playing about the yard, "I've been thinking about Lem Beeson. Once, I couldn't have believed I'd ever think of him without a curse and now there's no trace of bitterness left. If I was to see Lem coming across those fields, I'd be glad!"

Ruth nodded gravely. "I know, Harley, and what's more, when I think of him, I don't even see him as I used to—there's a softness in his face as if he were looking at our baby and loving him!"

When the new church was dedicated, it was Fanny's privilege to entertain the kindly, eloquent man who came from the big city to preach the sermon. Sitting before the cheerful fire, mentally reviewing his impressions of the day, he spoke thoughtfully.

"There are not many men who use their opportunities as your husband did, Mrs. Beeson. Of course, his means enabled him to give greater service, but not every man realizes that money is God's chance for usefulness!"

The minister thought he had never seen so sweet a smile as radiated the worn face before him. Almost as one beholding a vision appeared Fanny Beeson as she answered, serenely, "Yes, Lem's had his chance, thank God! Lem's had his chance!"

6
CHAPTER

STORIES ABOUT ANIMALS

"A good milk cow in a family is second in importance only to a good wife. A milk cow should not be compelled to stand around an old straw stack, in mud, filth, snow and cold rains, or housed in an old, cold stable that has not been cleaned out all winter and then expected to furnish good milk for your babies. If you love your wife and babies, you should take care of your milk cow."
—*The Idaho Farmer,* November 1915

Animals were as much a part of the American country scene in the early part of the century as houses and barns. There were relatively few large livestock, poultry, or dairy farms that produced beef, pork, eggs, or milk on a scale familiar today, but most farm families kept animals for their own needs. Cattle and hogs kept meat on the table, chickens supplied fresh eggs as well as Sunday dinners, and milk cows furnished ample stocks of milk and butter. A few animals, along with gardens and orchards, helped make most rural families relatively self-sufficient.

And horses were equally important, of course. Good horses afforded the farmer the necessary power for field work and drew the conveyances that both town and country families depended on for transportation.

The country magazines were filled with articles on animal care and production. There was plenty of advice on marketing produce such as milk, butter, and eggs. This was likely to be aimed at women readers; the poultry house and butter churn typically were seen as the domain of the farm wife. Cash from the sale of butter and eggs often was a significant source of income. Even the children were encouraged to start small-scale poultry production; articles of the "farm boys earn money from chickens" type were common. Improving the farm's stable of draft horses for field work was an accepted source of pride for the farmer, a challenge that accounted for considerable advertising in the rural magazines. Men engaged in breeding, selling, and trading horses for both fun and profit.

But rural Americans cherished their animals for reasons that went far beyond the utilitarian value of livestock and poultry. Animals offered companionship; they could be trusted and loyal friends. Unlike fellow human beings, animals demanded little in return for their friendship. They were placid creatures, as Walt Whitman had observed, lacking human worries over happiness and respectability and "the mania of owning things."

Animals appeared in rural magazines as subjects of fiction almost as often as topics for informative news and feature columns. Stories about animals could evoke remarkable passion. An animal-story plot might involve compelling adventure in an exotic location or dramatic heroism by a common farm dog. Or it might offer comic relief.

Most short stories about animals were about horses or dogs. The plot variations seemed endless. Horses could race or pull, dogs could hunt or save their masters from any unexpected danger. Stories about horses that were traded and dogs that were lost or stolen were popular. Wild animals turned up less often, and then usually as the object of man's determination to hunt and kill. An exception to this could be found in children's stories written to teach youngsters about wild animals. These typically were light-hearted yarns that endowed animals with human characteristics. The *Ohio Farmer*, in its "Little Folks' Story" section, drew lovable portraits of such animals as "Jacob Rhinoceros," while *Wallaces' Farmer* did the same for an underground mole named "Starnose."

Typical of selections the rural magazine readers had to choose from in the period from which this collection was drawn, three of the four animal stories included here are about dogs or horses. The fourth is about a wild animal subject to the hunt. Each represents a broad range of fiction from the period, and each might have appeared in virtually any rural magazine at the time.

THE RENEGADE

Elmore Elliott Peake
The Country Gentleman, January 1916

BANTRY Pettigrew—known to his parents and a few other staid adults as Foster—stood on the Harrodstown wharf boat, wearing a new straw hat with a blue band and an immaculate sailor waist. His cheeks were flushed, for he was only ten, and he was embarking for a visit to Grandfather Horton's, and Stub Hatch was going along.

Stub was a playmate of Bantry's simply by force of juxtaposition, he living across the alley from the parsonage barn. He was now Bantry's guest only because Alicia Pettigrew, Bantry's mother, had recently coaxed him into her Sunday school class. She had persuaded him at divers times since to surrender a greasy pack of playing cards, a rusty .22-caliber revolver, and a soggy remnant of plug tobacco; and she cherished a hope of clinching his reformation by a change of environment—Bantry having failed to inform her that Stub still spat brown on occasion and boasted that a fellow could gamble just as well with dominoes as with cards.

The wharf boat was a great, dusky, smelly inclosure, littered with bales, boxes and barrels, chicken coops, calf crates, and dozing Negroes sprawled about with their hats over their faces to fend off the flies. In the foreground a yellow dog scratched a flea-plagued ear at frequent intervals, incidentally beating a tattoo with his hock upon the oil-stained floor.

The boys surveyed the scene with interest, and finally Stub Hatch's black eyes rested upon the author of the tattoo. Disapproval, tinged with hostility, showed in his face.

"By cracky, Bant," he whispered, for the Reverend Homer Pettigrew stood near, "I wish Spot was here. He'd make mincemeat of that mongrel. Why didn't you bring him anyhow?"

"Father said I couldn't," answered Bantry regretfully. "He said he might chase grandfather's chickens. So he tied him up in the woodshed."

"Your daddy never wants nobody to have any fun," observed Stub discontentedly. "Spot could lick any dog we come across, and dig out gophers and woodchucks, and save our life besides if we should happen to scare up a wildcat—or a lion that had broke loose from a circus."

Presently a blast from the Valley Belle's melodious chime whistle set the summer air atremble, and the pair dove for the luggage at their feet.

"Put your bags down, boys—the boat is still below the bend," commanded Mr. Pettigrew. Though not an old man, his youth was aeons behind him; and now, as always, he looked calm and cool, in spite of the dog-day sultriness and a black alpaca coat buttoned to his Adam's apple.

"Let me finally repeat," he continued sermonically, "that you are on your honor as to good behavior. You, Foster, are to obey your grandparents' slightest command, and Charles is to do likewise. Any infraction of their rules will result in your immediate return. And do not presume upon their indulgence, for they have instructions from me to this effect."

Bantry assented with an obedient "Yes, sir," but Stub stood with hard, downcast eyes fixed upon the parson's square-toed boots—noticing which Alicia, who was fifteen years her consort's junior, said with a smile: "But have a good time and write home every week."

At length the Belle blew again, and the boys, who had begun to fear that she had struck a snag, were now permitted to gather up their traps. The boat was only a stern-wheel packet—the big sidewheelers having laid up on account of low water—but she fully satisfied the diminutive travelers' conception of grandeur as she headed into the wharf with clanging engine bells, hoarse exhausts, and the smoke pouring from her twin chimneys in velvety, inky swirls.

For ten minutes the black roustabouts, naked to the waist and glistening like seals, swarmed up and down the gangplank. Then the big bell on the forward hurricane deck warned Mr. and Mrs. Pettigrew ashore, after a hasty kiss; the hawsers were cast off the snubbing posts, and the plank was being hauled in when a streak of black-and-white crossed it like a shot out of a gun.

It was Spot, with the frayed end of a rope dangling from his neck; and without an instant's hesitation he bounded up the companionway and made straight for his master.

"Hold the boat, Captain Scott!" called Mr. Pettigrew, lifting his umbrella like a field marshal's baton. "That dog must be put off. Foster, bring him down at once."

But Spot's Scotch collie forebears had not studied human nature for countless dog generations for nothing; he detected a Judas Iscariot note in Bantry's reluctant call, and he fled. A merry chase followed, alow and aloft, fore and aft, which enlisted the whole bellowing, guffawing crew—cooks, pantry boys, and deckhands. Once, in the saloon, they would have nabbed Spot but for Stub Hatch, who slyly kicked open an outside stateroom door, giving the fugitive a fresh start of half a boat length.

Eventually, however, they cornered him in a coal bunker on the main deck. The bristling hair of his back and his gleaming teeth halted the crew members; but the Reverend Mr. Pettigrew, who had again boarded the vessel by this time, stepped into the bunker with that firm manner which he could so readily assume, seized the rope hanging from the dog's neck, and dragged him ashore on stiffened, skidding hind quarters.

But Spot was a dog who never said die; just as the boat was straightening up-river, a long, narrow head began to cut the intervening water some fifty yards above the wharf. The pilot saw it first, and he was a young fellow who must have loved dogs, for a sharp stroke of the engine bell stopped the wheel. The boat slowly lost way, and when the dog came alongside Captain Scott himself thrust a muscular arm over the gunwale, seized him by the scruff of the neck, and hauled him, dripping, aboard.

"I was afraid he'd get under the wheel!" he shouted to Mr. Pettigrew, who was

266

again vigorously waving his umbrella in protest. "I'll put him off up-river a piece."

"How far up-river, if you please, sir?" asked a respectful but anxious small voice at his elbow. "I wouldn't want him to get lost, sir."

"About seventy miles," answered the captain. "In the neighborhood, say, of Horton's Landing, where you get off."

Stub chuckled at the captain's strategy, but a troubled look clouded Bantry's face. "I'm afraid my father didn't understand that, sir," he demurred, though rather faintly.

"Perhaps not," answered Captain Scott with a wink at the mate. "But there's a law that forbids us from throwing a passenger from a boat while in motion, and as it doesn't say whether the passenger shall be two-footed or four-footed, I can't take a chance on a lawsuit. So I guess you boys will have to put up with this fellow on your vacation."

He stooped and, opening a big jackknife, cut the rope from Spot's neck.

"Why, Captain Scott, we'll be glad to have him," explained Bantry quickly. "It was my father who didn't want him to come along. But when I write home I'll explain about the law so my father won't think you deceived him."

"I wish you would," said the captain. As the boys moved off he added to the mate: "A damn nice little boy. But I've got no time for that old stiff of a sky pilot."

"Say, Bant," said Stub slyly, as he removed the irksome shoes and stockings which Mrs. Pettigrew had given him for the occasion, "didn't you know Spot would chaw that rope in two?"

"I didn't *know* it," answered Bantry gravely. "I *thought* he would. And if father had asked me I would have told him so."

The boat was a wonderland through which Captain Scott gave the boys a personally conducted tour, from the engine room—where the pitmans, like giant arms, thrust back and forth with irresistible power, spinning the paddle wheel as easily as a boy spins a top—to the pilot house.

The pilot let them hold the steering wheel a minute or two; and when, at his command of "Port your helm!" one pulled down with all his might and the other pushed up, and the jackstaff slowly swung to the left, their throbbing hearts fairly dyed their ears with blood. It was one of those supreme moments of which life is so chary later on.

To Bantry the conduct of affairs on the boat was even more thrilling than to Stub. There was none of the prudence, none of the punctiliousness which characterized the quiet, orderly parsonage. The mate bawled his orders as if addressing someone in the next township. The fireman slammed the doors as if trying to break them from their hinges. The roustabouts sang and hallooed, and sent barrels of apples whizzing down the stage plank with a recklessness that was fascinating.

When one of the barrels chanced to strike another one and burst open, showering the forecastle with Red Astrachans, Bantry held his breath, awaiting the penalty. But the merry crewmen scrambled for the apples, and Captain Scott, instead of being enraged merely said: "Go down and fill your pockets, boys."

Dinner was another big event. White-jacketed black waiters, popping through a swinging door, moved down the long, narrow saloon with incredible speed, balancing big trays of smoking dishes on one hand; and then, swiftly passing a towel beneath each dish, arranged them round one's plate in an ever-lengthening semicircle.

"Is this all fer me, you reckon?" Whispered Stub with glittering eyes.

"Of course," answered Bantry, who had eaten on a steamboat before. "There'll be more too—ice cream and cake and pie, and maybe watermelon."

Stub clutched his knife and fork with a beatific face. At home he often sat down to bread and potatoes.

It was a seven-hours' run to Horton's Landing, but to the boys, at least, the time passed all too soon. Owing to the low water they were disembarked upon a sandbar near the middle of the river. As the sun was now low they immediately fell to discussing ways and means, should they by any mischance have to spend the night there. But the Belle's three sonorous blasts had given Grandfather Horton due notice of his guests' arrival, and presently his skiff put out from shore.

At Grandfather Horton's there were many delightful things: The great kitchen where something appetizing was always cooking; the spring house with crocks of milk and butter sitting in the cold water; the garden with blackberries and raspberries along the edge, apple, peach, and plum trees; a poultry house where you could gather four dozen eggs a day; horses to lead to water; cows to drive home; a blacksmith shop at Horton's Corner, a quarter of a mile up the road; an ice-cream freezer with a dasher that whoever turned the handle could lick when the cream was frozen.

Yet the pair's favorite haunt was The Rocks—a wooded ravine with precipitous walls; caves that still smelled of wild beasts—if your smeller was good; ledges that a barefoot boy could creep along; jungly patches of ferns higher than your head, and a creek at the bottom along which little green herons flapped and squawked.

Yet, withal, it was a bosky, fearsome place, which made Stub bitterly regret the loss of his revolver. As a protector, though, Spot was not a bad substitute. No living thing escaped his eyes and nose. He had a certain bark that signified a snake, and his companions had perfect faith that any tramps, kidnapers, counterfeiters, or bad men in general who should attack them would be instantly torn to pieces by him.

One day the trio ventured beyond The Rocks into a stony, broken pasture which did not belong to Grandfather Horton.

Spot at once began to sniff the ground excitedly and presently dove into a copse like a dog on the trail of something worth while. When he began to bark furiously Stub suggested wolves. The boys halted, uncertain whether to advance or retreat. A moment later, however, a flock of sheep, bleating loudly and raising a cloud of dust with their flying feet, crossed the pasture in a panicky huddle. They piled up in a fence corner like a swift stream dammed by a fallen trunk. Spot leaped among them. They flew asunder like a living bomb, re-formed in a wild, struggling mass, and raced back toward their starting point.

At first the boys looked on admiringly. What finer testimony to his pure collie blood could Spot have offered than this instinctive effort to herd the first flock of sheep he had ever seen?

But when the flock again swung into view, with faltering legs and heaving flanks, the pair scented mischief. Moreover, Spot had undergone a strange change. His playful barking had ceased. He ran with a stiff, outstretched tail. Foam flecked his jaws; blood-lust glittered in his eyes, and he snapped savagely at the haunches of the flying animals.

Both boys darted forward in consternation to the rescue. But Bantry's loud "Hyuh, Spot! Hyuh, Spot!" was lost in the uproar; and when the flock again broke from the fence corner tragedy was revealed. A lamb lay on the ground, limp and still, and Spot, with a rigidly bowed spine, tore at its bloody throat.

"He's a sheep killer!" shrilled Stub accusingly.

Bantry stood with horror-sick eyes. It was the dreadful truth. Spot, the well-beloved, the upright, the pampered canine aristocrat of Harrodstown, had committed the crime of crimes in dogdom; had shown himself the degenerate scion of a long line of noble sires. To complete his infamy, he growled savagely as his master approached.

Now occurred one of those rare but violent ebullitions of temper so distressing to Bantry's parents, so antithetic to his equable disposition. With flaming face he seized a stone as large as his fist and hurled it with all his strength at the offending canine. It took him squarely behind the ear, and he instantly lost his appetite for raw lamb. Indeed, he rolled over on his back and showed the whites of his eyes in an alarming fashion. But after a moment he righted himself and crawled abjectly to Bantry's feet. The latter's anger instantly evaporated. His one thought now was to fly from the scene of the tragedy before the wrathful owner of the murdered sheep should appear with a gun and wreak vengeance on the murderer.

Twisting the thick hair of the dog's neck about his fingers—for he dared not trust him to follow—he dragged him toward Grandfather Horton's boundary line. Stub helped him bundle the dog over the rail fence. Then followed a breakneck dash down the steep side of the ravine—slipping, stumbling, stubbing their toes, bumping their heads.

At the bottom they paused for breath, but not long, for the wicked flee when no man pursueth. Up the other side they labored with thumping hearts, and then, with many a fearful glance behind, they struck out across the rolling land for home.

Stub, who was hardened to sudden flights, soon slowed his pace and before long was skylarking about in his usual manner—chasing butterflies, peering into bushes for birds' nests, ramming sticks into gopher holes. But all the long, hot way to the farmhouse Bantry never released his hold on the dog except to spell one aching hand with the other.

Under, over, or through fences, across creeks and ditches, through patches of tall, purple-flowered ironweed that viciously buffeted his face, he stuck by Spot's side until, by a circuitous route through the orchard in order to avoid the barn, they reached the tool house, where Bantry remembered having seen a dog collar and chain hanging from a nail. He secured the dog and then, with numb arms and throbbing temples and his rippling, auriferous hair flat and stringy with sweat, he threw himself upon the floor and wept.

Stub, who, unlike the poet, never wasted any time in looking before and after and pining for what is not, regarded their escape as closing the incident.

"What you bawlin' fer?" he demanded, whirling a tool grinder and touching a nail to the wheel to make the sparks fly. "That farmer will never know Spot killed his old sheep."

Bantry did not answer. His heart ached worse than his arms, and the dead lamb, so piteously still, was etched upon his brain in lines of fire. Foul murder had been done and his own hands were not clean. Had he warned his father that Spot would chew a rope in two the lamb would still be alive.

Nor was this the only cause of pain. The sinister transformation which had taken place in Spot in the pasture still griped him like a witch's spell. He now lay in a corner, but not in the attitude of sleep or rest. It was more like a crouch for a spring. Behind his slim muzzle, pressed to the floor, gleamed a pair of watchful, suspicious eyes. They seemed to say to Bantry: "Wait till I get loose. I'll kill all the sheep in that field. And I'll not forget that you struck me with a stone. Never again will I trust you."

"My stars and garters!" exclaimed Grandma Horton when the pair, at the summons of the dinner bell, appeared to wash up in the basin on a bench of the back porch. "Where have you boys been to get so hot and dirty and scratch up your legs like that?"

"We was over to The Rocks," answered the ready Stub, "and Spot chased a poor little rabbit and wouldn't quit when we called to him, and we had to ketch him and haul him home to keep him from chasin' it again, and we tied him up in the tool house to learn him to mind."

Bantry's lips parted to refute the lie, but no sound issued forth. To sign Spot's death warrant was beyond his power.

He ate little dinner. By this time, he supposed, the alarm must have spread throughout the countryside. His excited imagination pictured not one farmer but a posse of them, armed with shotguns and mounted on horses, in pursuit of the sheep-killing dog.

To keep a lookout he spent most of the afternoon in a lawn swing in the front yard. The sound of every hoof on the white pike beyond the osage orange hedge brought his heart to his throat. Finally, a man with a gun on his shoulder really did appear and Bantry, with a blanched face, sped to the tool house, resolved to defend his pet to the last extremity. But the man passed down the road.

At supper, though, the blow fell. Grandfather Horton was called to the telephone. When he returned he announced that Ash Whitehead had warned him to be on the watch for a stray dog that had killed one of his sheep. Grandfather's voice was always soft and low, but the knell of doom could not have impinged more stunningly upon Bantry's ears.

A dreadful silence followed—or so it seemed. Bantry imagined that his grandparents and the hired girl and all the harvest hands were staring at him accusingly. With his dilated eyes glued to his plate, he feared they would hear his pounding heart or see his trembling hands. Then he felt Stub's warm, bare foot press warningly upon his own under the table; one of the hands spoke of a barn dance to be given that night, and thus the crisis passed.

That night, after stripping off his few clothes, Stub bounced into bed without troubling to put on the nightshirt Mrs. Pettigrew had made for him. He knew Bantry would not tell his grandmother unless directly questioned. That was a remarkable thing about Bant. Bant never swore, chewed tobacco, or told lies; yet he never tattled on boys who did swear, chew, and lie.

As Bantry knelt at his bedside prayers—more protracted tonight than usual—Stub watched him with bright, unblinking, beady eyes. Stub, at Mrs. Pettigrew's earnest entreaty, had himself once tried prayers. But, in his own words, he had not found them what they were cracked up to be. He had asked for everything he could think of so as not to hamper God's beneficence, but had laid special emphasis on a shotgun and a bicycle, either new or second-hand. The result was nil. Even the humble request, on one occasion, that he might find a dime on the sidewalk the next morning with which to buy a fishline and hooks had come to naught, though he had trudged miles with his eyes on the ground.

Yet he had never known Bantry to miss his prayers on a single night. It was the more puzzling because Bantry was no fool, either. He was the first person to prove to Stub that toads don't make warts on your hands, that horsehairs don't turn into snakes, and that seventeen-year locusts don't bite.

"Stub," said Bantry, after blowing out the light and climbing in bed, "I think we'll go home tomorrow."

"And leave all these eatin's! What fer?" demanded Stub in amazement.

"Because I'm afraid they will kill Spot."

"Shucks! How they goin' to find out he done it? Nobody seen him but you and me. If they had, old Whitehead wouldn't have phoned your granddad about a stray dog."

"But I'm afraid Spot will go back to that pasture and kill another sheep. Dogs do that, I've heard, when they've had a taste of the blood."

"Spot won't—not after that crack you took him on the head," declared Stub confidently. "By jeeminy, I'll bet he seen stars. Anyhow, if we keep him tied up tomorrow he'll forget about that sheep. Tain't like an aig-suckin' dog. You can't cure an aig-sucker 'cause they suck so many aigs before you find 'em out. But this was Spot's first sheep. Mebbe he didn't know it was a sheep."

"Grandfather might ask why we kept him tied."

"Tell him you're punishin' him fer not mindin' you, like I told your grandmammy."

"But that wasn't true, and I'm sorry you told it to grandmother."

"You are, huh? Well, old Spot would be a dead one by this time if I hadn't." He yawned. "I'd lie fer a good dog like Spot any old time."

"Say, Bant," he asked a moment later, "did you pray tonight fer him not to be killed?"

"Yes," admitted Bantry after a pause.

"Do you think he won't be, then?"

Bantry reflected a moment. "He won't be unless God thinks it's for the best."

"What good will that do when *you* don't think it's fer the best? He's your dog, not God's. And I'll tell you something else too: When I prayed fer a shotgun and it didn't come, your mother said that God helps them that help theirselves. Accordin' to that

271

you got no license to think God'll save Spot if you don't try to save him too."

Before Bantry could extricate himself from this stalemate, Stub's regular breathing indicated sleep. But it was a long time—as time is measured in Boyland—before sleep came to Bantry. A flock of sheep raced round and round in his brain. Outside, the insect orchestra of midsummer buzzed and whirred and clacked. Ordinarily it was soothing to Bantry. But tonight the chorus of tree crickets, tinkling like millions of tiny sleighbells in fairy hands, struck a mournful note. And the katydids seemed to fiddle:

"Spot, he did! Yes, he did, he did! Spot, bad Spot! Bad, bad, bad Spot! They'll kill Spot! Yes, they'll kill, kill Spot!"

But along toward morning, by his own reckoning, Bantry fell asleep. At about the same moment Grandfather Horton was making his usual bedtime round of the stable with a lantern to make sure that none of the horses had a foot in the manger or was tangled in his halter. When he paused on his way back to the house to lock the tool house door, an appealing whine came from within.

Grandfather loved a good dog. Stepping inside, he was about to release Spot when he paused, as if struck by a thought, for grandmother had mentioned the boys' obvious excitement at dinnertime. Stooping and holding the lantern close, he examined Spot's lips. He discovered several kinky gray hairs which plainly had not grown there. These he carefully picked off. Next he drew a handful of waste from a drawer, wet it at the horse trough, and sponged a clot of blood from the white patch on Spot's breast. Also, he left the dog tied up.

The next morning he hitched white Fanny, who was too old to work in the fields, to the phaeton and drove over to Ash Whitehead's with his checkbook in his pocket. But no one except grandmother knew the nature of his errand. When the story of Spot's misdeed was made public he wanted it to come from Bantry, as he felt confident it would.

All that day the lad stole off by himself at every opportunity. He was very unhappy. Spot's danger was not the only element in his unhappiness; his deception of his grandparents was a close second.

As he lay in the tall grass beyond the hedge, watching the white cumulus clouds which seemed to bring heaven so near, the warble of a bluebird suddenly wrought him to tears. It breathed the sorrow which now burdened the whole world. The crowing of distant cocks, the lowing of cattle, expressed the same sentiment. Even the flowers looked sad.

So he would have loved to lay his head in his mother's lap and sob out his pain. But he knew that he would not have done it had she been there. There was no such heartsease for him. Confession, restitution, and sacrifice were the medicine for his sick soul.

People, looking at Bantry's blue eyes and burnished flaxen hair, often remarked that he was his mother's own child. Indeed, in addition to her physical features he also had inherited her sunny disposition, soft heart, and tender, yielding spirit. Now and then, nevertheless, his father's adamantine will and ruthless hewing to the line of conscience cropped through these milder traits of character as a boulder crops through a velvety turf. Thus it was that, about sundown, he came to a high resolution.

The next morning he refused a ride to the railway station with Stub and the hired man. The wagon was not out of sight before he set about his sacrificial business.

Calling Spot, he led the way to the tool house and buckled the collar about the dog's neck. The task was harder because Spot had both forgiven the blow from the stone and shown no inclination, when released the day before, to return to the scene of his bloody carnival.

The boy's hand trembled. But with set teeth he led his dog through the orchard, so as not to be observed from the house, to a point on the highway.

It was about a mile to the Whitehead place—a big, white house crowning a hill which Bantry had ridden past several times. The road descended a long slope from Grandfather Horton's, crossed a bridge over a creek at the bottom, and then climbed another long slope.

It was a beautiful road, bordered with goldenrod and asters and clumps of wild cherry trees. But today it was as gloomy to Bantry as the corridor from a death house to the gallows.

Spot tugged lustily at his chain and all but overturned his master when a half-grown rabbit leaped from a tuft of grass. Bantry did not see it. They met a group of urchins who looked askance at Bantry's sailor waist and blue-banded hat and assailed him from behind with cries of "Sissy!" But he scarcely heard.

Once his courage failed and, dropping heedlessly into the dusty roadside weeds, he wound his arms about his dear friend's neck and wept bitterly. He wished he might die then and there. Yet he rose at so trivial a thing as the sound of an approaching wagon and dashed the tears from his eyes with his sleeve in order that the man might suspect nothing amiss.

It was a woebegone little figure, dusty, tear-stained, and flushed, which the motherly Mrs. Whitehead opened the door upon ten minutes later.

"Why, you're Sarah Horton's little grandson, ain't you?"

"Yes, ma'am, and I'd like to see Mr. Whitehead, if you please."

"Why, certainly. He'll be glad to see you. You'll find him in the barn. But won't you come in and have a glass of nice cold milk first? You look hot."

"No, ma'am, thank you. I—I wouldn't feel right to drink any of your milk." After a pause he added in a tremulous voice: "And I'm afraid Mr. Whitehead won't be glad to see me when I tell him why I came."

She gazed down upon him sympathetically, suspecting his errand; for of course she knew of Elijah Horton's visit the day before.

"Oh, I am sure he will," she declared. "He likes boys. I'll go out to the barn with you, so you won't have any trouble in finding him." At the wide doorway to the carriage room she added: "You just wait here a minute."

He made a quick survey of the barnyard, wondering if the lamb's grave might not be there. He had heard of people so grief stricken over the loss of a lamb as to want it buried near them, and even to erect a tombstone over it. But to his relief no grave was in sight. Then the bearded farmer appeared.

"Good morning, sonny," said the man very kindly, and stooped and patted Spot on the head.

This unexpected attention to the dog all but unnerved Bantry. For a moment he struggled with something in his throat, and then he heard himself saying, in a voice that sounded strange and far-away in his own ears, as if some other boy were speaking:

"Mr. Whitehead, this is the dog that killed your lamb."

He recoiled slightly as he spoke, expecting an explosion of anger. But to his astonishment Mr. Whitehead's face scarcely changed its expression.

"You don't say so! Why, he looks like a good dog to me."

"He is a good dog, sir," exclaimed Bantry earnestly. "He never chases chickens or sucks eggs or fights other dogs unless they jump on him first. But," he faltered, "he killed your sheep. I saw him do it."

"How do you account for it?"

"Why, we took him into your field, but we didn't know there were any sheep in it. He never saw any sheep before, because he's always lived in town. He chased them, but we thought at first he was only trying to drive them home, for that is what Scotch collies are trained to do, you know. Then he got excited; I never saw him so excited before; and then—then he killed the lamb.

"I came over here because grandfather's hired man says some dogs are natural sheep killers, and that a dose of buckshot is the only thing that'll cure 'em, and that the law allows a farmer to do it."

"Does your grandfather know that you came?"

"No, sir."

The man stooped for a spear of hay and began to break it between his fingers. "Do you mean that you brought him over here to be killed?" he asked very gently.

The lad paled at the question. "I don't want to break the law, or to deceive grandfather and grandmother any longer, and you can kill him if you think it's right," he answered with a convulsive swallow. "But I love him, Mr. Whitehead," he urged, lifting a pair of fervent, appealing eyes, "and my mother loves him, and I thought if I promised to keep him chained up, or to take him home right away and pay for your lamb besides, that maybe you would forgive him."

"That's certainly a fair proposition," returned the farmer. "But I wouldn't want you to cut your visit short, and I'd hate to have the dog chained up this hot weather, with so many flies round. I don't believe that would be necessary anyhow. He doesn't strike me as a natural sheep killer, and I doubt if he would go back to that pasture again."

Whitehead paused. He had raised four boys of his own. He wanted to make it easy for this one, yet not too easy.

"As to paying for the lamb, how were you thinking of doing it? Have you any money?"

"No, sir; only enough to pay my fare and Stub Hatch's back home on the steamboat. But," he added eagerly, "I carry part of a paper route for a big boy in Harrodstown, and he pays me a quarter a week. I could send you that every week till the lamb was paid for. Of course, you might not want to trust me."

"Oh, I'd be glad to trust you," answered Mr. Whitehead. "But another plan occurs to me. We are going to pick peaches tomorrow, and we're short of help. If you care to hire out, a day's work would about square us—especially if your friend Stub came along."

"Why, I'd love to do that, Mr. Whitehead!" cried Bantry, with a joyous face. "I don't call picking peaches work."

"All right, then. Talk it over with your grandfather, and if he's agreeable be over here about eight o'clock in the morning. Now I've got to drive down to the Corner for some axle grease and you can ride with me. Spot will follow if you unchain him."

A wonderful change had come over the road. The flowers nodded gaily; a dickcissel sang from almost every fence post; bobwhites and meadow larks whistled on every side. Once again the world was brimming over with joy.

"You don't know how glad I am to have this settled, Mr. Whitehead," said Bantry as he climbed down from the buggy at the Corner.

"Same here, sonny," answered Whitehead with a smile. "I know now that no stray dog will kill any more of my sheep."

Stub Hatch awaited Bantry, seated on the horseblock and curling dandelion stems with his tongue. Bantry's story fairly stunned him; also streaked him with envy, for he knew his own nerve would never have stood such a test. But he only said:

"By cracky, Bant, you took a big chance. Some of these dodgasted cross old farmers would have blowed Spot's brains out. But I'll help you pick peaches. I suppose a feller kin eat all he wants to."

Bantry next sought his grandfather. Ordinarily he would have gone to his grandmother first, but this was largely a matter of business. Grandfather Horton, who was oiling a set of harness, wiped off his hands, lit his pipe, and listened with attention.

"That was done like a man, Foster," said he. "Now let me tell you a little story. Once, a good many years ago, I owned a young horse that never seemed to get bridlewise. I sold him to a man and told him the horse had never run away. But I didn't tell him that the horse seemed always wanting to run away. Well, it wasn't a month before he did run away and broke two of the man's ribs. I never felt right till I had paid that man's doctor bill and taken the horse back and refunded the money. My neighbors thought I was foolish, but I knew better. Peace of mind is worth all the money in the world."

"Yes, sir," said Bantry. "It's like the toothache. You hate to have your tooth pulled, but you're glad when it's out."

Rodney Thomson

THE HORSE THAT BROKE HIM

Jack Humphrey
Capper's Farmer, September 1920

S IDE by side the man from the East and the man from the West hunched forward on the hard seats of the grandstand. Before them in the dusty, hoof-torn arena, three men worked slowly about a sullen, brooding brute, saddling the man-killer. About them the crowded grandstand waited in quiet, tense impatience. It was the last day of the world's champion bronco bustin' contest at Juarez.

For three days the crowd had watched the varying contest between man and beast. Picked men, the best in all the range country between Montana and the border, had fought it out. Man had conquered and had been conquered and the crowd had ceased to gasp as the ambulance clanged in to carry out an unconscious rider and the victorious horse shook and twisted to free himself of the saddle and to dodge the ropes of the wranglers. It had ceased to shudder as crippled horses, broken in their mad fights, were dragged out to be shot. Only two men had come through that ordeal and now the last rider was saddling up.

In the arena the man-killer, blindfolded, his head snubbed over the withers of a sturdy cow pony, squealed in anger. A long, lanky cowpuncher industriously chewed one ear of the horse, while a companion held fast to the other ear with a two-handed grip. Carefully, slowly the rider raised and eased the saddle to the horse's back, pushed it forward, caught the cinch and drew it close. With the same methodical care he threw the bucking rope around the horse's flanks and tugged it snug. With both hands at the latigo he cinched the saddle tight. The horse squealed again, a high-pitched scream of rage, and the tension of the crowd snapped.

"God, how cruel," exclaimed the man from the East, as he scowled his disapproval.

The man from the West turned toward him resentfully.

"Cruel nothin'" he growled. "He's not bein' hurt. Just plain onery, I call it."

A final tightening of the bucking rope and the man-killer pulled back, threw himself sideways and fell. In the same instant the lanky puncher was on the horse's head and the preparations continued. Standing astride the fallen horse, his feet in the stirrups, the rider gave the word to cut loose. As the horse rose the rider caught his seat, the spurs sank into the animal's shoulders and the fight was on. In accordance with contest rules, the spurs racked back, and streaks of blood followed their path. The man from the East gritted his teeth.

"God, how cruel," he burst out again.

"Hunh," the man from the West frowned. "What'd you come for? That's not hurtin' him, much. Don't you know who's ridin' him? That's Joe Glenn. He's got the biggest heart for a horse of any man in the West. Joe's not cruel. That's his business and when it comes to horses Joe's got a love for horses that's bigger than anything you

277

can understand. Joe's been broke, body, heart, and pocketbook, by a horse that he hated and then loved, loved him so that he cried like a baby when the horse was gone."

For four minutes the horse pitched and plunged, with every trick known to the outlaw. Twice he came over backward, but Glenn was out of the saddle, and in again when the outlaw struggled to his feet. Old riders gazed, as breathless as the crowd, their admiration divided between the violence of the plunging, fighting outlaw and the man who rode him.

Suddenly, with one furious burst of rearing, plunging and twisting the outlaw quit. The crowd waited silently. The man in the saddle sat tight, sensing a new trick of the outlaw. Then as the horse stood dejectedly, head down, legs and body muscles relaxed wearily, the man slapped at his head twice, thrice. The horse did not move.

It is a common mistake of the public mind to believe that the smartest horses are the trained animals of circus and riding school or the high-bred pets of paddock and sportsman. The bad horse is and always has been the most knowing thing in horseflesh; otherwise, he could not be an outlaw. The outlaw knew he was beaten and that further fight was useless.

Glenn swung carelessly from the saddle and limped across the arena and as a megaphone voice boomed out, "Joe Glenn qualified on Funeral Wagon as champion bronco buster of the world," the man from the West yelled in the roar of applause.

"Whoopee, Joe's made his ride," he shouted into the ear of the man from the East.

"See that leg he's draggin'. Joe got that from a horse he loved, the horse that broke him. Let me tell you about it."

And while they trailed out with the crowd the man from the West spoke on:

That was a long time ago. Joe had his own ranch then. Just a big kid with his all sunk in a bunch of broom-tailed mares. Then he got a stud to mate with them. A real horse, too, the best I ever saw but one, his son.

That stud broke him, stole his last dollar and left him as you saw him there, limping through life and earning his bread working for the other man. The summer he got the horse that broke him Joe worked four months for old Cap Watts and never drew a cent. When time came to quit Joe said he wanted to buy a stud. Then Cap told him he could pick his bunch of colts for a wage or he'd pay him one hundred and sixty dollars in gold.

Joe picked the bunch and he picked with a knowledge of every horse old Cap owned. The colt he led away was a golden sorrel. His mammy was the best steel dust mare in the C. W. brand and his daddy the horse that made the brand famous through the whole Southwest. Pretty? That colt was a picture. Slim and trim with the muscles just rippling beneath his golden hide. Growthy, too, for his kind and with a head and ear that showed his breeding and his cow sense as far as you could see him.

Joe took him home and kept him in all that summer; handled him some, but mostly let him run and play. Next summer he turned him in a trap with a few picked mares and the next turned him loose on the range. The colt had grown, keeping all his beauty. His colts that came from the year before were perfect little pictures. Through the summer he led Joe's mares, a king in all his glory. In the fall he broke the round-up right at the corral gate, but Joe let him go, little thinking of the lesson.

The next year he took Joe's best mares and went up into the mountains. Never came to the ranch corral the whole summer through. Come fall and Joe rode out to brand the colts, and then came trouble. The stud remembered the lesson of the break at the corral gate. Quietly he went with mares and colts till they reached the open. Then he broke and took the bunch off with him.

Joe rode home and studied. In the days that followed he rode the range and located the dunging grounds that marked the horses' circle. He hired men and fitted horses. Then he laid a relay to run the wild bunch down. Three days they ran them, with hardly a breath of rest from light till dark. The mares had dropped out one by one until the stud was running alone. Then Joe took old Slim, the horse he had been saving. As the jingler brought him by and Joe rode out to take his relay, they were not three hundred yards apart. Away they went off toward the Pat hills, where they would turn west and south to where another man was waiting.

Joe disappeared, following the stud. When we found him next day Joe was unconscious. There he lay, and twenty feet below him was old Slim, head under, his neck broken. The marks told the story of how they'd run across a hog back and then half way down Slim had stepped into a dog hole and there they were—Slim dead, Joe unconscious and with a broken hip, and the stud nobody knew where.

From that time on the stud became a nuisance. He stole the best mares in the valley, ranged them over two big counties and never let a man get near. Every ranchman paid his toll to swell the herd running with him. Then the Association told Joe to get the stud off the range and Joe tried to do their bidding. He sold his mares to get money to fit his horses and hire men to make the run. For weeks he studied every move and every grazing ground the wild bunch favored. Then he set his men and gave the order to get him, alive if possible, but better dead than not to get him.

For days again they ran him. Each man taking the bunch for ten or twelve miles to where a fresh man and horse were waiting. These in turn passed them on to another, and so the relay kept them going from the first break of day until they were lost in the darkness.

This time again Joe was the last man. The bunch had dwindled to three-head—the stud, a grand black mare he'd stolen from old Cap Watts, and her yearling stud. And right here let me say that colt was sure a beauty. Just like the old horse but more so. His black mother had darkened up his coat until he shone like burnished copper. He had the build of the old horse but had more power. Even then, just a colt, he was still running wet when the mare and stud had been dry-coated for a day. And when a horse quits sweating you can figure he's near done his running.

But, as I said, Joe took the bunch from Billy out east of the Whitewater. He carried them north a ways, up toward the Pat hills where he got his limp before. This time, though, the stud was tired and was watching for a chance to quit the chase. Just ahead a mile or so there was a rincon and Joe could see by the way they headed that they aimed to cut in there and go to the mountains. Joe turned off at an angle for a hog back that let in beyond the entrance, to head them off.

I was watching through my glasses and Joe was trying hard. His horse seemed to be winded, for he gave but little to Joe's urging. The three ahead seemed to sense Joe's move and went on all the faster. Up and over the hog back, Joe dropped down right at their noses. But his horse was done and the three went by him. I saw Joe stop; a puff of smoke and the old stud went to his knees, fell, lay quiet. On off into the hills went the black mare and her colt—the old stud's son.

One would think that Joe had paid his obligation. He was broke, his horses were gone and there before him lay the stud that had done it. But off in the mountains went the colt that was to take more toll of work and time and money.

The colt grew up a whole lot like his daddy; darker, larger, faster, keener but with all the old horse's tricks and then some. The first year or so he ran with broomies, staying with a bunch until an older stud would run him off. Then he'd run alone until he found some other bunch and so it went until he reached his size and strength. From then on he had his own bunch. Picked them up where he could find them. Always he had them on the run and when one quit or was not fast he'd fight her off. In time he had a bunch of twenty-odd, the picked mares of the county. Some were branded mares and some were fillies, but one and all they were good ones. With this bunch he'd drop into a round-up only to break away and take the gentler horses with them. Little by little he made the horses wilder, until at length he had the whole valley outlawed.

While he grew Joe used to see him, for Joe was working for the Rods. As a colt Joe liked him. I remember Joe once said he'd give an arm for that horse four years old, sound and branded. But as the horse grew older, as the toll he took grew greater, every man seemed to blame Joe for him and with the blame Joe came to hate him. Joe'd come in after he had caught sight of the horse and he'd grieve and worry and almost fight us. "Ain't it enough," he'd say, "to lose my mares, break my bank roll, kill my stud and bust my leg, without having this hell hound track me? Every man along the valley seems to think I own him just because I owned his daddy. Yet he is a real one and I'd like to own him, sound and gentle."

Then came the summer of the great drought. With the drying of the outside water, the calf round-up was called off and all hands went to branding at the wells. A man or two at every well, according to its size, would watch the cattle as they came to drink and brand the calves that were unbranded.

Joe was working at the Whitewater well up in the valley where the Chiracahuahuas and the Pat hills come together to make a corner. As was his custom, he sat up on the windmill tower watching out over the valley in all directions. Out from the well went the cow trails like the spokes of some gigantic wheel. For perhaps a mile the grass was tramped thin or gone entirely. Then the green-gray guillata merged into the small brush, and beyond that was the bigger growth and then the mountains. Here and there the shifting mirage told its lie of plenteous waters while the little dust devils played up and down the valley. Without a breath of air the dust devils seemed to rise straight up to heaven, swirling columns of dust, writhing as though in torment.

One day as he sat on the windmill tower, gazing up toward the Pat hills, Joe saw a great dust devil rise. As he watched, it moved out into the valley, rose and swirled, but moved too regularly to be a real dust devil. He focused his glasses and watched to find its cause. First he made out a bunch of horses. They came on down to the Brady, found it dry and traveled southward. They were running as though they wanted water bad. Down across the valley, through the brush above the Scherer and straight for the 7D they headed.

The water at the 7D is fenced, and as the bunch slowed up to look things over before going in Joe could make them out. It was the young stud and his mares come in from the mountains. Afterward Joe told me of the thoughts that piled in on him. The young stud had come into the valley. Surely the mountain water must be dry. If that were true they'd have to come to the 7D right regular, for that was their nearest water. He thought of the horse and all the misery he'd caused him. And as he thought his hate grew hot and restless. With the thought and hate came plans for action, to make the stud's thirst cause his downfall.

Joe rode in to the Rods to quit his job and draw his money. The next day he went to the store at Four Bar and bought a pack of cheese, canned goods, and some crackers. Then he pulled out north for the brush that runs up to the west side of the 7D corral.

Out in the brush about a quarter from the water Joe made a dry camp and settled down to watch and wait and conquer. Along toward night he saw them coming. Down across the valley to the water, coming straight and fast, as though they felt sure of the ground before them. On they came without slowing until a couple of hundred yards away. Then the young stud caught the man taint on the air, threw up his head and snorted. Every mare and colt stopped short and ran a short way back while the stud looked things over. Back and forth he trotted with his nose thrown into the wind. Every little while he'd stop, look off into space and whistle. But as he watched and seemed to find nothing the demand of thirst told on the mares. One by one they slipped by him and into the water. When they had drunk they started back toward the mountains and the stud went with them, his thirst unquenched.

"You're on your guard today, boy," Joe whispered after them, "but the thirst will get you yet, and when it does you're mine."

Day after day the bunch came for water. Two days the stud went off without drinking, but the third day he looked things over, trotted in, snatched a swallow and ran back toward the mountains. After that he took more time and gave less thought to the man smell.

Days went by until the bunch would come to drink, and hang around to rest and drink again before they went back to their pastures. Then came the day that Joe thought the time was ripe to spring his trap and make his capture. When the bunch had drunk and gone, Joe went out and laid a rope from the corner of the great corral gate to the brush where he'd been waiting. He propped the latch so that it would drop and lock the gate, making the corral a prison. Then he covered rope and tracks with desert sand and went back to watch and wait.

With morning came a sky that was leaden. The air was heavy with a light breeze from the east that meant rain. Would the rain come to put water in the mountain holes and spoil his plans after all his work? Joe watched the clouds banking one above the other. Thank God the wind was from the east, so if they came it would carry to him and guard his trap the better. In the west the clouds grew darker and there came the flash of lightning and the low roll of thunder. But with it came the dust cloud for which he had been watching. Down they came, straight for the corral with its water. With never a halt they trotted by him and into the trap. That was Joe's moment and he jerked the great gate closed. With its bang came the first big drops of rain and then the storm broke over.

Little thinking of the storm, Joe went to tie the gate and make it doubly strong. Then he looked in at his capture. Round and round they raced and tried the fences. But the corral had been built to stand rough treatment and with each spring the horses were thrown back, only to run and try again.

The storm was over soon and then Joe went to work to brand his captives. One by one he cut the mares into the small corral adjoining, roped, threw and tied them down. With a cinch ring he drew the brand that marked them for his own and then turned them back to the bunch that waited. When the mares and colts were branded he worked the stud into the small corral and tied the gate against his struggles.

Joe stood and feasted his hate on the great horse's vain efforts to escape. But, as his gloating eyes wandered over the shining copper coat with its thousand glints and shadings, as they took in the play and ripple of the perfect muscles beneath the silken skin, noted the perfect form, the head, the ears, the back, the loins and the quarters, Joe's hate turned to admiration and then to love.

"You're a horse, you're a horse," he murmured.

Joe dropped down from the fence and went to the center of the corral with rope in hand and watchful. The great horse snorted and ran the faster. Joe let him run. To press him now would mean to start him fighting. Slower he ran and then Joe flicked his rope. With the move the horse renewed his efforts. Slowly the rope flicked and slowly the horse dropped back to an easy run. Each time, as he neared the gate, he slowed for an instant, seeming to hope that this time the gate would be open.

As he slowed at the gate in another circle Joe's rope shot out. The great horse reared and pawed but the rope seemed to reach up after him. It closed around his front legs at the knees and something pulled him over. With a crash he fell and lay there, winded, moaning. Before he caught his wind, lost in the fall, Joe had tied his feet together and the horse lay there helpless. Joe worked fast, to get the hackamore on before the horse could regain strength to fight. With the hackamore on and then a blindfold, Joe sat back and rested.

Slowly he fanned the fire that heated red the cinch ring for the branding. When it was hot he crossed the green willow sticks through its center and ran to the horse to brand him as his own. And then he stopped, backed off and looked at the horse he loved and hated and now loved again.

"You pretty lad," he said, "you're sound and mine but you are not gentle and I'll be hanged if I burn your hide until you are."

He threw the ring back into the fire and went to work to break the horse and prove his mastery. He loosed one hind foot and tied it high up to the horse's shoulder. Then turned the others loose and the horse bounded up, only to stumble and fall and try again.

At last he stood, three feet on the ground and one bound up and helpless. His head was thrown high and he seemed to try to look out through the blindfold. Joe took him by the rope that hung down from the hackamore. Gently he pulled and the horse reared to strike and fell. The fight went on until the horse heeded not the pull on the hackamore. With a blanket Joe slapped the horse from neck to tail. His fight seemed gone, for the horse did not flinch.

Folding back a fourth of the blanket in front, to make the saddle higher, Joe put the blanket on his back, well forward. Then he eased his saddle up, placed it, caught the cinch and drew it tight. All through it the horse did not move. Joe put a toe in the stirrup and placed a little weight on it. The horse jerked and tore loose. With all his might he struggled to loose that man-made thing from his back, great crooked jumps with a world of power in them. Joe watched and was thankful he was not in the saddle. As though with a final effort the great horse changed to long, straight jumps. Across the corral he went, straight into the fence that his blinded eyes could not see. Midway in his jump, high in the air, he struck it. There was a snap and the horse fell and lay still.

Joe ran forward, jerked loose the blind and tried to give help. But the neck was broken and the eyes were already glazing. Slowly Joe stripped loose the saddle and the ropes that held him. "Boy," he gulped, "you're sound and fine and—and, God bless you"—and Joe Glenn knelt by the horse he loved and cried like a baby.

WHITE

Edwin L. Sabin
The Farm Journal, April 1921

"BUFFALOES! Hey, boy! Buffaloes!" Before the last word was out, I had recklessly dropped the dish that I was wiping and, dishcloth in hand, had sprung to the door of the line cabin.

My cowboy partner, Tom, had come back in haste from an early morning canter on a little tour of inspection. We two were running things, just then, at this outpost of the Broke Arrow Ranch, Dakota Territory—"riding line" and keeping tab on the cattle while the two other cowboys, Dutch and Happy Jack, drove a bunch of beef to the railroad.

"Where?" I demanded. "How many? Did you see them?"

"Did I! First I heard 'em bellowing; but I wouldn't believe my ears, because buffaloes haven't been coming in here any more. Then I sneaked on 'em, up wind; and when I got where I could look over into Medicine Crow draw, there they were—some of 'em, anyhow. Get your gun. I'll be saddling your horse."

"Why didn't you down a couple, yourself?" I marveled.

"Well," said Tom, "I could have all right, maybe. But you want a whack at 'em, don't you?"

That struck me as mighty civil of Tom. Some fellows would have played their own game, and I was still a greenhorn in the cow camp.

By the time I had clapped on my hat, wrestled into my coat, grabbed the old Sharpe rifle with one hand, and stuffed a fistful of cartridges into my pocket with the other, Tom had brought in my horse and was throwing the saddle on him. We buckled the cinches in short order.

"Dutch's and Jack's eyes will be popping when they get in and see buffalo hides pegged out in front of the cabin," I exulted.

"Yes, siree! We can hang a hat on those eyes. But I don't know as we'll tackle the hides by our lonesome. We'll fetch in the tails and some meat first, as proof. All set?"

"You lead out, Tom," I bade.

"Nope. We can ride together. It's four or five miles straight-away to Medicine Crow. I'll show you when we get there. We'll have to charge right into 'em, so I can use this six-shooter. How many ca'tridges you got?"

"Six or seven."

"Shucks!" he grumbled. "This is a hefty outfit for hunting buffaloes."

And that was true. Dutch and Jack had taken the Winchesters. The old-timer single-shot Sharpe was a good gun, although limited in fire and a prodigious kicker; but the cartridges for it were scarce. And while Tom swore by the battered Colt that he toted at his thigh, the battered Colt was a short-range weapon.

285

"If we can't get in close, you can do business with your Sharpe, anyway," he proposed cheerfully. "But I spied a kind of wash that we can follow out into the draw, and so come smack at 'em before they know it. This belt cannon of mine is an all-right gun from the saddle if I'm near enough. Plug 'em behind the fore shoulder. That's the place, just behind the fore shoulder. But don't you wait on me."

The November air had a frosty tinge to it as we steadily loped across the wide, unfenced, broken and lonely plains of this Dakota land. The first snow lay in patches where there was shade from the sun. Winter was due again at any time.

Tom guided true. Suddenly he drew rein.

"Listen! Hear 'em?"

A dull rumble like distant thunder drifted down the thin air.

"They're there!" I panted.

"Bet your boots," he assured. "I'll take you for a look down on them—same place I was. Then we'll scheme."

Medicine Crow draw was not far now. Tom led for it through a shallow side draw; but before we reached the main draw he drew up short.

"We'd better climb up afoot for the look."

We left our horses and climbed on foot to the top of the side draw. The draw curved sharply at an angle with the main draw, so that by lying flat and taking off our hats we could peer into Medicine Crow.

"West'ard! See! Down to the west'ard," Tom whispered.

Those? Buffaloes? Must be! Straying down there in the broad bottom between the rocky, brushy slopes, they resembled black cattle.

I trembled. I could not control the funny feeling that seized me.

Tom laughed softly.

"I've been that way, too. You'll have to steady down or you wouldn't hit a red barn with a scatter-gun at ten yards."

"I'll st-steady down when we get to sh-shooting," said I, lips curiously stiff. "Where's your w-wash, now, that you count on?"

"Yonder. We'll ride back a piece, cross this ridge and make a sneak. Then if we can't rush 'em, you'll have a rest for your gun and—wait! Hold on!" His hand fell heavily upon my shoulder. "There's another bunch, closer in, up this way. See? Some old cow in with it, too—isn't there?"

Only four or five hundred yards down the slope and out into the bottom a second bunch of buffaloes had appeared. They were a small bunch, moving slowly through the draw as if to join the large herd. Now and again they paused to flick their tails and gaze about uneasily. Dark, shaggy creatures they were, except one; and he, or she, looked undersized and whitish.

Tom focused with all his eyes. They were keen eyes, plains eyes.

"May be cow critter," he muttered. "Sometimes they throw in with buffaloes, 'cording to the tell." He caught quick breath. "No! No, siree! A white buffalo! That's what! A white buffalo."

"It can't be!" I stammered.

286

"But it is—it sure is. It's no more cow than you are. And we've got to get him. He'll be worth a thousand dollars. Reckon we could get 'most a thousand for his hide. There was a Sioux once; he had a white robe and he wanted five hundred dollars for it. Even then the chiefs wouldn't let him sell it because it was a medicine robe. Come on."

"Where?" I implored.

"Circle down ahead and cut that bunch off from the main bunch. Act quick. The brutes have sensed something wrong already. See how they act? If they start running they'll stampede the whole herd before we get a shot. We can't make the wash. Too far. Lose time. There's a point that sticks out. Let's try that first. We can reach 'em from there when they pass. We sure'll have to head 'em at that point."

"And shoot him, Tom?" I puffed, as we tore for our horses.

"That depends. We'll try to cut him out, same as a cow, and turn him for the shack. If we can turn him and tucker him and put our ropes on him, I 'low we can corral him some way. But we got to get him, shoot or no shoot. Never mind the rest of 'em."

We galloped back out of the side draw and around to strike Medicine Crow where the point jutted out. The point was a little spur curving into Medicine Crow and it proved to be the very thing. Following the inside fishhook base, we were out of sight of the main herd as well as of the small bunch.

Near the tip we tumbled off our horses in order to crawl to the top and reconnoiter.

"You first, with your rifle," Tom generously ordered. "They're coming! Watch out!"

Amid my heart thumps I could hear the sound of thudding hoofs. The little bunch was scouring madly, helter-skelter, their heads low, their short tails extended and crooked, their hugh shaggy fore-quarters plunging. They were surging diagonally across toward our point, and in their wake streamed a bevy of bushy-tailed smaller forms.

All these latter were whitish; they were larger than dogs; they ran silently and swiftly. They were wolves.

"Lobos!" Tom snorted in disgust. "What d' yuh think o' that?"

"That spoils our chances?" I gasped. "They'll catch 'em?"

"Catching 'em hand over hand. Catching one, anyhow, and that's our Whitey. By thunder," Tom muttered, "if they only come within fair shooting distance!"

"Maybe they will."

No. The bunch had changed direction and were pelting straight down the draw for the main herd. But the white buffalo had lagged behind. He ran as if lame, and the wolves closed upon him rapidly. How they did eat the ground, those big burly lobos!

"Caught him!" Tom rapped.

Darting in, the leader of the pack had made his spring. But the furious leap just missed the white buffalo's flank as the little animal cleverly whirled.

"No they haven't!" I cried. "Come on, Whitey!"

For Whitey, evidently lame, was gallantly forging for the point again, as if he sensed the vantage of the high ground. Then, strange to say, another buffalo dropped back from the scampering bunch to be his mate. So presently the two were running side by side with the pack upon their heels.

The companion buffalo was the ordinary, larger kind. Tom hazarded a shrewd guess.

"That white is a yearling bull, and t'other is his mammy," he called. "Come on, Whitey! Come on, both of you!"

"No! They're going to fight!"

And they were. They had no other recourse. The wolves not only were leaping and snapping at their flanks and hocks, but were racing alongside and launching spring after spring at their lolling tongues.

In the twinkling of an eye the two running buffaloes had wheeled about and stopped. Braced flank to flank they stood, facing in opposite directions. A wolf, hesitating not the fraction of a second, flung himself full tilt at the flank of the brown mother. With astonishing quickness, the little white bull charged, met the wolf midway in the air, and sent him head over tail for a distance of twenty yards.

The first wolf lay writhing for breath. But another wolf sprang at the youngster— and was promptly bowled aside by the brown mother.

Tom cheered.

"That's the ticket! Keep at it. You'll lick 'em. Gosh!" he deplored. "If they were a little closer we'd try that Sharpe o' yours."

"It's a hot fight," said I, fascinated.

"Do we have to wait here, Tom?" I asked.

This broke the spell. Tom jumped up with decision.

"No. Let's get into it. That Whitey's pelt won't be worth stripping if we don't clean those lobos out the way." He shambled for the horses. "And I hate to see 'em all chawed up by the brutes," he confessed over his shoulder. "You let me dust those lobos with your Sharpe as soon as we get closer. Then I reckon we can fix Mister Whitey and his mammy."

At two hundred yards Tom reined in sharply and threw up the rifle. But our horses were dancing and shying, and sending the landscape dancing, too. The heavy ball puffed the dirt far beyond the battle.

"Hold my horse. Got to shoot on foot. Haven't any ca'tridges to waste." And Tom was out of the saddle.

He had reloaded, he aimed, fired. This time the ball hit. "Slap!" and we saw a wolf's body drive asprawl, fairly flattened by the blow. When a chunk from that old Sharpe struck it made quite a mess.

"One!" I exulted.

Tom only grunted, ran forward a few steps, aimed, fired, missed.

"They're jumping 'round so I can't hardly follow 'em," he complained.

He fired, fired again; ran and fired.

"Blamedest wolves ever I saw. Laid out three, haven't I? Rest are regular blood-crazy. Don't know whether we can charge in with these horses or not."

"Tom!" I cried. "Look out! The whole herd's coming!"

There had sounded the drum of many hoofs on our right. And here they did come, the whole herd, rolling in a black mass up the draw. With a startled exclamation of his own, Tom legged it to climb aboard his mount.

"Something's stampeded 'em. They're running up wind. Reckon the wind's changing. Mind your horse. They're liable to step all over us. Make for the point and you can shoot into 'em as they pass. If they don't see us or smell us, they'll keep right on going, regardless."

We waited a moment. The thunder of the hoofs welled louder. Even the wolves noted it. One by one they pricked their ears and gazed. They whined uneasily, sniffed the breeze and caught another danger sign, seemed aware, for the first time, of their nearer enemies. And as Tom waved his hat and shouted, away they loped, tails drooping, for the hills, leaving their quarry and their dead and crippled.

"We're next," Tom blurted. The buffalo avalanche was pouring for us. "Break to the point or we'll too late."

Our horses leaped to prick of spur and gladly tore for safety. Half way Tom glanced behind; he hauled upon the bit.

"Hold on. They've stopped. They've smelled us. Smelled something, anyhow. Wait."

Almost upon the battleground, where the two mauled fighters were standing, still braced, and uncertain as if not sure of their freedom, the leaders of the herd had set their hoofs, to stare and bellow. The mass of followers, jostling, rearing, bawling, also came to a stop.

Tom's voice rose high.

"Now's our chance, Billy! Charge 'em! Here's you gun. Turn loose on 'em with what you have, when you catch up with 'em. You take care of the meat and I'll tend to Whitey."

He whooped; I whooped. Together we charged, holding our horses to it. That was too much for the herd. With prodigious snorting, they wheeled about in another jostling mass and stampeded again, the little white buffalo and his mammy bolting after.

"Yip! Yip!" we urged.

"What did you say to do?" I shouted.

"I'll put my rope on Whitey. You get meat."

Our two horses asked no favor. They lengthened nobly; they had chased cows many a time before. The buffalo mother had won the herd, but the little white fellow was being distanced. Knee to knee we closed in on him. Tom began to take down his rope.

The youngster sensed the new menace and veered. As quick as a flash Tom's trained cow horse swerved on the new course—and I after. I forgot all about the meat.

"Can you hold him if you rope him?" I yelled.

"Sure. And I'll snag him all right."

Gradually we drew in. The little bull's breath was wheezy; his bulging eyes showed bloodshot when occasionally he glared backward. His yellowish white hide was stained with sweat and the crimson from his gashes. No, he was not pure white; he was "a dingy cream, about the color of weathered buckskin, and oddly mottled," I heard Tom accuse, as he sized him up at short view.

"You blamed little fraud, you! What do you call yourself, hey?"

Leaning forward, Tom cast. The ropes flew with the hiss of an arrow, opened precisely as the coils paid out, hovered for barely the tenth of a second over the little nose, and then settled down so that the bull ran his head into it. It clapped tight about

289

his stubby horns.

Tom's wise horse sprang aside and the rope stretched taut.

"Whoopee! Snagged him. No danger of busting his neck, I reckon." As everybody knows, to rope a running cow by the horns sometimes means a broken neck. But a buffalo's neck is short and thick.

Whitey suddenly awakened to the touch of the tether, as Tom turned his horse farther and farther out. The animal whirled and braced, and charged; and away went Tom, gazing rearward from the saddle and laughing. In a flash the little bull again whirled for flight. The rope whipped wire-tight before Tom could check his horse, spun the bull end for end, and "crack!" The back cinch snapped while the horse was dragged on two legs.

"Whoa-oa, Jo! He weighs a ton and he's quicker'n a bobcat," Tom yelped. "You'll have to get that rope o' yours on him, boy."

I circled warily, swinging my noose. The little bull was full of fight yet. He charged and charged, keeping Tom dodging. I cast, missed completely, gathered my rope—

"You get him or he's liable to get me," Tom wailed. His horse was well-nigh unmanageable, what with the tilted saddle and the furious lunges of that strange animal.

The little white bull's breath was coming short. He yielded for the moment, to brace himself weakly and bawl. I seized the opportunity and cast. Luck smiled, for the loop caught and we had him. Tom shouted triumphantly.

"Hold him! Now we can hold him!"

Whitey tugged and swayed, his eyes suffused, his tongue dangling, his shoulders and flanks muddy red. But from opposite directions we had him anchored. At least, we thought we did.

"Here's his mammy," Tom called across. "Just hold him and wear him down. Hope she isn't on the prod, for we haven't time to shoot."

Sure enough, the mother buffalo was loping and bellowing toward us. The little bull answered her hoarsely. In the distance the herd had halted, pawing and waiting.

Would the mother fight? No, she did not dare. She slackened her pace, approached more slowly, and sidled about.

"She's our meat if she doesn't watch out," said Tom.

Whitey surged bravely, tugging right and left, shaking his head and straining with his shoulders and hind quarters. He certainly did weigh a ton, in sheer strength. The ropes hummed. Tom's saddle was almost off, with him in it. I felt my own mount sliding hither-thither.

The buffalo mother lowed encouragingly. Her heart was warm, but not hot enough to tackle these monsters. The little bull bawled, half-choked by his efforts. He gave one last mighty struggle, caught Tom's rope in a momentary slack, and with a report like a pistol shot it parted.

"Look out!" he yapped.

My alarmed horse sprang back, so that the little bull was whirled around as he attempted to gallop for freedom. He essayed to charge me, his second tormentor; he stumbled, his fore legs collapsed and he plunged to his nose.

"Hold him now!" Tom was forcing his horse in, his revolver aloft. But before I could tauten rope and keep the rascal's nose in the dirt, he was up again.

There he stood, propped astraddle, and quivering in every limb. By his trembling and his wheezing and his slaver he was about done.

"Can you lead him?" Tom demanded.

I pricked my horse.

"No!" For the little bull was resisting with all his tortured fibers.

The mother had sidled nearer, pawing and challenging, but helpless. Tom cocked his Colt.

"Hold him, then. We'll have to down him for his meat and hide. We can't fool longer."

Jabbing with his spurs and hauling on the bit, Tom forced his mount in still closer for a sure shot while I held the bull. Whitey moaned piteously as he tried to face this new flank attack; and I felt rather sick. But on the range animal life is cheap.

In a minute all would be over. Then on a sudden the big revolver exploded viciously down along the little bull's heaving ribs—my rope jarred and parted and my horse reeled to his haunches.

"Watch sharp!" Tom's voice rang commanding. He leaned and slapped the cringing youngster's scarred flank with his hat. "Get away, you!" he bade. "Git!" And he spurred in flight from another charge.

For a few breaths Whitey stood dazed and snorting. Presently he shook his dusty head to glare about for his enemies. He tottered forward two or three steps, and rumbled.

"Come on," he seemed to defy. "Where are you?"

Tom laughed.

"You're sure a bundle of nerve," he praised.

The little bull, rumbling belligerent, backed. He turned around, and at a leisurely and not undignified limp made off, his rope ends dragging. Now and again he paused, half to turn and bellow and paw. His mother met him, she sniffed him over, lowed gently, licked him. Painfully they loped on to the main herd.

We waited. The herd opened, let them in, closed upon them. And on they all went at a steady gallop down the draw.

Tom looked at me and grinned.

"Where's your meat?" he queried.

"Where's your bull?" I retorted.

"Aw," said Tom, sheepishly, "he wasn't plumb white. When I saw he'd just been rolling in some alkali wallow I reckoned we didn't want him. Better let his mammy clean him up. I'm no wolf," Tom growled to himself. "Always did like a fighter, anyhow."

THE IMMORTALITY OF DRAKE

Warren H. Miller

Farm and Fireside, December 1920

"I tell you, Gosh, you got tu shoot that there boar houn'," declared the overseer harshly. "Shoot him, or send him away. The doctor's wild oveh this ram-killin'! 'Tell Gosh to dispose of that brute, immediateleh'—that's what he's telephoned me from Town House. He's comin' out in the cyar, d'rectleh."

Gosh leaned against a veranda post of the plantation overseer's bungalow, chewing a straw in dejected misery. The wild turkey slung over his shoulder, which he had brought in as a peace offering, dropped unheeded to the porch, its bronze glories of wing and breast feathers falling in limp array.

"Ef 'twarn't that buckketty ole ramgoat that ma Drake-dog killed, I hain't got a word to excuse him," he retorted glumly. "He ain't never touched no sheep before. But thet old rip-snorter—sho' spilin' fo' a fight, he was! No wondeh Drake kinder forgot hisself! Waal—hit's done, now."

"You bet its done—good and plenty!" replied the exasperated overseer. "The doctor set gre't store by that impo'ted Beloochistan ram. Stood him over eight hundred dollars to get him heah from England, Gosh. Hope you done tied up that dawg of yourn! The doc's mighteh quick-tempered, an' jist the sight of him—"

Gosh's green eyes glared under the pulled-down brim of his felt hat—he'd like to see *any*body try to shoot Drake! But he *had* tied the dog up. There was no question as to who had killed the doctor's imported ram the night before. Only one dog on the plantation left such enormous tracks as did Drake; old Tad and half a dozen of the stock-house Negroes had seen the fight—the massacre, rather. Babbling, with rolling eyes, they had described the whole affair—the pugnacious ram just arrived from England stamping about in his pen, his bucking challenge, Drake's mighty leap over the palings, and then the single slash of his inch-long fangs that had cut the ram's throat. Before a soul could interfere, Drake had vaulted back over the fence and bolted for his kennel.

"Waal, Ah's makin' maself mighteh scarce," resumed Gosh, after a long, awkward pause. "Tell the doctor that Ah'm mighteh pow'ful sorry. Give him this yere turk. Henry-dawg run him up yesterday, down by the branch, an' Ah got him flying with a load of sevens. So long! Ah'll be back in mebbe a week, when he's had time to cool off. Ah'll try tu git him a piney hawg fo' a make-peace."

Gosh turned away and slouched across the cotton fields toward Great House, leaving the overseer to await the doctor's car hastening wrathfully out from Piedmont. Brevoort was a smallish plantation of about seven thousand acres, but it was the doctor's pet, his trying-out ground for dozens of new agricultural experiments before putting them through on a large scale down at his twenty-thousand-acre main plantation of Gadsen. Siberian hogs, Beloochistan sheep, Aseel game cocks, Japanese pecans, Manila hemp, Kabul indigo, Siamese pepper, Hedjaz dates—all sorts of overseas subtropical products were experimentally cultivated here, for it was the doctor's firm belief that Brevoort could grow anything found on the thirty-sixth parallel around the whole world.

Gosh was just Gosh. If he *had* a last name, no legal mention of it existed. For generations his family had been the plantation hunters and game-keepers of Brevoort. Slender but wiry, leather-faced, with green eyes and high cheek bones, there was a strong dash of Cherokee or Choctaw in him somewhere. He generally clothed himself in some ragged, cast-off flannel shirt of the doctor's and a suit of old clothes from the same source. His black hair, cropped short in a circle around his red neck by Crambo Yow, the plantation Negro barber, had that intense blue-black luster that comes with Indian blood. Perhaps thirty-five years old, all his life he had been a swamper, fisherman, and hunter for the plantation, keeper of the doctor's dogs and his own pack. Up to a year previous he had lived in a lonely shack "up the branch," with Drake and his hound pack as sole companions. Lately he had been given a cabin up near "Gret Huis," the better to look after the doctor's own bird dogs.

Gosh hurried thither now, for he had no desire to face the first fierce anger of the doctor, driving in from Piedmont by way of the overseer's bungalow. A dread that something irrevocable would happen to Drake if the dog were found at his kennel near Great House urged faster his long, tireless strides.

As he approached the plantation manor, a doggy chorus welcomed him. The diapason of Drake's ferocious, deep-chested roar served as an undertone to the musical belling of the hounds and the higher pitched barks of setters and pointers. But it was to Drake's kennel that Gosh hastened. The giant boar hound leaped up with exuberant affection, his paws on Gosh's tall shoulders, his bearded, fuzzy head over-topping the man's by six inches.

"Down y' ole scoundrel, down!" he ordered, laughingly disentangling himself from the chain links. "Quiet, y' ole fool! We gottu git outen heah, right smahrt sudden!"

He unsnapped the chain hook, and Drake bolted off in ecstacies of delight, his progress marked by flying clouds of guinea fowl and scuttling bevies of long-legged game cocks.

"Come back heah, Drake! Heel, you great devil!" yelled Gosh, blowing his whistle. Drake came lumbering back, nearly knocking his master over with a ropy tail as he wheeled to position at the man's heels. They set out through a young pecan grove for the nearest creek branch. Gosh had no certain objective. To flee from the doctor's first wrath and lay low for a time in the old swamp cabin, then to round up with Drake's help and shoot a "piney hawg," as the wild boars of the region were called, by way of further peace offering—this was as far as the bewildered hunter, overwhelmed by his sea of troubles, could plan.

The pair melted into the cane brake, the only thing still thick and green amid the December browns and yellows of myrtle, briers, and broom grass that bordered the tall cypress forest of the swamp. Out near a "pawnd"—an islet of long leaf pines in the limitless fields—a Negro was singing to his mules as they turned ground for the winter sowing. Here, in the dense leafy cane, under giant long-leaf pines and bottle-trunked Carolina ash and cypress, they could move along unseen, unreported by the Negroes at their third cotton-picking, unobserved by any mammy on her shack "po'ch"—she whose garrulous tongue and beady eye scanning the world over black corncob pipe usually gave the whereabouts of Gosh to the doctor's scurrying plantation flivver.

Mile after mile Gosh and Drake threaded through the laurel and bay thickets of the creek, the man dodging ropy vines armed caterpillar-fashion with spiny thorns, the dog snuffing game tracks and passing them by with indifferent snorts. Only one track ever interested Drake—piney hawg—unless it might be an infrequent black bear. He ran mute—an inestimably valuable quality, for a wild boar can run like a deer and a howling pack of hounds will give him warning enough to scare him out of the county without the hunters ever having sight of him. But Drake's method of attack was a silent rush, until at close quarters with the boar, when his rapid volleying bark would hold the creature at bay and give Gosh time enough to come silently up and administer the only death shot that would kill him—a solid ounce ball from a twelve-gauge shotgun.

It was toward nightfall when they reached Gosh's former home up in the bayous of the Santee. An old clearing, grown up since the war with loblolly pine, was hemmed about with the tall cypress tops of the creek branches on every hand. A freedman Negro had once lived here. Then the general shrinkage of cultivated land all over Brevoort that had followed the war had abandoned this spot to nature. Its gray roof of split shakes, its weathered walls of rough-sawn yellow pine, with sashless windows and pine-knot hinged door, greeted Gosh's eyes as he pushed out toward it through yellow broom straw, waist-high. Small wild animals scampered out of the abandoned kennels and burrowed into the underbrush as they approached; a corn snake weaved swiftly for his lair under the shack.

Opening the door, Gosh started a fire in the rusty stove, while Drake lay down before the cold hearth of the mud-and-stick chimney. Sundry tin cans of cornmeal, coffee, sugar, and beans were opened from Gosh's store in a pantry closet and a brace of quail, shot on the way down, were split and set to grilling in a greasy black frying pan that no period of disuse could rust. Then he started a fat-wood fire in the chimney and prepared an ash cake of corn grist and water.

Drake watched the proceedings with intelligent eyes. His master began talking to him, as was his wont after long and severe periods of reflection.

"Drake, yu ole snoozer, yu've gotten me intu a peck of trouble, this time! But yu and I is goin' tu stick it out til the doctor gits oveh his mad—you heah me, you ornery scoundrel?"

Drake thumped his tail on the boards with loud applause. This expedition was, of course, for piney hawg. He understood that; this was their usual headquarters on such trips. Odd that Master had not mentioned the beast by name—but those emphatic tones referred to a killing on the morrow, that was certain!

"You ain't no sheep killer, Drake," went on his master. "No critter could sass you like that ram-goat done, without havin' tu eat his insults. I don't blame yu a bit! The doctor'll see it that way, when he's had time to think. 'Twarn't your fault, Drake-dog. No-sirree-bob!"

Drake pricked up his ears. He didn't quite get the drift, but show him a fresh piney-hawg track and you could depend on him! He watched Master interestedly as the man swept away the coals from the hearth and spread out a circle of green oak leaves. On them was dumped the moist corn cake from its pan, and the heat immediately curled the leaves over the top of it. Raking a layer of ashes over them, Gosh heaped up a pile of live coals and then lit his pipe with one of them.

"Yes, suh, Drake," he continued between puffs, "you may be a mistake, but yu sho' is the dearest of all ma dawgs tu me!"

The "mistake" reference was to Drake's ancestry. His mother was an enormous Irish wolf hound, imported by the doctor ten years before in the early stages of his various experiments. There had been a mesalliance, but Drake had received his aristo-cratic name before the taint in the litter of pups had been discovered. Drake had then been begged for by Gosh, and the rest of the litter drowned. Distemper took the mother before her next litter, so Drake had been the sole survivor of that venture. Raised by Gosh from a clumsy, waddling pup, he had been the one big pride of the hunter's life. He was just like his mother all over again, except for certain defects that only a fancier could discern, and the trait of running mute that the unknown interloper—probably a shepherd dog—had given him. But to Gosh he was the dog of dogs. No better boar or bear hound ran on four legs, if you asked him! To Drake he owed half his living, for piney hawg drew nine cents a pound when sold to the gentry of the neighboring planta-tions, and there were plenty of them to sell, even after his feudal obligations to the doctor's own smokehouse had been discharged.

"You is royal-blooded, Drake! Wuth any twenty of them furrin rams—the doc'll realize that too, when he cools down. Perk up, dawg!" he chirped, seeing that Drake's ears had fallen somewhat over the minor tones that had crept into his voice. "Ah reckon the ash cake's 'bout raidy."

He swept off the live coals and pulled out the charred bundle of leaves. As he peeled them off, a glazed surface, dusted with white ash, came to view. He washed it off carefully and broke the steaming bread, tossing great chunks into Drake's huge jaws. The bony remnants of the quail, more plentiful than their meat, were disposed of the same way, and then Gosh went out into the clearing to think, leaving Drake dozing before the fire.

He relit his corncob and sought a convenient stump. He knew that he had not faced this whole problem fairly and squarely, even yet, but was building on the vaguest hopes of the doctor's relenting. The round red moon rose, enormous through the trunks of the cypress, and the hoot of a barred owl and the squall of a raccoon came from some distant fastness of the swamp, as the man sat buried in thought.

"Ain't no man kin make me kill ma own dawg, nohow!" he declared, soliloquizing to himself. "Ah knows dawgs as no one else in this county knows 'em. Some's jest dawgs—jest animals. But when a dawg grows up with a man, like Drake has, lives with him day by day, thinks as he thinks, feels as he feels—Gawd, man, that dawg grows him a soul! Ain't I seen it? Look at Drake, here—fed and raised with me from a puppy. Part of him's jest dawg; but part of him, an' the biggest part, is more than dawg. Danged ef it ain't a part of ma own soul, growed oveh into him! Danged ef it ain't!"

He ruminated pleasedly for a while on this novel theory. To Gosh it explained a good deal that had been mysterious in his dealings with his own dogs: their capacity to read his thoughts like a medium, for one thing; their intense partisanship with him, for another; their utter devotion and sympathy—why, otherwise, should a creature of a totally different order of nature be so wrapped up in human joys and sorrows as to become a veritable reflection of his master's state of mind, as does his dog? Who are we, to these beasts of a lower order even than the apes, that they should be so mindful of us, unless our dog really bears part of our own soul through his tour of life with us?

"It's nat'ral that it should be!" insisted Gosh to himself, after further reflection. "We does sho'ly transplant part of ourselves into a critter that we love as I do Drake-dog. Ef I shoot him, Ah kill part of maself—mebbe the best part!" He grinned momentarily. "No, suh, Ah jest nat'rally cayn't do it!"

Then he thought on the other horn of his dilemma, his loyalty, his duty to Brevoort. His father had served Brevoort all his life; his grandfather had fought for her. They had all been born there, raised on the plantation. He himself had never gone out of the county expect for an occasional trip to Piedmont with a load of game for the Town House. But Drake had killed the doctor's imported ram, and ruined a cross-breeding project that might have meant much to the future of wool-growing in the South. There was no guarantee—except his death—that he would not do it again. Who was Gosh and his dog to stand in the way of a momentous agricultural experiment like that? If this hot-country sheep could produce a strain that would thrive in the South, and yet yield wool equal to the best Northern-grown—

"Dag-*gone* it all!" he muttered exasperatedly. "Ah never was so worried in ma life! Ah've either got to shoot him or cl'ar out!" A kind of terror seized him. To leave the friendly protection of Brevoort and go out into the cold world, a wanderer, a woods savage—and all for a dog! Every big plantation had its own hunter; even if he could find a vacancy, how long would he last at it with Drake and his sinister reputation following him?

"Jest the same, Ah ain't shootin' him, nohow!" he averred resolutely. "I'll go tu trappin' fer a livin', fust. We'll lay low. Mebbe Ah'll think of somethin'.."

But even sleeping on it failed to produce any satisfactory solution. Drake must go, to end this menace, once for all. There was no other way. Next morning at dawn, while they were preparing breakfast before the day's hunt, a peremptory message from the doctor reached him. A little Negro suddenly appeared at the door of the shack, poked in a folded note, and ran off before Gosh could collect his wits to stop him. He opened it:

Doc says shoot drake or clear out. He's wild. Better do it quick and come back and eat crow, or he'll sack you, anyhow. J. Edsall

It was from the overseer. Cowardice, the first Gosh had ever known, assailed him. To be deprived of the doctor's friendship and patronage, to be driven from Brevoort, to be jolted out of his easy gamekeeper ways and have to fight into the fierce competition of trapping, with its uncertain returns and its certain fights with men already in possession of all the good trapping grounds—he felt as if all the props of his life were being pulled out from under him. It was easy to fall in with the doctor's point of view—that Drake was an intolerable nuisance, an impediment to progress on the plantation that would have to go, just as would a pet bear if Gosh had taken into his heart to raise one. The doctor had never forgiven Drake for not running true to strain; it had only been Gosh's wheedling importunities that had saved him from the fate of the rest of the litter. Why not take the common-sense view of this matter? The doctor was the most genial of feudal lords, adored by all the Negroes, looked up to by the neighbors, respected by his white employees, from the overseer down. He was never unjust. If he saw that it was necessary to get rid of Drake, why oppose him? To send him away would not do; they had tried that once—shipped him two hundred miles, only to have him turn up a week later, gaunt and ribby, but pathetically glad to see them again.

No, the only way was to —

Gosh slipped a couple of ounce ball cartridges into his gun and chirruped to Drake. He would pretend that they were going after piney hawg, and then, when a good chance came —

"Here Drake! Hie on! Ssuey, pup! Go git'em!" he called, waiting on the porch for Drake to dash out to hunt. No response came, and he stopped, astonished, to look in at the door.

It was uncanny! The dog lay with his great brindled head erect, but his fallen ears and the troubled expression in his eyes told Gosh instantly that the dog had read his mind. He did not offer to budge, as Gosh strode in and laid hands on his collar, and it took a deal of coaxing even to get him to his feet. Standing thirty-six inches at the shoulder, Drake could have killed the man, right then, with a single snap at his throat; instead, a look of deep humility, pitiful worry and fear hovered in his brown eyes. Was this the Drake that used to dash out to the boar hunt with a frantic eagerness, utterly unrestrainable until he had capered off a surcharge of high spirits in the first wild rush out of the cabin door?

Gosh's heart smote him as he slipped on a leash. He felt that Drake could and should have killed him, then and there, for the treacherous thoughts, the odious purpose that lay back in his brain. Instead, the dog slunk resignedly along, trembling in every limb, glancing up woefully at his master, a wondering, piteous expression in the honest brown eyes that spoke his soul out under the shaggy brows.

"Gawd! He knows I mean tu kill him, as well as I do!" shivered Gosh to himself. "O Gawd! O Gawd! Forgive me! I'll neveh do it!"

Fearful to fail in his resolution, he made haste to tie Drake to a small long-leaf pine sapling at the edge of the clearing. Then he sought the depths of the cane, where an ambush could be had, and Drake would never know the instant of his death.

In vain! The dog's eyes followed him, seeming to penetrate the thickest hiding places. When the tubes were finally leveled on him, with quaking arms, they looked right into those unflinching yet pleading eyes, it seemed to Gosh, as if with a telescope. Drake faced him, with ears fallen, with a sacrificial humility of soul streaming out of those yearning eyes that had never looked at Gosh before with any other expression than that of adoring love. An air of self-sacrifice shone about him, as if saying: "Here am I, Master. I do not know why this is being done to me, but if you know best, then do it! My life, my soul, my all are yours!"

Gosh lowered the gun. "I cayn't! Gawd in heaven—I *cayn't* do it!" he groaned through his tears. "I ain't no murderer! Drake! Drake-dog! Forgive me, ole pardner!

Forgive me!" he wept, dropping the weapon to burst through the cane and fling his arms around Drake's big rough-coated neck. "Never! Drake-dog, never!" he sobbed, while Drake's tail swished soberly in the broom straw and he licked at Gosh's face solemnly. There was still a pained expression in his eyes. In his doggy heart he could not fathom all this at all; but Master was in deep trouble, and he himself was some way mixed up in it—that was certain.

"We'll cl'ar out, honey! We'll leave Brevoort foreveh. We two kin make a livin'! C'mon, boy! Hip! Ssssuey! We'll git the doctor a piney hawg and then, daggone him, we're quits with him! Hie on, dog! Sssuey!"

Their ancient war cry now seemed to reassure the dog completely. Master's trouble, whatever it was, was over; they were really and truly going boar-hunting this time! Oh, but a dog can read the human voice tones! Gosh's rang true, now—no faintest hint of hypocrisy—and Drake started off confidently into the swamp, worrying not at all that Master had repossessed himself of his double gun. They crossed the branch on a down tree and gained an uplands of bear and turkey oak, small, scrubby trees whose plentiful crop of small acorns strewed the wire grass. Here, at night, the wild boars came out to feed, retiring by day into the deep fastness of the swamp. Gosh strolled along, just outside the brier border of the branch, Drake quartering the high ground assiduously, his immense, iron-gray shape loping across Gosh's watchful eyes, and now and then stopping to look back for a reassuring wave of Gosh's hand. In his poses his immense fuzzy head resembled some super-Airedale.

Suddenly he dashed off down a narrow, muddy game trail toward the swamp. Gosh started to run at once, for in the mud of the trail he saw the fresh, cloven-hoof prints of a wild boar. Drake disappeared into the cane, silent and vengeful, while the man tore after him, his breath panting, his heart thumping so that he could hear its beats through his open mouth. It was silent team work that they both understood well. There were rustlings and dashings hither and yon in the dense, thorny undergrowth; and then, somewhere on ahead, came the rapid, volleying bark of Drake at the attack. Gosh pressed on, cursing his way stubbornly through thorny vines that raked him, and crossing the winding creek twice on precarious bridges of cypress knees and prone water-ash saplings. To the constant barking ahead was now added the angry, animal squeals and grunts of the boar, and a rank, musky odor pervaded the forest. Gosh judged that he was on the wrong side of the creek, and forced his way out through a thicket of bay bushes that overhung its deep, rapid stream. He leaped for a mossy cypress knee in midstream and was making the other bank with his momentum when a ropy vine encircled him about the waist and hurled him backward into the water.

"Hold him, pup! Sssssuey!" he yelled, floundering madly out of the embrace of the vine. He crawled up the banks and burst through the cane—to face the boar, not thirty feet away, at bay and slashing with his long, sharp tushes at the agile Drake. The hog was all of six feet long, huge and shiny black, with long coarse hair that covered invulnerable shoulder plates more than an inch thick. A high-power rifle simply left no chance at all to the man who fired it at this range—the boar would surely charge, and his tushes disembowel the hunter before the bullet could shatter his vitality. But the smashing blow of an ounce solid ball usually knocked the creature down to stay.

Gosh leveled the tubes on the raging boar and the roar of his right barrel rang out. The boar squealed a furious challenge and started for him, Drake springing in and seizing an ear to hold him back. Gosh steadied himself and planted the sights full on the thick, hairy chest, under the gleaming eyes that burned over wicked, slavering jaws. At ten paces he fired. Malignant fury glared in the pig's eyes—he was charging to kill, still coming on with the last ounce of his vitality. Drake loosed his hold on the ear and made a desperate snap at the boar's foreleg to trip him. Fatal move, and the dog knew it! With a savage slash of the boar's head, a long glistening white tush went home into the dog's side and there was a horrible sound of ripping and tearing, of snapping and breaking ribs, as Drake yelled in agony.

Gosh whipped out his smoking, exploded shells and frantically shoved in fresh ones, snapping the gun shut and firing both barrels from the hip. The boar rocked from side to side, grunted, sighed, and lay over, kicking feebly.

Gosh rushed forward, sobbing with sickening anxiety, and flung himself on giant Drake, who lay gasping, with stiffened, convulsive legs, on the moss. Drake looked up at him, the life-light dimming in his eyes, while he feebly tried to lick the tears that rained down his master's cheeks. He was ebbing fast, but to die thus, looking in humble adoration up into the eyes of the man he had loved all his life, seemed contentment. Gosh had no words. Sobs of anguish, despair, impotent regret, shook his frame. It seemed that part of his own soul was being torn out of his body. He bent his head down and smothered Drake's leonine one in a frenzied hug, clasping the silken face of his dog tight in his arms as, with a faint shudder and a last, feeble thump of his loyal tail, Drake passed on.

For a long time Gosh made no move. He could not believe that Drake, his Drake, the superb, the magnificent, was—dead. The body was still warm; it moved limply. Surely some faint spark of life still smoldered somewhere in that great frame! The hot sunlight streamed down through the whispering cypresses, and still he had not moved, had not relinquished the loving clasp of that royal head in his arms. Gosh had never heard the story of Drake's own forebear, Gelert, but surely all the pangs of King Llewellyn were his!

The red life blood had long since ceased to ooze from Drake's torn side and a certain stiffness had set in in the limbs before Gosh finally stirred.

"Good-bye—ole pardner!" he whispered huskily, his lips quivering as he tried to form the words. Reverently he covered the poor form with green bay leaves, and then, without a single glance at the boar, picked up his shotgun and started for Great House.

During all that march he did not trust himself to utter a single word, for it had brought a flood of tears. As he came up to and started to enter his own cabin, heedless of the vociferous welcomes of the dogs, the overseer came around the corner of Great House veranda.

"You, Gosh!" he called out. "Whar's Drake?"

"He's—daid," choked Gosh. "Died—like a—hero—" and with a sudden spasm of emotion he dashed into his cabin bedroom and flung himself face downward on the couch.